The Damage

Howard Linskey

NO EXIT PRESS

First published in 2012
by No Exit Press,
an imprint of Oldcastle Books Ltd,
PO Box 394, Harpenden,
Herts, AL5 1XJ

www.noexit.co.uk

A CIP catalogue record for this book is available from the British Library.

ISBN
978-1-84243-502-1 Print
978-1-84243-648-6 Kindle
978-1-84243-649-3 Epub
978-1-84243-650-9 PDF

4 6 8 10 9 7 5 3

Typeset by Avocet Typeset, Chilton, Aylesbury, Bucks
in 11.5pt Garamond MT
Printed in Great Britain by Clays Ltd, St Ives plc

For Erin & Alison, as it ought to be

ACKNOWLEDGEMENTS

I would like to thank the following for their support and friendship during the writing of this book; Adam Pope, Andy Davis, Nikki Hurley, Gareth Chennells, Andrew Local and Stuart Britton. Thanks also to David Shapiro and Peter Day.

A very big thank you to Ion Mills at No Exit for publishing *The Damage*. Thanks to Alan Forster for the cover design and Claire Watts, Chris Burrows, Jem Cook and Alexandra Bolton at No Exit for their hard work on my behalf. A massive thank you to Keshini Naidoo for her intelligent and insightful editing.

I have huge respect for the team at Marjacq Literary Agency, particularly my agent Phil Patterson, whose time, help, advice and friendship are greatly appreciated by me. Thanks also to Isabella Floris for her efforts in foreign markets and to Luke

Speed for his work on the TV option. A special thank you goes to David Barron and Stevie Lee at 'Runaway Fridge' Productions.

Finally, a massive thank you to my loving wife Alison and beautiful daughter Erin, for their love, faith and support, which means everything to me.

PROLOGUE

Glasgow

The body was propped up in a sitting position on the park bench, head back, arms splayed wide, as if the victim had been trying to embrace someone right before the bullet struck. The entry wound was the soft tissue of the right eye, leaving the rest of the face completely intact. If it were not for the dark, bloody hole where the eyeball had been you might have thought the victim was merely dozing. From the back it was a different story. The high calibre round, meeting little resistance, had gone through the man's skull, tearing off the back of the head and taking most of his brains with it. The exit wound was a gaping, ragged and bloody mess the size of a grapefruit.

Detective Constables Jason Narey and Eamon Walker had been the first officers on the scene and Narey had winced when he saw the damage. The only positive thing about dying like that, reasoned Narey, was that you wouldn't know a bloody thing about it. You'd be here one second and gone the next, dead in less than the time it took someone to click their fingers.

It was a strange sight. Most victims of gunshot wounds ended up lying on the ground. This one was still seated on the wooden bench he'd been occupying when the bullet struck, causing everyone around him to scatter, screaming in panic as they ran from the park. Someone managed to retain the presence of mind to call Strathclyde Police to tell them the Sandyhills Sniper had struck again. As luck would have it, Walker and Narey were nearby, following up a lead in an unrelated case and, from what Narey could make out, there was nothing here to contradict the caller's assessment. Everything about the crime scene indicated this killing was down to the sniper.

The municipal park was eerily empty now except for the two Police officers and the murdered man. The detectives proceeded cautiously at first, even though they both knew the killer would be long gone by now. That was the MO of the sniper. Set yourself up so you are well hidden, select a target somewhere off in the distance, preferably a face in a crowd, to cause maximum hysteria after the shot, then take them out. There'd been three previous attacks, on seemingly random and entirely innocent victims. As soon as the shot was taken, the sniper disappeared into thin air, leaving no clues for the Police to pick up on, not even a spent cartridge. The only real evidence they were left with was the bullet, which invariably passed through the body of the victim and was found nearby, embedded in the first solid object it met. Ballistics reckoned the ammunition in the earlier killings was .308 and Narey had no reason to doubt they'd find an exact match to that calibre in the undergrowth somewhere close to this poor sod.

Both men had taken a cursory look at the victim but you

didn't have to be a GP to know he was way beyond anyone's help, so they retreated, to spots some distance away, standing either side of the body, their primary aim to secure the scene against any pain-in-the-arse-passers-by or make-a-name-for-themselves-journalists whilst they waited for the SOCOs to arrive.

Narey chose a spot by some trees, just in case. The sniper might be long gone but twelve years in the force had taught him to be cautious. Narey could still see the victim clearly enough from this vantage point. He looked like someone sleeping off a liquid lunch but the gelatinous brain matter plastered over the wall behind him told a different story.

'Poor fucker,' he said.

'Wouldn't want to be the one that's got to clean this up,' Walker called from his spot at the opposite end of the open ground between them, 'he certainly picked the wrong day for a walk in the park.'

Narey couldn't argue with that. If the victim had stayed in that afternoon or gone round the shops instead, he'd still be alive now, for this crime was about as indiscriminate as it gets.

The guy on the bench looked to be in his early forties, appeared respectable enough for this part of Glasgow and was dressed casually, in t-shirt and combats.

Narey wondered if the corpse had a wife somewhere. There'd be kids most likely and friends, colleagues from work, mates down the pub and all of them would be shocked rigid when they found out what happened to this guy. He was unlucky enough to have become the fourth, entirely random victim of the Sandyhills Sniper. These motiveless attacks, on unconnected victims from distances of hundreds of yards away, had shocked Glasgow into a kind of paralysis. People were afraid to be out on the streets, some were too scared to go to work and even pubs were reporting a downturn in business.

And the Press, as always, were sticking the knife in, 'Baffled

Police left clueless,' being just one of the more helpful headlines that morning, followed by the strapline 'Police can't guarantee Sniper won't kill again,' as if anybody could guarantee that. Now there was a fourth victim, which meant the tabloids were going to have a field day. Fucking journalists, all they ever did was sneer. He'd love to get some of them to try and find the bloke responsible for this and see how they got on. They'd be bloody clueless, the lot of them.

Everyone was freaked out by this killer, because they knew they had just as much chance of being picked off by him as the next man. The Sniper didn't care who he killed. So far there had been a van driver, filling up his vehicle on a busy petrol station forecourt in Sandyhills, which is why the Press had dubbed the killer the 'Sandyhills Sniper' even though he shot people from all corners of the city. Next, a middle-aged business woman in a trouser suit was gunned down walking home from work during the evening rush hour, closely followed by a young guy shot from his bike while he pedalled down the middle of the street on his way to get his exam results; straight As of course, the Press loved that bit and now this, a fourth victim in ten days; a poor, harmless bloke out for a stroll in the park on a Sunday afternoon.

Thank God they had McGregor on the case. Narey's boss, legendary Detective Chief Inspector Robert McGregor already had a theory. He reckoned the perpetrator was copying the Beltway Sniper attacks of 2002, when thirteen luckless souls were gunned down randomly in Washington and Virginia by a nut job called John Allen Muhammad. 'We've definitely got ourselves a copycat,' DCI McGregor told a room packed with detectives, who were hanging on his every word, shortly after the second murder victim was positively identified.

At least the brass had been sensible enough to put their top man on it, temporarily commandeering McGregor from his duties looking into Glasgow's gangland killings. Everyone knew McGregor would want this case. He may have been brought back to his native city to tackle the gangs, following a stint breaking up firms in London, but he would relish being reassigned until this one was cleared up, 'And cleared up it shall be,' he assured the officers in the briefing room.

Now here he was, striding purposefully down the hill towards them. Trust McGregor to get here before the SOCOs, his entourage of medium-ranking detectives trying and failing to keep up with him; tall, strong, powerful, his trade-mark, long, dark raincoat flapping behind him in the breeze. No wonder the tabloids called him 'The Caped Crusader'.

As McGregor drew closer, Narey straightened until he was almost at attention. There was something the guvnor possessed that made you strive to do a good job for him, almost made you want to be a better man after you'd been in his vicinity. Narey supposed that was called leadership. McGregor wasn't like other senior officers. All they worried about was managing their own careers but it was obvious McGregor cared passionately about the job and he had an incredible instinct. People said he could think like a gangster and was hard enough to take them down himself, being unafraid to get his hands dirty or his knuckles skinned. The stories about him were legendary. What man in the force wouldn't respect that in a boss?

DCI McGregor drew alongside Narey, his burly frame almost blocking out the light. Some of the detectives were out of breath from the yomp across the park but McGregor looked like he'd just stepped from his car.

'Jason,' he said, 'how's the family?' There was warmth in the question and it caught the younger man by surprise. After all, there were surely bigger priorities.

'Good, thanks boss,' a quadruple murder on his hands and McGregor still had time to ask after his well-being, amazing. Frankly he was astounded the guvnor could even remember his name, let alone the fact that he had a family.

'How old's your little girl? Eight?'

'Yeah, she is,' beamed Narey, 'you've got a good memory boss.' McGregor was probably able to recall the name and age of the kids of every man in CID.

'My advice? Enjoy the next five or six years before she starts running you ragged. Now,' he commanded, as if suddenly remembering they were all there for a reason, 'lead the way.'

I'd be proud to, thought Narey but he managed to avoid saying it, instead he said 'Mind how you go there, Sir. It's a bit slippy,' but DCI McGregor was already clambering down the grassy bank towards the victim.

'Beat the SOCOs to it, did we?' McGregor snorted. 'Probably still struggling into their little white gimp outfits,' and there were chuckles at that. 'Let's take a look at this body shall we? Don't worry, I won't *touch* anything,' he added, his tone drippingly ironic, as if they thought he might start frisking the corpse. This attitude would never have been tolerated in any other officer but McGregor would get away with it, as he always did.

They stopped a few yards from the body and the whole party waited patiently for McGregor to take a look, then deliver his verdict. He didn't disappoint. 'A middle-aged bloke out on his own walking in the park,' he began, speaking softly, as if to himself, 'is he dodgy, I wonder? We should check that. Just because he's unlucky enough to become the latest victim of the Sandyhills Sniper doesn't mean he wasn't out here looking for kiddies to fiddle with, leaving a trail of Werther's Originals right up to the back seat of his Rover 75.' They all laughed lightly at the chief's gallows humour. 'But I doubt it. I think we'll find this poor fucker is probably divorced, not his idea either, and it wasn't his weekend with the kids. He probably didn't know what to do with himself until it was time to go to his local.'

Narey hadn't thought of it like that but, all of a sudden, it seemed to fit. The boss had painted a vivid and believable picture of the victim, based on little more than a glance, and Narey found himself trusting in it unreservedly. Why else would a man be wandering in the park on his own, unless he was missing his kids?

DCI McGregor pointed at a scrunched up, brown paper bag at the victim's feet that Narey hadn't even noticed. 'He dropped that when the bullet hit him. It's empty, which shows he's respectable, old fashioned, wouldn't dream of littering the place with the bag that contained the bread he was using to feed the ducks.'

It was quite a forlorn image really, if the guvnor was right. Some poor sod whose life fell apart when his wife kicked him out, reduced to plodding through the park, making friends with the local bird life. 'I wonder if he had a dog?' mused the DCI, 'might be worth checking the park to see if one ran off when the shot was fired, which brings me to the angle....' He left the sentence unfinished, instead bending down to examine the bullet wound, peering closely at the obscene hole in the socket where the eyeball used to be. He looked like a golfer surveying a particularly tricky putt on the eighteenth green at St Andrews. McGregor rose and went round the back to check the exit wound and he took a long, hard look. He retraced his steps and went down low again, resuming the golfer's stance as he looked once more into the bloodied eye socket, then he turned his head to look behind him.

'So many possibilities; office blocks with flat roofs, those new apartments and the tenements,' McGregor turned back to the corpse, as if checking something, then faced forwards once again, 'but I don't think so,' he bit down on his lower lip while he was thinking, 'beyond them, those tall high-rise blocks way back there. What do you think Peter?'

DI Peter Blaine at least had the balls to offer a half-hearted contradiction, 'Not sure about that boss,' he offered quietly, 'looks a bloody long way from there to here.'

'Could be out of range but I bet you a pint and a chaser that it isn't.' The disagreement was amiable enough. McGregor wasn't the sort to make his officers look bad in public. 'There are rifles these days that can take a man out from a thousand yards. I'd say it's almost out of range, but not quite. Not for someone who's had training, a veteran, Iraq or Afghanistan maybe.' That was one of the theories they'd all been working to; that some unhinged former member of the armed forces, scarred by his war experience, had gone postal. Not that they were making that theory public, for fear of the backlash from the Press. 'We should check those balconies,' McGregor continued, 'see if he left anything behind. You never know.'

'Yes Guv,' answered Blaine.

Narey stared at the three high-rise buildings McGregor had indicated. They were set back a long way from the crime scene, but they were still tall enough to tower over the park, affording a perfect vantage point of the bench. It would have been a simple enough matter to fire a shot, then disappear before anyone noticed. Narey didn't know about rifles with a thousand-yard range but believed his boss knew what he was talking about. One thing he did know however; in those flats, the chances of anyone cooperating with the 'Polis' was next to zero, no matter what the crime.

McGregor glanced back at the victim, looked up again at each of the three high-rises in turn and squinted, then he rose slowly to his feet. 'Gentlemen, I think you will find that the fatal shot came from there,' he said, pointing at the block of flats to their left. Narey didn't turn away from McGregor, which was just as well or he would have missed what happened next. There was a distant, muffled crack and Narey flinched as something zipped past his left ear.

Before anyone could move, the bullet caught DCI

McGregor flush in the centre of his chest. He was catapulted backwards and a thick clot of blood expelled from his mouth as he gasped at the impact.

Narey looked down at his guvnor's body. McGregor had landed on his backside, his body propped against the park bench, head slumped against the last victim's knee, eyes wide open, a look of complete shock on his lifeless face, the trademark black raincoat puddling around him in the mud. 'Jesus fucking Christ!' someone shouted, and then all hell broke loose.

1

Newcastle – one year later

The legendary Peter Dean, appropriately enough for a porn baron, had gone down in the world. He looked up from the chipped basin he'd been spitting into, at the end of another spectacular coughing fit, and took in his tired, lined face in the old bathroom mirror. He stared at the unwashed greying-brown hair and squinted at the mercilessly receding hairline that was cutting a swathe over the top of his head. 'Christ almighty,' he murmured at the bald patches, wondering again if it was too late for a hair transplant at his age. He noticed his sallow complexion and sunken, watery eyes, 'too many fags,' he concluded gloomily, then immediately reached into his pocket for another one, struck a match several times with shaking hands and eventually lit it. Dean took a rejuvenating drag, then exhaled, deliberately blowing smoke at the mirror until his image was obscured.

He ambled back into the lounge of the one-bedroom-flat he called both home and office and sat down on the ancient battered armchair, attempting to ignore the cold by folding his arms across his chest. He was trying to avoid spending money on luxuries like heating, and he wondered whether he should put on a second pullover, while telling himself for the thousandth time that it would all work out somehow.

It hadn't always been like this. There was a time when he and Bobby Mahoney had made good money from his little film production studio; a lot of money in fact. But that was when Bobby was still a wannabe gangster, making his way in the world with a little armed robbery there, some protection here, a bit of grass and a few whores on the side, before he went on to run the entire city. In Newcastle, back in the late seventies, Peter had been a player and, hard as it might be to imagine it now, was once on an almost equal footing with the man who went on to control Tyneside's biggest criminal organisation. Back then, Peter was the go-to guy for all manner of adult material.

'Angel Productions' started out as a supplier of cine films. Those big, round loops of film that were spliced onto cumbersome, plastic wheels and ran on noisy projectors that could be beamed onto screens or, if your gathering was less discerning, plain white walls. Peter did well because his stuff was stronger than the material so beloved of the dirty mac brigade down in Soho. You could hardly show his stuff in cinemas. This was back in the days when, if you were really daring, you went to see, *No Sex Please, We're British* or *Confessions of a Window Cleaner*, and Robin Asquith was considered the height of naughtiness. Of course, most respectable people didn't watch anything that strong but, as Peter assured Bobby, 'There are always some folk out there who want their sex dirty and real.' For Peter, those people were manna from heaven.

Long before the advent of the internet, if you wanted to see actual sex performed in front of you by real people, it was sleazy, illicit and expensive, and Peter Dean was the man who could get it for you. He'd sell you his films under the counter at his studio or in the back room of one of Bobby's pubs and they'd cost you. 'When you take these home,' he'd tell you, 'you keep them hidden from your wife, your kids and the law. And you don't know me. You've never met me, not once, do you hear?'

These days, you can watch stuff a hundred times more explicit than those old films on the internet, and all of it for free, which is why Peter Dean found himself living in reduced circumstances, renting a squalid flat above a branch of Blockbusters, an irony he seemed wholly unaware of.

Peter's fall from grace had been a gradual one. Having ridden the crest of the cine film era, he initially adapted well to the VHS age, when the films got naughtier and nastier and he found he could sell more and more of them. He even ran some large shops at one point, partly funded by Bobby's largesse. Bobby Mahoney ensured there was plenty of cash available for Peter to keep on paying the girls and making the films that were recorded onto those black, plastic cassettes that seemed so portable then and so bulky now, in the digital age. His stuff usually consisted of grainy footage of 'Wives next door' performing pathetic little stripteases before half-heartedly playing with themselves, until the window cleaner turned up, caught them at it and 'punished' them in the only way he knew how, with a good, hard shag. Bobby Mahoney continued to fund Peter because he knew a universal truth; where there's sex there's money.

In the eighties Peter was minted. He had the cars and the big house and he held legendary parties, with proper champagne and the finest quality drugs. 'Pure Bolivian!' he'd assure everybody.

Where there's money and drugs and parties, there's girls, and Peter had more than his fair share of them too. He had his pick in fact – and not all of them porn stars, though he did insist on 'auditioning' all of those as well. 'You've got to show me what you're capable of love, before I go to the time, the trouble and the expense of filming it,' he'd tell them solemnly. Some walked, but most of them shrugged and let him get on with it. Not a single girl appeared in Peter's films without first performing on his casting couch. 'Not a bad way to earn a living is it?' he confided to Bobby with a wink.

But the high life couldn't last, and things got a lot harder for Peter with the advent of the DVD. The stuff he was churning out all of a sudden seemed old and a bit pathetic. He was loyal you see, perhaps a bit too loyal, keeping faith in the same lasses who'd paraded for him in skimpy schoolgirl uniforms in the eighties and 'reinventing' them for his 'Bored Housewives' series. By this stage, his housewives looked bored even while the window cleaner was giving them one on the kitchen table. Sales dwindled and 'Bored Housewives 14' actually lost money, which was unheard of in porn.

By the time the internet caught on, Peter was really struggling. How could he compete with his 'Northern MILFS' on DVD at £20 a pop when your discerning viewer could watch Pamela Anderson or Abi Titmuss doing stronger stuff? 'You've got that Paris Hilton and Britney Spears showing their growlers for nothing these days,' he told Joe Kinane in disgust, while explaining his latest business setback, 'no one's even paying them to do it!'

The sensible thing for Peter to have done was retire but he didn't have quite enough put away for that. He regretted splashing so much cash around in his thirties; all those parties, all that champagne and all that coke didn't come cheap but

Peter hadn't worried about any of it at the time. The money had been pouring in back then and he had thought it would all go on forever. Porn doesn't come with a final salary pension and, like many of the 'actors' in his little films, Peter wondered what he could do afterwards, once the gloss had gone from his empire. So, near bankrupt and thrice divorced, he sold his house and, instead of buying a little bungalow in Barnard Castle, rented a tiny flat above the video store and ploughed what was left of his money into the reincarnation of 'Angel Productions'.

'Ladies and Gentlemen, I give you Phoenix Films!' Peter Dean was back.

Times may have changed but it wasn't too late for Peter to change with them. He still thought of himself as an ideas-man, and now he was going to cater for the extreme end of the market. He would sell movies to 'connoisseurs' of the hard stuff. 'We'll cater for all tastes, no matter how weird they might appear to the so-called *normal* man in the street.'

There were little movies about barely-legal babysitters caught in the act of self-love by couples returning home early who were 'punished' in sadistic threesomes, fake 'snuff' movies in which the actresses appeared to have been brutally raped then 'murdered' for real afterwards, except the 'actresses' weren't good enough to fake fear quite as well as they faked their orgasms, and the same faces tended to crop up again and again to be murdered over and over in front of Peter's camera. 'I will make films on demand on any subject you desire,' he'd tell potential backers, 'it's all dependent on the price.' There was rape, torture, masochism, sadism, onanism or bestiality. The sex was middle aged, old aged and under aged, with first timers, part timers and old timers. There were threesomes, foursomes and moresomes, and household items crammed into every orifice. Peter set up rooms full of girls and boys who swapped with each other, then forgot who they'd been shagging just moments earlier. The drugs helped with that. Nobody remembers anybody in the hard core porn world, except the name and number of their dealer.

Trouble was, whatever Peter Dean did, no matter how filthy, it was never quite enough. He just couldn't compete with the internet. Every dirty thought Peter had in his sleazy life was already out there, magnified a thousand times and all just a mouse click away, most of it uploaded for free by Joe Public and his filthy 'ex-girlfriend', motivated by revenge on each other after they'd split up or, if they were still together, fuelled by the illicit thrill of knowing their most private, intimate moments were being watched every night by millions of strangers they'd never meet. How could Peter rival that?

He didn't see it coming. Now, in his sixties, Peter Dean was a poster boy for failure. It took a couple of years but slowly, steadily, the money began to run out. That was when Peter decided on one last desperate throw of the dice. He went to see David Blake.

Bobby Mahoney hadn't been seen around in a while, so there was no way Peter could speak to the man himself. Bobby was in semi-retirement somewhere hot, or so the story went, though there were other, more cynical voices than Peter's who claimed he was really six feet under, killed by a rival gang or an ambitious lieutenant. Peter didn't believe that but either way he realised he would have to deal with a new face in Bobby's firm. The main man these days was David Blake; still a young guy, mid-thirties, clever enough by all accounts but not a hard man particularly, though it seemed that the real hard men in the Mahoney crew were more than happy to work for him. Blake gave the orders now, anybody who was anybody in the city knew that, and so Peter Dean had his receding hair cut neatly at a proper barbers in the town, then put on his best full-length dark brown leather coat, the one that made him feel like Humphrey Bogart playing Philip Marlowe, and set off to speak to Blake at the Cauldron, an old nightclub that doubled as an HQ for Bobby's lads.

He was more than a bit put out on arrival to be told by a shaven-headed man in a leather jacket that, 'a meeting with the boss is impossible. You didn't make an appointment.'

'Fuck that,' he replied, because the bloke didn't look particularly scary, 'I know Blake's here. I've known him for years and he'll bloody well see me,' then he'd tried to push by, an act that proved to be ill advised. Peter was stunned to be lifted off his feet, spun round and planted very firmly against the wall, his glasses falling to the ground and his cheek grazed by the brickwork until it drew blood. It said a lot for Peter's parlous situation that he was more concerned about the condition of his spectacles than his own physical state. Bones could mend but he couldn't afford a new pair of glasses.

At that point David Blake himself walked out into the corridor to see what was happening, spotted Peter being pressed against the wall and actually laughed at the sight.

'Put him down, Palmer,' he'd said, 'you wouldn't touch him if you knew where he'd been.'

It was an ominous start. He was however released from Palmer's grip. 'You've got five minutes, Peter,' Blake told him as he was admitted to the great man's office and they both sat down either side of an imposing wooden desk. Peter looked round the room. Half a dozen of Blake's associates were there but he hardly recognised anyone. The guys he was used to dealing with were all gone. These fellas were all hard-looking bastards in their twenties and thirties, who looked like they had just stepped off a night club's doors. Except for Kinane, the firm's legendary enforcer, and Hunter, who was one of the few old guard remaining, a man who had virtually grown up in

Bobby Mahoney's crew, Peter couldn't have put a name to any of them.

Blake was young to be running a firm, but then everybody looked young to Peter these days. Peter guessed he was in his mid-thirties, around six feet tall, dressed in a smart suit with no tie and in possession of a full head of dark hair Peter immediately envied.

'What do you want to see me about?' asked Blake without any preamble.

Peter launched into his practised spiel, including the jargon he'd learned from the business books he'd been reading lately. 'I have a bit of a liquidity problem,' he explained to Bobby's young protégé, 'but all I really need is some working capital. If you can provide the start-up cash then I can leverage an amazing new idea, one that promises a very high return on your investment.' It was a fine speech, even if he did say so himself, and he was pretty certain Blake was interested, judging by the faint smile that played on the younger man's lips as he listened.

'Go on then,' he urged Peter, 'what's the big idea?'

He knew Blake was hooked then. Peter leaned forward in his seat, but not too close because Palmer adjusted his position at the same time, as if to intercept him before he got too near to the boss. God these security types were jumpy.

Peter cleared his throat and pressed on, 'What's the most successful adult site on the world wide web?' he asked.

Blake blinked like he had never given it much thought, 'YouPorn?'

'Correct!' said Peter, wagging his finger at the younger man, as if Blake was a particularly bright student, 'and why is it so successful?'

'Because it's free,' answered Blake, 'obviously,' and Peter was unable to hide his disappointment.

'Well no,' he said, 'I mean, yes it is free but that's not the reason it's so successful.'

'Isn't it?' Blake gave him a questioning look and then raised an eyebrow at the guys in his entourage, who chuckled sycophantically. 'Then what's the reason Peter? You tell me.'

Peter spread his palms, 'The name,' and, when there was no acknowledgement of his powers of perception, he explained further, 'that's how everyone knew where to find them. There's millions of porn sites out there on the internet but 'You Porn' took a name that was almost like one of the massively successful non-porn sites already out there,' he paused, 'You Tube, you know?'

'Yeah, I know,' admitted Blake, 'that was a clever gimmick but I think the fact that they were the first to supply bucketloads of hard core porn for free, was their *actual* USP, don't you?'

Peter didn't know what a USP was so he just nodded, 'Perhaps, but I still think it's the name. It's all in the name,' he said grandly, holding a hand up and sweeping it across an imaginary billboard in front of him.

Blake sighed and said, 'Peter, you have sixty seconds to get to the point. I have a flight to catch.'

'Right, yes, of course, no problem,' and Peter reached into the large, black document case he'd brought with him and fished out the A3-sized bit of card he'd had mocked up for the occasion, with what little remained of the cash from the sale of his house. He took off the cloth cover that obscured the art work and handed it to Blake reverentially. On it was a graphic artist's rendition of the website Peter was going to create using David Blake's money. Here was the idea that was going to put Peter right back where he belonged; at the very top of the pile.

Blake looked at the mock-up. He took his time and he peered at it intently. Peter held his breath. First Blake seemed to frown and Peter's heart sank but then his face broke into a smile and it felt as if a great burden had been lifted from Peter's shoulders. Thank God, he thought, the man with the money likes my idea. Everything was going to be alright after all. Peter's troubles were over. He was so happy he could have leaned over and kissed Blake but, just then, something odd happened; Blake's smile turned into a broad grin and then, horribly, unbelievably, it morphed into a chuckle. Blake looked at Peter and laughed, he looked back at the art work and laughed some more, then he started to really let rip. Blake showed the art work to Palmer and he laughed too, then they all leaned over, took a good look at it and joined in, all of them, everyone in Blake's pathetic, arse-licking, little crew of tough guys started to laugh at Peter and his brilliant idea. What the fuck was wrong with these people?

Blake finally stopped laughing and said, 'Thanks Peter, it's been an absolute pleasure, no, it really has. Funniest thing I've seen in ages but I've got to go now. Like I said, I've a flight to catch. See you around eh?'

And with that Blake rose to his feet and was gone, the posse of bodyguards melting from the room after him, all of them still chuckling. Peter looked down at the art work that had caused so much hilarity and genuinely struggled to understand how such an intelligent man as Blake, a successful man, a so-called entrepreneur, could fail to see the sheer goldmine potential behind a porn site called 'SitOnMyFacebook'.

Peter Dean went home and crawled; first into bed, then into a deep depression. He avoided meals, dressing and washing and failed to return calls from the very few acquaintances he had left. Bills and junk mail began to pile up on the mat. He contemplated suicide on a number of occasions and in increasingly imaginative and impactful ways.

Two weeks later, Peter finally emerged to take the phone call that would change his life forever. There would be money, a voice on the line explained, a lot of money and Peter would gain powerful new friends into the bargain. It seemed Peter Dean's dreams would be realised after all and it was all so simple.

All he had to do was kill David Blake.

2

I have to be lucky all the time. They only have to get lucky once. That's the thought that's always with me these days, the one that gnaws away at my brain in the small hours until I finally give up on sleep and climb out of bed, leaving Sarah breathing softly behind me.

I woke early as usual, my rest fitful, interrupted by dreams so vivid they covered me in a sweat that pooled on my chest and chilled my body, despite the heat. There seemed no point in lying there reliving nightmares, so I put them from my mind and climbed quietly out of bed, being especially careful not to wake Sarah, because she needs her sleep more than most. I thought I'd woken her when she stirred and muttered 'Davey' but she rolled over immediately, still fast asleep, just calling out my name in her own dreams, as if I was the only one she knew who could save her from them.

I padded quietly down to the kitchen and made coffee,

reminding myself, as I do every morning, that I really am a very lucky man in so many ways. I have my health, I have money, more than I could ever spend, and I have Sarah Mahoney.

And there's our place in Hua Hin. Not many people get to make their coffee in a kitchen the size of most people's flats. The sun was just coming up, turning the sky a grey-blue colour that you only ever see at the beginning of the morning. The scene outside my window looked like a watercolour. Soon the sun would be high in the sky and before long the heat would begin to cook the ground we walked on. Sarah likes it like that. She can sit out in the sun for hours in one of her bikinis that are little more than three tiny triangles tied together with string, her arms and legs covered in oil, her whole body turning a rich golden brown as she slowly bakes under the Thai sun, but I'm not too keen. I can't sit outside for long before I get restless. I'm not comfortable out there basting like a turkey and I can't relax with the bodyguards standing around us. Our ex-Gurkhas keep a discreet enough distance and it's not as if they lech at Sarah – though I could hardly blame them if they did, she is a stunner after all – but I like a bit of privacy, and that's one of the things I've had to sacrifice since I became the boss, so I prefer to swim in our indoor pool.

I spend a lot of time in the house while Sarah suns herself outside. I have a room set up with a bank of computers that help me keep a track on all of our legitimate investments. I am careful not to leave anything un-coded or incriminating on them that relates to the other side of our business though, the side that makes the real money. Most of our legitimate stuff is there for show; the restaurants, clubs and bars, the spa and fitness centre, even the two taxi companies we recently purchased and the bureau de change. They aren't really businesses in their own right. They tick over okay and they make a bit of profit between them but they are only really there to serve one purpose; to do our laundry. They make us look respectable and we can plough the money that keeps on rolling in from everything else we are involved in through them and wash it all till it's clean. My biggest headache is trying to find new ways to put the bent money through the system without anyone noticing it. Anybody who is involved in my world will tell you the same thing; the more money you earn, the bigger the problem, because you have to be able to explain every penny to the authorities if they come knocking on your door. It's a problem as old as my profession. Just look at Al Capone. If he'd bothered to pay some taxes they'd never have got him.

The proceeds that flow in from the drug deals, the escorts and massage parlours, the protection we offer to local businesses and smaller firms who operate on our patch, along with the occasional armed robbery, all has to be cleaned and laundered. Having too much money isn't easy. You might think this is a good problem to have but you'd be wrong. One mistake from me and I'll be staring at four grey prison walls for the rest of my life. I live with that stress constantly.

That's why I am about to make a change to the Gallowgate Leisure Group. Soon we will go global. We are about to become Gallowgate Offshore – then we really will have a licence to print money. But not yet, not until I can sort out a few issues closer to home; like the new luxury hotel we are building on the Quayside and the club we are about to open, which will be the largest nightspot in the north of England. More importantly, I have to sort out the heroin drought. My biggest wholesaler of coke and H has just left the market-place, suddenly and permanently. He thought it would be a good idea to import more than a tonne of cocaine into the UK in a single transaction, cutting the risks he endured with multiple trips from his base in Amsterdam. The stash was huge, and around ninety per cent pure, so it could be cut to make seven times the amount before it reached any users, which made that particular cargo worth more than two hundred and fifty million pounds on the street. It wasn't all for us, of course, but we were going to take a sizeable amount and, as he had been supplying us with most of our heroin and cocaine for the best part of two years now, his arrest was a disaster for him and for us.

A shipment that size doesn't just get stuffed into a cupboard, it was built into a hidden compartment behind the galley, but someone tipped someone else off and SOCA got on its trail. The Serious Organised Crime Agency used to be regarded as a bit of a joke in my world, but not any more. They've sharpened up their act. They impounded the yacht and dismantled it bit by bit until they found what they were looking for. It took SOCA three days to locate the drugs but eventually they were able to parade a haul on the TV news bulletins that amounted to around twenty per cent of the entire UK market and our wholesaler was facing a nailed-on life sentence. I wasn't concerned about him talking, he was old school and knew the risks, but I was worried about a product drought on the horizon. If the drugs dry up my money dries up too – and there are a lot of people on my books who have to be paid on time.

That's why the Turk and I are about to go into business together. Barely a month before, I was sitting in a little family restaurant in Istanbul, putting the finishing touches to the biggest deal of my life. It was the usual set-up. He and I shared a table while our bodyguards stood back and eyed each other suspiciously. I had brought Kinane and Palmer with me. No other customers were allowed in the place and the owner had made himself scarce. I'd forgotten what a smoke-filled room was like, all of the Turk's guys smoked and it hung around us like a veil. The room was oppressively warm, no air con and I could feel damp patches of sweat under my arms. I was hoping to get out of that room quickly.

The Turk was, in point of fact, actually a Kurd. Because he was based in Istanbul, Remzi al Karayilan had become known as 'The Turk' and the name had stuck. He didn't seem to care, but then he was doing pretty well by it so why should he? He was thriving because he had found a way to bridge two worlds; he knew people in Europe who wanted pure heroin and he had the contacts in the east to get it.

It takes guys like the Turk an eternity to come to the point. First you have to break bread with them, talk family, all that bollocks. He was a portly bloke who wore the fat round his belly like a badge of prosperity but you could tell he was a strong and powerful man underneath it. I'd had him checked out and I knew he had killed men with his bare hands. Now I was sitting opposite him, I could see how he'd managed to climb to the top of the heap in this city. He had the look of a man you definitely wouldn't want to cross.

The Turk shovelled a couple of dates into his mouth and chewed them noisily. Before he'd finished them he asked me, 'You have a wife, Mister Blake?' I shook my head. The guy looked at me like I was a freak, but I wasn't going to mention Sarah. I didn't want him to know about her.

There were small plates laid out on the table, each with a different dish, Turkish meze; white cheese, hot peppers, dolma, kofte, squid and figs. I ate some to be polite before he finally got down to business.

'I'm curious to know,' he asked me, 'what you think you can give to me, apart from your money?'

'Isn't that enough?'

'Not now, maybe before when I did not have enough, but not now. I don't want to be a rich man who dies in prison,' he explained.

'You know what I can bring. You wouldn't have sat down with me if you didn't. I can guarantee safe passage of your product from the Balkans to Amsterdam and beyond, right into the eastern ports of the UK. From there it goes straight to the estates and high rises of my city. I have a network of dealers working for me who can dispose of a dozen kilos at a time, with no interference from the police. That's what I bring to this deal. Now convince *me* you are worth my investment.'

'Me? I bring nothing Mister Blake,' and he eyed me contemptuously, 'just friends where you could not even step, without your throat it is cut,' his accent might have been strong, and he jumbled his words, but his message was clear. 'The Afghan tribes who grow the poppy trust me and the border officials in Iran live in my pocket. How many men do you own in those countries, Mister Blake?' I was getting a bit bored of his faux-formality but he made a fair point. Most of the heroin used in Britain comes from Turkey these days, so his Afghan connections were critical to us.

'And the Americans?'

'Don't give a fuck,' he assured me, 'as long as I am not Taliban, as long as I don't talk about the prophet, they don't worry what I do. All they care about is extremists. Years of Americans in Afghanistan and what has this achieved? Now the country produces ninety per cent of the world's heroin,' he shrugged, 'the Americans tolerate this. They tolerate any one who is not Taliban. The only alternatives are the tribal warlords who make most of their money from the poppy.'

'Most of the product comes out through Pakistan. Why don't you use that route?' I asked.

The question seemed to irritate him and he shrugged dismissively. 'A country more corrupt than mine, even than yours,' he told me with mock wonderment.

'You're saying Iran isn't corrupt?'

'I find it useful to work with governments that want to saturate western cities with heroin. Iran wishes for everyone in the west to become an addict. They won't stop me helping them to achieve that. So long as I pay big money to the right people, my shipments will always go through Iran.'

'Then on into eastern Turkey,' I told him, 'via the province of Agri where the product is collected by your men at Gurbulak and loaded onto oil tankers, before they smuggle it into the Balkans.'

He did not disguise his anger at my knowledge. 'What are you,' he slammed his hand down hard on the table, 'a policeman?'

'If I was, you would be in big trouble. I'm just a businessman who does his homework before he enters into a deal.'

'It is not a good idea for you to know so much about my business,' he said, wagging a finger at me, 'maybe I don't like that.' Abruptly he drained his drink and stood up. 'One million Euros in advance English, to show good faith, then we talk about your first consignment.' He stood up. It was the signal that our brief meeting was over. He and his men left without a word. There was no handshake.

The Turk is convinced his process is impregnable. I hope so because I am about to trust him with a great deal of my money. Even for an organisation our size, one million Euros is a lot of loose change.

I can't worry about that now though because today is the day that Pratin calls. I always pay Pratin on time, and the numbers are substantial. He comes down from Bangkok every month, regular as clockwork, and leaves carrying a nice big briefcase packed with currency – and none of your Thai Bahts either, this is strictly 'US Dollar American' as he calls it. Since Sarah and I relocated to Thailand I have got to know Pratin pretty well. He is *Roi Tamruat Ek*, which means he is a Captain in the Royal Thai Police, but his influence extends far further than his rank. Pratin knows people who matter. He is just another insurance policy I suppose, one more Drop that has to be paid, just like the monthly sum we still pay to Amrein, our high-level fixer back in the UK. Obviously I also have to shell out a considerable amount to my Gurkha bodyguards who patrol our compound night and day, making sure nobody can get in. They aren't cheap either, but that's one number on our balance-sheet that I never question because they are keeping me alive. That's what it's all about these days; insurance, protection, safety. I pay people to guard me, keep me out of jail, and tell me what my enemies are doing to get at me. It all costs big bucks, some of it in 'US Dollar American'. I suppose you could call it the cost of living.

This is the bit no one tells you about when you are on the up. Before I started running Newcastle, I assumed my predecessor Bobby Mahoney was absolutely minted. I'd seen the figures; the amount of money coming in was vast and much of it was undeclared income. I knew what he paid out to employees of the firm and how much we spent on the Drop. There should have been plenty left over to live the high life but I'm telling you, lately, the cost of business has gone up and up. The more our empire has expanded in the little over two years since Bobby died, the more I have to pay out to avoid being killed or stuck inside a prison in the UK or Thailand for life, so I am always thinking. Am I paying the right guy the right amount? Should I be paying his boss or some other guy I'm not even aware of? If I fuck up it's all over for everyone.

I try not to think about that as I surf the main news channels while I drink my coffee; Sky, BBC, CNN, though I don't bother with Fox obviously. I can't relax until I've surfed them all. Only then, when I am sure that the planet is still rotating safely on its axis, do I feel like I can properly start my day.

I was just about to change the channel when another news item claimed my attention. The trial of Leon Cassidy, aka the Sandyhills Sniper, was about to begin. The Sky News reporter told us earnestly that 'Cassidy will stand trial on five counts of murder, including the killing of Detective Chief Inspector Robert McGregor.' I was back in Newcastle when the sniper started picking off his victims and it had been a massive news story at the time. 'Police are not looking for anyone else in connection with the killing,' the reporter told us, in a poorly-concealed code that was designed to make everybody think 'they've got the bastard.' So much for innocent until proven guilty, I thought, but they did find the rifle in his flat, so it looked like Cassidy was going down.

I turned off the TV, then changed and went for a swim in the indoor pool. That alerted the stone calm figure of Jagrit to my presence, but he wasn't the sort to overreact to my sudden arrival. He didn't even flinch. I could see him standing there through the huge windows that overlooked our grounds. With his olive-skinned face and dark, watchful eyes he looked like he'd been carved out of jade. Jagrit is one of my Gurkhas chosen, like his comrades, because of their innate loyalty and legendary hardness. They were the perfect guys to look after me; honest, decent, honourable men but vicious bastards who could creep up on you and slice your throat open without you hearing a thing. Nobody could get into our compound with them watching out for me. These elite fighting men were probably the only reason Sarah and I got any sleep at all these days.

The water looked inviting enough so I did a few lengths, counting them off each time my hand touched the end of the pool. I did this most mornings to stay in shape, but I also liked the way it cleared my head at the start of the day. I can think in here and not in a way that makes me regret the past or feel anxious about the future. Who needs that? Deal with all of the shit you've seen and done and move on, that's what I say. It's the only way. Fretting is for old women and fools. Looking back on what might have been just drives you mad in the end.

I felt better after my swim. I dried myself and put on a robe, then made more coffee, before going into my office to check my messages. There was a new one from Kinane and I frowned at the screen as I read it. He wanted me to come back to

Newcastle as soon as possible. I didn't like the sound of that. It must have been something important if he couldn't handle things with Palmer and my brother Danny. That was the whole point of living out here with Sarah, thousands of miles away from the shitty end of the stick. They were supposed to look after everything. That's what I paid them to do.

Kinane's message said he would call me on a web phone later so I went up to check on Sarah. She was still fast asleep, breathing deeply, and I was pleased. She hadn't been sleeping well for months now. Instead she gets up in the night and goes quietly downstairs. I'm usually relieved when I hear her weight stir on the bed, then listen to her feet pad down the stairs. I sleep lightly these days too, and I get more hours on my own without her tossing and turning next to me and, if I have one of my nightmares, I don't really want her to know about it. So I usually leave her to it, unless I hear her crying downstairs and, if she sounds worse than normal, I'll go and see if I can do anything to help, even though I know by now that I can't. She just has to get through this somehow. She's not a drama queen, and doesn't wake me intentionally, but there's something about the pitch of her weeping that makes me pick it up in my sleep every time.

Some people don't look too good when they are sleeping but Sarah looks like a Princess from a fairy tale; like Cinderella or, well, Sleeping Beauty. Right now she looks so peaceful, if I took her picture it'd be like one of those adverts for a restful foreign holiday.

I should have been getting on with stuff but I didn't move. Instead I took a moment to look at my girl, to actually see her. She looked so lovely that, just for a moment, I completely forgot all of the doubts and negative thoughts that have been plaguing me lately. The sun was beginning to stream through the thin material of the linen curtains. In a little while it would wake her but, right now, it was putting colour in her face, painting her with its glow, making her seem even more young and beautiful than normal and that's some achievement. I thought that I might just be with the most beautiful girl in the world.

Glancing down at Sarah, seeing her there, looking so calm and peaceful and lovely, like the world could never harm her, I could hardly believe it was almost two years since I blew her father's head off.

3

Peter Dean thought long and hard about who he could use to get at David Blake. He finally settled on Billy Warren, who may not have been the first choice of many, but Peter had his own reasons for selecting him to arrange the hit.

Billy Warren was a slippery little fucker who'd been with Mahoney's crew for more than a decade, starting out as a young thug stealing cars to order. As he grew older he started breaking into houses, taking everything that wasn't too big to carry. If it looked like you were on holiday when Billy called round, he'd come back with a van and take your furniture – earning him the nickname 'Pickfords' which stuck, right up until the day he was finally caught. The lad did his bird in the right manner, head down, mentioning no names, like a proper, honest crook.

'No, your honour I do not remember the name of the man I sold the stolen goods to. It was just some bloke I met down the pub. No, I do not have his address,' Billy went on to deny there was any truth in the rumour that he was allowed to operate on his turf in return for a substantial kick-back to bent Police officers and further tribute money paid to an anonymous local crime lord, rumoured to be a certain Mister B. Mahoney of Gosforth, Newcastle. The judge quickly lost patience and Billy got three years, served two in Durham jail, then was released back into the community as a completely reformed man. As a reward for his loyalty, Billy was given the option of a career change by the aforementioned Mister B. Mahoney of Gosforth, Newcastle, who persuaded him that there was no real future in house breaking.

'I'm offering you a new job, Billy, as "a vendor of class-A substances",' Bobby told him.

Billy Warren's face creased into a confused frown. 'Eh?' he said.

'I want you to sell some Blow, Billy,' Mahoney clarified, 'because I think you'd be good at it.'

And he was. It all went swimmingly at first. In fact for a few years Billy Warren enjoyed the good life. He never got nicked because half of the law tasked with putting him inside was already in Bobby Mahoney's back pocket and though the other, more honest, half didn't like what they saw, it didn't mean they were going to shop their mates. Billy had never met a copper yet who wanted to put his colleagues inside for corruption.

So life was sweet. Billy had enough to rent a decent flat, get the car he needed to impress the birds and more than enough cash to go out on the town with his mates whenever he wanted. That's pretty much as good as it needs to be for a man in his early twenties but, over time, his outlook began to change. It's amazing what you can get used to. Billy went from being a man who never had enough; enough money, enough food, enough booze, enough dope, to a man who had all of that and still wanted more. In fact Billy started to question whether he was really getting his fair share. A lot of money passed through his fingers. He was building up contacts, selling a lot of blow and it wasn't just the coke that he was flogging. Billy could get you ketamine, meth amphetamine, crack, he could even get you a bit of 'H', just don't tell Bobby, who had a big time downer on heroin. Bobby thought heroin would damage the community. Ha, as if there was such a thing as 'community'.

Like everyone in Bobby's crew, Billy Warren had a few things going on the side. It was known, accepted even and everybody did it, they just didn't talk about it, especially in front of the boss.

'The secret is not to be too greedy,' Geordie Cartwright told him, 'you can rip off the big man just a little bit and he'll let you get away with it, as long as the major part gets kicked upstairs to him.' That was the one big, unwritten rule. But Billy had started to think about the future and things didn't look quite as rosy as he would have liked. Sure, he had money, but not big money, and certainly not the wedge required to live like a 'face' in this city – but it wasn't just that. There was one other thing Billy lacked, something that had been eating away at him for months. Nobody respected Billy Warren. The guys in Bobby's crew took the piss out of him constantly. Billy knew he wasn't the brightest bulb on the Christmas tree but, nonetheless, he did know what he was doing.

If you wanted someone to persuade a young, flash business type to part with way too much of his salary on far too much cocaine, then Billy was definitely your man. But despite the money coming in to him, Bobby Mahoney treated Billy like he was some sort of court jester. As soon as Billy walked into a room the jokes and the sledging would start. They'd question his short stature and slim build, call him 'Shortarse' and 'Sammy Shrink'; they'd take the piss out of his low-slung jeans and hooded tops, labelling him 'Gangsta'; they'd ask him when he last got laid, knowing it was likely to have been a while back, because Billy wasn't that great with the ladies, unless he paid them, so they'd call him 'Virge', short for Virgin.

Worst of them all was Jerry Lemon, a tattooed armed robber turned Mahoney lieutenant who tormented Billy in a way that thoroughly disturbed him. Lemon would call him 'the little queer boy', even though Billy wasn't a homo, or he'd insist on naming him 'Bunny' Warren, which made Billy sound like a total queen. Lemon would blow kisses at him in front of the rest of the crew and, when he looked freaked out by this, would ask 'what's a matter Bunny, gone off me, have you? Don't you like a bit of boy no more? That's not what I've heard. They say you was everybody's best bitch in Durham.' And the whole crew would laugh at him then and the shame would burn into Billy's face.

He was pretty sure that it was actually Jerry who 'liked a bit of boy' as there was something bordering on the sexual in the way he taunted the younger man, but Billy would never dare say anything back to him. Jerry was an out-and-out hard case who would have killed Billy for fun, then shrugged an apology at Bobby, merely for inconveniencing him.

There was another reason why Billy wouldn't dare challenge what was said; because he was worried that Jerry really did know something. Billy was no queer but he had been forced into doing some stuff by a cellmate in Durham that he definitely did not want to do, or be reminded of, ever again. The shame of that memory had led him to snort a good deal of his own product. But what could Billy do? Refusal was not an option at that point and the alternatives would have been far worse, so Billy had done what he had always done; he'd survived.

Did Jerry know about this or did he just guess it had happened? Could he read it in Billy's eyes? If Jerry did know there were two worrying possibilities. One; he would tell everybody in Mahoney's crew what had happened and Billy would be even more of a laughing stock for blowing a murderer in Durham jail. Two; Jerry was keeping the information to himself, so he could use it against Billy, most likely by making him repeat the act on Jerry – and that was an even worse prospect.

The day someone chose to blow Jerry Lemon's head off was one of the best days of Billy Warren's life. His tormentor had finally got what he deserved. Life might have been sweet but Bobby's head of security, David Blake, discovered that Billy had done a coke deal without Bobby's knowledge. This meant Billy Warren now owed his life and continued livelihood to Blake, and he began to hate the man.

'I can't take a piss in Newcastle without this fucker's permission,' he told Kinane.

Kinane looked hard at Billy through narrowed eyes. 'You're lucky Blake lets you carry on breathing, Billy. If it was me you'd tried to rip off like that, I'd have taken you ten miles out into the North Sea on a fishing boat and thrown you overboard.'

'I never meant nothing by it man, honest like,' Billy stammered.

'I'll do it too,' Kinane told him, 'if I ever hear you say another bad word about David Blake. You got that Billy?' and Billy nodded, as if his life depended on it, which of course it did.

In the scheme of things, that exchange might not have been too significant at the time but Peter Dean had been in the bar that day and his ears pricked up. He loved a bit of gossip, did Peter and, if Kinane was taking the trouble to terrify people on his behalf, it showed just how far up Bobby Mahoney's organisation Blake had travelled. Peter recalled that conversation before he decided who he was going to approach for money for his internet venture. He remembered it again now, as he eased his car into one of the communal parking spaces beneath Billy's flat.

4

Jaiden Doyle had a spring in his step. Perhaps it was the weather, which was milder than usual for the time of year, maybe it was having some money in his pocket, or possibly it was to do with the new threads. There was something about the right clothes that could make you feel like you fit in. The ones he'd just bought seemed to have had the right effect on Palmer and Kinane. Things had definitely not been anything like so pally the last time they'd seen him.

A month earlier, he'd gone to the same Quayside hotel with messages from the Sunnydale estate and a word or two about the week's takings, along with a request for some more stash. You would have thought the supply of junkies willing to pay top dollar for H would eventually become exhausted, even on these shithole estates, but they couldn't get hold of the drugs quick enough. Jaiden thought that David Blake's two closest lieutenants would have been happy to hear that but, when he met them, in the bar of one of the Quayside's fanciest hotels, they had torn Doyle a new arsehole.

'What do you think you look like you scruffy fucker?' growled Kinane before Jaiden even opened his mouth. The firm's enormous enforcer was giving Doyle a look like he was contemplating snapping him in half.

'Eh?' It took Jaiden a moment to realise they were talking about his clothes, and he wondered if Kinane had a problem with his eyes. Scruffy? Everything he had on was brand spanking and all of it killer reem. Doyle reckoned he looked pretty slick. There was a yellow, hooded Southpole top over a Super Dry T shirt and FUBU jeans worn so low over his hips that everyone could see the black letters of the Calvin Klein logo on the elasticated band of his undercrackers. He was particularly chuffed with his box-fresh bright white Nikes that didn't have a scuff mark on them. The final addition was the long, thick gold chain round his neck and he kept the hooded top unzipped, so everyone could see it and the designer T-shirt it hung low on. He kept the hood up over his head. Where he grew up you didn't want to be recognised by the police, remembered by a witness or spotted by a rival gang if you strayed from your home patch. Doyle thought an old hand like Kinane, a proper gangster who'd gone right to the top of the tree, would understand this but, instead, he gave the teenager a look of disgust.

'Are you asking to get arrested?' added Palmer. Kinane's bulk made Palmer look small by comparison but, in reality, he was an average-sized bloke with a bigger than average reputation that revolved around the words 'special forces'. Reputed to be a former member of the SAS or SBS, with a drawer full of medals and dozens of 'Black Ops' to his name, before quitting the forces and 'coming over to the dark side' as Braddock put it, Palmer was a muscly, shaven-headed, softly-spoken Scot with stubble on his chin; his accent was part Glasgow, part

Geordie, thanks to his adopted home. Doyle didn't know too much about the smaller man, except for the whispers on the street about his military career, but he did know he was just as senior as Kinane and was apparently 'nails'.

'Palmer's been in wars and shit and killed, like, hundreds of people,' Doyle's mate Shanks informed him just days before the meet. It was true that those who worked in Bobby Mahoney's firm afforded Palmer just as much respect as they did the far larger figure of Kinane. Doyle was careful to watch his mouth around both men, and certainly never set out to piss either of them off intentionally, but he couldn't understand what their problem was. Dressed like this, Doyle reckoned he looked like Eminem or maybe a white Tinchy Stryder; proper Gangsta and a man not to be fucked with. His mates had all been impressed by his style but it seemed Kinane and Palmer didn't share their enthusiasm.

'What's the matter?' he asked.

'What's the matter?' Kinane growled the words back at him and Doyle experienced the fear that came with them, 'You look like a complete cunt, that's what's the matter. You might as well walk in here with a bag full of H and an Uzi.'

'You can't come into a hotel like this, looking like you just stepped out of the Hood,' Palmer explained. 'You're carrying a sign saying 'Arrest me I'm a drug dealer'. Look around you, you tool.'

Doyle turned his head from side to side and looked at the other people in the bar, some of whom quickly averted their gaze like they'd only just stopped staring at him. The place was quiet, except for the sound of very dull piano music coming from the speakers, and the low chat of the other customers, all of whom were dressed like they were going to a wedding. They all had on jackets, and trousers, some even wore ties. All of a sudden it dawned on Doyle how out of place he looked. It had never before occurred to him that looking like a dealer, when you actually *were* a dealer, was a disadvantage.

He looked back at Palmer and Kinane. Both of them were frowning at him.

'Soz and that,' he stammered the apology and they continued to frown, 'I didn't know like.'

'Well you know now,' Kinane told him.

Palmer reached into his inside jacket pocket and started to write something on the back of his drinks receipt. 'If you want to carry on being our eyes and ears at Sunnydale, get yourself down here pronto and buy something proper. I mean a jacket, trousers and some shirts. The kind of stuff we're wearing. No hoodies, no trainers and no Bling. Understood?'

'Yeah,' he was nodding like a madman, desperate to keep his privileged and protected position as the messenger, the go-between for these men of power and Braddock, the man who ruled the Sunnydale estate on their behalf.

'Blake gets his stuff from there. It's quality,' Palmer told him, 'not that you'd recognise that if you saw it.'

'And another thing,' added Kinane.

Doyle had frightened rabbit eyes by now, 'What?' he asked.

'Get a fucking haircut.'

Doyle returned from that meeting a month ago a chastened man. He still wore his own gear for working on the estates but, as soon as he could, he went down to the designer clothes 'emporium' Palmer had told him about and bought the clothes they had asked him to buy; trousers, jacket, some shirts. And he got the haircut. If Kinane told you to do something you weren't stupid enough to wait until he asked you twice. He felt a bit foolish wearing those clothes as he left the estate but he had to admit that, once he was in town, he felt a lot happier. Doyle caught his reflection in a shop window as he passed by and he looked sharp.

Palmer and Kinane must have thought so too because they

didn't say anything about the way he looked, not at first. Instead they listened, hearing him out without interruption as he told them the latest take from the Sunnydale estate, which was down on the usual amount by a fair sum.

'Who gave you that amount, Doyle?' asked Palmer.

'Braddock,' answered Doyle, 'it's always Braddock that gives me the amount.'

'And did he give you a reason?'

'No, he never said anything about it.'

Kinane and Palmer showed no emotion at this news. They asked him a couple more questions, the usual day-to-day stuff, then they let him go. As Doyle reached the end of the bar, Palmer called out to him, 'Oi Doyley,' and he turned back to be told, 'you look almost employable.'

Doyle beamed at Palmer then immediately felt self-conscious, turned and left the bar.

Doyle crossed the hotel foyer, silently cursing himself for looking so uncool in front of the big men. He'd smiled like a simpleton as soon as he received a bit of back-handed praise from a street legend. He left the hotel wondering if they would ever take him seriously.

Doyle was about to cross the road to follow the riverside path back towards the Quayside. No one, least of all Doyle, saw the gunman as he emerged from the shadows behind him, raised his hand, pointed his Makarov pistol and shot Jaiden Doyle twice in the back.

5

'They want me to set up a job for them, using a local man,' explained Peter Dean.

'Who does?' asked Billy.

They were sitting at a table in Billy's flat, a chaotic place that made Dean's tiny flat seem ordered by comparison.

'Never you mind Billy,' said Peter, '*they* want to remain anonymous. That's why they are paying me. You can think of me as the client, if you like.'

'Yeah, well, I don't care, do I? All I care about is the money and what the job is…' Billy seemed suddenly to recall that nobody had actually told him what was required yet, 'What kind of work is it?'

Peter Dean took a deep breath and said, 'A hit.'

'A hit,' Billy laughed, but then he noticed that Dean wasn't laughing, 'you're fucking joking, aren't you?'

'I'm deadly serious,' said Peter.

Billy's mouth opened like he was about to form the words of a reply but he didn't say anything. Instead he thought for a moment and finally said, 'that's not what I do. I just deal.'

'You don't have to pull the trigger yourself, that's the beauty of this. I just want you to find a local man who can do it for us, tell him all about the fella these guys want to remove, give him some inside information to help him complete the job, then pay him and see him on his way.'

'Why don't these people just do it themselves then? Why pay us?'

'They're not from round here and, like I said, they want to remain anonymous.'

'Right, I see,' said Billy, 'well it's their money I suppose,' he took a drag on his cigarette, tapped it against the ashtray, then added, 'talking of which, what are they offering?'

Peter told him and Billy whistled like he couldn't believe it. 'Who is the bloke then? The one they want removing?'

For the second time, Peter Dean took a deep breath. This was the moment where he risked everything, up to and including his life, on a single roll of the dice. If he had misread the situation, if Billy didn't really despise David Blake, or was too scared of him, if he simply wanted to get back into Blake's good books by telling him there was a plot against his life, then Peter Dean was a dead man. But then Peter was as good as dead anyway, without the funds needed to prop up his fading empire. So he told Billy Warren who the target was.

'David Blake? Are you sure?' Billy's eyes widened as Peter nodded, 'Jesus fucking Christ man!'

There was a moment when Peter fully expected to be asked if he was mad, before witnessing the nightmarish prospect of Billy picking up the phone to David Blake or, worse, Joe Kinane, then Billy said, 'that's a hell of a risk you are asking me to take.'

Billy didn't believe that though, not really. He was used to ducking and diving, always had been and he was already pretty sure he could sort this, without actually going anywhere near the sharp end himself. Delegation; that was what was required here. He could put a lot of space between himself and this job if he planned it right and the money was, well, astounding. When the amount was mentioned, Billy couldn't believe his luck. Jesus, who did they think they were going to kill, the Prime Minister? Peter explained he would receive half once the hit man had been approached and engaged, and the rest once the job was completed.

'Interested?'

'I might be.'

'But can you do it?' asked Peter. There was a worried look on the older man's face like he suddenly thought he might have overestimated Billy's contacts. 'Do you know the right man to make this happen?'

'Oh yeah, no sweat,' answered Billy, 'I know a bloke that would do it easy,' he assured Dean, 'in fact he's exactly the man for this job.'

'So,' asked Peter, failing to hide his nervous excitement, 'are you going to do it?'

Billy took another long drag on his cigarette, 'I'll have to think about it,' he answered, 'won't I?'

'What's so important I have to drop everything and fly over there? I was with you a couple of weeks back,' I was in the computer room on the first floor taking the promised call from Kinane. 'I thought you and Palmer could handle everything.'

I turned my seat while I listened and looked down through the open window so I could see Sarah's slim shape cutting gracefully through the water, rolling from side to side as she powered towards the far end of the pool.

'I know,' Kinane admitted, 'we can, usually.'

'It's not Braddock again, is it? You're not still banging on about him.'

'No it's not him,' he assured me, 'but while we are on the subject I have to say…'

'We are not on the subject,' I told him firmly, 'you just said it wasn't him. You know my view on Braddock. Just leave it.'

'Yeah and you know my view an' all,' he told me, but my silence was enough to shut him up, 'it isn't Braddock.'

'Well?'

'We've got some problems,' he sounded almost sheepish.

'What kind of problems.'

'I don't know where to start.'

Sarah finished her lengths and climbed out of the water. She walked over to one of the loungers and picked up a large white towel, then began to dry herself with it.

'Start with the bad news,' I said, 'then give me the other bad news.'

'Amrein's been on,' he said, 'says he has to have this meeting with you about the Gladwells. It's urgent, he reckons.'

'Yeah,' I sighed, 'I know. I've been stalling him. I don't really want to have a cosy chat with him about the Gladwells.'

'Can't say I blame you,' Kinane admitted, 'what do you want me to tell him?'

'Tell him I'll talk to him when I'm back in the country,' I conceded, 'which sounds like it's not going to be far away. What else have you got for me?'

'It's Toddy,' he said, like he couldn't quite believe it, 'it's not looking good.'

'You're kidding me. I thought Fitch was all over it.' My lady lawyer was the dog's bollocks and harder than most of the men in our crew.

'She is, big time. I know she always runs the Police ragged when they drag you in for questioning,' said Kinane, then he added, 'but it's her that's telling me it's not looking good.'

I had pinned all of my hopes on our expensive lawyer picking the Police procedure apart on this one, looking for anything that might have made evidence inadmissible or violated Toddy's human rights in some way. Ever since he had been lifted by the Police on the Sunnydale estate months ago, we had been fighting a losing battle to get our Toddy off the hook. Mainly because he had three kilos of H in the boot of his car.

'The Polit found a lot of product on him,' Kinane reminded me, 'she thinks he's on for a stretch.'

This hit me hard. I always thought something could be done to get Toddy off, or minimise the sentence if he was sent down. Maybe he'd only get a year or two and he could handle that. We would look after him, take care of his mum and his girlfriend, compensate Toddy for the time served and make sure he had a future when he got out. That way he'd be less likely to cut a deal. If he had any notion his sentence was likely to be a long one he'd be far more open to offers from SOCA, to name names before disappearing into a witness protection scheme.

'What are we telling Toddy?'

'Nothing,' said Kinane, 'just that it will be alright. He'll probably get off on a technicality.'

'He believes you?'

'Don't know, yes, at least I think he did.'

'As long as you're sure then,' I told him, but he didn't seem to detect the sarcasm.

I realised now I'd placed too much faith in the lawyer. Susan Fitch was expensive but she knew her stuff. She was a formidable adversary and had torn more than one Police officer apart in the dock before now. They'd arrive there all brash and cocky, with a notepad full of concrete evidence, just waiting to send a villain down. Then they'd be confronted with a hard-faced analytical mind just waiting to pounce on any tiny little detail, blowing a contradictory or misrepresented piece of evidence out of all proportion until they were dizzy from it. Susan Fitch was known for getting even the most hopeless cases off scot-free. The Police bloody hated her for it. But not this time it seemed, at least according to Kinane.

'I still can't believe it,' Kinane had reason to be disbelieving. We paid good money to ensure the Sunnydale estates were way down the Police's list of priorities. Like me, they took a realistic view of the heroin trade there. It had been going on for thirty years and was never going to end, so why fight the inevitable? We were the ones who got rid of the low-lives dealing there and replaced them with our men. The estates had become a huge money earner for the firm. Our move into the Sunnydale high-rises was so successful we expanded, branching out into every other estate in the city. Now we were a presence in every run-down hell-hole in Newcastle, but better us than the alternative. Obviously the people who worked for us weren't saints. How could they be? They dealt drugs and, on occasions, used violence. But we made sure they never went too far. People didn't get killed on our watch, we didn't deal to children or get teenage girls high for free then pimp them out so they could pay for their addiction, and the drugs we sold weren't cut with strychnine, rat poison or household bleach. We cleaned up the trade, ending the tendency to settle every minor dispute with a drive-by killing. Sure we had to get rid of the local hoodlum who ran the patch before we moved in but they usually got the message, eventually, and the short, sharp shock we administered was a small price to pay to bring order where there was chaos. Even the Police understood that. It wasn't exactly junkie nirvana on the estates now but, in the real world, it was about as good as it gets.

Because the Police knew we were the best-worst option they left us to it. So at first we couldn't work out why Toddy had been lifted. Panicked phone calls were made, as we demanded to know what the hell had gone wrong. It was only then we realised just how unlucky Toddy had been.

'Jesus Christ,' I tried not to show my exasperation but this wasn't going to be an easy one to fix, if Susan Fitch couldn't pick holes in the arrest then no one could, 'this is all we need.'

'Tell that to Toddy,' said Kinane.

I ignored him, 'you said there was more bad news.'

'You could call it that. Doyley has been shot.'

'What?' This, if anything, was even more startling news, 'Jaiden Doyle? Where?'

'Outside the hotel and in the back – right after the usual meeting with Palmer and me.'

This one I just didn't get. Doyle was a low-level operative in our firm. He ran a team of dealers for Braddock in some of the high-rises on the Sunnydale Estate, but that didn't make him a target for anyone. This didn't make any sense.

'Is he dead?'

'He'll live. The bullets went through him, just missed his lung and his heart, assuming he's got one. To be honest, I don't give a fuck about his well-being. His sort are ten a penny. What worries me is that someone had the balls to have a go at him. Everybody knows he's on our payroll, so he was protected.'

Kinane was taking this like a personal affront and well he might. If you took a pot shot at one of our lads you were basically giving Joe Kinane the finger. You were saying you didn't give a fuck about our enforcer coming after you – and Kinane wouldn't take kindly to that attitude from anyone. He had been right to call me. Right now it was hard to imagine anything worse than Toddy facing a stretch and someone having the nerve to shoot one of our guys on our own doorstep. Even so, the last thing I needed right now was another long-haul flight back to the UK, with a load of shit to deal with at the end of it. I'd always thought that, as time went by, I'd be able to delegate more and more of the day-to-day business but it seemed that there would always be some things in our world that only the boss could sort.

I sighed, 'I'll take a flight in the morning.'

6

Sarah put her book down and asked 'What's up?'

'Nothing,' I said, 'I've got to go back to Newcastle though.'

'When?'

I shrugged, 'May as well be tomorrow. The sooner I sort things out, the quicker I'll be home again.'

'Doesn't sound like nothing,' her voice was calm but I could tell she was worried. We were both playing the same game, assuring each other that we weren't really concerned about anything; that my short-notice business trip to Tyneside was a routine one and she was merely taking a passing interest.

'It's just stuff,' I managed, 'you know.'

'Yeah,' she said, 'I know. Stuff…'

'Make sure you eat properly while I'm away,' Sarah had a bad habit of not bothering to eat if I wasn't there to share it. Like a lot of girls, she thought toast was a meal.

'I will.'

'Five a day,' I reminded her.

'Is wine part of my five a day?'

'It's made of grapes, so I'll let you have that.'

'You're the expert on matching it with food, which wine goes best with Maltesers?'

'Hey, I mean it. Eat proper food or you'll waste away. Then you'll lose that great figure of yours and I'll go off you completely.'

'Thanks. I'm getting fat anyway,' and she surveyed her impossibly flat stomach for the umpteenth time that week, scrutinising it critically.

From where I was standing she looked good. Very good in fact. And it was a shame she wasn't feeling well at the moment because I was about to fly off for a few days and I quite fancied a going-away present. Fat chance of that though. In fact, about the only time I got to see her body these days was when she was wearing a bikini. It was strange, I'd seen Sarah naked dozens of times but when she stepped from the shower that morning and saw me, she immediately covered up before I got so much as a glimpse of her. I didn't understand what that was all about, but I'd come to the conclusion there was a great deal I'd never understand about women.

'Be a good girl while I'm away,' I told her as I bent to kiss her on the forehead, 'try not to sleep with the Gurkhas.'

'I'll try,' she smiled sweetly back up at me, 'but I can't promise. I get so bored and what's a girl to do?' This time I bent lower and kissed her on the lips.

'Thanks for that comforting thought.'

Being the boss has its advantages. Wherever I go these days I get treated like the head of any decent-size corporation, which of course I am, and I'm shown straight into the first class lounge before I board the plane. It's fine in its own way but I am getting a bit too used to this sort of thing to really enjoy it.

A pretty young thing appeared from nowhere and gave me a smile like I was the centre of her universe, but it was all in the lips, her eyes were expressionless. I wondered how many fat, bald chief executives fall for this and try it on with her.

'Champagne or orange juice, Sir?' she asked me, and her ruby-red, heavily-glossed lips formed themselves into an inviting 'O' as she said 'orange' and, for a moment, I wondered what those lips would be like around me and if her blonde, tied-back hair would stay in place while she moved her head up and down. Christ, I am going to have to do something about the drought I'm in. It's not Sarah's fault that's she's suffering from depression. I understand, I really do, but this no-sex thing is turning me into a dirty old man.

'Champagne,' I answered, and she took a long glass by the stem and handed it to me. It's daft really. I've got cases of the stuff back at the house in Hua Hin and all of it better than this bought-in-bulk inferior fizz the airline offers, but there's still a poor, Northern boy trapped inside me somewhere who would shout 'don't be daft man, it's free!' if I refused it. I don't think my mother ever had a glass of champagne in her life, except maybe at a wedding.

I sat for a while waiting for my flight to be called and tried to read a book. Somewhere there's a serial killer on the loose and a maverick detective with a liking for hard drink is tracking him down. Years ago I could have read the whole thing on my flight home and enjoyed it for what it was, but I just can't get into it. I've got a lot on my mind, what with Sarah not doing so well. Then there's Toddy's case and now even Jaiden Doyle has given me something to think about. Who would want to shoot one of my men? Lots of people probably, for a whole variety of reasons, but I have to work out who stood to gain most from the act and actually had the balls to go ahead and do it.

*

I glanced out of the window and watched as the large black Lexus pulled up outside the café. The driver parallel-parked it, taking a moment to get the vehicle straight against the kerb. There wasn't much room between the two vans but he rocked it quickly back and forth until it was slap bang in the centre of the space. The car came to a halt, the driver's door swung open and out stepped the hardest man in the north-east of England.

Joe Kinane was so big he made every car he drove look like a toy. He reminded me of Noddy in fact, always out of scale, far too large for the car he drove around in. Kinane stretched like he'd been cooped up in the car for too long, then he glanced towards the window, saw me sitting there, nodded and walked up to the café, frowning all the way.

The door swung open like someone had just kicked it but that wasn't misplaced aggression, it was just Kinane's natural awkwardness. Here was a bloke who really didn't know his own strength. Joe Kinane was around six-four in his socks and weighed in at about two hundred and forty pounds. He was in his early fifties but remained undiminished for it. There was no sense that Kinane had seen his better years and was on the wane. Certainly no one was brave enough to suggest this to him. Pride alone would have forced him to knock them into a different post code.

Kinane had been talent-spotted by Bobby Mahoney while still a young man. Back then Bobby hadn't been the top dog. He was still an emerging force, carving out a name and a reputation for himself. He had reached the stage where he had earned respect from those within his profession, but there were a number of candidates who could just as easily have taken on the role of Top Boy in the city and he was merely one of them. Another candidate was Alex Clarke who, along with his two brothers, came from a long line of criminal stock. They were hardened villains whose father and uncles had been frightening people for two decades before they came along. The rise of the

Clarkes seemed almost pre-ordained in those days. Certainly Bobby was aware of them and would have been wary of their reputation, which involved a ruthless and enthusiastic use of violence.

The Clarke brothers decided to take over a pub they'd taken a liking to. It was on the outskirts of town but doing well because it was right opposite a thriving club they also had their eye on. The brothers gave the owner an ultimatum; sell to them for way below market value or stay put and have the place burned down around him, but the owner refused, so they decided to pay him a visit. They didn't realise that a new man had started on the door that night. That man was Joe Kinane.

I can't remember the other Clarke brothers' first names; they are just a footnote in Geordie criminal folklore – but I do know that Joe Kinane killed one of them in the fight and paralysed another. Alex Clarke got his face and throat slashed with the broken bottle he tried to use on Joe, who took it off him and turned it against his attacker. At least he was able to run from the building. The police found Alex by following the trail of blood and got him off to hospital before it was too late. It was rumoured that one of the senior detectives investigating the whole bloody affair actually shook Joe Kinane by the hand and said, 'if it was down to me, son, they'd give you a medal,' before they led him away. Joe Kinane became a legend on Tyneside that night.

Kinane was charged with murder at first, but only for five minutes or so; this was the Clarke brothers, after all, and the charge was soon dropped to manslaughter. There were mitigating circumstances, everyone knew the reason the Clarkes were in the bar that night and people were prepared to testify about it now that one brother was dead, another in a wheelchair and the third had gone missing, Alex having hopped onto a train to London as soon as his wounds had healed. Eventually far lesser charges were brought and Joe

Kinane was given just eight months for what would now be described as affray. He only served four and, when he was released, with everything he owned in a brown paper parcel, he emerged blinking into the sunlight to find Bobby Mahoney and Jerry Lemon waiting for him outside the prison walls. They gave Joe a lift into town in Bobby's Jag, bought him drinks and a meal, lent him money that didn't need to be repaid to 'get him back on his feet' and finally talked idly about finding him a bit of work when he was ready for some.

A week later, Kinane started on the door of the Cauldron but it soon became clear his talents would be better utilised elsewhere and, along with the late, great Finney, he soon became one of the firm's two enforcers. With them at his side, Bobby Mahoney's rise was unstoppable.

I would never say this to Kinane's face but he and Finney were very much alike and, possibly because of this, they never really got on. Each one thought he was harder than the other man and itched for the opportunity to prove it. Seven or eight years ago now they almost got the chance. There was a row, the details of which have been lost in the mist of time and been clouded by myth, but it involved money, a dust-up with some rival villains and an argument about who exactly did what to whom, when, and on who's orders. In the end, Bobby sided with Finney and Kinane was banished from the inner circle, forbidden to earn a living in any way that might impact on Bobby's business. Most people with Kinane's talents would have left the city at that point but Kinane clung on, opening a ramshackle gym which kept him going during the wilderness years.

I had managed to avoid falling out with Kinane, despite being one of Bobby's trusted lieutenants, and he was the first person I brought into the organisation when I took over. When Kinane walked into a room with me people shut up and they listened.

'Found the place okay then?'

'Eventually,' he told me, and he looked around the room, as if he was about to start addressing everyone in it, 'why anyone would choose to live down here is beyond me. It's a shit-hole.' He said it loud enough for a couple of people to look up from their plates, but they soon looked back down again once they realised who was doing the talking. The area we were in was Kings Cross, which used to be a shit-hole but was well on the way to full gentrification, transformed by the renovation of the St Pancras Hotel, the building of up-market apartments and the European rail link. I suspect Kinane disapproved of it all simply because it wasn't Newcastle.

'Get yourself a brew, Joe. You've come a long way.'

He nodded and walked over to the counter just as a manager emerged from a side door. The girl who'd served me was clearing cups and wiping tables, so the manager served Kinane. The manager was young and keen and almost as shiny as the five grand's worth of gleaming espresso machine behind him, which looked like it could power a steam train.

'Yes, sir, what can I get you?' he chimed.

'Coffee, white, two sugars,' ordered Kinane.

'You mean you want a white Americano?' the young man corrected him with a nod towards the tariff behind him. Kinane looked at the man with distaste then squinted at the tariff with its Grande-this and Frappe-that, scanning the dozens of Americanised-pseudo-Italian phrases, looking for the simple word coffee. When he couldn't find it, he gave up and turned his attention back to the manager who was looking a little impatient now.

'No,' explained Kinane quietly, 'I do not want an Americano, you soppy cunt. I want coffee, white, two sugars. Got that?'

The manager stared at Kinane and nodded quickly, 'Yes sir.'

'Go on then.'

And the young manager quickly put his head down and got

his arse in gear. Seconds later there was a steaming cup of coffee with milk added, resting on a saucer on the counter between them. The manager did not stop there. He even came out and fetched two sugar sachets from the self-service section, returned to the counter, tore them open and poured them into Kinane's coffee, then stirred it for him. Kinane paid him with a gruff, 'There's a good lad.' The manager gave him his change, quietly thanked him and quickly retreated through the side door again.

Whenever I can, I prefer to drive. Public transport is a disgrace in this country. Okay, I don't have to worry about the cost like most people, but think about it, go by plane and you stand around waiting for an age to board the bloody thing. Then there's that intrusive paper trail with passports and boarding cards; all easy to trace later, which isn't ideal in a world where you'd really rather nobody knew where you were going or what you were about. And don't get me started on the trains. Last time I bought a first-class ticket I told the bloke behind the counter I wanted to buy a seat not the whole fucking train. So much easier to just climb into your car when you want, and go where you want.

I don't normally expect Joe Kinane to drive all the way down here to pick me up but he wanted to talk and this was as good a way of doing it as any.

'Is Palmer back from the Turk?' I asked.

'No.'

'Taking his time, isn't he?'

Kinane's ludicrously broad shoulders shrugged, 'It's a tricky business, isn't it?'

'It *was* a tricky business,' I agreed, 'initially. Negotiating with a new wholesaler always is, but this meet was supposed to ratify what's already been agreed. I don't know why it should take this long,' I observed.

'I don't either but he's carrying a million Euros. He's got to be careful, hasn't he?'

'I guess so.' I conceded. I didn't know what worried me more; that Palmer was late back from carrying a one million Euro deposit intended for our new drugs wholesaler or that Kinane had got a bit sniffy with me when I queried this. Kinane was showing a commendable loyalty to Palmer; considering they worked together a lot that was understandable, but his first loyalty was supposed to be to me. I didn't want the two of them becoming too close – a firm within a firm. The fact that it had never entered Kinane's head that Palmer could have done a runner with the money, or been killed by the Turk for it, concerned me too. You need imagination to stay alive at the top of our profession. That's why they need a guy like me running things, so I'm trapped, because they won't survive for five minutes on their own without me. Right now I just wanted to get back to Newcastle, so I could sort out the mess as quickly as possible, then take the first flight back home to Sarah. I was getting the nagging feeling that it wasn't going to be that simple.

7

We stopped halfway for a break. Kinane chose a truck stop because he 'wasn't going to pay over the odds for a fucking Panini and a muffin. Not when I can get a proper fry-up for half the price.' We sat at a formica-topped table that was in need of a wipe-down. There was a plastic sauce bottle shaped like an over-sized tomato with congealed ketchup on its nozzle. Through the grubby lace curtains I could see rows of lorries parked up outside. We were the only ones who'd arrived by car.

A good fry-up was one of the things I missed the most, along with a proper pint. Kinane lived off this stuff and I joined him. We both ended up with plates piled high with bacon, sausage, fried egg, fried tomato, fried bread and baked beans, washed down with mugs of piping hot tea. By the time I'd finished I could almost feel my arteries hardening. Kinane chuckled to himself as he mopped up the remnants of his egg yolk with his fried bread and stuffed it into his mouth.

'What?' I asked.

'I almost forgot.' He mumbled while he chewed, 'Peter Dean wants a meeting with you.'

'You're not serious? Not after the last one. I hope you told him "No".'

'I would have done but…'

'Christ, Joe. I rely on you to keep old timewasters like Dean away from me. Haven't I got enough on my plate already?'

'Hear me out,' he said, 'you want to be rid of him and his stupid schemes, don't you?'

'Of course.'

'Well now's your chance. Peter has found a backer.'

'A money man?'

'Apparently.'

'Are you telling me someone is about to invest in Peter Dean?'

'So he says.'

'And you believe him?'

'He reckons he has the man and the money all lined up.'

'Well good luck to him,' I said, 'but what the hell has that got to do with me and why does he need a meeting?'

'Because the Gallowgate Leisure Group owns fifty per cent of Phoenix Films.'

'You're kidding me?'

'Nope. I checked. It's true. Bobby must have chucked him a bit of wedge for old time's sake or out of charity or something.'

'Doesn't sound like Bobby. So Peter needs my permission to receive investment?' I still didn't get it.

'According to Peter, this backer of his wants to buy us out.'

'But the company is valueless.'

'Peter has persuaded him otherwise. According to him, this mystery backer will pay one hundred thousand pounds for a controlling stake in Phoenix Films, so fifty grand is ours if we agree to walk away.'

'Fifty grand? You're joking. We'd walk away for nowt. We've walked away already. I didn't even know we owned a stake in his so-called company.'

'Then this will be the easiest fifty thousand we've ever made. All you have to do is meet Peter and sign his papers.'

'That's fine with me,' I told him, 'if someone wants to throw their money away then who am I to dissuade them, but I don't want to go to that disgusting flat of his. Set something up elsewhere.'

'He asked to meet you in Chi-Chi, on the terrace there.'

That figured. I could imagine Peter Dean sitting on the terrace outside Chi-Chi, pronounced "she-she", an establishment that, like him, had delusions of grandeur. He'd be wearing his sunglasses whatever the weather, dreaming he was really on La Croisette at the Cannes Film Festival instead of peddling smut on Tyneside.

'Alright,' I agreed, 'but make it a drink, not lunch. I'm not eating at the same table as Peter. He makes my skin crawl. Fuck knows what he's riddled with. Get Councillor Jennings to join me there for lunch after, no later than twelve-thirty. Half an hour with Peter is long enough, even for fifty grand.'

On a good day I can imagine Bobby Mahoney is looking down on me and he understands. I can convince myself he knows I had no choice but to do what I did. He is pleased, in fact, that I am taking care of his daughter, while simultaneously preventing anarchy on the streets of his beloved city and, consequently, he is not likely to pay me a disapproving visit in the night, like the ghost of Hamlet's dad. On a good day, I can calmly evaluate the facts behind his death and my involvement in it. I can coldly and clearly state that I had no choice and that Bobby Mahoney understood this, right up to the point when I pulled the trigger and killed him.

Bobby had watched as Tommy Gladwell got a former

officer of the Russian Spetsnaz, called Vitaly Litchenko, to press a gun against my head. He told me he would kill me if I made a wrong move. He then handed me a Makarov pistol with one bullet in it and ordered me to shoot Bobby. If I accepted he would let me live. If I refused he would kill me. I was given ten seconds to make up my mind and at the end of them I chose to live. I killed Bobby. I think about that moment every day. If I hadn't done it, Tommy Gladwell's Russians would have killed us both. That's what I tell myself.

No one was more amazed than I was when Tommy didn't go back on the deal. He let me live, stuck me on a train to London and told me never to return. No one was more amazed than Tommy Gladwell when I came back and killed him and his Russian thugs. Well, no one perhaps, except me.

'Do it,' Bobby ordered me, right before I killed him, 'you'll be doing me a favour,' and I believed that at the time, because I really wanted to believe it. 'Get out of here, find Sarah and take care of her.' That was the last order he ever gave me and I obeyed it. I found Sarah and I have been taking care of her ever since. I console myself with that fact. On a good day.

But not all days are good. Some mornings I wake and recall, with awful clarity, a recurring dream I have, where I am back in that room down at the derelict factory with Tommy Gladwell and his Russians and, this time, the words coming out of Bobby's mouth are very different. He's asking me if I am really going to kill him just to save my own skin; if all the years I've known him mean nothing to me; if I am such a coward that I am actually going to go ahead and do this? Then I do it anyway, but this time it all happens slowly and in vivid Technicolor. I shoot Bobby in the head and every streak of blood splashes in slo-mo against the white walls behind him. Then I wake with such a start, I sit straight up in bed before I realise it's a dream and the very first thing I see when I open my eyes is Bobby's only daughter lying next to me, blissfully unaware that I am the man who pulled the trigger on the father she loved so dearly.

But not this time. Today, when I wake from that dream, I am alone in a hotel bedroom and, for a moment, I'm so disoriented by jetlag that I don't even know what part of the world I'm in. I look around me, then remember I'm in my hotel on the Quayside with a view that would overlook the Tyne river if I hadn't drawn the curtains to blot out the afternoon light so I could get an hour's rest.

I stumbled groggily to the bathroom, ran the cold tap and caught water in my cupped hands. I brought it slowly up to my face and it had the desired effect. It jump-started me back to the present. I looked in the mirror at my pasty face, with its contrasting bloodshot eyes, and contemplated going back to bed for the whole afternoon but I resisted. I had things to do.

My first call was to Susan Fitch. I told her my concerns regarding Toddy and his case.

'I'm a lawyer, Mr Blake, not a miracle worker,' was her considered response.

'Should I remind you how much we paid your firm last year, Mrs Fitch?' I asked.

'And should I remind you that Martin Todd was caught with three kilos of heroin in his car, which makes him not just a dealer but a heavy-duty one? He will be damned lucky if I can get him out of a life sentence.'

I had to admit she was right. It didn't look good for Toddy. 'Look, just do your absolute best for this guy, okay? Will you do that?'

'Of course, but will you also do something for me?'

'Name it.'

'Stay away from Martin Todd. You can't do anything to save him and we don't want you appearing on his friends and family list right now. You may think my firm is expensive Mr Blake but this is one piece of advice I am giving you for free.'

8

I took a cab out to my brother's house. Our young'un, as I always called him, had a new place. Until recently, my older brother had been content with my old apartment, which was a whole lot better than the one he had been living in before I employed him. Then, abruptly, he said he wanted somewhere bigger, with a garden. I just laughed at him. I couldn't see it really; my big brother Danny tending his petunias. Anyway I took the piss out of him but I didn't argue. It was his business what he spent his money on.

He'd been in the new place a few weeks now and when I pulled up outside he was in the front garden cutting back the hedges with one of those big electric trimmers. He had his shirt off while he worked, revealing a tanned and muscular torso, covered with long-faded Parachute Regiment tattoos on his arms and back. On his chest he had the cap badge with a motto underneath; the Latin words 'Utrinque Paratus', which translates as 'ready for anything' and was as suitable a motto for our firm as any I could think of. On his back was a huge airborne forces emblem of Bellerophon atop a winged Pegasus wielding a spear to kill the Chimera. I knew fuck all about Greek mythology, but I knew that story. I could still remember the day Our young'un first showed me his new tattoo. He'd not been in the Paras long and was about to go off to the Falklands, a war that completely fucked him up for thirty years or so, before I finally got him straightened out. He came home pissed one night, woke me up and pulled off his shirt to show me the fresh new tattoo. I was only about seven and it scared the shit out of me. I don't think I really understood what he had done. It felt like that bloody man with the spear somehow owned him after that. The tattoo had faded, but the childhood memory was still vivid.

It was a warm day, but not hot enough to strip to the waist so I reckoned it wasn't down to the weather, and it turned out I was right. I paid the taxi and walked towards his front gate, just as a woman came out of the house next door, carrying a little tray with a cold glass of beer on it. I'd say she was about forty; quite tidy in her own way, with a gym-toned body and expensive hair-do with blonde streaks in it. She had a look that must have cost a few bob to maintain and, as she smiled at Our young'un, I wondered where her old man was right now. My guess was he worked away somewhere, sweating to earn the money she needed to keep looking so fit.

'I thought you looked thirsty,' she announced, offering the tray over the hedge towards him.

'You read my mind, pet,' answered Danny and he wiped his brow with the back of his hand theatrically, then reached out and accepted the beer. 'Ta very much.'

Danny still hadn't seen me, which was why he stood straight, raised the bottle and took a long slow drink from it, giving the woman plenty of opportunity to check out his muscles. She looked like a cat eyeing a bowl of cream.

'Now then, Danny!' I called and he almost choked on his beer. 'How's it hanging bro?'

He actually coughed then, as if the beer had gone down the wrong way. He managed to keep his composure while he introduced me. 'This is Davey,' he told the woman next door, 'my little brother.' He put a bit more stress than was necessary on the *little*, like he always did when he was narked at me. He forgot to tell me her name so I simply leaned over the hedge and shook the hand not holding the tray.

'I'm Stephanie,' she said, before adding unnecessarily, 'Daniel's neighbour.'

'Daniel?' I asked and he gave me a look, 'very pleased to meet you Steph,' I told her, 'hope I'm not interrupting,' and she looked a little flushed.

'Not at all,' she assured me, 'Daniel was trimming his bushes so he offered to do mine while he was at it.'

I stifled a smirk and made out like I was admiring his handiwork, but she was still standing right behind the shrub I was looking at. 'Nice tidy bush,' I told him.

'Thanks,' he told me stiffly, 'were you just passing, like?'

''Fraid not,' I said, 'need a word,' then I looked at her, 'the family business.'

'Of course,' she said, 'I'll leave you men to it then. Unless you'd like a cold beer too Davey?'

'No thanks, I'm fine, but it's very kind of you to offer.'

'No trouble at all.'

'Thanks Stephanie,' he told her retreating rump as she sashayed back into the house, closing the door behind her.

'Careful Our young'un, wouldn't want you to get caught up in her clematis.'

He picked up the hedge trimmers and waved them at me like he was about to cut my head off with them, then we both walked towards his garage so he could put them away. I wasn't going to let him off that lightly.

'Oil rigs?' I asked.

'Eh?'

'Her husband? Aberdeen is it, or is he a travelling salesman?'

He smirked like he was about to 'fess up to something, 'Dubai.'

'You dirty bugger,' I said, 'you're like one of those randy blokes from "On The Buses", always trying to get your end away with some other bloke's bird.'

'What?' he mock-protested, 'I haven't done anything.'

'Yet.'

'Hey, it's not my fault if she's after my chap. I'm not encouraging her.'

'Apart from taking your shirt off and offering to trim her bush for her.'

'Alright Finbarr Saunders, you can stop with the bush jokes now,' he told me firmly. 'Besides, she's too old for me.'

'She's a few years younger than you,' I reminded him.

'Yeah, well I prefer 'em young,' he said, and from what I'd heard he was getting them too. It was an amazing transformation. Two years back no woman in Newcastle would have given our Danny the time of day. He was broke, unemployed, drinking too much and he lived in a shit-tip but now his life was turned around and all because he was working for me. He had money, nice clothes, he wasn't drinking anything like as much as he used to and everybody knew who he was. Not every girl in the city wanted to go out with someone in his line of work but there were enough who did like a bad boy to keep him going. They wanted to be seen with him and he was lapping it up.

'Well, be careful, she looks like she'd eat you alive.'

'She's alright,' he told me.

I figured we'd wasted enough time on small talk so I asked him, 'What do you know about Doyley getting shot?'

'Not much. We followed it up, obviously, but there's no strong lead, no one with any major reason to follow him down to the Quayside and shoot him, or pay someone to do it for them. I even went and saw him in the hospital and he has no idea who did it. He's scared shitless, obviously, and a bit delirious with all of the drugs pumped into him.'

'I'd have thought he was used to that,' I said.

'At least Doyley lives up to his nickname,' he said ruefully, 'now he's got holes in him.'

'Braddock wouldn't want him out of the way for any reason?' I asked.

'It's possible, I suppose, we'd thought of that. But why would he go to all of that trouble to get rid of a member of his own crew outside a hotel on the Quayside? Much easier to do it on the estate where no one sees anything.' I'd thought of that too, of course, but I'd wanted to hear what Danny had to say about it, 'I'm not saying that Braddock isn't a toerag, pain-in-the-arse, because he is, and he needs sorting,' he added, 'but him shooting Doyley makes no sense.'

'Has there been a lot of heat on us?'

'The Police have gone a bit mental about it, as you can imagine. They don't mind that much if a drug dealer gets shot on the Sunnydale estate or any of the high-rises but they ain't too keen when he's gunned down outside a tourist haunt in the Quayside.'

'I figured as much. Who came to see you?'

'Who do you think? D.I Clifford,' and he snorted, 'I think he is losing the plot. He kept demanding to see Bobby, of all people. He's got it into his head that Bobby is back in Newcastle.'

'Bloody hell.'

'Anyway he left a message for Bobby,' he said.

'Which was?'

'It was a bit rambling but it was all about keeping the streets of Newcastle safe for the good folk of the city and how he wouldn't tolerate another shooting.'

'That bloke is a heart attack.'

'Agreed,' he said and he glanced at his watch, 'so you're back,' he said solemnly, 'and I haven't got any plans for the afternoon. Are you finally going to show me it or what?'

Danny drove us down to the nightclub in his Jaguar XF. He tried to pretend he wasn't that arsed about his new car but I was sure he secretly thought he looked like the DBs behind the wheel. We parked outside the new club, which had been custom-built on an old lot on the Gateshead side of the river. We'd bought an old club that had been forced to close down, demolished it brick by brick and put the new building up in record time. It was a cavernous place. 'Jesus Christ,' said Danny, I've seen aircraft hangers smaller than this ...'

The club still needed a bit of work; a lick of paint in places and the attention of a sparky but we were almost there. Our young'un was looking round, taking in the huge lighting rigs, the glass lift to the VIP area and the podiums. 'Amazing,' he announced, above the din of the workmen.

'A lot of it was down to Sarah.'

'How's that? She's never even set foot in the place.'

'I showed her the plans and I got a bloke to do me a virtual version, you know a 3-D mock-up on the computer. She took one look at it and went, "No, that'll never work" and "what you need is one of these" and me being a mug I listened to her. She had some great ideas, really transformed the place. None of them were cheap, mind.'

'You really think we can compete with the Diamond Strip? I thought the Quayside was dying on its arse these days.' The so-called Diamond Strip was an area of pubs and clubs north of the Quayside at the top of the hill, centred around Collingwood Street. It was the place to be seen since it became the preferred venue for rappers, footballers and Z-List reality TV personalities.

'If this club does what I expect it to, we'll drag the whole party scene back across the river,' I assured him.

Danny looked unconvinced. 'Must have cost a friggin' fortune.'

'It did,' I admitted.

He shook his head, 'I'm sure you know what you're doing, bro', but I can't see how you're ever going to make any money out of this place.' I laughed at him and Danny looked baffled. 'What's the joke?'

'It's not supposed to make any money, Danny,' I assured him.

'I don't get it.'

'The whole place is one huge launderette,' I explained, 'the money from the sale of our product comes in and it goes through the books as admission money from non-existent customers and their proceeds from the bar. The club can be half full, making a massive loss and I don't give a shit, just so long as we can wash our dirty cash and it goes out the other side clean and ready for the accountant to wrap it up in a bow.'

Danny thought for a moment. 'That's bloody genius.'

'It's one of my better ideas,' I admitted, 'do you want to hear another one?'

'Suppose so,' he wasn't looking at me. His eyes were wandering round the place again and he looked like a kid in a sweet shop.

'Once it's open, I'll need someone to run the place.' He looked at me now. 'Do you know the kind of person I'm looking for?'

He grinned at me, 'A handsome, rock hard, former para who'll leave the hard men quaking and the ladies sliding off their seats?'

'No, a crude, thick fucker who'll do what he's told because

he doesn't know any better.'

Danny beamed. 'When do you want me to start, like?'

'Opening night,' I told him. I was relieved he was so up for the job. Along with Palmer and Kinane, Danny had been my main muscle since I became the boss, but I was keen for him to take a bit of a back seat now. Doyley getting shot had reminded me how tough this business we had chosen could be. I liked the idea of Danny being the face of our club, no longer the guy out there collecting protection money or taxing our local villains. I could trust him to keep a proper eye on the club and it would keep him safe.

'What are you going to call the place?' he asked.

'"Cachet",' I told him. I'd not long decided on a name but I liked it. It was short and snappy, a one-word depiction of style, which I reckoned would fit the bill.

'Should call it "The Laundry",' he told me.

9

We've got twenty-three pubs in Newcastle and Gateshead. The Mitre was one of those pubs and tonight we had the big upstairs bar to ourselves. The lads were downing pints and, as usual, Hunter had put himself in charge of the old-fashioned jukebox. None of the boys minded because they couldn't be bothered to change the tunes themselves and he kept us entertained, his lazy eye scrutinising the track lists as he sought inspiration. Trouble was that he thought nobody made decent music after 1985, so the choices were a bit limited. The boys enjoyed Meatloaf's *Bat Out of Hell*, followed by Fleetwood Mac's *The Chain*, because they could play air-guitar to them, then he gave us some Cult and a bit of AC/DC, followed by Bryan Adams' *Run to You*. It was like we'd all suddenly gone back in time in one of those crap TV series.

I watched Hunter choose the next round of tracks. These get-togethers were virtually the only time we ever saw Hunter dressed in anything but overalls. That night he was wearing a pair of jeans and a blue pullover his missus probably picked up for him in Marks & Sparks at the Metro Centre. He didn't look much like a hardcore criminal from this distance, but he had seen some things in his time and he'd dealt with a lot of shit for the firm. He was tall and stocky and his hair was now more grey than brown. He would have had a forgettable enough face if it wasn't for that lazy eye. When Hunter looked at you, one eye was fixed on yours and the other seemed to be staring at a spot somewhere over your left shoulder, which could be a little distracting. Hunter was our Quartermaster, and his cover was the body shop he had in the arches under the railway bridge. If the boys needed a piece they went there to see him, their comings and goings easily explained to the police by a duff radiator or burned out clutch.

The whole crew was there that night. More than twenty of our most-trusted faces. I like to get them together from time to time. Bobby used to do the same thing. Put them all in a room with free beer on tap and watch them. I didn't have an ego about it but I needed them all to see men like Palmer, Kinane and my brother Danny deferring to me on business matters. That way, no one was likely to forget who I was or where I fit into the scheme of things.

We'd been there a couple of hours when Palmer walked in, straight from the airport. He got an ironic cheer for making the effort even though he was late and he waved to acknowledge it. When he saw me at the bar he came straight over. He was wearing the long black leather coat he always wore these days. It was the only thing I could ever remember him spending any money on and he virtually lived in it. It had been raining outside and the drops clung to his shoulders and the top of his head. He'd given up on his thinning hair and spontaneously shaved it all off one day then turned up the next morning 'looking like Yul Brynner,' as Kinane put it. That was the kind of thing Palmer did. He didn't bang on about it, or even discuss it with anyone. One minute he had hair, the next he was shaven headed and sporting a thin layer of stubble that, if anything, made him look even harder.

I was relieved Palmer was back from his meeting with the Turk. I took a quiet table in the corner so we could talk before we rejoined the rest of the lads.

'How'd it go?'

'Easy. It's a shame we're not in the Euro.'

'You're not serious.' It was the first time I'd heard that view expressed in the UK in a while.

'A million Euros weighs a lot less than a million pounds,' he explained, 'and you can fit it all into one bag.'

'I meant how did the meeting go?'

'Okay,' he said.

'Any hitches?'

He shook his head, 'No.'

He took a sip of his pint and I took a sip of mine.

'You were gone a while.' I noted.

'They do things slowly over there. You have to meet everyone before they even sit down to talk business, you know that.' I didn't know that, but then I had only met the Turk twice. I left the rest of it up to the men I trusted. 'I lost count of how many cousins he introduced me to but they all work for him. His is a big operation. I had the deposit on me for three days before he agreed to accept it. I slept lightly with that amount of money in my room I can tell you.'

'So why did it take so many days to shake hands on the deal? You did shake hands on it?'

'Yes we did and I told you, they do things slowly out there.' Palmer seemed a little edgy. Was he nervous because he had something to hide or nervous because he didn't and the last thing he wanted was me to think that he had? Maybe it was just me. Perhaps I was the edgy one these days. 'He wanted certain assurances for starters.'

'What kind of assurances?'

'The usual kind; are we secure as an organisation? Do we have a safe, foolproof route to get the product into the UK? Did we have enough money to buy that amount of product from him each and every month?'

'We've been through this countless times.'

'I know,' he said, 'but he's cautious. You would have to be in his shoes.'

'And what did you say?'

'I told him we'd been in business with the Haan brothers for years without a hitch and they were more than satisfied with our credit history.'

'Was the Turk happy with that?'

'Yes and no,' he said, 'happy we could pay, but not too happy I'd reminded him our former suppliers were looking at life sentences.'

'He knows that comes with the turf,' I said.

'Maybe he thinks we had something to do with it?' he offered.

'Not if he has done his homework. If he has checked us out, and he will have done, he'll know we are not undercover cops trying to make a name for ourselves and we don't grass,' I took another sip of beer, 'well, not about anyone that actually matters.'

'Yeah, I know that,' he agreed, 'if he'd thought I was an undercover cop I'd be floating face down in the Med.'

'So the deal is on?' I asked him.

'The deal is on and the first shipment is on its way. Our million Euros saw to that and he needs two million more by the end of the month to establish a line of credit.'

'He'll get it,' I assured him.

'Then we are back in business.'

'Thank fuck for that. Another eight weeks and we'd have been out of product completely.'

It had taken months of delicate negotiations with the Turk to get us to this day and we were almost out of supply. Newcastle would have been open to anyone with product in his back pocket and, sooner or later, they would have taken over. That's how vital it was that Palmer shook the Turk's hand in Istanbul.

Danny was in a good mood that night. Turning my older brother's life around is the achievement I am most proud of. If you'd known him a couple of years ago you wouldn't recognise him now. Back then he was a basket-case and nobody really knew why. All we did know was that he'd had a bad experience in the Falklands War when he was still a teenager and it had somehow messed up his life. He could never hold down a job after he left the Paras and, by the time he hit forty, he was walking round like a zombie; no job, no partner, no prospects, no money, shit flat, shit life. He basically mooched round the grottier pubs in Newcastle living off benefits and whatever money I threw him. That all changed when I was in the shit. Nobody could argue that when I really needed Our young'un he was there for me. Virtually everybody I knew and trusted was dead at that point. We had no crew left so I had to rebuild from scratch.

That was when men like Palmer and Kinane earned their stripes. They stepped up and stood alongside me to take on Tommy Gladwell and his Russian henchmen. Danny was right in there with me. He stood by me and I made sure he got his reward.

We all had a few pints that night and Danny got a bit loud. Nothing like he used to be when he was into the sauce but just enough to be embarrassing. He was banging on about our childhood, when we had no money and he had to look after me because our Ma told him to.

'I tell you I couldn't get rid of him. He'd follow me every-fucking-where.' The lads who worked for me were lapping this up, which only encouraged him. 'If I wanted to go to the pub with me mates, he'd still be tagging along. We'd tell him to go and sit in my pal's car and if he didn't come inside we'd bring him out a bag of crisps. It was the only way I could ditch him.'

'And he never did bring me any crisps,' I told them.

'And we never did bring him any crisps,' said Danny, as if I hadn't already spoken.

'We'd come out hours later when it was dark and he'd still be sitting there, bubbling.'

I could really do without this. In my line of work I don't need anybody questioning whether I'm a soft arse, so the image of me crying, because my brother was a twat to me when I was a nipper, wasn't doing me any favours. I knew why Our young'un was doing this. It was the last thing he had over me, the only remaining point where he could still say he was a bigger and better man than me. Those days are long gone and I could crush him in front of the guys in an instant, with a few carefully chosen words. I could say that it's just as well I am more generous with his wages than he used to be with his crisps, otherwise he'd starve. I could basically make it clear that I own Danny, but what would be the point of that? Danny realises he owes everything to me and, even though I know he is grateful, on another level that has to hurt. No one really wants to be in debt to their younger brother. You don't have to be a psychiatrist to understand that.

'He was horrible to me when I was a kid,' I tell them all, smiling like it was such a very long time ago, 'I think that's why I'm such a cunt now.' And they all laughed at that one.

Were they laughing because it was funny or laughing because I was the boss? I honestly couldn't tell you. Hunter changed the record on the jukebox. Somewhere far away Tom Petty and the Heartbreakers were singing about an *American Girl*.

10

We used to take the Drop down to Amrein's home; a huge country house in Sevenoaks that had state-of-the-art security and rooms for all of his bodyguards. We don't do that any more. I think his faith in the place was dented when we broke in and left Tommy Gladwell's severed head on the windowsill of his summer house.

You could describe that as the low point in our business relationship but we are both realists and we moved on. Amrein needs me to keep sending the Drop every month and I need the information, influence and protection it buys me. It's what's known as a symbiotic relationship. We don't have to like each other, and Amrein certainly doesn't like me. Not after that little incident. But he knows he was bang out of order. He betrayed me by going behind my back and giving information to Tommy Gladwell and withholding it from us. He knows I could have – maybe should have – had him killed for that, and for the blessing he gave the eldest Gladwell boy to take over our operation when he was supposed to be on our side. I think, if his superiors had known what he was up to, they'd have saved me the bother of killing him. His little bit of entrepreneurialism would have been the death of him. So, although Amrein undoubtedly despises me for scaring the crap out of him the way I did, he also understands that I was well within my rights and, if I'd handled things a little differently, it would have been his head on the windowsill not Tommy's. So there's an uneasy truce between us these days but, like I mentioned, we don't meet in Sevenoaks any more. Instead he prefers nice, big shiny hotels in neutral cities, places with wide open spaces and lots of witnesses. Today though, he is meeting me on my patch, in a conference room at the Malmaison in Newcastle. They think he's the MD of a Financial Services company. Me? I'm wondering why he is affording me the courtesy of driving all this way from Kent to see me in my city to talk about the Gladwells. It can't mean anything but bad news.

The two of us sit together at the end of a large conference table, his bodyguards stand against one wall, rigid, like they are about to come to attention on the parade ground. My lads are opposite them. They look a bit more laid back, but they're just as alert, ready for anything. They have to be with Amrein and I am sure he feels exactly the same way about me.

We have a corporate video running in the background to drown out anyone who might be trying to listen in. Just as the video cuts to shots of prosperous and youthful-looking retirees with perfect teeth, striding across a foreign golf course, we get down to business.

'Arthur Gladwell is dying,' he told me.

'I know.'

'Indeed, but he hasn't got long,' he cleared his throat and I wondered if he was still nervous about mentioning the

Gladwells in front of me, 'it's only a matter of days, which is why I need to facilitate a meeting as soon as possible.'

It strikes me as ironic that a man like Arthur Gladwell, who has controlled most of Glasgow since the mid-seventies, when he brutally murdered his predecessors and their lieutenants, chopping them into small pieces while some of them were still alive, should meet his final end like this. Lung cancer has ravaged his body and it looks like he is about to succumb. The nastiest, most violent man in three decades of the Glasgow underworld has finally been defeated by the debilitating power of a cigarette.

Like Amrein says, it's only a matter of time for old Arthur. There are those, however, who say it isn't the cancer that has seen the old buzzard off but the grief for his eldest son, Tommy, the apple of the cruel old bastard's eye, the man destined to be his heir, but that isn't my problem. It is another irony that, if Tommy Gladwell had been patient enough to cling on for two more years, he'd have inherited his old fella's empire in Glasgow and he wouldn't have needed to take over our city. In other words he'd still be alive, but hindsight is perfect vision.

'Alan will take over?' I asked.

Alan Gladwell was the second son. Harder, nastier and, I was reliably informed, more intelligent than his elder brother. Not the best choice as far as we were concerned but I assumed his rise to the throne was inevitable.

'Yes,' acknowledged Amrein.

'What's on your mind?' I asked him, 'or his.'

He straightened his little wire-framed glasses on his nose before coming to the point. I got the impression he was choosing his words carefully.

'Alan Gladwell has approached us,' he was using the word *us* instead of *me*, trying to make it all sound impersonal. I didn't worry too much about Amrein being in league with another

Gladwell. I figured he'd learned his lesson and he knew not to fuck with us again. I'd made it pretty clear what would happen to him if he did, 'he would like a meeting with you, with your organisation,' he corrected himself and I let him. He must have known by now that Bobby Mahoney was a dead man. Amrein would have looked for him, if only to satisfy his own curiosity about who was really in charge of our firm these days. If Amrein's organisation could find no trace of Bobby then he was bound to be dead. Amrein knew I was the boss – and I knew he knew.

'The meeting would be held on neutral territory, assuming you agree. You would bring your people and he would bring his, the same number so there would be no imbalance. We would handle the security.' He meant he was guaranteeing my safety and that, similarly, if I tried to have a pop at Alan Gladwell, it would not be tolerated. I was less concerned about the security arrangements than the purpose of the meeting.

'What does he want to talk to me about?' I knew Alan Gladwell was no mug either and, by now, he and half of Glasgow's underworld would know that his elder brother Tommy had been made to disappear by a rival firm in Newcastle. That fact alone should make me wary of Alan Gladwell, whose brutal methods were well known in his city. He liked to use pliers and blow torches on his enemies and I didn't relish the notion of him using them on me.

'What does he want to talk to me about?'

'Edinburgh,' he told me.

I hadn't seen that coming.

When Amrein and his bodyguards had left we stayed behind to talk it through.

'What did you make of that?' asked Palmer.

'From a business perspective, without any emotion attached, it makes complete sense. Edinburgh is an open market since

Dougie Reid was jailed. It's chaos up there. Between us we could control the place.'

'Yeah but there is emotion,' Danny reminded me.

'Do you think I don't know that?' Towards the end of our meeting with Amrein I had struggled to listen to the details of Alan Gladwell's proposal because I had been completely thrown by it. Why would he want to share a city with the crew that had killed his brother? Wouldn't you have to be a total psycho to even contemplate it?

Whatever I decided to do it put me at risk. If I didn't go into business with Alan Gladwell in Edinburgh he would probably take over the city on his own. Then his empire would be huge and even closer to our backyard than before. I didn't relish that notion, 'I need to think about this one.' I told them all in a tone I hoped was final enough.

'In any case, we have more important stuff going on in our own city right now,' said Kinane.

'You mean Doyle?' I asked.

'No, not Doyle,' he said impatiently, and I realised he had been building up to this, 'I mean Braddock.'

'Oh not again Joe, not now. Can we please stop talking about Braddock?'

'But he is taking the fucking piss!' Kinane shouted, his eyes bulging and his teeth bared, 'and he is taking it out of me, you, and every last fucking one of us!'

'I know he is Joe.'

'You know he is?' He said it like this was news to him.

'Of course,' I assured him, 'but what do you want me to do about it?'

'What do I want you to do about it?' he looked like he was about ready to burst a blood vessel, 'something! That's what I want you to do.'

'Like what Joe?' I was talking quietly to him in the vain hope this might calm him down a little. It wasn't working. He banged his fist on the table and I admit that even I flinched at the impact.

'Something!' he demanded, 'I want you to do something. Christ, man, I've been asking you to do something about this for months, or let me do something about it at least.'

'Want me to have a chat with him do you?' I asked.

'A chat?' he looked at me in disgust. 'No, we've tried that, haven't we. I've told him, my lads have told him, Palmer's tried to put him straight and you've been to see him so no, not a word.'

'Thought not,' I said, 'so what then? Rough him up a bit? Give him a bit of a kicking; think that will be enough to get him back on side?'

'Back on side?' he was booming at me now. Even Palmer was looking a bit concerned, as if Kinane might completely lose it and accidentally snap me in half before he realised what he was doing. Everyone knew the tales of the big man and his temper. 'No, a slap is not going to get him back on side.'

'I thought that too,' I said calmly, 'which is why I ruled it out. I reckon once he'd recovered he'd defy us even more. He'd keep all of the money and all of the stash, try and get a supply from someone else, then go to war with us; him and his whole bloody army of scum bags. We'd win, of course, but we'd be fighting gang members in hoodies for weeks on those estates before we restored order. The Sunnydale estate would be our Afghanistan. I'd be committing men, money and resources way beyond the value of the outcome.'

He was looking at me closely now, like he was trying to spot a hole in my argument. When he couldn't see one he said, 'Well, exactly.'

'So then, not a word and not a slap, which leaves what?'

He didn't reply.

'Go on then,' I told him, 'say it out loud. You want me to kill him.'

Kinane folded his arms, 'You'll hear no argument from me.'

'Great, thanks for that Joe. You've just reminded everybody why we don't let you make the decisions,' if Kinane had looked like he had the hump before he seemed about ready to explode now. I was the only person in this city who could get away with talking to him like that and I never did it lightly, but there were times when I had to reassert a little authority over guys like Kinane, men who could literally tear me apart with their bare hands if they chose to. My only chance of surviving as boss was to outwit and out think them. I had to make them realise they wouldn't survive without me to hold their hands and wipe their noses for them. 'Think about it. If we kill Braddock, he'll instantly become some fucked-up urban martyr, a cross between Reggie Kray and Robin Hood. Rightly or wrongly, he has managed to win the hearts and minds of those vermin on the estate. They think he is the king of their court. If we kill him there will be a riot and there'll be no proper business done for weeks.'

I could see by the fact that Kinane was quietening down that he agreed with what I was saying, but I wasn't finished yet. 'Secondly, when he's in the ground, who are we going to give the job to, eh? Who is hard enough, sneaky enough and nasty enough to control Sunnydale and, more importantly, before you start looking round this room, who would want the bloody job? Do you want to sit there every night in Braddock's flat sending out runners everywhere to terrorise the local heathens? Thought not. Perhaps one of your sons would like a go at it, eh?' he opened his mouth as if to say something then frowned and closed it again. 'No, didn't think so.'

'Braddock is an eighteen-carat bastard,' I said, 'I don't like him, you don't like him and I doubt anyone in our organisation likes him, but we don't have to like him. Who but a complete cunt could keep order for us down there? Now, he's dipping and he's taking too much, I know that and you know that and he bloody knows it too, which makes him a crook and a thief but then we are all crooks and thieves, so what can we expect? As it stands, I am getting good money out of Sunnydale. Not as much as we would like, or feel we deserve, but the alternatives are far more expensive. So, here's what we are going to do. We are going to let him carry on for the time being. We are going to keep letting him know we ain't happy, until he finally gets the message and doesn't step over another line.'

Kinane held up a hand. All of a sudden he was normal again, like an ocean calmed after a storm has blown out, 'I hear what you are saying, I do, and I understand it. You might not think I do but I'm not stupid. All I am saying is; it's a risky strategy.'

'Everything we do is risky, Joe,' I reminded him, 'and I live with that risk every single day.'

I stood up and told Palmer we were leaving, so I could draw this one to a close. We all made for the door and in the foyer of the hotel I stopped to speak to Kinane again, 'I never said you were stupid Joe,' I assured him, 'I just don't want you making all of the decisions. Let me deal with Braddock.'

He nodded but he didn't look convinced.

I needed some time on my own to think, so I took one of the firm's cars and pointed it north. The Merc made short work of the road and I soon left the city behind me. I was driving on autopilot and I couldn't remember a mile of it afterwards. I was too busy churning it all over in my mind. I didn't relish the prospect of entering into business with a family whose eldest son I'd killed. There was no easy answer to my problem. The Gladwells were never going to go away. They would cast a shadow over my city for years whether I agreed to become their partner or not. This was one deal where I was damned if I did, and damned if I didn't. I knew either way, I would always be looking over my shoulder.

11

Nobody seemed to have the faintest clue why someone would want to shoot Jaiden Doyle. For a drug-dealing low-life, he had surprisingly few enemies and there were no rumours of a falling out with Braddock, though it was hard to get the inside info on his crew because they were so tight-knit.

It was time to have a word with Maggot. Barry Hennessy, aka Maggot, was a long-standing member of the firm, but that's not to say he was indispensable. It was Maggot's job to make sure that our 'sports injury clinic' on the outskirts of town kept ticking over and making money, while avoiding the close attention of the law and pissing off the neighbours. The sports injury clinic was a loose cover for a massage parlour that did a little bit more than unknot your damaged muscles.

Elaine, as always, was on the door. I didn't know how long she'd worked there but I reckoned she'd probably been a fixture since the early eighties. She had probably been one of the first girls to give a massage there when Bobby opened the place. These days she was in her mid-sixties and we employed her as the 'housekeeper' which meant she looked out for our girls.

'He's out back,' she said, before I even mentioned I needed a word with Maggot. I followed her from the reception desk through the large, dark windowless area that served as a waiting room for clients and girls alike. It was empty, so the treatment rooms must have been busy. We climbed the stairs and she showed me into Maggot's office.

'What's new then, Maggot?' I asked the pot-bellied, bald man in front of me. He looked a bit guilty when he saw me, like he'd been up to no good, which was likely, but then Maggot always did look a bit shifty.

'Oh, nowt much,' he assured me. Then he pointed a nicotine-stained hand at a chipped china cup and asked 'want a cup of tea?'

'No, ta,' I said, 'I just want a word, actually.'

'If it's about the take I was going to come and see you,' he blurted out suddenly.

I leaned back in my chair and folded my arms, 'Go on,' I said, pretending that it really was about the take, as he was clearly worried about it.

'It was just a loan, honest,' he said, 'to tide me over, like. I had a spot of bother and I just needed a couple of hundred, to see me right.'

None of us had realised that Maggot had stolen more than usual from the take but I wasn't going to let the thieving bastard off the hook by admitting that.

'It won't do, Maggot,' I told him, as if that was the reason for my sudden appearance, 'you know that.'

'Yeah, I do,' he admitted, 'but I was desperate. I'm sorry.'

'If you were desperate then it was a lot more than a few hundred. How much have you stolen from me Maggot, this year I mean? Tell me, or I'll ask Kinane to come down here and do an audit on you with his tool box.'

'Please,' he said, 'there's no need for that,' and he swallowed nervously, 'it's three grand, give or take.'

'Let's call it four then, shall we? If you're admitting three it must be at least five so I'll be nice to you and meet you in the middle. I'll do a repayment plan for you and if you miss one payment I'll get Kinane to drill another hole in your head.'

He looked terrified. Maggot still bore the mark of a close encounter with Finney, who had allowed an electric drill bit to glance off the middle of Maggot's forehead, leaving a deep red welt, which, over time, had turned into a rust-coloured scar.

'I won't miss,' he said.

'Good,' and I got to my feet as if our business was concluded, 'oh, and by the way, as you're a man who always knows what's going on,' I told him, 'and since I'm already here, tell me all about Jaiden Doyle.'

'Eh? Jaiden Doyle?'

'You've seen him around, haven't you?'

'Yeah,' he admitted, 'what do you want to know about him?' he looked shifty again already.

'Not much,' I said, 'I just want to know who gave the order to have him shot, that's all.'

Maggot's face creased into a confused look. He eyed me suspiciously for a long time, then finally said, 'you mean to say it wasn't you?'

So much for Maggot knowing everything that went on in this city, I thought. After I had wasted my time with him I headed for the front door but, when I reached the waiting room, I stopped dead in my tracks. There, sitting on one of the sofas, dressed in a simple black dress and strappy high-heeled shoes was one of the most beautiful girls I had ever seen in my life. She was slim, yet curvy, and she had long, jet-black hair. I glanced over at her, took in her presence, then instantly zeroed in on her again, the sudden movement making her turn towards me and stare back defiantly. She didn't look remotely fazed by my presence but I was stunned by her.

Now the girls who worked in our place aren't dogs, they can't be. If the punters found them unattractive they wouldn't keep coming, and nobody would make any money. So our lasses are well groomed and well turned out but they are not exactly Playboy centrefolds. If we described them on our web site as 'late twenties' it meant they were really thirty-eight. If we said they were mature, then they were forty-five, at least. They kept their figures by watching what they ate and some of them had gym memberships, but the effects of gravity were there to be seen, in a drooping breast or a broadening of the hips and, without make-up on, frankly one or two of them could look a bit startling up close, but not this girl. She was young, early twenties at most, and classy, you could tell that by her poise alone. It was the way she carried herself. If she hadn't been wearing the little black dress, I'd have thought she was a lawyer, come to serve us with an order to close the place down. She was so atypical in fact that I think my mouth might have actually been wide open while I surveyed her.

'Can I help you?' she asked, which made her sound even less like she belonged here. The voice was cool and gave away her education. What the hell was she doing in our joint?

'I don't think we've met,' I managed to say.

'Have you got an appointment?' she asked me curtly, 'if you haven't I can't see you. I'm booked.' There was a touch of the head girl about this one. Her careers officer would have had a heart attack if he'd seen her in here. For some reason she made me feel tongue-tied. Most of the girls in here treated me like I was the boss, because I *was* the boss.

'What's your name?' I asked.

'Call me Tanya,' she told me. It was a command, not a request.

A side door opened and a familiar figure emerged.

'Hello Mr Blake,' called Nadia, all formal, like I was her husband's boss and we'd just bumped into each other at the firm's Christmas do. It wasn't that long ago I used to have a laugh with Nadia. She even told me to fuck off once, but then she had good cause. While chasing Maggot through the brothel I accidentally burst in on her and a client while she was in the middle of administering a happy-ending. I don't know who was more shocked to see me. Actually that's a lie. The client was definitely more shocked. Nadia was just pissed off that I'd interrupted a delicate moment with him. The punter almost shat himself and that was hardly surprising, as he was a town councillor.

Councillor Jennings had been extremely helpful to us ever since. So much so, I'd even arranged for Nadia to visit him a few times in hotels we booked and paid for; a little reward for services rendered. He was mightily relieved I'd not shopped him to the tabloids, particularly as I'd convinced him we had film of the act. I also made some generous donations to his re-election fund. And Nadia? Well, she didn't mind. I paid her way over the going rate to go and see the councillor and made sure she got a taxi home on the firm.

Perhaps Nadia felt indebted to me for the extra work, which would explain the formality. 'Fancy a cup of tea? I'll make you one,' she asked.

Normally I'd have said 'no thanks' and I'd have gone on my way, but I wanted to find out more about Call-Me-Tanya so I said, 'Thanks Nadia, milk and no sugar'.

'Right you are,' she said quaintly, suddenly sounding like a character from an old Ealing comedy. Nadia disappeared to boil the kettle. I sat down on the sofa opposite Call-Me-Tanya.

'I'm David.'

'I said I'm busy,' she reminded me, 'but if you wait here one of the other girls will attend to you, in due course.'

I'd never met a hooker before who used the words 'in due course'. Where did Elaine get this one from?

'Now that we've been introduced, I was hoping we could start over,' I said.

'Start over? But I have a booking.'

'I meant we could be more honest with each other,' I told her. 'You could start by admitting you know I'm the owner of this place,' I said, 'then maybe I could get your real name.'

'Maybe I did know,' she answered, 'perhaps I just didn't care.'

'Oh you've established that,' I said, 'other girls rush off and make tea for me, Nadia's probably hunting in the cupboard for digestives as we speak, but not you. You don't care that I'm the boss and you want me to know it.'

'I don't want you to think you own me just because …'

'Just because?'

She looked me straight in the eye, '…just because I let strangers fuck me for money in your brothel.'

I held up my hands, 'I don't own anyone. You're free to leave any time you like.'

'Really?' she sounded sceptical. 'Well, let's say that for the time being it suits me to work here. Now if you'll excuse me, I have an appointment.'

I watched her leave. There was something almost equine about the way she walked; straight-backed, head up, long, graceful legs moving in measured steps as she took the stairs down into the spa area. I watched her close the door behind her.

'Bloody hell,' and I realised that though I'd said that to myself, I'd done it out loud. I glanced around but nobody had heard me. I walked down the corridor and found Elaine sitting behind her little check-in desk.

'Tell me about Call-Me-Tanya.'

'Oh that one,' Elaine said, 'not much to tell. She came in here a few weeks back, out of the blue, which was a bit of a surprise.'

'I'll bet.'

'She said she wanted to work here, so we had the chat.'

'The chat?'

'The one we always have; where I make sure the girl knows what the job entails and can handle the work.'

'And you were satisfied with her, obviously, or she wouldn't be working here?'

'I had my doubts, at first, but she had her reasons.'

'Which were?'

'The usual,' she said, 'money worries and a twat of a boyfriend. You'll get the same story from all of them, the lucky ones anyway.'

'The lucky ones?'

'The lucky ones have managed to get rid of the boyfriend, so all they've got left are the debts. Usually they have no job, no money and no prospects.'

'And the unlucky ones?'

'The unlucky ones have all of that, but they are still carrying the useless bloke they're with.'

'Why would they do that Elaine?' I asked, as if she was the fount of all female knowledge, 'I've never understood it. If you know a guy's a waste of space and is never going to change, why would you stay with him, eh?'

'It's a little thing called love, deary,' she said, 'not foolish enough to subscribe to it myself these days but I'm aware of its existence. It makes people fall for hopeless cases, men and women both, so you be careful,' she cautioned.

'Don't worry about me. This bloke of hers,' I asked, 'ex-bloke I mean. He ever turn up here?'

'No,' said Elaine, 'I've never seen him, although…'

'Although?'

'She insists on getting the bus home. The stop's over the road. I've seen a big flash car pull up a couple of times like the guy is offering her a lift, but she never gets in.'

'You get a look at him?'

'No. He's got those blacked-out windows.'

'Does anybody else show up looking for her? Anyone take a shine to her.'

'Men do, punters I mean,' she admitted, 'well they would, wouldn't they? You've only to look at her to see that, but she won't do regulars. Won't even see them twice unless I tell her she ought to, and she's usually so bloody rude to them I'm surprised they stick it. I was a bit worried at first, you know, that she was too beautiful for this place. Girls like her, well, men get attached to them don't they, fall in love and such like. Remember we had that young Russian girl here? Lovely looking she was, but too pretty really, that one. She had a habit of making men do what she wanted them to, which isn't ideal, not for us. No, I prefer them plain and normal-looking, like Nadia. She's got her regulars and she doesn't scare away the new boys. But I must say, Simone's been as good as gold since she came here.'

'Simone?'

'Tanya's real name,' she explained, 'Simone Huntington.' It was a name that sounded like it should come with a coat of arms.

'No trouble between her and any of the clients then?'

'Like I said, she can be a bit lippy with the punters but I think they secretly love it. I call her "Mistress Tanya". They'd let her walk all over them in her stiletto heels most of them, even the ones who ain't into that sort of thing normally, I mean,' and she chuckled, 'she's dangerous that one.'

12

The 'Second Chances' centre was a nondescript grey building that used to house a call-centre before they relocated it to India, so the rent was cheap. We were due to have its official opening, but in reality we had been taking people in for more than a year. You could be fresh from prison that day and we'd have a look at you. In fact, that was the purpose of the place. We'd interview you to see what you could do and you'd get a bed there for a few nights if the manager thought you could be trusted. Without wishing to sound like a total wanker, I was using 'Second Chances' to try to put something back into the community – well mostly.

We took guys who wanted to go straight and stay clean, we gave them menial jobs they could handle and we paid them a proper wage for their work. That might involve clearing up derelict patches of land and planting trees or flower beds, mowing lawns and trimming hedges, scrubbing graffiti off walls or painting over it. The really promising guys would visit schools and talk to teenagers about the perils of drug use and the pointlessness of a life of crime.

We didn't care what you did or how long you served, as long as it wasn't messing with children. We drew the line at putting kiddie-fiddlers to work in the local community – our lads would have killed them in any case – and we expected you to be drug free. That might sound hypocritical coming from me, after all, it could have been the drugs we sold that started you robbing and stealing in the first place, but that wasn't the point. We couldn't employ heroin addicts to mow an old lady's lawn if they were likely to rob her dinner service afterwards.

We ran the Second Chance centre as a voluntary, non-profit-making business and managed to achieve charitable status on the back of it mainly, I suspect, because my name wasn't on the submission papers. The money we ploughed in there came from one of our holding companies and the parent was a British Virgin Islands registered trust.

We could also launder money through the scheme because we could inflate what we actually paid for goods and services, or fail to actually declare the true cost of materials we had negotiated a price on. We could place phantom workers on the pay roll too. Soon we had forty ex-cons who were genuinely on our books, most of whom would probably beaver away at this unspectacular work for the rest of their uneventful lives and look gratefully back on the day they were offered their very own second chance, when nobody else would even look at them.

As usual with us though, there was an angle. Second Chances was a great scouting ground for new talent. We could find out all about a guy under the umbrella of the programme then, if we thought he was suitable for more skilled labour with the firm, someone outside of the Second Chance centre could come along and offer him a legitimate-sounding job in another branch of our organisation. This was how Palmer recruited Robbie, who headed up our little group of 'watchers on the shore' as I called them, after the Stan Barstow novel no one else in our firm had heard of. Robbie was an IT boffin, an electronic whiz kid who could make computers talk to him. Here was a young lad who could break down firewalls, hack into systems he had no right to and plunder information for us without anyone knowing about it. He'd learned the importance of that the hard way, after he was sent down for a year for fraud and insider trading.

I used to say I was like Robbie, a strictly white-collar criminal who'd never hurt a fly. When he was sent to prison he was petrified. He thought he'd be raped or murdered, or both, but Palmer had read all about his case and been impressed by his skills, even if he had been caught in the end. Palmer arranged for some protection for Robbie and made sure he knew who was looking after him on the inside. When Robbie came out of jail we gave him a place on the Second Chances scheme and left him alone for a while, until he realised we were his only real shot. He was never going to get a legitimate job anywhere with his tarnished CV.

By the time I met Robbie and offered him a job he was already halfway to the dark side without even realising it. He chose to throw his lot in with us and it worked out great. Palmer loved working with this geeky little bloke with his Joe 90 glasses and the slight stammer when he got nervous. His sideline speciality was electronic surveillance. 'When I was in the regiment, I used to dig a ditch and sit in it for days, not moving, shitting in bags, just waiting for a glimpse of the target,' Palmer told me, in a rare reference to his SAS career, 'these days Robbie can get a bead on someone from miles away, using a satellite and their mobile phone signal. It's a modern fucking miracle.'

The Second Chances scheme was the reason I was attending

a meeting of belligerent football fans at a pub in the Bigg Market. We were packed into an upstairs room, clutching pints of beer, listening to a politician who was standing on his metaphorical soap box. The venue may have been a long way from the oak-panelled corridors of Westminster but veteran Newcastle MP and former Home Office Minister, the Right Honourable Ron Haydon, was still in full sway, assuring us he shared our hatred of 'the buggers who have brought this once proud club to its knees and turned us into a national joke in the process!' before adding 'they have run this club with all of the style and grace of a pimp in charge of a brothel, well, no more!' that got him his first round of applause. 'They…' he was pointing in the direction of St James' Park, which was a couple of blocks away, '….have rebranded a hallowed shrine until it resembles little more than a cash-and-carry…*they* are men who know the price and cost of everything but the value of nothing.' There was some positive murmuring at this sentiment, 'I'm talking about society, community, a shared history where a father and son go to the match together to watch their local team for generation after generation.' I wondered when he had last seen them play; probably years ago. 'What they don't…what they fail to understand…' he was jabbing his finger at us now for emphasis, '…is that no one ever really owns a football club…they are simply custodians for future generations!' I was pretty sure he'd nicked that last line from a magazine ad I'd seen, but it didn't matter.

Ron Haydon concluded his rousing speech by appealing for a more democratic world, which involved fans owning their own football club and bringing the game back into the community, but I couldn't see it myself. Why would a fat billionaire listen to the fans when he patently didn't have to? He got a round of applause just the same.

'I was wondering if you'd received my letter,' I told my MP after I'd waited ten minutes for the back-slappers and gladhanders to disperse, 'about attending the launch of the Second Chances centre, the home of our prisoner rehabilitation programme,' he looked right through me, 'we believe in offering convicted criminals the opportunity to turn their lives around through gainful employment.'

He gave me a big grin, 'Spoken like a politician,' he told me, 'you should join the party, son. You've got the gift of the gab.' This didn't sound like a compliment, but I carried on regardless.

'We were hoping you might choose to grace us with your presence when we open the building later this month in Dunston, but we have yet to receive a reply to our letter from your constituency office.'

'I got your letter alright, but I won't be attending,' he told me. The smile had gone now, 'I don't mix with criminals.'

'We prefer to see them as former criminals.'

'I wasn't talking about them, son,' he said it low and threatening, 'I was talking about you.'

'Me? I'm a company director of the Gallowgate Leisure Group, a legitimate...'

'Don't waste your breath,' he interrupted me, 'you're forgetting I was a Minister at the Home Office, so I've seen the files on your outfit,' he was speaking quietly, so the other guys in the bar couldn't hear us and he'd planted a half smile on his face so a casual observer might think we were discussing the state of the Euro, 'I don't like gangsters in my city,' he said that bit like he truly believed it was *his* city, 'but I'm glad we've had this chance to meet Mr Blake because I want to tell you face to face what I am going to do about you and the rest of Bobby Mahoney's firm. I am the newly-appointed chairman of the Police Authority and I am going to see to it that the Chief Constable makes you his highest priority. The day you go down, I will be standing on the steps of the court house with a bloody big grin on my face.' And he gave me a look that told me he was going to relish that moment.

'You know, I only really came over to offer my commiserations,' I assured him, 'they say all political careers end in failure and you are certainly living proof of that. An MP for twenty-nine years and you couldn't get into the Government till it was on its dying breath. Why was that Ron? A lot of the ones who made it into high office turned out to be numpties but they all got their chance before you, didn't they? All those years on the back benches and you only got in at all because you changed your vote on his little war in Iraq.'

'Haddaway and shite, man,' he was resorting to Geordie bluster when he couldn't think of a better denial.

'You'll be in your mid-seventies before Labour sorts itself out again and that's way too old for high office. Now it's back to constituency work; all those MP's surgeries, line after line of lunatics pleading for help because no one has collected their rubbish and the grass verges need cutting. You must be going out of your mind with boredom.'

'You've got no idea son, you really haven't,' his face had reddened.

'Enlighten me then. It's not much to show for all of those years in politics is it? Bobby Mahoney used to say you could stick a red rosette on a monkey up here and everybody would still vote Labour. You could sodomise a schoolboy in front of Grey's monument and they'd still rather vote for you than a Tory and you know it. What a bloody waste of time and effort your whole life has been. You want to bring me down? Well good luck with that.'

'Is this the bit where you threaten me, son? I wouldn't do that if I were you, bonny lad, because I don't scare easily. They used to send me in to sort out the local union convenors when they wouldn't tow the party line and there's no bigger bastard than a proper full-on Union man, everybody knows that. More than one took a swing at me and I always knocked them down where they stood, in front of all their pals. I might be older than you but we can go out back and settle this right now if you want.'

I laughed, 'Oh please, you look like you're about to have a heart attack just saying that.'

'I'm warning you…'

'No, I'm warning *you*. I can see why you need a hobby these days but I'd recommend fly fishing or golf, not us.'

I turned and walked away, leaving the pub without another word. As I walked out into the street a man emerged from the shadows and stepped out in front of me.

'Jesus Christ, Palmer, you nearly gave me a heart attack.'

'What?'

'Lurking in the dark like that and leaping out on me. I thought my number was up.'

'Sorry,' he said.

'What do you want?'

'I had to tell you something,' he said, 'and you are not going to like it.'

'What is it?'

'The shipment didn't arrive.'

13

'Will you calm down?'

'I am calm,' I lied, but it had taken me two very swift drinks in the hotel bar even to get me to this stage and I was still boiling, 'I just don't like being arse-fucked by a Turk who's stolen a million Euros from me. I'm old-fashioned like that.'

'Can you not shout at least?' asked Palmer, looking around him, presumably expecting undercover cops to leap out from behind the potted plants that dominated every corner of the bar.

'I'm not shouting,' I told him, but out of the corner of my eye I noticed the cocktail barman was watching me. I glared at him and he suddenly remembered something he needed to do out back.

'Then will you at least lower your voice while you talk about drugs, Turkish dealers and missing Euro millions,' he added reasonably.

'Fine,' I said and I realised we must have sounded like a couple of old queens having a lover's tiff, 'I'll keep my voice nice and low if you get back on to the Turk tonight and tell him I want him to send me either the shipment or the money but definitely not the excuses.'

'It's difficult,' said Palmer, 'there's a lot of stages he has to go through to get the product out and any one of them can cause a delay.'

'Who are you working for, Palmer?' I asked him.

'What?'

'Him or me?'

'I'm just saying.'

'Well don't.'

Palmer just blinked at me and fell silent, his face an unreadable mask.

When Palmer left, I took my third drink with me into the restaurant, a dimly lit so-called brasserie that had attracted two other diners that night, both solitary males on business trips. I could have guessed the contents of the uninspiring menu without opening it and I settled on a medium steak with fries and a béarnaise sauce. I travel a lot, so solitary meals in hotels are nothing new. They also give me time to think and, for some strange reason, my mind kept coming back to Simone and what she was doing working at the massage parlour. It wasn't as if I didn't have enough on my plate already; what with Doyle getting shot, Braddock taking the piss, Gladwell wanting a partnership and the Turk holding out on me but, despite all of that, I'd started wondering if maybe I could help her. If I could save Danny, I reasoned, then surely I could do something to alter this girl's life for the better.

Was I attracted to her? Of course, who wouldn't be? She was a stunner, but it wasn't just that. A lot of girls have a nightmare boyfriend when they are young, but they don't all end up doing what she was doing. Simone had her whole life ahead of her. It seemed a shame to waste it like this.

I made a decision then. I was going to take Call-Me-Tanya on, as a kind of personal project. This girl would give me a chance to do the right thing for once and I knew she'd thank me one day.

I wouldn't normally go near the Sunnydale estate – and not just because it is a shithole. I didn't want anyone to make the link between me, the high-rises and the product. Most of our supply issues were handled by Kinane's sons but, from time to time, if there was a problem or a dispute, I had to step in. This was definitely one of those times.

It was up to Braddock to keep order on the Sunnydale estate, which he did with some considerable skill, mainly because he employed the hardest people in the high-rises and he, in turn, was tougher than all of them put together. He should have been the ideal guy for Sunnydale, but the gaping holes in our accounts said otherwise.

The drugs business won't vary that much. Your customer base doesn't suddenly elect to spend its money on something else. Addicts have a need for the same amount of hard drugs every single day of the week. That's why it's called a habit. You would expect the revenue from heroin or crack cocaine to be, at the very least, static, with possible growth potential, as new customers discovered the joys of drug-induced oblivion. Not so, on Braddock's watch. He would explain to Kinane and his sons that times were difficult, that some junkies had gone into rehab, others were in jail and still more had died, but he was always a little vague when it came to actual names. He'd tell us the product he was expected to sell was too pure or not pure enough, it was the wrong drug at the wrong time and his customers didn't want it as much as the same shit being sold on the estate next door by another gang of dealers we also controlled. Braddock would explain that deals had to be done cheaply in order to dispose of the stash before a new consignment arrived. His evidence of a sales slump was vague and anecdotal but to hear him talk he couldn't give the stuff away.

We all knew this was bullshit. He was stealing from us because he thought he was in an untouchable position. In a way he was, but I couldn't have him keeping all of the profits. I would be expected to come down on him hard. That, of course, was easier said than done when he manned his territory with the nastiest fuckers in the city and was never on his own. In fact he left the estate less and less these days, despite his comparative wealth, except to visit his old mum. He might pick a woman up in the city from time to time but more and more he seemed to prefer to live like a king on a mountain of shit than move out like a normal person. Instead he sat in his flat at the top of the high-rise that gave him the best view of the whole estate. As we drove in there for an unannounced meeting, I knew Braddock's look-outs would have tagged us before we'd gone ten yards.

I made sure we arrived mob-handed that morning in four cars; Palmer, Kinane, Hunter and Danny were with me in the Range Rover; Kinane's sons and some of the lads from his gym were in the other cars. It was an inflammatory gesture turning up en masse like that but I wanted Braddock to remember who he was dealing with.

We took the lifts to the top floor. They worked but stank of piss.

'You'd think he'd sort this out,' suggested Kinane, wrinkling his nose, 'he virtually has the place to himself.'

Kinane wasn't exaggerating. The top two floors had been commandeered by Braddock as his command centre. The residents had been bought out or threatened off and nobody from the council was ever going to have the balls to come down here and look into it.

Braddock greeted us at the door. He was a tall, muscular guy, the right side of thirty, who dressed more smartly than the low-lifes in his crew. With his unscarred face, athletic build and designer clothes he could have passed for a pro-footballer, and he had a reputation for attracting the women. People said he could really smooth-talk them. I heard he kept an apartment in the city just to entertain his women. Braddock was all smiles, but his eyes were darting all over the place as he took in Kinane, Palmer and the rest of the group. A bunch of guys from Braddock's crew were lounging about the place, drinking beer, smoking dope, watching Sky Sports on a Plasma TV or playing pool on his garish blue-baize table. They all stopped what they were doing when we walked in. I'd counted ten guys hanging out here and they all looked like they'd been fighting every day of their lives. They probably had to if they were brought up on the Sunnydale estate. There was only one girl. She was thin and pretty and dressed in a T-shirt and denim shorts, but she had that pasty, junkie look about her, like she hadn't seen sunlight in weeks.

His HQ was an odd-looking place. Braddock had even removed some of the walls to turn the top floor into a big open-plan flat that he and his crew could hang out in. He didn't worry whether they were supporting walls. He just replaced them with heavy metal props to keep the ceiling from falling in. The big open space he'd created was a warren of interconnecting flats. There was crap lying everywhere; empty bottles and cans and containers from last night's takeaways littered every surface, along with overflowing ash trays.

'Turn that off!' barked Braddock and the gangsta rap that was pumping from a pair of enormous speakers ceased abruptly, 'do the guys want a beer?' he asked.

I shook my head, 'we're not stopping long. I'm just doing the rounds.'

I asked him how business was, and he peddled the same old

shit about times being hard, as if the drug-dealing trade was just another victim of the recession.

'You seem to have this place well under control though,' I told him.

'It's locked down,' he said, 'I'm in complete control. A pigeon can't shit in here without me knowing about it. Isn't that right boys?' There were murmurs of agreement and indistinct comments from his group of knuckle draggers. He was deliberately bringing them into the conversation so I could see what a tight group they were, hoping I'd be intimidated by them.

'That's good to hear. You'll know who shot Doyley then.'

'Doyley? Yeah, well, that didn't happen here did it? Doyley got shot on the Quayside.'

'Police weren't too happy about that,' I said, 'makes Newcastle look like the wild west.'

Braddock shrugged, 'it doesn't happen every day, but now and then someone gets hosed in Newcastle. The papers bang on about it for a few days, then it's all forgotten.'

'Unless it escalates of course, you know, reprisals, tit-for-tat killings, that sort of thing. You weren't planning any of that?'

'No,' he said, 'how could I when we haven't a clue who popped him?'

'Sure you've got no idea who was behind it?' I was looking directly at him.

'I mean who'd want to shoot Doyley?' He said it like Jaiden Doyle was a simpleton.

'Don't know,' I admitted, 'a rival dealer maybe, someone on your patch who's jealous of Doyley's position, a complete stranger he pissed off at a drive-though McDonalds. There's a few theories for you to be going on with; figured you'd like to look into it on our behalf.'

'Yeah,' he said, 'I will.' Was it just me or was Braddock acting like he already knew who'd done it and didn't give a shit?

'Then you'll come and see Joe, yeah? With a name, I mean. I don't want you to go after someone in the street with an Uzi. We don't need the heat, especially right now.'

'Course not. I'll come to you. I mean I'll come to Kinane,' he corrected himself.

'I must say you're taking this very well,' I said, 'someone's just shot one of your lads. I thought you'd be bouncing off the walls.'

'Like I said, I don't know who did it, so I can't go off on one, can I?'

'No,' I said, 'suppose not.' I said nothing for a moment, then continued, 'like I said, I'm just doing the rounds, checking up on the businesses but, while I'm here, there was one thing.'

'Go on.'

'You remember I told you that if you did well here, if you kept order and ran the place like it should, there'd be a bonus in it for you?'

'Er, yeah,' that got his interest right enough.

'How does forty grand sound to you?'

'It sounds pretty fucking good from here,' he said, grinning, and there was a bit of laughter from his guys at that.

'Good,' I nodded, 'well I reckon you've earned it, don't you?'

'Sure have.'

'Well done,' and I looked around me as if our business was concluded.

'So, er,' he wasn't sure what was going on, 'where is it, like?' and he looked at my boys as if one of them was just about to hand over a briefcase full of cash.

'I already gave it to you,' I explained, and he looked bemused, 'just this minute I gave it to you. By that I mean I'm not going to ask you for the missing money. You can keep it. That's your bonus for nailing everything down so well here.'

'Missing money? I don't get it.' The smile had vanished.

'It's really simple,' I explained very calmly, 'the take is forty grand light. That's the difference between the street value of the last few consignments and the amount you handed over to Kinane's lads.'

'Are you saying I'm skimming?' he flared. I could tell our lads were suddenly more alert, like it was all about to kick off. Around us, Braddock's lads seemed to stiffen, ready to react to the affront, exuding menace like they would on the street. I ignored them.

'No,' I said, 'you're not that stupid. I'm saying that someone is. Not you, but somebody must be short-changing you or there would be more money in the take.' He didn't know how to answer that, 'now you've just told me you've got this place nailed down, so when you retrieve the missing money, you can keep it. I can't say any fairer than that, can I?'

He didn't say a word. He just looked a little bit sick.

'Just make sure that whoever is selling you short learns the error of their ways. You need to make an example of them. We can't let some chiselling, little low-life cunt get away with stealing from us. It would be taking the piss big style and we can't afford that. Can we?'

Our eyes locked for a long moment. 'No,' he agreed eventually.

'Good. I've every faith in you. I know the take will be right next time.'

He mumbled something and looked down as he pulled on the cuffs of his shirt.

'Sorry?' I asked.

I was deliberately challenging him now, giving Braddock his opportunity to take me on. There was a moment when I thought he was going to rise to it, then he looked up at me and said, 'Yeah, got it.'

'Good,' I said, 'then I'll see you around.'

As I made to leave, I stopped and turned towards the young lass who'd been keeping a low profile in the background. 'And what's your name, pet?' I asked her.

'Suzy,' she told me, her voice almost a whisper. I reached out a hand and she just blinked at it. Then, slowly, she put out her own cold, pale hand and I shook it like we were in the line-up at a wedding.

'Very nice to meet you Suzy.' I said.

When we were back in the car Kinane said, 'On the one hand I can't believe you let him keep the forty grand, but on the other, it was worth every penny to see that stupid grin wiped right off his fucking smug face. That moment will stay with me. Oh yes!' Kinane was jubilant. At least I had his seal of approval, which meant he might stop bitching about Braddock for five whole minutes and I could turn my mind to more important matters.

Danny chipped in with, 'it was worth the forty grand to keep the peace and remind him of his responsibilities,' and I appreciated his supportive comment.

'I don't know,' Palmer cautioned, 'I get the feeling it's far from over.' That brought me crashing back down to earth, because I reckoned he was right.

From the tiny balcony, Braddock watched Blake's convoy pull away from the Sunnydale estate. 'Who the fuck does he think he is?' he asked.

'He thinks he's the boss,' answered one of his crew without thinking and Braddock snapped.

'Well he isn't, is he?' Braddock rounded on Dwayne Fletcher.

'No,' Dwayne agreed hastily, 'not round here. That's you, isn't it? You're the real general on this estate,' Dwayne assured him, 'the only boss down here, where it counts, on the streets.'

Braddock knew Dwayne was laying it on thick, kissing his arse because he feared a kicking, but 'the General' was a nickname Braddock liked. And Braddock *was* a general. He was the only one round here with the brains to keep a lid on the

Sunnydale estate, a living, breathing, self-contained world cut off from the rest of the city, filled with dealers, users, foot soldiers and civilians and every one of them under his command. Braddock knew things, he read books, unlike the Muppets who worked for him; biographies of real generals, histories of the Third Reich and the Roman Empire and he knew he was destined to be more than just one of David Blake's minions. Braddock knew Blake slapped him down in front of his men like that to remind him who was in charge, but Braddock didn't really need Blake. As far as Braddock could make out, David Blake had never earned the right to be Top Boy in Newcastle. He might be able to hold his own in a hotel meeting room but what had he ever done on the streets? Braddock knew how to make moves on the streets and, one day soon, he was going to make a very big move against David Blake.

14

I was sitting at one of the tables outside Chi-Chi. The weather was nice for once and there were a couple of other people enjoying a rare chance to drink their coffee in the open air. Peter Dean was late, but I wasn't too bothered. I figured he'd show up eventually and I was glad of a few moments to myself. Palmer had driven me into the city and he'd been sitting next to me reading the paper when the waiter walked up and gave him a message. Apparently Kinane had called the place and needed his help with something. I wondered what description Kinane had given to help the waiter find Palmer. He had once described our former soldier as, 'a short, squat, muscly bloke who looks like SpongeBob SquarePants.'

'How do you know what SpongeBob SquarePants looks like?' I asked him.

'I've got grandkids,' he told me, 'my daughter's bairns. So I'm familiar with Bob's work.'

I had forgotten Kinane had a daughter. I knew he had three sons; Kevin, Chris and Peter, all born in the 1980s and each named after a Newcastle player; Keegan, Waddle and Beardsley. 'I almost changed our Chris' name by deed poll when Waddle signed for Sunderland, fucking Judas,' he told me.

When the waiter left, Palmer reached into his jacket pocket for his phone. 'It must be serious if Kinane is admitting he needs help,' he said.

'Particularly from you,' I agreed, 'why didn't he just phone you?'

He frowned at his mobile, 'bloody signal's always shit down here.'

'Go on,' I told him, 'I'll be fine. I don't need a bodyguard to meet Peter Dean, do I? An immunisation of some sort perhaps, but not a bodyguard.'

I watched Palmer leave, and when he'd gone I turned my attention to the people passing by and did a bit of human-watching, wondering who they were and what they did for a living. What did they think when they saw me I wondered; businessman, marketeer, entrepreneur, killer? Take your pick, I thought. I'm a little bit of each. I watched as a bloke ambled towards me. He wore a pair of Morrissey-style glasses and he was carrying a battered, brown leather satchel on his shoulder that looked suitably studenty and weather worn. Doubtless there would be a copy of Jean Paul Sartre or Proust in there to compound the image of the right-on intellectual. He was a walking cliché. I would have paid him a little more attention if I hadn't been distracted by something behind him.

There were two guys on a motorbike and they just didn't look right. Not at all. Fucking amateurs, I thought, getting out of my seat without taking my eyes off them. They were wrong on just about every level. Here were two big blokes sharing one motorbike, both dressed in full leathers and black helmets with mirrored visors pulled down, but the gear they were wearing looked brand new, like it had been bought that morning. It was too hot for leathers and the bike was one of those high-powered bits of kit designed for a fast getaway, but it was dawdling along towards me, like they were trying not to draw attention to themselves. A man with a bike like that usually knows how to handle it and rides accordingly. This guy looked unsteady, like he'd never ridden the thing before. Why was he going so slowly? So the passenger riding pillion could scan the road ahead looking for someone and, like as not, that someone was me.

I didn't hang around to see if I was right. I left my drink unfinished and walked briskly away. As soon as I left the restaurant I heard the bike rev and I knew they'd seen me and were coming after me. Suddenly the message from the waiter made sense. Someone had dragged my bodyguard away from me and set me up. I didn't have time to worry about who. I didn't fuck about and I didn't care how it looked because I knew what was going down. I broke into a run. Behind me I heard a scream, and the unmistakeable sound of a motorbike careering at full speed. They almost knocked down a pedestrian in their haste, and I wished they had because they would have probably turned and fled. As it was, I was left with the unlikely prospect of outrunning a motorbike with a hit man on the back. Jesus Christ, I'd been stupid. I was too relaxed sitting on that terrace waiting for Peter Dean. I'd let my guard down for a moment and now I was completely in the shit. I sprinted flat out to get to the end of the street so I could lose them.

There are a bunch of little cuts and sidestreets round here, near the old city walls, and I chose one with stone steps that the motorbike couldn't handle. I took them two at a time, thankful I'd kept myself in good shape. Fear was driving me along and I knew I needed to put enough space between me and the road or they'd just aim up at me and gun me down right there on the steps. I could hear the motorbike's engine getting louder and I kept running upwards. The sound was piercing for a moment, then abruptly faded away.

Maybe I'd lost them, but it wouldn't be for long. They'd know I'd gone for higher ground and they'd be after me, moving at a far greater speed and using the main road to loop up to the road above me. I didn't have the nerve to double back down the steps the way I had come, in case they were waiting for me. When I reached the top of the steps, I pegged it across a cobbled courtyard that doubled as a hotel car park, so I could make a sharp right turn and get back down into the quayside where I'd be surrounded by people. The cobbles were slippery and I almost fell flat on my face but forced myself to keep going.

I'd been stitched up, and I didn't even know who'd done it. I took another flight of old stone steps back downwards at a rate of knots and managed to reach the steep hill that drops down to form a side street.

I had to get off the street and lose myself and I spotted my best chance straight ahead of me. Halfway up the hill there was a little gap between two old buildings, a restaurant and a pub. I knew that gap and where it led to. If I could dart down it, I could keep on going until I emerged on the other side, into a vacant lot full of builder's rubble that had been empty for years, covered in old bricks and full of weeds. It was one of those brown-belt developments that no one wanted because it was hidden from view and you wouldn't get any passing trade. The council had shown it to us when we talked about opening the club, and I told them they were having a laugh, but I was bloody glad I'd seen it now. No motorcycle was capable of following me over that rubble.

I made short work of the cobbles as I pegged it down the hill, and had almost reached the safety of the little sidestreet when I looked up and, abruptly, the bike swerved into view, its rider struggling to keep control of it as it came round to face me. They'd seen me and I now had no choice but to trust in my plan. I ran flat out across the road towards the cut. The bike made a low rasping sound as the rider revved it and shot off down the hill towards me. I had to get across the road, into the cut and out through the other side again before they caught up with me.

I made it across the street, my unsuitable leather shoes almost giving way as I ran. I reached the cut and came round the corner so fast I was halfway down it before I realised something had changed. When the man from the council had walked us down here months earlier there was a twenty yard stretch of unblocked pavement, except for a couple of wheelie-bins and some litter that had blown in there. Beyond that, there'd been an old brick wall just a couple of feet high that was left there to ensure the demolition rubble stayed put. It was so low I would have been over it in one bound. The scene that confronted me now was very different. Straight ahead of me was a high, sturdy, wire fence with a metal gate in the middle of it.

I carried on running towards it because I had no choice. It was too late to turn back to the main street now. I would have run straight into them. The fence was too high to climb and the gaps in the wire looked too small to plant my feet into them for toe holds. Even if I could manage it, I would have been halfway up as the bike turned the corner. To my right and left were the two high, sheer walls of the buildings either side of me. There were no conveniently opened doors to dart into, and the only windows I could see were so high I couldn't reach them. My only remaining chance was the gate. If it was unlocked I could still get through it and be over the rubble and away. It looked solid, but I couldn't see a padlock, so I sprinted flat out straight at it, expecting to hear the motorbike behind me at any moment. I got there and pulled hard on the metal handle. It was designed to slide to one side, releasing a long, flat metal bolt so you could push the door open. The bolt gave way and I felt a surge of relief flood through me, but it didn't last long. It moved but only a couple of inches before it met resistance with a loud clang. It was locked. I was trapped. I was also a dead man. I knew all of this in the time it took for the echo of the clanging metal to die away.

In my panicked state, even though I knew it couldn't possibly work, I tugged at the bolt. I tugged again and again, praying I could somehow force it to open by sheer bloody will alone, but it wouldn't give. And that's when I heard the motorbike behind me.

15

I span round to face them and watched as the rider drew the bike to a skidding halt at the end of the alley. All I could see of his face was the jet-black glass of his helmet's visor, but I knew he was staring straight at me. Then the second man leaned round and looked at me too. He patted the rider on the shoulder and the guy tilted the bike to allow him to dismount. For a man who was about to kill me he didn't look to be in a big hurry, but then he didn't need to be. He knew I had nowhere to run. I felt sick. All I could do now was wonder if it would be quick and whether there would be a lot of pain. As I watched him climb from the bike, I thought of Sarah and the grief I would cause her because I'd been stupid. I'd fucked things up and I'd cost us everything.

The man who was about to kill me was off the bike now. He had both feet planted firmly on the ground next to it and he was reaching into a leather satchel, the kind that motorcycle couriers use. I watched as he carefully drew out the gun and I took a deep breath. In the absence of any plan, idea or clever solution, I was trying to at least look defiant. It was the only thing I had left. I knew he wouldn't let me reason with him. I was wondering if I had the guts to run at him, or maybe just stand there and shout 'fuck you' as my last words, or would I lose all my dignity at the very end and blub like a little girl.

The man who was about to kill me briefly examined his gun and took a step forwards.

I reckon he had taken about three steps when it happened, another two or three and he would have been in the cut. Right then, I heard the loud revving sound that indicates a car accelerating at top speed. The rider turned towards the sound and tried to climb off the bike, as the man who was about to kill me turned on his heel. I watched him put both hands up in a vain attempt to cushion the blow.

Palmer's car hit the bike full-on at speed, smashing into it, sending the bike, the man trying to dismount from it, and the man who was about to kill me flying towards the far wall of the alley. The two men, the motorcycle and the car all collided with a sickening impact that must have killed both men outright, or at least severely injured them. Their bodies were slammed against the brickwork like they'd been thrown there by a giant hand. Blood fountained up the wall and limbs were bent and twisted under the car's wheels, but Palmer wasn't taking any chances. He was out of the car, crouched low with his pistol drawn. He fired twice into the rider's body to finish him off, then he aimed at the shooter. Amazingly, considering the impact of the crash, he was still moving, but I doubt he could have troubled anyone now. The gun was nowhere to be seen. It had been catapulted from him at the moment of impact. He must have been dimly aware of Palmer's presence though, because he tried to hold up a hand, but his arm fell limply back down by his side. Palmer shot him twice; once in the chest, then a second time through the visor of his helmet and he finally lay still.

Palmer was calling to me but I couldn't hear him, so he called again, louder this time. My ears were ringing and I couldn't make out what he was saying to me. I knew we had to go but I was rooted to the spot. I couldn't believe what I had just seen or how close I had come to death. If he had been ten seconds later it would have been me lying there instead of them.

Palmer started frantically beckoning me then, and he was clearly shouting 'Come on! Come on!' at me. Somewhere, not very far from this spot, a siren was wailing. I realised it was a Police car and it was getting nearer. That snapped me out of it and I set off, making short work of the yards between us. When I reached him, he grabbed me by the arm and hauled me towards the car. He tore open the rear passenger door and threw me onto the back seat, slamming the door behind me, then ran round the car and climbed in. He started the car and slammed it into reverse. There was a horrible sound of twisted metal grinding, but the car wouldn't budge. It was stuck fast on the wreckage of the motorcycle. Palmer tried once more; there was an acrid burning smell as the clutch started to burn out but the car still didn't move. I could hear the normally unflappable Palmer swearing at the car now, his voice becoming louder and more desperate.

Palmer gave it one more go, revved the car till it made a terrible wail of protest and slammed it hard into reverse. There was an almighty grinding sound as the car lurched a few feet to the rear, the bike was dragged along under its wheels and then, with a bump that nearly jolted me off the seat, the car jumped backwards and shot out into the road.

I couldn't see a thing but I could hear shrieks from the people in the street, as they scrambled to get out of the way.

Right then I'd have accepted Palmer ploughing through a crowd of pedestrians if he could just get us both out of there. I lay still as the car raced back up the hill and looked up in time to see the iron arches flash by above me as we tore across the High Level Bridge, the shriek of the Police sirens receding in the distance behind us.

16

As soon as Sharp got the call from Blake, he went straight over to Peter Dean's flat. The whole city was buzzing with rumours about what exactly had happened on the Quayside that morning; Newcastle had its rough spots, but no one had ever tried to gun down a crime boss in broad daylight just yards from the city's best hotels, bars and restaurants. Coming on the back of the shooting of Jaiden Doyle in the same area, this constituted a crisis for the Police, and the Press were all over it like a rash. Every detective in Northumbria had been dispatched to look for leads. Of course newly-promoted Detective Inspector Sharp was one step ahead of them all – because he was on the payroll of the intended victim.

It wouldn't be long before someone discovered that David Blake was meant to meet Peter Dean that day, so it was important Sharp got to him first. At the very least Dean had a lot of explaining to do.

The door to Dean's apartment was to the rear of the video store atop a metal staircase that rose to a first floor gantry. Sharp was cautious by nature, but Dean wasn't muscle in anyone's eyes, so the detective didn't hang about. He climbed the stairs, reached the flimsy wooden door and tried the handle. The door was locked, but Sharp didn't bother to knock, glancing right, then left, and giving the door a sturdy kick. It popped open like it was made of balsa wood and Sharp went straight in, expecting to find Peter cowering on a sofa, pleading that it had all been an unfortunate misunderstanding.

Peter Dean was in the room, but he wasn't seated on the couch.

'Fuck me,' said DI Sharp aloud, as he took in the scene before him. Peter Dean was swaying ever so slightly. His eyes were bulging wide open and his arms hung straight down by his side. The dining chair was upended on the floor, because Peter must have used it to get high enough to thread the drawstring he'd torn from the curtains around the old, metal light-fitting in the ceiling. He had tied the other end around his neck, in a noose that tightened sharply when Peter kicked the chair out from under him.

Whatever role Peter Dean may have played in the plot to kill David Blake, he must have panicked when he learned it had failed. He wasn't going to be talking to anyone about it now.

'You were right about the CCTV,' Sharp was telling me what I already knew, 'it was down. There's no footage of anything on the Quayside all morning. It all crashed about an hour before you arrived there.'

We were standing out in the open air on the roof of the Cauldron. Sharp had flashed his badge at the manager of the Chinese restaurant next door, then gone through his kitchen and up the fire escape so he could meet me without being seen. His information about the cameras being down was no surprise to me. You wouldn't plan to shoot somebody in broad daylight in the Quayside unless you could be sure the CCTV was out of commission. Only someone in our league could have pulled off that stunt. The only question was who.

'Your lot are investigating that?'

'Too right,' said Sharp, 'it's all kicked off at our place. No one likes firearms being brandished in the city centre. They're not partial to hit men being flattened in hit-and-runs either, if I'm honest. Journalists all over the country are onto this one, trying to paint Newcastle like it's Dodge City. Our top brass have been taking a right kicking from government. Now they are passing the bollockings down the line to us and demanding answers.'

'What do they know?' I asked, 'or what do they think they know?'

'Not much without the CCTV, but…'

'Go on.'

'They know it's you,' he admitted, 'the intended victim, I mean. A lot of folk saw you pegging it through the streets. A few of them will have known you and were prepared to tell us, as long as it was on the QT.'

'Don't suppose your lot are too happy with me right now, even though it wasn't my fault?'

'No,' he said simply.

I knew the Police would blame me for this whole thing. They'd figure I must have done something to deserve it. So I was the one endangering the local population and putting the kibosh on a few promotions in the process. Now they'd be mad keen to find anything that could be used to put me away.

'Did they ID the shooters?'

'Yep. Andy Tate is ex-Royal Marines. They booted him out, also ex-Foreign Legion and ex-dodgy freelance contractor, selling his skills all over Europe to the highest bidder. He's a serious, professional operator by all accounts, at least he was.

The younger man was Jimmy Dane; basically a thug with convictions for robbery with violence and GBH but nothing like this before.'

'Tate? I know the name,' I said, 'is he local?'

Sharp nodded grimly, 'Yeah. One of the lads thinks he might even have done a job for Bobby a few years back.'

I was trying to take all of this in. Even the hit man had been local. What the hell was going on? Who was after me?

'What about our car?' I asked.

'Witnesses described the make and model but nobody got the full reg number, maybe because Palmer was reversing into them at speed.'

'Good.'

'Anyone ID Palmer?'

'Nope,' said Sharp, 'the best description we have is "a scary looking bloke in sunglasses".'

'I dunno,' I said, 'sounds pretty accurate to me.'

'This is serious, you realise?' said Sharp.

'Do you think I don't know that, Sharp!' I shouted at him. 'Try it from my fucking perspective. I was the one they were going to kill, remember?'

'I know. I'm just saying that my lot are fuming. They were sure they'd be able to at least get you tagged as the victim. They reckoned you'd have to admit to illegal activity or beg them for protection.'

'Don't know me very well then, do they?'

'No,' he admitted, 'they don't.'

'Find out who took out that CCTV system.'

'Okay,' he said, but he looked uneasy. I reckoned Sharp was finally starting to realise how deep he was in with us.

'Did you get anywhere with the waiter?'

'He confirmed what you already knew. He took a call from a man purporting to be Kinane with a message for Palmer. Clearly it wasn't Kinane…'

'Clearly,'

'….I think they chose the venue because the mobile signal is so bad in there,' he explained. Even so, I thought, we shouldn't have fallen for such a simple trick. If Palmer hadn't phoned Kinane from his car en route and realised the message was bogus, I would have been gone.

'And Peter Dean?' I asked, 'you sure he hanged himself or did he get a little help?'

He shrugged, 'Doesn't much matter, does it?'

'No,' I sighed, I don't suppose it does.'

The Police showed admirable restraint under the circumstances, waiting twenty-four hours before they hauled me in but, thanks to Sharp, I knew that was more down to lack of evidence than anything else. I was interviewed by a new DI I'd never come across before. He told me his name was Carlton.

'It's usually DI Clifford who drags me all the way across town when you lot want a word. What's happened to him?'

'Detective Inspector Clifford has elected to leave the force,' he said stiffly, 'on medical grounds.'

I nodded as if I understood, 'that's a shame. I rather liked Clifford. His heart was in the right place. Stress was it? I shouldn't wonder. He used to get stomach ulcers. He was a bit of… an obsessive. I hope you are not like that, DI Carlton.'

The Police officer who faced me was a well-built man of around forty with a local accent and a humourless expression. 'If you mean will I be using my holidays to jet off round the world looking for Bobby Mahoney? Then no, I won't. DI Clifford might have believed that Mister Mahoney is alive and sunning himself in Morocco or the Algarve, but I don't. I reckon he's six feet under and it was you that killed him.'

'Me?' I asked incredulously. I knew that DI Carlton was fishing. He knew nothing about the demise of Bobby Mahoney, but such a direct accusation from the new man threw me a little. I was used to dealing with Clifford, the expert chaser of wild geese. We always knew where Clifford was going for his holidays because we arranged for informants to tell him that Bobby was living in retirement out there. Clifford would jet out on vacation and return a week or two later with nothing more than a tanned face and another ulcer to add to his collection. 'Why would I kill Bobby Mahoney?'

'Because he was in the way and you wanted to be Top Boy, but spare me your denials. How about you waste my time denying you were in the Quayside yesterday morning instead?'

'No,' I assured him, 'I was there. I had a coffee at Chi-Chi.'

'Then you went for a jog?' he prompted me.

'Not a jog, no,' I clarified, 'but if you are referring to the fact that some people may have seen me running through the streets afterwards, that's because I had an appointment with my accountant and I realised I was late. No harm done. A brisk run helps combat the jet lag.'

'The jet lag?' he sighed. 'Yes, I was coming to that. On the TV, Policemen are always asking suspects not to leave the country but I'm going to tell you the exact opposite. We don't want you in the city Mr Blake. Your presence here offends us. We want you to fuck off back to whence you came and stay there for a while, so we can fully investigate the circumstances behind the recent attempt on your life by two hit men on motorbikes who were themselves killed by one of your crew.'

'Is this the bit where I say, "What a vivid imagination you have, Detective Inspector"?'

'Don't bother. I knew bringing you in here would be a complete waste of my time, but the brass insisted. I thought I might as well use some of it constructively to inform you that you're going to be on a plane tomorrow. You see our Chief Constable has the severe hump. His eyes are firmly on the prize right now, and that prize is you. He wants you banged up for life.'

'So why allow me to flee the coop?'

'Oh we're not. We just want you out of the way until we find enough evidence to arrest and charge you, that's all. We are coming for you and your business interests; the club, the new hotel. It's only a matter of time, so get your affairs in order; write your will, put some money aside for the nearest and dearest, that sort of thing, because you are going down for life. That much has already been decided.'

I was angry now and I didn't care what I said to him. 'Do your worst,' I told him, 'you haven't got jack-shit on me or we wouldn't keep having these fireside chats. You're just the latest empty threat in a suit. I've heard it all before. I'll fly out if it makes you feel better about yourself, but not tomorrow. I've got too much to do right now, but don't worry, I'll be gone in a few days. I could use a break from this place. Don't be deluded though. You can't hurt me. The club and the hotel aren't in my name, they are not even owned by Gallowgate Leisure. Those deals are funded by venture capitalists using legitimate shareholders with deep pockets and very nasty lawyers. Try and block those projects and you'll get a firestorm of court orders, injunctions and writs for damages. The bureaucracy will keep you in the station for a year,'– he looked like he didn't take too kindly to that – 'and if you get any ideas about coming over all Gene Hunt and planting evidence on me, my lawyers will fucking destroy you. When they are through, the only job you'll ever get will be holding one of those placards on street corners that advertise golf sales.'

Carlton rose then and brought his arm across his chest, then unleashed it in an arc so that the back of his open hand shot out and smashed into the side of my face. It was a meaty blow, but it was worth it to know I'd rattled him. I could feel blood inside my mouth and I spat it onto the desk in front of me. Then I smiled at him through my bloodied teeth and said, 'Nice one, Carlton! Good to see you've got a pair! Normally I'd take myself straight off to be photographed and the lawyer would skewer you, but you can have that one on me.' I was pleased to see his fury. Anger clouds the judgement. I got to my feet like we were done. 'You want to be careful though, DI Carlton,' I warned him, 'you'll give yourself an ulcer.'

17

Kinane was waiting for me in the car. I could tell by his face that something was up. As soon as I climbed in, he said 'Jack Conroy has been in touch.'

'Bloody hell. What does he want?'

'Exactly,' Kinane seemed relieved I was taking it seriously, 'he wants to have a meet.'

'Who with?'

'Well that's just it, with you,' and he cleared his throat, 'and only you.'

There aren't many people in our business who unsettle me. You have to learn to carry yourself with absolute authority when you are around these guys. Otherwise they will sense your unease, feel your fear; then they'll chew you up and spit you out. So I act like the Top Boy should, and after a while you get used to the company of killers, but there is definitely something about Jack Conroy that unnerves me.

*

You could never have guessed what Jack Conroy did for a living. He dressed like a working man; plain black coat with a collar, sweat shirt, jeans, black shoes. You might have said he was a builder, unless you got a close look at those hands. They were big, and there was strength in them, but they weren't the rough hands of a labourer. That was the only clue you'd get about his true profession, that, and the eyes. I don't believe that bullshit about eyes being the windows of the soul but, if I did, I would have assumed that Conroy didn't have one because there was nothing behind his eyes.

We agreed he could come and see me but we met him in numbers; Palmer on the door to pat him down, Kinane close behind, Hunter and three of Kinane's lads between me and him, all of them armed, and Danny close by my side.

Jack Conroy simply spread his hands wide and gave us a resigned smile, 'I'd have to be daft to be carrying in here,' he told us.

'And I'd have to be stupid not to check,' I informed him.

'Fair enough,' he said.

Palmer finished frisking Conroy for weapons, then he got him to remove his coat and leave it on a chair. We were using the Cauldron and its blacked-out windows gave me the level of privacy I needed.

We had used Jack Conroy before, on more than one occasion, because he was good, very good in fact. If you gave him a job, he carried it out without fail, often making it look like an unfortunate accident. If you were a business rival of Bobby's there was no point looking over your shoulder. You still wouldn't see Conroy coming. He was particularly adept at arranging car crashes or hit and runs with no witnesses. He could throw you off a building and make it look like a fall, fake a suicide and leave evidence of gambling debts or mistresses that the Police would jump on to conveniently explain your sudden removal from the world.

Sometimes though, we didn't want a killing to remain secret. In those cases we would prefer people to know it was a really bad idea to take us on. Conroy would shoot you, stab you or kill you up close with those deceptively soft, white hands of his. Man or woman, he would not fail, which is why I afforded his talents the absolute respect they deserved by placing half a dozen members of the firm between him and me.

Palmer indicated a chair in the middle of the room and Conroy regarded it wryly, but walked slowly towards it and sat down. He placed the palms of his hands on his knees where we could see them. He must have figured we were jittery so he probably did this as much for his own safety as for my peace of mind.

'So what can we do for you Jack,' I asked him, 'it's been some time since we did business together.'

'Aye, it's a while back,' he said, as if we were discussing a painting and decorating job and not the murder of a town councillor. The fool not only failed to oil the wheels of the planning department, like he'd promised when he took Bobby's money, but even threatened to tell the Police all about it. Bobby was so incensed he got Conroy to make the married councillor's death look like the suicide of a tortured, closet homosexual. There was poetic justice in it, I suppose. Councillor Barry had been one of the most bigoted blokes ever to join the Labour Party. I don't suppose his wife and family saw the funny side though when they were told he was found with gay porn, the numbers of several male escorts programmed into his phone and 'love letters' from a young man of dubious character.

'This isn't a social call though,' I told Conroy, 'not from the tone of your message.'

'No,' he said, 'not a social call.'

I cocked my head slightly and gave him a questioning look to prompt him.

'I had a visitor a few days ago,' he explained.

'Did you now?'

'Aye. It was a go-between, a cut-out, you know.'

'Yeah, I know,' he was telling me he didn't know the identity of the client who wanted to hire him.

'Anyway, I knew the guy right enough, we all do, but I was surprised as he's not into that game normally. I mean, *you* wouldn't have sent him to talk to me. He asks me straight out if I'd be interested in a job, someone local, somebody "high profile" as he put it, and I said "well that depends". He asks me on what, and I say "on who it is and how much we are talking" and that's when it got interesting.'

'Go on.'

'He told me there was fifty in it for me if I did this particular job.'

'Fifty grand? That's a lot of money Conroy.'

'That's what I said,' he paused for a moment and then bit his bottom lip before continuing, 'until he told me who it was he wanted doing.'

'And who was that?' I asked him, even though I knew the answer already.

'Well,' he said, a little nervously, 'it was you.'

One of Kinane's lads took a step forward like he was about to give Conroy a belt across the face, which would not have been a wise move.

'Hey,' I cautioned.

'Get back in your box,' his voice was a low growl as Conroy stared Kinane's son down.

'So,' I asked Conroy, 'what did you tell him, your cut-out.'

'I told him to fuck off.'

I just looked at Conroy, trying to make my face expressionless, and I kept quiet. Bobby taught me the value of silence years ago. It makes people uncomfortable. Sooner or later they feel the need to fill the void and sometimes they tell you things.

'Honest to God I did,' Conroy assured me. 'Why do you think I'm here?'

'Don't know,' I told him, 'why are you here?'

'To tell you about it, obviously.'

'Why come to me? Why didn't you just send this guy packing and keep out of it? Must have been tempting.'

He thought for a moment before answering, 'well it was. I did think about that, to be honest, but I figured you wouldn't take too kindly if you heard I'd been offered a hit and didn't come to you about it. I mean, I operate on your patch don't I? I live here, this is my home and you, well you're the boss,' he looked a bit nervy there, like he'd just revealed a secret nobody was supposed to know, so he added, 'I mean sort of.'

Was I surprised that Conroy knew I was the boss? Not really. People were bound to speculate when nobody had seen Bobby Mahoney for two years.

'Is that why it took you so long to come here?' I asked him, 'because you were thinking about it, weighing it up? You've been playing a risky game, don't you think?'

Conroy looked about as nervous as I'd ever seen him. We outnumbered him big style and we were on our home turf. One word from me and he'd be bundled into the boot of a car and his body thrown to the pigs, and he knew it.

He swallowed and licked his lips, 'you were abroad, so I was led to believe, so how could I contact you any sooner? I wanted to speak to you direct about this, not one of the lads. In the end I had to talk to Kinane because I heard you were back.'

'You mean you heard someone tried to kill me the other day and you were worried I might have heard they approached you first.'

'Aye, well, right enough, but you have to understand the business I'm in. You don't get work if people know the minute they ask you to remove someone you go running off squealing to their targets about it. Like I said though, you're a special case. This is your city,' he looked around the room as if he was including everybody in the 'your city' but he meant me. It concerned me that the guy who acted as the cut-out had described me as 'high-profile'. I thought I was about as far removed from the day-to-day as possible, living out in Thailand for most of the year, but I guess the lads had been conducting business in my name, which is the same thing as me being right there in the room. I could see it now, 'Blake wants this to happen', 'Blake needs that to happen' and pretty soon I am the guy to get rid of if you want to take over the city. 'I wanted to warn you,' he concluded.

'You could have done that through Kinane.'

He chose his words carefully, 'when someone's out to kill the boss, who can you trust to tell him but yourself? No offence, Joe.'

'None taken,' answered Kinane, because Conroy had a point. He could have been warning the man who'd arranged the hit.

I changed tack, 'who was the cut-out?'

'Well, that's what I came to tell you,' and he looked around the room again, 'it's why I wanted to see you on my own.'

I laughed and shook my head, 'like that's ever going to happen.'

He shrugged as if he finally realised it had been an absurd notion. 'Fair enough,' he said.

'Stop stalling me, Conroy,' I told him, 'give me the name of the cut-out.'

He exhaled and took an eternity before he spoke. I reasoned that grassing on anyone was anathema to him. Finally he said, 'Billy Warren'. I almost fell off my chair.

18

I didn't need to give the order to find Billy. That much was obvious. With everyone in our organisation out on the streets looking for Billy, we'd get him before the day was out, even if he didn't want to be found.

As to what had suddenly possessed Billy Warren to become the middle man between a hit man and whoever wanted me dead, I could only imagine – but it seemed I had completely misread him and that worried me, because Billy was about as one-dimensional as it got. I had always thought I'd put the fear of the devil into Billy when I caught him betraying Bobby. He knew I could have killed him for that, but I let him live and kept him on the payroll; admittedly with his wings clipped, but I would have thought that was a small price to pay to carry on breathing.

Now it seemed I'd misjudged Billy Warren. He was too ambitious to put up with earning a fair day's pay for a fair day's work. He wanted more, and was willing to kill me to get it.

I parked my car with two of its wheels on the grass verge. I got out, climbed over the gate and trudged across the field, cursing the long wet grass and Sharp in that order. When I reached the opposite end of the field there was another gate. I climbed over that too, crossed the road and climbed into Sharp's parked car.

'Do we have to go through all of this "Smiley's People" bollocks every time we have a meet these days?' I asked him.

'Yes, we fucking do. Have you got any idea of the heat you are attracting right now? If I'm even seen with you I'm finished.'

'What have you got for me?' I demanded, 'and it better be good since you just ruined a nice pair of shoes.'

'Officially, nobody knows who was involved in taking down that CCTV system. There are no suspects and, even if there was one, it wouldn't be admitted.'

'Go on,' I urged him, 'why not?'

'Because,' he said solemnly, 'bent coppers are an embarrassment.' He spoke with no discernible trace of irony.

'Give me a name, Sharp.'

'I can do better than that,' he told me, reaching into his case and pulling out a photograph. It was an eight-by-ten, black-and-white surveillance photograph and it showed the image of a stocky man in his mid-thirties. He looked more like a gangster than a copper. 'This is Detective Sergeant Ian Wharton from the Drug Squad. It seems he visited the offices of the CCTV operatives a few days before the system abruptly went down. It is alleged he went to the building with another man, though Wharton denies this, and ordered the security guard to admit them so they could review footage. Wharton showed his credentials and ordered the guard to leave them to it.'

'Giving the second man plenty of time to hack the software and close down the system at a point in the future?' I offered.

'That's my best bet.'

I thought about this for a moment. 'What's going to happen to DS Wharton?'

'Nothing,' Sharp said, 'for now. It seems the security guard got it wrong.'

'How do you mean?'

'At first he told a young investigating officer that Wharton was accompanied by another man. When he was brought in to discuss it further, he admitted he had made a mistake and Wharton was really on his own. There was no second man at all.'

'I can see that would be an easy mistake to make.'

'The investigating officers weren't quite as sympathetic as you. They grilled him about it for quite some time but he wouldn't budge, and of course DS Wharton lacks the necessary technological expertise required to hack the city's CCTV system all on his own, which means nothing can be proved and he is no longer suspended.'

'Where is Wharton now?'

'He was encouraged to take some leave. I don't know where he has gone but he's no longer in the city.'

'Shit, he could have been the one man who might have been hired without a cut-out. Give me that picture,' I demanded.

'What are you going to do?' he asked me, looking anxious as usual.

'Nothing,' I assured him. 'I'm just going to ask around.'

Palmer wanted to speak to me alone so we drove out to his house. I sat at the kitchen table while he made us coffee and I looked around.

'How long have you been here now?'

He shrugged 'about three years.'

'The place looks like you moved in yesterday.' It was amazing how few things Palmer owned. I paid him well, but I was hard-pushed to identify anything in here that looked like it truly belonged to him. He had the 42-inch plasma TV on the living-room wall and a Playstation tucked underneath it with a few games but even his sofas came with the house. It was a former show home and I swear he only bought it so he could take all of the furniture as part of the deal. There was a laptop on the dining-table and he switched it on.

'Mrs Evans keeps the place pretty clean for me,' he said. I wasn't talking about his cleaning lady and he knew that, but this wasn't a conversation he was comfortable with. The no-possessions thing was an aspect of Palmer's personality that I found intriguing, and in a way I envied him for it. He didn't seem to have any baggage at all. There was an ex-wife, but no kids, and he barely mentioned the former Mrs Palmer, except to acknowledge she was probably right to give up on him as a bad lot. We'd see him with a woman now and then but he always held them at arm's length and they were usually history by the time we got used to their names. It suddenly struck me that one day I might drive out to this house and find Palmer gone without any explanation.

'What's on your mind?' I asked him.

'Jaiden Doyle,' he said.

'Oh yeah,' I answered him dryly, 'in all the excitement I'd almost forgotten about Doyley.'

'At least we have footage of that one.'

'Not much to go on though, was there? At least that's what you told me.'

'I did,' he agreed, 'but then I had another look and there's something I want you to see.'

He turned the screen to show me the frozen, black-and-white image of Jaiden Doyle leaving the hotel. Palmer clicked on the arrow and the image started to move. I watched as

Doyley walked away from the hotel. He managed a few steps and then a dark and indistinct figure stepped into the frame, carefully pointed a gun and shot Doyley twice in the back. Doyley fell to the ground, the man left the scene and the image froze once more.

'What do you think?'

'I don't get you.'

'Look again,' he said, and I did.

'What am I looking at?'

'Who does he look like?'

'The shooter?'

'No, Doyley.'

'Doyley?' I asked, 'what do you mean? He looks like Doyley.'

'Okay,' he said reasonably, 'describe him then. Pretend you don't know him.'

'Why?'

'Humour me.'

'Alright. He's about six feet tall, fairly slim build, short dark hair, wearing sunglasses, a smart jacket and trousers, for once, and a pair of black shoes. Er, that's it.'

'Who have you just described?' he asked.

'Doyley,' I answered impatiently.

'Yourself,' he corrected me, 'you've just described yourself, to a tee. I think we've been barking up the wrong tree. It was a botched job. I think the shooter that took down Jaiden Doyle thought he had you in his sights.'

I looked again at the frozen black-and-white image of the smartly-dressed, tall, slim man in the sunglasses and saw it anew. 'Well, fuck me,' was all I could say.

We sat in Palmer's garden and drank a beer while we went over it again.

'So, where do we go from here?'

'You know what I would prefer?' Palmer said.

'You want me to leave the UK until you get to the bottom of this.'

'Yes.'

'You're the second person this week who's asked me to leave the country. The Police told me to go too, and I will. I'll fly out very publicly in a couple of days. I'll have a few days back in Hua Hin with Sarah, then I'll come back again. But this time it'll be under their radar. No one will even know I'm here. Not at first, not if we play it right.'

'I think you should stay out there for a while.'

I shook my head, 'And how are you going to find out who's trying to kill me if I am stuck in a compound five thousand miles away, not daring to show my face by my own swimming pool?'

'I'll find a way,' he assured me, but he was a little slower than usual in answering me.

'I don't see how. We all know there's a long list of people who would benefit from my death and none of them can make a move against me if I'm out of the country.'

'Which is why it makes sense for you to leave on the next flight,' he interjected.

'You don't get it,' I told him, 'I would like nothing better than to leave here, disappear and stay out of the line of fire but, if I do that, the problem will never go away. The only chance we have of getting to the bottom of this is if I stay here with you and Joe and Danny and we find out who is behind it. Someone in this city must know something and that's the only way we'll ever discover who's behind this. Then you can put them down before they put me down.'

'You realise how risky that is,' he was looking at me like I was a mad man, 'you want to flush out a hit man so we can find out who put the contract on you. But what if the next hit man is too quick? What if I can't get to him first?'

'You'll be out of a job,' I assured him 'and I'll be six

feet under. Any more daft questions?'

He snorted, 'No.'

'Look, I'm good at this. I've known this city all of my life and I've done it before.' This time it wasn't missing money I was looking for, but a contract killer so we could find the man behind the hit. It wasn't going to end because Palmer had gunned down two assassins in the Quayside. This would go on until either the man who hired them was dead, or I was. There was no third option. I had to see this through.

'I used to do this for Bobby, remember?' I said.

'Yeah,' he admitted, 'I remember.'

I was glad he resisted the temptation to remind me how that turned out.

19

I told myself I went down to the sports injury clinic that afternoon to try and get a lead on the whereabouts of Billy Warren from Maggot, but that wasn't strictly true. It was a dead end, as I suspected it might be, but when I left Maggot's office and went down into the lounge, Simone was sitting there.

'I'm glad I bumped into you,' I said, not sounding as calm as I would have liked, 'I wanted a word.'

She made a show of glancing at her watch, 'I haven't got long.'

'I don't need long,' I told her, 'have dinner with me. How's that for getting to the point?'

She laughed, 'No.'

'Why not?'

'Because you own this place.'

'But I don't own you.'

'Exactly.'

'I'm talking about a meal here, maybe some conversation, nothing more.'

She raised her eyebrows and I laughed, 'Well, to begin with. Don't rush me woman,' and at least that got a smile. It was progress of sorts.

'Look, say "yes" to dinner. I would like to talk to you, and I can't do that here, can I?' She hesitated, so I added, 'but I will not let you sleep with me, you hear,' she actually laughed then. 'I mean it,' I said, acting stern, 'it's just not going to happen. Can you cope with that?'

'I'll try,' she was still eyeing me suspiciously, 'so when then? I'm working every night for a week.'

I didn't want to think about that so I said quickly, 'the next time we're both free.'

Billy Warren had disappeared – or so they told me, but I didn't believe that for one minute. He just hadn't been seen round his usual haunts, half a dozen places he hung out in when he was between deals; pubs that sensible people avoided or clubs that let in the guys who'd been barred from everywhere else in the city. I doubted Billy had taken flight though. I reckoned he had never left Newcastle in his life, not even for a holiday. He probably didn't have a passport, so I knew he'd turn up soon enough once the word was out. I had people everywhere ready to pick up the phone to us. It was only a matter of time. Trouble was, I needed answers quickly.

'Come on,' I told Kinane, 'it's time we went for a chat with Golden Boots.'

The party was at its height when we arrived. Golden Boots' house was full of footballers, hangers-on and wannabe WAGs, but you could tell it was still early because they hadn't paired up yet. Most footballers are lazy. As soon as they get bored of the music or the atmosphere they grab the nearest girl that takes their fancy. It's easy, since the girls attend these parties for one of two reasons; so they can tell their mates they shagged a Premier League player or, the holy grail for them, they are actually going out with a man who is paid sixty grand a week to swear at referees, blaze shots several metres over the crossbar and kiss his badge minutes before demanding a transfer. Why the world continued to worship these vacuous tossers was beyond me. They'd sign five-year contracts worth millions and, if their clubs were lucky, they'd get two good seasons out of them before they lost their hunger and slid into obscurity.

Golden Boots' parties were very popular. He liked to get people together. He saw himself as a middle man between the players, the women and the Charlie, as he liked to call the coke we sold him, which was heavily cut with baking soda.

The house had cost him two million, which was small change to Golden Boots. It had a massive glass frontage, which shone light down onto the usual assortment of black leather sofas and armchairs, and there was a huge plasma TV in every room, including the kitchen. He didn't seem to be able to cope with silence or being on his own. I reckoned he had ADHD.

Golden Boots face dropped when he saw us, but he quickly transformed it into the cheesy smile of a man greeting two old friends.

'David Blake,' he said, pumping my arm, 'and Joe Kinane… my main man!' He pretended to shadow box my enforcer. Kinane looked at Golden Boots like he was someone he couldn't even be bothered to hit. There was a reason for all of this faux camaraderie. Technically we were in business together, because Billy Warren sold coke to Golden Boots that he then sold on to his Premier League mates and their entourages, which in turn made us a lot of money and gave Golden Boots the gangsta cred he craved. However, the main reason for his obsequiousness went back to the first day we met Golden Boots at Billy's flat. I had Finney with me and he almost finished the gobby bastard's career because Golden Boots thought he was harder than we were. It was fun watching the Premiership's finest crawling on the floor begging Finney not to break both his legs, then thanking him for teaching him some manners afterwards. We'd moved on since then, and now Golden Boots acted like it had never happened, but you could tell he was shitting himself every time we showed up.

'Drink, guys?' he offered, 'Mandy!' His latest pneumatic blonde almost jumped out of her skin when he shouted her name, 'get them a drink, you lazy bitch,' he nodded at us and she broke away from her mates sharpish. They all looked at the walls and the floor while she legged it to the kitchen, looking flushed and humiliated. No one said anything.

'That wasn't very nice,' I told him, 'you forgot your manners.'

'What?' he genuinely didn't know what I meant. 'Sorry lads, did you want something else?'

'That your girlfriend is it?' I asked him.

'Yeah,' and he grinned, 'well, sort of.'

'Shouldn't speak to her like that then, should you?'

'Eh? Oh,' and he looked like a little boy who was being told off by the headmaster, 'S'pose. I'm a bit stressed, you know, business and that.' He was playing the gangster again, blaming his piddling coke deals for his appalling behaviour.

'No excuse,' Kinane told him, 'you'd better apologise.'

'Of course,' answered Golden Boots and he turned to me, 'I'm really sorry you had to see that.'

'Not to us, you twat,' I said, sighing. 'To her.'

'Yeah, yeah,' he was nodding, 'I was just about to.'

At that point the blonde returned and handed beers to Kinane and myself. We both made a point of thanking her and I looked at Golden Boots, who was already having trouble remembering his promise. The girl was walking away when he called, 'Babe,' and she reluctantly turned and walked back. 'I'm really sorry, babe', he said and he pulled her to him in an embrace, 'I don't know what I'm doing. I'm stressing about everything. I'm really, really sorry babe, love ya.'

She looked like she couldn't believe it. I doubt he had apologised to anyone since the day Finney threatened to smash his legs in, least of all to one of his girls. She beamed, 'That's okay babes.' When she'd gone, Kinane said, 'That's better. Now we need a word with you.'

Golden Boots looked worried. 'We're looking for Billy,' I told him, 'you're having a party and Billy always comes to your parties. So where is he? Where's Billy Warren?'

'He does usually, yeah, but I've not seen him tonight,' and he looked put out by this, 'he was supposed to sort out a couple of my mates, if you know what I mean.'

Of course I knew what he meant. 'You might have missed him,' I said, 'in a place this size. You don't mind if Kinane has a look?'

Most people would mind if Kinane was clomping round their house during a party but he was in no position to argue with us, 'Course not,' he said, '*mi casa su casa*,' he added self-consciously. We left him to it. Kinane took the upstairs and I wandered outside towards the pool. There were lots of pretty boy footballers and glamour models out here, showing off and preening in their designer clothes.

'You're not a footballer,' said a voice accusingly. It was a skinny brunette in her mid-twenties with a stack of eye make-up on. She was lying on a lounger in a bikini top and shorts. 'So what are you then?' she waved her glass of champagne at me and narrowed her eyes, as if I might be a spy sent from a tabloid.

'I'm an agent,' I told her.

'A football agent?' she asked and she literally sat up at that point like she was paying attention to me now. I nodded, 'Looking after this lot?' her eyes were wide and hopeful.

I surveyed the young trash in front of me, 'some of them,' I told her. It was partially true. We had invested some start-up cash in a guy who had made some inroads in the agent world. He wasn't that much brighter than Golden Boots but he had a way with words and his baseless threats that one of his young players was about to be spirited away by Spurs, Chelsea or Manchester United usually had chairmen scurrying to increase their wages to a new level of obscenity. It was the easiest, most legal cash we took, though, in some ways, it was grubbier than the drug money.

'You must be minted then?' She was clearly wondering whether it was worth cutting her losses on the players who were goofing about by the pool with younger girls.

'I get by,' I told her.

She climbed to her feet and put the glass down on the table, 'we should have a talk,' she said and she put her arm through mine like we were about to go for a walk along the beach together.

'Now?' I asked her.

'No time like the present, honey,' she laughed a stoner's laugh, but it reminded me of the girls we employed as lap dancers down at Privado. They were trained to fleece guys, twenty quid a time, though she wanted it all and wasn't as patient as they were.

'Where?'

She shrugged, 'where would you like to go?'

'For our talk?' I asked. She nodded. 'How about the bedroom?'

She giggled, 'okay.'

Kinane appeared. He shook his head to indicate there was no sign of Billy. He didn't react to the presence of the girl, who was hanging on me like a barnacle. 'He can come too, right?' I asked her and she looked up to see the bigger, older man with the pock-marked face.

'I don't know about that.' She sounded unsure.

'He always does,' I assured her, 'whenever I talk to a girl, you know, about money and the like.'

'Right,' she wrinkled her nose up as she contemplated this. She obviously didn't want Kinane anywhere near her, 'if you're sure.'

'Why not?' I asked her all innocently. 'We could all three of us go up to one of the bedrooms for our chat, then I could let him beat you up and we'll both roast you. One of us at each end. How does that sound?'

'You what?' she let go of my arm, 'what you fucking going on about? I ain't doing that.'

'Then how about we start again while I remind you that you don't know either of us or what we do for a living. You were this close to going up to a bedroom with us and we could have done anything we liked to you and no one would have heard you scream because of the music. The next day you'd have cried rape but you wouldn't know who you were accusing because you didn't get my name. I'm not a football agent love, I'm a postman and he's a serial killer. Have you got it now?'

'You're horrible,' she told me, 'why don't you fuck off?'

'You know what,' I said, 'I think I will.' And I took a last look at her, 'you're a bit old for me.' And I left her to digest that comment. She crossed her arms over her chest defensively and padded off towards the footballers by the pool. We could see she was telling them all how horrible I'd been to her and a couple looked like they wanted to do something about it but they soon simmered down when they saw Kinane standing there next to me. Instead one of the footballers came up behind her and pulled her shorts and bikini bottoms down to her knees. She squealed as she tried to grab them and, while she was pulling them back up, his friend pushed her into the pool. They all burst out laughing.

'They're vermin,' said Kinane, 'all of them, every last one.

They think they can do anything they want.'

'So do we,' I reminded him.

'But we're not like that,' he reasoned, 'you can't say we're like that.'

'No,' I conceded, 'we're not like that.'

We watched as the brunette splashed to the opposite end of the pool and tried to climb out of it while trying to pull her clothes back on. Her make-up had run till she had panda eyes and her hair was a dripping mess. None of the girls went to help her and the group was laughing at something else by then.

Kinane was right. We weren't like that. It comes to something when footballers behave worse than gangsters and nobody does a thing about it. The girl ran round the pool and disappeared into a side door of the house.

20

Billy lay back on the soft pillow on the hotel bed, staring contentedly up at the ceiling. Billy Warren had never had money before. Not proper money. He'd never been minted. Not like this.

Sure, he'd done a few decent deals with the Premier League lads, and that was money for old rope. Some of these guys earned thirty, forty grand a week, more even, yet there was one thing none of them could buy in the shops. Billy could provide that, and it wasn't just the drugs either. He gave them the gangster glamour they all craved. That's why Billy had the nerve to look Golden Boots in the eye and, straight-faced, give him a price for a kilo of blow that regular cokeheads would have laughed their cocks off at. Golden Boots had looked at him for a moment then answered, 'So, when do we get the stuff?' in a mockney voice that proved he'd been watching too many Danny Dyer DVDs.

These guys wanted people like Billy Warren at their parties. They wanted to nudge their mates and nod at Billy, who'd be standing at the edge of the room, then say, in a world-weary voice, 'that's my dealer, he'll sort you out.' And they'd watch as their friends traipsed over, looking like virgins walking up to a hooker, about as scared and excited as it is possible to be, hoping to pick up a bit of something forbidden.

That's the kind of thrill you need when you play football every week in front of tens of thousands of foul-mouthed fuckers, earning a weekly wage that would be the windfall of a lifetime to most people in the process. When you have a stunning model or a singer for a girlfriend, yet *she's* the one who never takes her eye off you in a club, because she knows there's a wall of fanny queuing up to take her place the minute her back's turned. What else is there to excite you when you don't have to try to score goals, not when it comes natural and always has done, when you can shag every girl you meet, and you have a garage full of Ferraris, Porsches and Astons? Billy had seen the cars, some of them with just a few hundred miles on the clock before the owners got bored with them and moved on to the next flavour of the month their mates are driving into the training ground. Billy has seen Bentleys and Maseratis gathering dust, their owners too stupid even to put a cover over them. So what do you do when you have already earned more money than you could ever spend and you're twenty-two years old? Where can you possibly get your thrills from then? Billy, that's where.

Doing something forbidden, something where the risk is so high that if they were caught their whole world could come crashing down around them is about the only thing that gets them truly hard. They are like the bank manager who defrauds his company, then leaves his wife and kids to run off with a Ukrainian hooker less than half his age; or the married career politician who goes looking for rough trade on Clapham

Common, getting a blow job from a complete stranger who might mug him or kill him. Billy knew enough about life to know that the best thrills are the ones that come with a little bit of risk, because it makes the pay-off all the sweeter at the end.

Billy Warren spent his free time at parties with spoilt, twenty-something millionaires and their hangers on; as drug dealer to the stars he should have been rolling in it. Instead, because of the tight leash Blake had him on, he was lucky if he made a few quid out of it.

The longer this went on, the more he began to resent David Blake. Who was he anyway? Just one of Bobby's 'yes' men. He wasn't hard. It was Kinane who did all of Blake's dirty work for him.

Then Peter Dean had showed up at Billy's flat with his plan. All Billy had to do was set Blake up and he was in for a massive score. It would make the coke deals with Golden Boots look like nowt by comparison. And the beauty was the upfront part of the deal; half as soon as he approached the hit man and half once Blake was removed from the scene. It was amazing. He was being paid a shedload of money to get rid of the one man who had stopped him earning a decent living for the past three years. Talk about sweet.

Finding the hit man hadn't been difficult. Everyone in Billy's world knew what Jack Conroy did for a living. When it came to sitting down with the guy and talking to him though, that was when Billy had earned his money. Sitting in the apartment of a man who had killed countless other men gave him the creeps. Then Conroy had turned down the job.

'What do you mean, man?' asked Billy, 'the money's bloody amazing.'

'It is,' agreed Conroy, 'but I don't shit where I eat.'

Baffled by this response, Billy made sure Conroy understood that their conversation had never happened. Conroy just laughed, 'don't worry, Billy. I'm like a grave. Nothing gets out.'

Billy left Conroy's place in a hurry, then spent a good while racking his memory, trying to dredge up someone else who could take Blake out for them. Then he remembered Tate, a borderline psychopath who'd killed two mental Albanians for Bobby because they'd been trying to take over his vice operation and weren't prepared to do a deal or listen to reason. Tate had managed that easy enough, so he was surely the right man for this one. Billy had gone to see him and, as soon as the money was mentioned, Tate signed on.

With the first part of the job done, Peter Dean came to see him and he paid what was owed. Dean looked nervous, and well he might, but there was nothing to link Billy to the hit and he decided to use some of that money to lay low for a while. First he booked himself into the poshest hotel in town under a fake name and turned off his phone. Then he went shopping for some new threads down the fancy shops with all of the labels. New shoes, suit, shirts, even socks and underwear. He'd gone for all of the brands his Premier League clients favoured; Moschino, Prada, Armani, Boss and a pair of Ferragamo shoes. He paid cash, and made the bemused girl who served him cut the tags off everything while he was still wearing it, then plonked his old gear on the counter, telling her, 'shove that lot in the bin, pet'.

Next stop was a jewellers for an Omega. He could feel its reassuring weight on his wrist when he walked and it made him feel like a player. He went back to the hotel and waited for news on Blake. The sirens outside told him the hit had gone ahead so he turned on the radio to BBC Newcastle and waited. Sure enough, the news report announced there'd been a shooting in the Quayside and two men were believed dead. Two men? That rattled Billy. He decided his best bet was to hole up in the hotel for a few days, living off room service and watching porn on the in-house service. He wasn't too worried at this point. He just thought he should probably keep his head down till the dust settled and he found out exactly what had happened.

Trouble with porn, though, is that it isn't as good as the real thing, and he was flush now, so he called down to the concierge. He'd heard they could get you anything and, sure enough, the bloke gave him the number of an up-market escort agency.

'Escort agency', Billy sniffed, they were still hookers when it came down to it. He dialled them anyway.

'I want a bird,' he informed the woman who answered, 'actually, no, make that two birds, but they've got to be quality.'

'All of our escorts are exceptional ladies for men of discernment sir,' the refined voice assured him.

'Yeah, right, well, that's what I want then,' he told her, 'what you said. How much?'

The woman gave him a price for each girl. There was a cost per hour and a cost for the whole night. The cost for the whole night was colossal but he had the readies and he had promised himself something a bit special; the kind of night Premier League players had every Saturday.

'Alright, you're on,' he said and he told her the name of the hotel he was in, before adding 'I want a blonde and a brunette,' then, almost as an afterthought, 'the blonde has to have big tits and the brunette's got to have long legs.'

'I'll see what I can do, sir,' said the woman with little enthusiasm.

'And they've got to be mucky, I mean, proper filthy,' he said, before adding, 'in bed like.'

'Sir, I don't think you understand our role here. We simply arrange the company of our girls and they provide their time.'

'Company?' asked Billy in disbelief. 'Time? I don't want company love, it's a shag I'm after and for what you charge it ought to be fucking guaranteed!'

'Anything you arrange between yourself and the girls is entirely at their discretion,' she told him, seemingly between gritted teeth. This sounded more promising, but Billy wasn't entirely convinced.

'Right, I see, but just make sure they're broad-minded like. Don't send them if they are not prepared to go down on each other when I tell them to.'

There was a click and she was gone.

'Bollocks,' said Billy out loud. It seemed there were still some things that money couldn't buy in this town. He should have known better than to choose some poncin' arsed agency. It didn't leave him many options though. It was a bit of a risk ringing one of the old timers but, really, where was the harm? He used the hotel phone to call Tommy Bailey.

'Two mucky birds, eh Billy? No problem, if you have the cash.'

'Oh I've got the cash Tommy, don't you worry about that.'

Now Billy was lying on the bed, still dressed in his new gear, looking the part, a proper Face. He was no longer Billy Warren, small time coke dealer, figure of ridicule in Bobby Mahoney's firm, the one they took the piss out of and treated like shit all the time.

There was a gentle knock on the door then. It was Tommy Bailey's girls and they were bang on time too. That was the other advantage of paying for birds, you didn't end up waiting around for them for ages. Billy sat up, then took a deep breath. God he was going to enjoy this. For the first time in his life two very fit lasses were about to get stark naked and do anything and everything he asked them to, and all because he had the wedge to make it happen. It would be the kind of night his millionaire footballers were always bragging about. Well it wasn't going to be them in the middle of a fanny sandwich this time. It was going to be Billy Warren; Player, Face, Top Boy.

Billy got up from the bed and took his time before answering the door. These girls weren't going anywhere, after all. He took a long look at his reflection in the full-length mirrors on the wardrobe doors, pulled down his jacket and smoothed it against him, then smiled to himself. He walked towards the door and opened it, still smiling. Then, abruptly, his smile vanished.

'Now then Billy,' said Joe Kinane, 'what have you been up to?'

21

The lock-up we used for this kind of thing was an old red-brick building with a low roof, a steel door and no windows. The place was an out-building, situated yards from a former electricity sub-station that had served the rural community round here before it closed down years ago. We picked the site up for next to nothing with a view to converting it, but we delayed starting the work when house prices dropped. For the time being it served as a useful destination for men like Billy Warren. Here we could have a quiet word, knowing no one could hear a thing because it was miles from anywhere.

Kinane went to collect Billy as soon as we got the call from Tommy Bailey. Now Billy Warren stood in the empty out-building, beneath the glare of a single, bare light bulb, squinting at me and rocking nervously back and forth on his heels. When he moved the bulb cast exaggerated shadows on the floor behind him. Billy knew why he was here but he was trying to act like he was an entirely innocent party. He didn't quite have the balls to challenge me about it though.

'Nice suit, Billy,' I told him.

'Eh? Oh yeah, thanks.' Then he mumbled, 'been saving for it,' and he looked down, not meeting my gaze.

Only Billy Warren would be stupid enough to go on a spending spree as soon as he pocketed the money he was given to set up a hit. If there had been an ounce of doubt about his guilt, it was removed as soon as we got word from Tommy Bailey that Billy was ordering up hookers two at a time and shipping them out to a four-star hotel.

'Hold out your hand, Billy,' I told him.

'What?'

'Your hand.'

Reluctantly, Billy Warren did as he was told. I took hold of his hand as if I was going to shake it, then, with the other hand, I slid back Billy's sleeve. Beneath it was a gleaming Omega.

'Save up for the watch too did you?'

'Yeah,' Billy's voice was a squeak.

'Oh I see,' I said, 'and there was me thinking you paid for it with all the money you got for setting up a hit on me with Jack Conroy.'

Billy's eyes widened, 'You what man? God no, who's been saying that. I'd never…'

'Jack Conroy's been saying that. He came to see us, Billy, told us all about it. *He's* not stupid enough to go against us. He knew what would happen if he did. He knew we'd find out about it and when we did, we'd kill him.'

'I don't know what he's been saying, Davey, I really don't but he's mad. He must be puddled. I'd never get involved in anything like that. I don't set up hits. I just deal.'

'How much of your own product have you been using these days Billy? What were you thinking? You should have stayed just dealing. If you had you might have had a longer life.'

'Jesus man, you don't want to listen to Conroy. He's never liked us, never…'

'Who paid you to set me up? That's the only thing I want to hear you say. Give me a name.'

'I don't know what you're on about Davey, honest. I swear on my mother's life!'

'Your mother's dead Billy,' and I turned to Kinane, 'go and get the tool-box Joe.'

'No, please, there's no need for that,' Billy was panicking now.

Kinane walked away towards the door.

'Shut up Billy,'

'I'm begging you man,'

'Shut up,'

'Please,' he was sobbing now, 'we go back years, known each other ages…'

'Listen to me Billy,' and when Billy Warren tried to interrupt again, 'listen…listen…listen,' and Billy finally fell silent, 'I want you to calm down so you can listen to me while I tell you what's going to happen.'

'Okay,' he said uncertainly.

'Kinane is going to walk out to his car and he is going to fetch his tool-box,' that was Kinane's cue to leave the room and Billy started to silently shake his head, tears rolling down his face, 'and you know what that means, don't you?'

Billy Warren watched Kinane leave, 'Jesus Christ.'

'You have until the time it takes him to reach the boot of his car and walk back in here with his tools to give us a name.'

Billy looked up into my face, but he couldn't read me, 'will you let me go?' he asked eventually. He was wide-eyed, desperate. 'If I give you that name, will you let me go?'

'No.'

Billy's face sagged and his mouth fell open. 'What…?' his mouth was too dry to speak coherently.

'It's a simple choice Billy. When Kinane returns he'll have his tool-box and a gun. If you give him the name, for old times' sake,' I assured him, 'he'll only use the gun.'

And before Billy Warren could find the words to reply, I turned on my heel and walked out of the room. As I closed the door behind me, I heard the single, sobbed word, 'please.'

I leaned against the wall of the building and fumbled in a pocket for my cigarettes. I lit one, took a deep drag and looked around me. It was so quiet out here. The air was crisp and there wasn't a sound except the wind stirring the trees and Kinane's slow, measured footsteps as the big man walked towards his car. I watched him pop open the boot, then reach inside. He drew out the large, metal tool-box that was his signature. Everyone in our world knew about Kinane and his tool-box and feared him for it. If you are an enforcer, if you had to make men tell you things they didn't want to tell you, sometimes you had to use brutal methods. I don't care what the liberals say, torture works. I've seen it. I've watched hard men broken, over time – sometimes it can take days, but everybody spills in the end. They just get to the point where the only thing they want any more is for the pain to end, even if what follows is death. A man like Kinane can hardly walk around with weapons in the boot of his car. If he's caught with knives or knuckle-dusters on him he'll be looking at serious jail time, so why run the risk when you can get exactly the same effect with hammers, nails, chisels and hacksaws. Ever hurt yourself putting up some shelves? Then you'll understand what I mean. So Kinane doesn't go anywhere without his tool-box. Sometimes all I have to do is mention it and we get what we need. Fear is as potent a weapon as pain, maybe more so.

This time however, it's different. Joe is carrying. I asked him to. I watched him take the Glock out of a holdall in the boot of his car. Then he walked slowly back with the gun in one hand and the tool-box in the other. He carried the Glock openly. Who was going to see it out here? As he walked past me his face was a dispassionate mask. I wondered what he was thinking and what he was going to say to Billy Warren. We had both known Billy for years, but none of that mattered now. We all knew he had stepped way over the line.

Kinane didn't look at me as he went by and walked on into the room. He closed the door behind him. I took another long draw on my cigarette and waited. It was cold, but I wasn't thinking about that right now. I waited some more. I smoked my cigarette right down to the filter and then I lit another. I waited so long, in fact, that I was starting to wonder if my instincts were wrong on this one but then, finally and so suddenly, there was a muffled explosion from within the lock-up. It was the sound of the Glock going off in a confined space. It was louder than I would have expected but there was still no danger of anyone hearing it from the road. It was the sound of Billy Warren dying, but his passing was so quiet the birds didn't even bother to leave the trees.

22

We walked to the car without saying a word. We fastened our seatbelts and both waited for the other to speak. In the end I asked, 'What name did he give you?'

Kinane shook his head, 'Peter Dean.'

'Shit. Didn't he know anyone higher up the chain?'

'No,' Kinane said, 'he would have told me.'

I didn't doubt that. We'd gone round in a circle. All we had were the names of two cut-outs. Both dead. One died before we could get to him and the other knew nothing.

'What are you going to do now?' asked Kinane.

'Me?' I didn't know what my next move was. I just felt indescribably weary of it all. 'I'm going home,' I told him.

The heat was oppressive, and I wanted to get out of it and into the house. I wanted a cold drink with ice in it and the air con on full. I didn't want to move for a while. I figured I'd surprise

Sarah, so I opened the door quietly and walked into the house, closing it gently behind me. I couldn't hear anything but I sensed I wasn't alone and the guards had told me she was in the compound. I climbed the stairs. She didn't hear me. I knew if she had she would have come running.

I opened the door to our bedroom without knocking, looked in and saw her. 'What the fuck are you doing?' I demanded.

Sarah was angry with me, spitting the words out. 'You can be a bastard sometimes, do you know that? So fucking cold.'

This hurt me a little, because it is not the first time a woman has said that to me. My ex, Laura, used to accuse me of being cold but I defy any man not to be when he has seen all the things I have. Other people's problems can seem trivial by comparison. So, when I answered Sarah, my voice was calm and I tried to explain my anger to her in a rational way. I wanted her to understand why I reacted the way I did when I walked into the bedroom and saw what she was doing.

'I might be cold,' I explained to her, 'but I have to be. I have to be cold, calm and clever, because that's what keeps us alive. I can't afford to make any mistakes. You of all people should know this. After what you went through, after what we *both* went through, I thought you would understand that.' She lowered her head, not exactly shamefaced by my words but she was listening at least. 'Everything I do is geared around keeping you safe so we can lead this life we have together. Neither one of us can ever let down our guard, you know that,' I reasoned, 'at least I thought you did.'

'I do,' she protested, 'it's just... I get so lonely stuck here on my own.'

'Stuck here?' I was stunned. The place was a palace compared to the shit holes most people Sarah's age lived in, 'Your mate Joanne lives in a one-bedroom flat. You live in a fucking compound with a pool and your own private beach!'

'Yes!' she shouted back at me, 'I know! And I can never leave it! It's got to be the most beautiful bloody prison in the whole frigging world!'

'Is that how you see all this? Like it's some sort of prison? Tell me you are kidding me?'

'It's alright for you,' she said, 'you get to go out, you get to fly back home for your meetings, you see old friends and hang out with them, you go out on the town, don't tell me you don't. I haven't been back there since Dad died. You won't let me go. You won't even let me shop in the markets round here.'

'Yes I will.'

'Not unless I take Jagrit and his mates with me, and that's not the same,' she argued. 'Do you know what it feels like looking at stuff, knowing there's a bodyguard walking a few yards in front of you and another two behind you? I feel trapped.'

'The alternative is a lot worse love, believe me.'

'I knew you wouldn't understand.' We didn't argue very often, but when we did we quickly reached a stage where we were completely at odds with each other's opinions.

'I do understand,' and I did. At least I was trying to. Sarah was still a young woman. She had been used to going out with her friends and doing whatever she wanted whenever she wanted, but all that had changed suddenly and forever, and there was no going back now, not for either of us. Sarah had no idea what would happen to her if my enemies ever worked out where she was. If she knew what some of them would do to her, just to get at me, then she would never leave the compound again. 'But I don't know what the alternative is, Sarah. You are Bobby Mahoney's daughter and my girlfriend, which means your card is marked. You get the privileges that come with that, but you can't live the life you lived before because there are people out there who will come after you, to hurt me,' I concluded. 'We have talked about this before.'

She couldn't argue with that because it was true. Instead she just said, 'Did you really have to smash my laptop?'

I looked over at the wreckage of Sarah's laptop, which exploded pretty spectacularly shortly after I ripped it out of her hands and hurled it against the far wall of our bedroom. There were sharp, black plastic shards on the carpet and the screen had become entirely detached from the keyboard. There was a massive crack right across it and a big gouge in the plaster where the corner of the laptop had impacted with the wall. I surveyed the wreckage and realised I had been more angry than I cared to recall. In retrospect, my fury must have been pretty frightening.

'I'm sorry,' I admitted, 'but it's just...I mean...what were you thinking?'

'It was only a Facebook page,' she pleaded, 'and I wasn't even using my real name. I'm on there as Sarah Phoney and I only used it to connect with some old Uni mates and a couple of friends from back home. Joanne was practically the only one who bothered to message me. I don't understand why it's such a big deal to you.'

'Because there are bad people out there who employ clever IT guys who are constantly looking for weaknesses in my organisation, something they can use to bring me down. So you having a Facebook page is the cyber equivalent of going out for the day and leaving the back door wide open. That's why it's such a big deal to me.'

She looked up at me, 'I'm sorry. I am. I just...I'm so lonely.' I didn't know what to say. I thought I'd created a paradise for us and it turned out I couldn't have been more wrong. Worse than that though, I didn't have the faintest clue how to fix it.

I went to her then. I sat on the bed next to Sarah and put my arms around her. She pressed her face against my chest and held on to me tightly.

'It's alright,' I assured her, 'I know, and I'm sorry too. You know I'll get you another laptop, just no Facebook page this time. eh?' She half-laughed and half-cried at that.

'And if you just give me a little more time I'll figure this out for us,' I reassured her. 'You know I can do that, don't you?'

'Yes,' she said, 'I do.' She was lying but, just now, I needed to hear the lie.

That night I phoned Sharp, 'I've got another job for you,' I told him.

'Christ,' he said, 'what is it now?'

I had a week in Hua Hin with Sarah. We spent a lot of time walking on the beach and talking, mostly about the future. We avoided dwelling on the past, for obvious reasons, and the present was too complex to sort out with just a few words.

I took calls from Sharp, Palmer and Kinane, but none of them had come up with anything new. Billy Warren and Peter Dean were dead and it seemed we'd hit a brick wall. I kept churning it all over in my mind, but I just couldn't piece it together. There were some obvious possibilities; Alan Gladwell wanted to meet to talk peace and cooperation but he could just as easily be trying to kill me at the same time; neither the man nor his family could be trusted. Then there was the Turk, whose shipment had been mysteriously delayed again while I was out of the country, despite the fact that he was sitting on one million Euros of my money. With me gone, he wouldn't have to give it back, and men have been killed for a lot less than that. Kinane kept telling me Braddock wanted to take me out, and you could sense Braddock wanted to be Top Boy just by looking at him. Killing me would be the quickest route to the top, whether he was up to the job or not. Then there was Amrein, our fixer, the man I had scared, threatened and humiliated. I knew Amrein wouldn't grieve for me. In fact I was sure he wanted me dead after what I did to him, but did he have the balls to take me on a second time? I truthfully didn't know.

Gladwell, Amrein, Braddock and the Turk. Four of them, and they were only the most obvious candidates. I hadn't even included members of my own crew, not to mention the crime families in every other city in the country. How many people had I blocked or frustrated with my business dealings, how many had I insulted, snubbed or annoyed along the way? If I wrote a list of people who wanted me dead it would probably have filled more than a page.

'I don't know what you want me to do,' she told me, 'I don't know what's expected of me.'

'Nothing's expected of you.' I was looking straight ahead, both hands on the steering-wheel to make sure we didn't ram the back of the tourist bus that was hobbling slowly along in front of us.

'Then why bring me along?'

'It's your presence he's expecting. I told you he's an important man. That's why I am going out to the airport to meet him and why I have asked you to come with me.'

'But I don't speak any Japanese.'

'Nor do I,' I reminded her, as I finally found a gap to pull out and overtake the bus.

'And I don't know any of the customs. They've got all of these rituals, haven't they, all that bowing and handing over business cards like they're family heirlooms.'

'He isn't expecting any of that, I promise.'

'And tea,' she was stressing out now, 'they make such a pigging nonsense over a cup of tea. They have a whole ceremony for it, all that kneeling and bowing. We just have PG Tips sent over from home. He's not going to be happy with a pyramid bag is he?'

'Don't worry about any of that. I've got housekeeping on stand-by. Please just relax and smile at him when he arrives. That's all I ask. I don't ask you to do much but I need you to do this for me.'

'Okay,' she said, 'you're right, you don't. I'm sorry, I'll try to chill out.'

We made the airport in time for the arrival of the private jet that had been chartered for the occasion. Sarah couldn't relax, so fretful was she about screwing up my big meeting with Mr Hakaihamo of Dogobari International. She was wearing a dress, and looked older because of it. Apart from bikinis she usually just wore shorts and T-shirts.

The plane took an age between landing and hooking up to the arrivals gate, but eventually the light went on above the door to indicate all was ready. I was watching Sarah out of the corner of my eye. She was staring at the gate intently, waiting for the first glimpse of Mister Hakaihamo.

There was a hissing sound, then a pop, as the hydraulics on the door engaged and it swung open. There was no sign of Mister Hakaihamo. Instead, a young woman was standing there with a huge grin on her face. She beamed at Sarah. Sarah's eyes went wide, 'Wha- ?' was all she could manage.

'Don't just stand there, you lazy cow,' shrieked Joanne, 'give us a hug, then help me with me bags!'

Sarah turned to me and I said 'Surprise', smiling at the look of utter shock on her face.

Before she could respond Joanne chipped in again, 'Come on, you lot,' and another eight people filed out of the door.

'Oh my God,' Sarah's hands went up to her face.

It had been fairly easy tracking all of Sarah's friends down. Not a difficult job for a man of Sharp's talents. They had all jumped at the chance of a couple of weeks' free holiday in Thailand, particularly when they found out I was flying them over on a private jet. There were a lot of hugs and screaming, tears and excitement. Kiet our housekeeper arrived then. He handed me the bag I'd entrusted him with. 'I'm going back on the return flight, but you are in safe hands.' I introduced them to Kiet, 'Drivers are waiting to take you to the house. While you are staying with Sarah, please treat it like your own home.'

'Oh God, I can't believe this,' said Sarah. 'I can't believe you're all here,' then a frown creased her forehead, 'but what about the Japanese bloke?' she asked me, 'there is no Japanese bloke, is there?'

I kissed her then. 'You know, for such a beautiful and intelligent young woman you can be quite thick sometimes.'

'Thank you,' she said, mock annoyed, but I'd not seen her looking this happy in ages, 'and thank you for *this*.' And she hugged me. 'I love you,' she told me.

'I love you too,' I said, and I meant it.

23

I came back into the country quietly, using a different identity and rented a hire car. The Police would know I was back soon enough, but I wasn't going to make a song and dance about being here. Not when they were so pissed off at me.

My first task was to meet Palmer at the offices we rented for Robbie and his watchers. We'd set them up to look like an IT help-desk team and the small group of four guys had computers, monitors and TV screens around them so they could keep track of the whole city. It was the screens that Palmer was keen to show me.

'Give him a demo, Robbie.'

'Okay, name me a place in the city.'

'Bigg Market,' I said and Robbie tapped something into his keyboard, his fingers becoming a blur. The screen we were watching changed, and there was a bird's eye view of the Bigg

Market as seen through a CCTV camera mounted on a roof somewhere.

'Name a street somewhere,' urged Robbie.

'Stowell Street,' I said, and his fingers darted over the keyboard again. Up popped an image of Rosie's Bar and the Newcastle Arms pub.

'That's bloody amazing. I can't quite believe what I'm seeing,' I said, delightedly. 'Robbie, have you hacked the CCTV network for the entire city?'

'Erm..yes…I h..h..have,' he stammered.

'Good lad,' I said.

Palmer smiled with the satisfaction of someone who has seen his protégé achieve the status of genius. I just shook my head in wonderment. 'I'm stunned. We can keep our eye on everything now.'

'And no one w..w..will know because all we are d..d..doing is tapping in and tapping out. It's untraceable,' Robbie assured me.

'I've got something else that might interest you,' Palmer said, beckoning me into an empty office and holding something tiny between his thumb and forefinger. It was no bigger than the SIM card from a mobile phone, and looked like it was made of plastic and metal, but it was so small I could barely make it out.

'What is it?'

'A tracking device,' he told me, 'you can hide it in someone's car, or attach it to the outside, then you can monitor them remotely from here,' he nodded at the screens. 'You'll know where their vehicle is twenty-four-seven.'

'Sounds useful.'

'It is. I think we should chip everyone's car. In our firm, I mean.'

'Everybody's?'

'Well, we don't know who to trust right now. This could be our only way of finding out.'

'They're not going to like it.'

'They won't know, and even if they do work it out, fuck 'em. We've got too much at stake here to piss around. Someone is trying to kill you. This could be the best chance we have of finding out who.'

I hesitated, but not for long. 'Okay,' I said, 'but Palmer, don't chip my car.'

He gave me a pained look. 'It would be easier for us if you'd let me.'

'I don't want you knowing where I am, all of the time,' I told him, 'that's not negotiable.'

We were walking around the perimeter of the square in front of the cathedral, ambling along like a couple of work colleagues out for a lunchtime stroll in the autumn sunshine. Behind us, Amrein's bodyguard and Palmer kept a discreet distance, keeping an eye on us and, no doubt, each other.

Meeting Amrein in Durham City seemed a sensible idea. I wasn't persona non grata with the local plod there and we could lose ourselves amongst fresh-faced students and gaggles of foreign tourists craning their necks backwards so they could photograph the cathedral.

'I don't know what you are telling me,' I said.

Amrein side-stepped a couple of students who were walking along arm-in-arm with big grins on their faces, then he spoke. 'I'm afraid there is nothing.'

'There must be something.'

He seemed surprised at my certainty. 'May I ask why? Do you have some knowledge you would like to share with me? It would certainly make our investigations easier.'

'Human nature,' I told him, 'because he's a politician, because they are all bent as nine bob notes, every last one of them. Ron Haydon has been one for nearly thirty years, so he has to have something hidden away that we can use. I know it.'

'I assure you, he hasn't,' Amrein explained calmly, 'I have had two journalists investigating him full-time since we got your call and they haven't found a thing.'

'Two' I asked, 'full-time?'

'Yes,' he told me.

I stopped walking and he came to a halt. 'Amrein, if you want me to think you are taking my problem seriously, you should have *twenty-two* journalists on it permanently. Do that and I might start to actually believe you are on my side – and not just hoping I'll be locked away for life so you can replace me with someone you'd prefer.'

'I assure you…'

'Assurances are like excuses, they mean nothing. Get me what I need on Haydon or I'll start to wonder why I pay you.' He looked worried then. 'Don't worry, Amrein, I won't kill you. I'll just stop sending you the Drop, and that amounts to the same thing.'

'I'll redouble my efforts, of course,' he told me quickly, before adding, 'are we done?'

'We're done,' I said and he walked off, followed by his bodyguard.

'What was that all about?' asked Palmer, as we watched them walk across the square, dwarfed by the massive presence of the ancient cathedral.

'Just business,' I told him. I didn't want Palmer to know that I had just threatened a man whose organisation made the Mafia look like a street gang.

24

We'd barely ordered our food, and the sommelier had just finished pouring the wine, when she asked me, 'So, what do you want to talk to me about?'

'Straight down to business? No small talk?'

'I'm used to that these days,' she said mirthlessly.

'You've not even given me time to compliment you on your appearance.' She looked good. She was wearing a black trouser suit that neatly contrasted the pseudo-cocktail dress look we encouraged at the massage parlour. I could see our reflections in the huge mirrors on the restaurant's walls. We looked natural together, smart, prosperous. Nobody in the room could have guessed how we both made our living.

'Perhaps I prefer it that way. I've had compliments before.'

'I'm sure you have.'

'And they didn't mean much when it came down to it.'

'Okay, you want the truth? You intrigue me.'

'I'm not that intriguing.'

'I think you are. Nobody can understand why you work down there.'

'At the massage parlour?' She was challenging me to say it out loud, seeing if she could embarrass me in public.

'Yes, at the massage parlour.'

'Because I am so much better than that?'

'Yes.'

'What about the other girls who work there? Aren't they too good for the job? Am I better than them?'

'I don't know about that, but I do know that you could walk out of there today and find something better in a heartbeat. They would all do that too if they could, and they wouldn't look back'

'But they can't.'

'No.'

'Why?' she challenged me, 'because you won't let them leave?'

'God no, we never stop anyone from leaving. Is that what you think? That we keep girls working there against their will?'

'I don't know,' she frowned, 'I've never tried to leave. It's just something one of the girls said, that she kept trying to leave but she couldn't. Not ever. She was resigned to it, she seemed sad.'

'I suppose she meant she needed the money. Most of the girls have debts or mortgages, or something that stops them from giving it up. There are other jobs but they don't pay as well. I'm not saying it's nice work, you know that better than I do, but the girls choose to be there. I mean they might feel they have no choice but they can quit and do something else any time they like.'

'I see,' she said.

'I understand *them*. It's you that's got me intrigued.'

'Why?'

'Like I said, you have options. A woman that looks like you, sounds like you, it's obvious.'

'What is? How do I sound?'

'Educated, refined.'

'Refined?' She did a cute thing with her eyes, dipping her head and raising her eyebrows at the same time and looking up at me. 'I haven't heard that word since I was a girl. My mother was always telling me to sit like a lady, don't slouch, be refined, such an old-fashioned word.'

'The fact that your mother even used it proves my point. You've not got the usual background.'

'What else do you think you know about me?'

I could tell she was starting to enjoy this little guessing game, maybe because it was about her. Most women like to talk about themselves. Men who understand that can sometimes find a way in.

'No accent, so you went to a "good" school. I'd guess you have qualifications, a degree?' She nodded slowly. 'So I'm assuming something happened?'

'Like what?'

'Don't know,' I admitted, 'something bad though. I mean women don't end up working there…'

'At the massage parlour,' she reminded me in a voice that was a little louder than our conversation.

'At the massage parlour,' I said it back to her at the same level, calling her bluff, 'if something good has happened to them. They don't walk through our door and say "I just got a degree, met the man of my dreams and won the lottery. I'd like to come and work here."'

'What do they say?'

'I don't know,' I said, 'Elaine handles all that. She has a good long chat with the girls beforehand, checks that they really want to do it. She makes sure they understand what's involved. You know that. She had the same chat with you.'

'You checked, did you?'

'Yes.'

She didn't seem too happy about that, 'and what did she say about me?'

'Not much,' I conceded, 'just something about a guy.' She folded her arms defensively. 'Hey, it's none of my business.'

'You're right,' she told me, then unfolded her arms and took a sip of her wine.

'Okay then, how about your name? Do I get to know that at least?'

'Are we pretending you don't know my real name? Elaine must have told you.'

'I'd prefer to hear it from you. I'd like your permission to call you by your real name and not just "Call-Me-Tanya".'

'Simone,' she said. 'Yes, I know,' she looked a little embarrassed, surprisingly, 'my mother named me after Simone De Beauvoir.'

'Oh God.'

'I'm afraid so. So what does that make her?'

'Serious, liberal and amazingly posh.'

'I don't know about amazingly posh,' she protested in a voice which just made her sound even more like a Duchess, 'but yes, she was quite serious. She studied philosophy and I gained the impression she was quite liberal, in her younger days, before she met *him*.'

'*Him* being daddy?'

'Him being daddy,' she confirmed.

'And what's wrong with daddy?'

'Oh absolutely nothing,' her tone was dripping with sarcasm, 'he's perfect; works in the city, with money. Comes home late at night after everyone has gone to sleep, goes to bed and probably dreams about money; the perfect father, never around to stop me from doing anything I wanted to do.'

She was challenging me again, waiting to see what my

reaction to all that would be.I suspected that whatever I said would be wrong and she would seize upon it. So this wasn't just about punishing the ex-boyfriend, it was about putting two fingers up at daddy too. He'd neglected her over the years and ground down her mum, so now she worked in a knocking shop to get back at him. I thought that was a peculiarly female logic, akin to cutting off your nose to spite your face.

'So that was daddy,' I said simply, 'what about this boyfriend Elaine didn't tell me about.'

'He was a bastard.'

'Aren't all men?' I asked her dryly.

'Yes,' it was my turn to raise my eyebrows, 'aren't they?' She seemed serious, but she was probably just challenging me again.

'No, not all of them.'

'Are you the exception?'

'God no, I'm a total bastard, an eighteen-carat bad boy, the kind of bloke your mother warned you about. You should steer well clear,' she was laughing again, which wasn't a bad thing. 'Should I have lied about that do you think?' I asked, mock innocently.

'Might have been a better tactic.'

'I don't know about that. Women are always telling men all they want is for someone to treat them right and make them laugh, but that's total bollocks. They don't want that at all.'

'And what do we want?'

'Something far more stressful, dangerous and uncertain. They want a man to run them bloody ragged, then leave them not knowing where they are. Only then will they be convinced he is the one for them, so they can set about changing him into the nice chap they could have had if they'd chosen better in the first place.'

'You could be right about that,' she admitted, 'judging by my track record, but then I may not be representative.'

'What about your bastard then? Is he still on the scene?'

'If you mean am I still sleeping with him? No. Is he still around? Well, he lives in the same city but other than that...' She let the sentence trail away.

'Treat you badly, did he?'

For a moment she looked like she might start to cry but she kept it together, 'very.'

'Fell hard?'

'You could say that.'

'That doesn't answer the question.'

'Which question?'

'The one about why you work at the massage parlour?'

'I need the money.'

'Because of this guy?' she nodded, 'what happened?'

'I told you, he was no good. We were seeing each other. I thought it was love. I loved him so much that I gave him money. We broke up. He didn't give any of it back.'

'Was it much?'

'Enough.'

'What's his name, this guy?'

'Why do you want to know his name?'

I shrugged like it was no big deal to me, 'Don't know,' I said, 'I might know him, that's all. I could have a word, about this money of yours, maybe get it back for you.'

She snorted, 'I don't think so.'

'Why not?'

'Because he is not the kind of man you have words with. He's a big scary guy and he throws his weight around. It's not just women he scares, believe me.'

'Well, he wouldn't scare me.'

'You're sure about that are you?' She sounded doubtful, then she looked at me as if seeing me properly for the first time. 'Well Mr Blake, if you are not scared of my ex, even though I've told you what he's like, then that makes me wonder about the kind of man you are.'

'The kind who doesn't like to hear about a lady being ripped off by a thug.'

'So I'm a lady, am I?'

'Yes.'

'Not a whore?' she was challenging me again.

'I suppose, technically, you're both,' I told her and there was a pause while she digested that one, then she laughed again.

'You're a charmer,' she said.

'I tell it as I see it,' I told her, 'and so do you.'

'Okay, so maybe you're not scared, but I'm still not going to give you his name.'

'Why? Regular gangster is he?'

'He thinks he is.'

'A lot do in this city.' I wanted to explain that five minutes alone with Kinane and this guy would be begging for the opportunity to pay her money back with interest, but I didn't think she'd be impressed by that.

'I am not going to give you his name because either you would end up getting hurt or he would,' and she peered at me intently, 'and I'm starting to suspect it might be him.'

'What do you care? He stole from you.'

'It was my fault. I was the fool for lending him the money. And anyway, I don't want him hurt, not in that way.'

No, I thought, you just want him to find out you are working in a brothel, like that's really going to ruin his life.

'You must have lent him a fair amount if you had to work at the parlour to pay off your debts.'

She sighed, 'I lost my job because of the lifestyle we were leading; the hours and the partying,' she meant the drugs, 'I almost lost my apartment, but I knew about the massage parlour, so I thought I would give it a try. I mean, I had nothing more to lose did I?'

'Getting money from darling daddy was out of the question, I suppose?'

'You suppose right,' she said with such steely determination that I let it go, but I couldn't understand how bad things would have to be between a girl and her father for her to prefer having sex with strangers than go to him for money.

'How did you know about the place?'

'The ex told me. I said he was a bad man. We drove past it one day and he said, "you see that place, it's a knocking shop" and I remember we laughed about the kind of women who worked in a place like that. I didn't give it another moment's thought until I had no money and they were going to repossess my apartment.' She was talking like she was in total control but she had started to unconsciously play with a long loose strand of her hair.

'I went down there, and I was too terrified to walk through the doors at first, but somehow I managed to pluck up the courage to go inside. Elaine was there, she seemed okay. I mean she's a tough one, but if you've been to a girls' boarding school you've experienced far worse than Elaine.'

She stopped playing with her hair for a moment, picked up her wine glass by the stem, took a long drink and continued, 'I almost didn't go through with it, on the first night, I mean. I couldn't even decide what to wear, isn't that crazy? I spent ages staring at the contents of my wardrobe, trying to find something *appropriate*,' and she laughed without humour at the word. 'I mean the men aren't down there because of the clothes you wear. It's not as if you even keep them on for long. I knew that but...' she trailed away and blinked at the absurdity of caring what she wore in a brothel.

'But I went through with it. I'd reached a stage in my life where I figured I was never going to let a man near me again anyway unless I made him pay for it. The first night I did five massages. Only one of them wanted more than a "happy ending". That first time was...' she took a moment to choose the right word, '...difficult, but I made enough money so I went back the next night. After three days Elaine said I could stay.'

'Because you were earning,' I meant for the house, and she nodded.

'Paid off your debts yet?'

'Not quite.'

'Will you leave when you do?'

'Why would I? I have to earn money somehow.'

'Yes, but you don't have to earn it like that. I'm not being a moralist here, but there must be easier jobs.'

'Than working for you, you mean?' Strangely, I hadn't actually viewed what Simone did as working for me. I may have been the main guy in our firm now that Bobby was gone but we had a lot of things going on and the massage parlour was just one of them. I'd even toyed with the idea of closing it down, but it was a decent earner so I'd kept it going. I didn't really get involved other than to count and launder the money. I supposed I was living off immoral earnings, though the money from the massage parlour was a tiny percentage of my income. In the eyes of the law I was a pimp, but really we were providing a service here. Everyone in that place was either a man who couldn't get sex elsewhere or a woman who needed to earn more than minimum wage. I provided a safe, clean environment to get them together, where no one got robbed or beaten. That was all.

'Some of the men are okay,' she said, by way of justification, 'most of them are polite. Nearly all of them are nervous and that makes them easier to handle. I thought they'd all be cocky, wanting to enjoy it for as long as they could, but they want to get it done and be away as soon as it's over. There are only some who are difficult, but then there's always Max.'

Max was the man we paid to sort out anything the girls and Elaine couldn't handle. He would hang back in the shadows unless there was trouble, but we made sure he was a visible presence. Seeing him there was usually enough to ensure everyone paid up and treated the girls with respect. Max probably had the easiest bouncing job in Newcastle, but occasionally a customer would misbehave and we couldn't run the place without a man like him on the site, because we couldn't afford the parlour to get a bad name and attract the wrong kind of attention from the authorities. If there was any bother he'd step in and stop it pronto.

'A lot of the guys are scared to death,' she said suddenly, as if she had only just realised it, 'they don't want to be there. They *need* it of course, they can't help themselves. All men are like that, like dogs. They want to get it out of their system and be out of there as quick as they can afterwards.'

'You have a low opinion of men, don't you?'

'Yes.'

'How do you handle it then?'

'With most of them, I just take off my clothes, give them a massage, give them a hand job and that's all they need. They don't even touch me and they don't take long.'

Another sip of wine, then she realised her glass was nearly empty. I refilled it and she carried on. It was funny, I couldn't get her to talk at all at first, now she didn't seem to want to stop. 'Some of them want full sex and I have to let them. I mean that's what they pay for, but I just lie there and turn my head away. They don't like it, but they don't get any more from me than that, ever. They want a Girl Friend Experience,' and she snorted at the notion, 'they want me to kiss them, put my tongue in their mouths, they offer to pay more.'

'But you won't do that?'

'Never,' she told me, 'no one gets that.'

She sipped her wine some more, looked at me as if waiting for a comment and when I didn't say anything she said, 'One guy kept going on at me, saying I was liking it. "Loving it," in fact, "You're loving this, darling",' and she snorted at his stupidity, 'he actually thought I was getting off on him because I was wet. I laughed at him and told him "you're dreaming pal. That's just the KY." I shouldn't have done that. He didn't like it, me laughing at him. Men don't like being laughed at. They take themselves too seriously, especially in bed. I thought he was going to hit me. Reckon he probably would have as well, if he hadn't been worried about Max and what he might do.'

'I guess you meet some strange guys.'

'There's this one guy has an appointment with me once a week, all he wants to do is look at my feet. Not interested in any other part of me, just my bare feet. Doesn't need to see me naked, just looks at them for a while, plays with himself, gets off and leaves.'

The starters arrived at that point. If the waiter overhead that last snippet he did a good impression of someone who hadn't. There was foie gras for me; something leafy and expensive with a slice of parmesan on top, which looked like it came straight out of a salad bag from Morrisons, for her.

'What if I found you something better' I asked, 'for the same money?'

'Like what?'

I shrugged, 'I don't know yet, but I'm pretty certain I could utilise your talents in a better way,' she looked at me suspiciously, like I was proposing to sell her to an Arab sheik or a Russian billionaire, 'with your clothes on,' I added.

'No.'

'Why not?'

'Because I don't want you to,' she was in defiant mode again.

'Why don't you want me to help you?' I asked calmly.

She frowned at me again. 'You think I'm something I'm not.'

'You can read my mind now, can you?' I retorted. 'So, what do I think you are then?'

'Something broken you can mend. Something damaged you can fix with your money.'

'But it's not that simple?' Maybe she had me pegged, but I was still sure I could help her.

'No.'

'Why not?'

She sighed, 'because I'm fucked in the head.'

It was hard not to laugh at that. She sounded like a drama-queen teenager, but I knew that arguing with her in this mood was pointless. Instead I just smiled at her and said, 'Eat your rabbit food.'

25

The following afternoon, I walked into the Strawberry Pub, where Kinane was waiting for me with the news. He was sitting in the corner on his own. I sat down next to him. He'd already bought the beers.

'Toddy's had a jolt,' said Kinane sadly.

My heart sank, 'How long?'

'Twenty-one years, minimum recommendation fourteen,' and he shook his head, 'he'll be in his fifties before he gets out, even if he only serves the minimum.'

'Christ,' I said. Toddy had been incredibly unlucky and now his whole life was ruined. There was nothing I could do about him spending his best years inside, but at least he hadn't spilled. If he had I'd have been in there instead of him. 'Make sure he's looked after, as much as we can.'

'There's his lass,' Kinane reminded me, 'he's been shacked up with her.'

Toddy knew we'd pay out to look after her, but I wondered how long she'd stay around, realistically, once she realised the sheer hopelessness of it all. I mean, if she wanted kids.

'And his old mum?'

'Obviously,' I agreed. This was the one thing you had to do when your men went inside. It would cost us a lot of money to put a mum and girlfriend on our payroll with no return from them, but I had no option. It wasn't just the right thing to do. Not doing it would send out the wrong message to everyone who worked for us. 'David Blake doesn't give a fuck about us if we're caught, so why should we give a fuck about David Blake?' At least we could get word to Toddy not to worry about his ma having a roof over her head, her bills paid and a few bags of groceries left on her back step every week.

I nodded at the third pint on the table.

'Where's Palmer?' I asked.

Palmer was outside having a fag, leaning against the side wall of the pub. He'd been smoking more lately. I joined him.

'You thinking about Toddy?'

'Can't get my head around it,' he admitted, 'so much time. I mean, you only get one life,' and he shook his head, ' stuck in the same place, no drink, no woman, shit food, surrounded by psychos and rapists. I'd go out of my fucking mind.'

'It's the risk we take,' I said and immediately regretted how harsh that sounded. 'We'll do everything we can for him,' cursing myself for talking like a doctor who'd just announced he was going to do his best for a terminally-ill patient.

Let me tell you how unlucky Toddy was. A bust rear light cost him fourteen years jail-time. He was driving down to the Sunnydale estate with three kilos of H hidden in the boot of his car. It was early evening and the daylight was starting to fade, so he turned his lights on. He was carrying the stash but he had nothing to worry about because there are never any coppers round there. It's a complete no-go area. The Police can't patrol it after dark without being attacked. They get pelted with missiles from the balconies if they even try to leave their cars, so they've given up on the place, unofficially of course. Officially they are tasked with ensuring the same level of law and order exists in the notorious Sunnydale estate as it does in Northumberland Street, but you don't see any one dealing H outside Marks & Spencer's. Virtually everyone in those estates is addicted to something; alcohol, pills, solvents, cocaine, heroin or methamphetamine, you name it. Hardly anyone has a job, unless you count nicking, which I don't. There are one or two decent people living there, but the vast majority are low-life vermin who just want to get high all of the time so they can forget about their shit lives. That's where we come in. It's a simple case of supply and demand and, as I keep telling our lot, if we weren't supplying them someone else would. At least with us there's order, and we keep the stupid gang feuds under control.

So Toddy drove down there without a care in the bloody world. He didn't even notice the marked Police car parked up by the side of one of the high-rises but, for no other reason than bum luck, it chose that moment to pull out and drive down the same road as Toddy. He noticed it then, of course, it was right behind him. The next thing he saw was the flashing lights and there was a short burst of the siren as he was pulled over. He must have thought about doing a runner at that point, but where could he go with them right up his arse, radioing for back-up? Nowhere; so he figures they won't find anything, or we can smooth it out if they do, so he takes a gamble and rides it out. Toddy pulled over. I wonder if that is what he regrets most now; that, or the fact he came to work for me in the first place.

It was two coppers, both very young and polite at first,

everything was all 'Good evening sir, did you realise you have a broken rear light, sir?' and he's all 'I'm sorry officer, no I didn't. I'll get it seen to at the first available opportunity.' Maybe it was his manners that made them suspicious. Police officers aren't used to apologies on the Sunnydale estate. Whatever it was, they asked him to please get out of the car. At this point Toddy was still gambling that he didn't look like a wrong 'un, so he climbed out and stood there with his hands on the roof of his car, while one of them searched it and the other asked for ID. There were a few rudimentary questions about where he had come from and where he was going, but nothing a pro like Toddy couldn't handle. Of course he would have been nervous when the one doing the searching started poking around in the boot, but there's a compartment in the side for the stash, which is specifically designed so that you shouldn't be able to open it if you don't know what you're looking for. But somehow, the copper doing the searching manages to pop open the hidden compartment – and what does he find when he manages this? Three kilos of street-level-purity heroin.

Before Toddy could react, they slammed him hard against his car and cuffed his hands behind his back, bundled him into the back seat of the police car and radioed into the cop shop. They were so excited, acting like they'd just won the lottery and Toddy was reeling, looking at serious jail-time.

When news of his arrest broke, the shit hit the fan big time. Even their own senior officers didn't know whether to promote these two, give them a medal, or fire them for some ill-defined breach of the Police code. And us, well we went into overdrive. We're phoning lawyers, Amrein's people and bent Police, wanting an explanation for all of this from someone. After all, we pay a lot of money to ensure this kind of thing can never happen. We were wondering if we had a grass who had tipped off these two young coppers about Toddy's stash.

It turned out to be just plain old, rotten bad luck. The two coppers who picked up Toddy were a couple of wet-behind-the-ears dimwits who'd come straight out of training and been sent out together because they were getting on a Sergeant's nerves. Normally they wouldn't be allowed anywhere near a squad car without the supervision of a jaded veteran but, because he wanted a quiet life that afternoon, he told them to take one out and patrol. It was a mid-week match day and he instructed them to make sure no away fans were organising fights in secret locations on the wasteland down by the river. They fell for this bullshit and went off looking for 'Faces' from the away fans' firm.

After an hour or so of staring at concrete, watching weeds growing out of it, they decided to 'use their own initiative', as one of them put it in his report. They picked the roughest estate they'd heard of and drove down there, parked up, somehow avoided being lynched by the local plebs and waited for the first car that came past with a light out before pulling it over. Poor bloody Toddy wasn't even arrested by a crack team from SOCA or the drug squad, just a couple of virgins in blue uniforms.

I knew Palmer had been thinking about Toddy. We all had. He's a good bloke, and he did the right thing, he said nowt. And what did that mean for him? It meant he took the full brunt of a judge's fury and was handed a sentence that made him out to be the drug lord of Sunnydale. The Chief Constable stood outside the court afterwards and praised his fearless young officers to the skies, the fucking hypocrite.

Once the press coverage has died down, all we will have left is Toddy, stuck inside for a long stretch, with plenty of time to wonder what he could have done differently that day that might not have involved him going to prison. He'll be cursing his luck and thinking about his woman, knowing there is no way that any lass on this planet is going to stay faithful to a jailed drug dealer for fourteen years. Before too long, she's going to be in another man's bed. I mean, if she's a good 'un she might wait a while; six months, maybe even a year, but it's going to happen eventually and he knows it. That's just the way it is and there's absolutely nothing Toddy can do about it, not when he's on the inside.

Three days after Arthur Gladwell's funeral, we had a sit-down. The atmosphere was no more respectful than normal.

'You still here?' Ray Fallon asked Kinane across the conference table of the Copthorne Hotel. 'I heard you'd retired years ago.' Fallon was Kinane's opposite number and as legendary in Glasgow as our Joe was in Newcastle. The Gladwells didn't do all of their own dirty work. They left some of it to the six-foot-four steroidal bouncer who was taunting Kinane. Fallon's inky prison tats on his bulky forearms and biceps stretched as he jabbed his finger accusingly at my enforcer. Fallon's nose had been broken so many times it was almost flat against his face and his eyes were filled with hate. He was baring his teeth like an attack dog, which was basically what he was.

'I'll retire you if you come a bit closer. I'll tear your fucking arms off and beat you to death with them, you cunt,' Kinane growled.

'Maybe twenty years ago you could have,' Fallon admitted, 'but then I was only ten. What were you? Forty?'

'Twenty years ago?' Kinane pretended to ponder the question. 'I was busy bitch-slapping benders from Glasgow with big mouths. It's a hobby of mine.'

'Alright you two,' I interrupted them, 'we'll get a ruler out later and measure both of you to see who has the bigger cock, but right now put your handbags down and behave yourselves.'

I looked over at Alan Gladwell, who smiled to himself, then nodded at Fallon, who looked a bit aggrieved to have been silenced by me. We were here to discuss business, not start a brawl in one of Newcastle's nicer hotels. The main players sat down, including Alan Gladwell, Fallon and the remaining Gladwell brothers, Malcolm and Andrew. Amrein was between us, acting as the chair of the meeting. His bodyguards lined the walls of the room to ensure the two sides couldn't suddenly launch themselves at one another. 'Shall we begin?' he asked.

I looked at Alan Gladwell. He was watching me intently and I was struck by how much he resembled his old man, unlike his older brother Tommy. He had the same long nose as Arthur, eyes like a rodent and the coarse stubble of a five-o'clock shadow on his chin.

'Amrein approached me about this meeting. He said you wanted to discuss some business with us and I agreed to hear you out. I'll listen to what you have to say, but there's something we need to do first.'

'And what's that?' he asked.

'Clear the air.'

'Go on,' he challenged me.

'Your brother Tommy came down to Newcastle too, but he didn't come to talk and he never went home. You and I both know that. We can pretend we don't, but we'd be kidding ourselves. You know he tried to take over Bobby Mahoney's territory and you know he failed. I am surprised you would want to do business with our firm, under the circumstances. There are some who would view that with suspicion.'

Alan Gladwell took a long while to answer. He bought time in fact, reaching for one of those heavy, glass bottles full of sparkling water and pouring himself a glass, then he settled back down in his seat and looked at me. It seemed like he was trying to contain his emotions.

'Tommy was my older brother, and I loved him...' he coughed, like he was attempting to prevent his voice from betraying his feelings, 'and when he didn't come back, we all grieved for him, me included.'

'His…' he was searching for the right word now, '…disappearance…caused my family a lot of pain. We had to take care of his children. I had to explain things to them, things no small child should ever have to hear. Losing Tommy took years off my father's life.' He was looking directly at me now. It was if there was nobody else in the room but us. 'But I never lost sight of one thing,' he coughed again, clearing his throat, 'Tommy was bang out of order. What he tried to do was wrong. He was taking the piss and no one could say he didn't pay a very big price for his ambitions.'

'Fair enough,' I said.

'If I was going to go to war with you over something, it wouldn't be that. Tommy did what he did and Bobby did what he felt he had to do. I don't have to like that, and I don't, but I understood why it happened. If we were going to come after you we'd have done it by now, but my Dad didn't see any mileage in it for any of us. Feuds cost money and good people from both sides end up dead. What matters is staying one step ahead of the Polis and all the wankers out there who want a slice of what we've got. Am I right?'

'Couldn't have put it better myself.'

'And there's another thing,' he told me, looking up at Amrein uncertainly. Amrein nodded reassuringly.

'The room's been swept,' Amrein assured him, 'you can talk freely.'

'The killing,' Gladwell said, 'I want it to stop.' I must have looked unconvinced, because he continued, 'it was my Dad's way. He thought it was the only way to stay in charge of a city like ours, and maybe it was, but times have changed. You can't just go around murdering people and expect the Polis to turn a blind eye any more. I mean they're not all bent, not these days. So where does it get you? My father stood trial for murder twice and missed a life sentence by the skin of his teeth. I don't want that stress. My father killed people, and I did too, but I am saying there's another way. We shouldn't be so casual about it, taking a man's life, I mean. It should be the last resort, know what I'm saying?'

I did, and was conflicted because he was echoing my own view, but was he just telling me what I wanted to hear?

'I'd be happy if I never had to do it again. Sure, if someone steps out of line they get a beating, but that ought to be enough. Now, I think you, me and Amrein can agree to it and, more to the point, it will be good for business because the men in uniform and the politicians will leave us alone if they think we are policing our own patch.'

'It makes sense,' I admitted.

'Then I suggest we talk about how we are going to work together on this Edinburgh thing because, if we don't, then sure as hell someone else will come in and pick up where Dougie Reid left off. I don't know about you, but I don't want a near neighbour of mine getting rich on Edinburgh's heroin, eyeing up what I've got, then planning to take it off me. I know you will have had the same thought.'

'I have.'

'My father is dead but I don't want anyone to be in any doubt about who is in charge. I'm the only one with the men, the muscle and the cash to control an operation the size of ours.'

He took another swig of water and I wondered if he was nervous, or just thirsty. 'In Edinburgh it's different. The Polis got lucky up there and they took down some high-level players, so we now have something that looks a lot like anarchy. Wannabes dealing a bit of Blow here and a bit of H there and when a dealer crosses over a boundary, people start getting nailed to garage doors or thrown off bridges. The Polis don't like that.'

'You've had talks?'

'Informal discussions, with senior men we've known for some time,'

Amrein interjected, 'in meetings brokered by us,' – as if I doubted it. He wanted to remind me how he earned the Drop.

'They are not stupid men,' Gladwell went on, 'they know there's a gap in the market and, if someone doesn't fill it, Edinburgh will soon start to look like downtown Kabul. Last week a bullet went through the hood of a baby's buggy, missed the little mite by inches. It ended up on the front page of all the tabloids. The Press are saying the Polis have lost control, there is no law or order in Edinburgh.'

It was a similar story in Newcastle, thanks to the attacks on me and my men, I thought, but I let him finish. 'The Polis don't like that kind of thing and I assured them I would do what I could to restore order, but I already have one city to run.'

'So do we,' I reminded him.

'Yes but…between us…' He didn't have to elaborate. 'I suggest you think about it. I'll provide some people, you can do the same, we can agree a split but you already know it makes sense. We've practically got permission to go ahead.'

I nodded. 'I'll give it some thought,' I assured him.

'Do that,' he urged me, 'I can let you have some time, but not much. Amrein can set up another meeting for us and when I come back here I'll need your answer.'

'Fair enough.'

The deal made perfect sense to me except for one last lingering doubt. Could I really trust the man whose brother I'd sliced up with a machete? Did I honestly believe Alan Gladwell was a reformed character, or did I just really want to believe it?

I was sick of hotels and hotel food. I was tired of looking down corridors worried that someone was going to come at me from the shadows before I had a chance to turn the key in the lock. I didn't want to bunk up at Palmer's house or stay with my brother. I relished the prospect of being on my own, in fact. All I wanted to do was buy a few things and cook them myself, wash a meal down with a glass of wine and maybe watch an old movie. I was too weary for anything else.

When we finished the meeting with the Gladwells, I walked to my car with Palmer. 'I'm going to use the town house tonight,' I told him, 'you can get me there if you need me.'

'Okay,' he said, but that was all he said, and there was something in the ensuing silence that alerted me.

'It didn't arrive did it?'

He shook his head slowly.

I took a deep breath. 'I don't believe this fucking guy. Who the fuck does he think we are? A bunch of amateurs selling a bit of puff to sixth-formers?'

'I don't reckon he does think that, no.'

'Then why is he taking me for a mug? He's been in business for years with a reputation for delivering, yet the minute he takes our money he's incapable of dropping a consignment into Amsterdam. Come on, Palmer, this is his bread and butter.'

Palmer shrugged, 'he says there's a hitch getting the product out of the country. One of the officials he's dealt with for a long while has just been lifted. He says it's nothing he can't fix.'

'And you believe that?'

'Why would he lie?'

'Then tell him to fix it. You tell the Turk it's very simple. Either he sends us our product or he gives us our million Euros back. There is a third way that we could conclude our business but I don't think he would like that option.'

'Careful,' cautioned Palmer, 'I told you he has a big operation. We don't want to go to war with them.'

'Then what do you suggest?'

'I know you're not happy, but I think we should give him more time.'

'Do we even have a choice?' I asked. It was a rhetorical question.

*

I met Sharp in one of our city-centre flats.

'You want me to do what?' he asked, as if I'd suggested he should step off a high building. 'Are you serious?'

'What do you think?'

'You want me to spy on Alan Gladwell? Have you got any idea how dangerous that is for me? You've heard the stories about him. Alan Gladwell has been the real force behind his father's empire since Tommy died. And *he* doesn't leave the dirty work to his hard men.' I assumed that was a dig at me, but I didn't react, 'he does it all himself. He enjoys inflicting pain. He cuts people up, he sets them alight. He castrated one guy!'

'Yeah, I heard that story.'

'It's not a story, it's true. The last guy who tried to take Glasgow from Arthur Gladwell got his dick and balls cut off by Alan Gladwell, personally!' I waited for him to calm down and carry on, 'he's a bloody psychopath. He doesn't care if you're a civilian, a villain or a cop.'

'Then he's a fool and it will bring him down in the end.'

'I don't think so,' he told me, 'I am not going to follow Alan Gladwell around Glasgow, his home patch, and wait for him to notice. I've seen the pictures of the guys he's fucked with over the years and it's not pretty, believe me. So no thanks, not this time.'

I could tell Sharp was shit scared of Alan Gladwell for real because he'd completely forgotten his place in the scheme of things. 'First of all, Sharp, I am not asking, I'm telling.' I told him through gritted teeth.

'Now hang on...'

'Shut up,' I told him quietly and at least he had the good sense to fall silent. 'You don't have to drive round Glasgow tailgating Alan Gladwell's car. I just want you to find out everything you can about him and report back to me.'

'Right,' he said, 'sorry, it's just I...'

'But don't go thinking you can get away with reading a few Police files and talking to a couple of bent coppers up there. I need you under his skin and you have to find something.'

'Find what, exactly?'

'Something I can use!' I barked. 'Right now Alan Gladwell holds all the cards north of the border. He owns Glasgow and, with or without us, he will soon be the main player in Edinburgh. So it would help my bargaining position if he had a weakness, but I won't know what it is until you find it. Come on, you know what I'm talking about here. Lift up stones and tell me what crawls out from under them.'

'Okay, I'll do my best.'

I'd had about enough of dealing with all of the pressure on my own. I walked over to the chair Sharp was sitting on. I put my hands on the arms and leaned in close. I had to contain my anger because I felt like I was about to explode. Whatever he could see in my face seemed to alarm him. 'Your best won't do, Sharp. Get me something I can use, otherwise there's no point keeping you. You'll be just another expensive luxury I can't afford, and I'll cut you adrift. Got me?'

He nodded quickly, 'I'm on it.'

'You'd better be,' I warned him.

26

Hunter turned the key in the front door but, before he opened it and stepped through, he glanced back behind him, squinting down the darkened driveway, certain he had seen something.

Nothing, and, even if there had been, what the hell could he have done about it? He paused for a moment, then started to feel foolish. This was ridiculous. Hunter was a veteran of the firm and here he was, standing on his doorstep like a frightened schoolboy, waiting for the Bogeyman to jump out and grab him.

'Fuck this for a game of soldiers' he said to himself as he opened the front door of the home he shared with his wife, the kids having both grown up and fled the nest. Mary was at her old mum's house, cooking dinner and making sure she got to bed alright, a ritual she went through every evening. He turned on the hall light, then did the same in the lounge and the kitchen.

Mary would have left him something in the fridge to microwave, but he wasn't hungry. Maybe it was the stress of seeing everyone in the firm permanently on red alert these days, or possibly it was the meeting with the Gladwells that had unsettled him. Perhaps he'd just pour himself a drink, relax with the paper for a few minutes, then get off to bed early. Going to the whisky bottle for a decent Malt was a routine move, done almost automatically.

Hunter poured a generous measure into a glass tumbler, flicked the light switch to illuminate the room and slid open the door. It moved smoothly to one side and Hunter stepped into the large conservatory that was tacked onto the back of his home. He placed the tumbler of whisky on the table in front of him, grabbed a cushion from the sofa and dropped it onto the armchair opposite the TV, though he didn't turn it on. He'd had Sky TV for years now; the kids had wanted it for the music stations and American shows when they were younger, but the only thing he ever watched on it was the football. When Hunter had been a lad there were only three TV channels; BBC1, BBC2 and ITV. Try telling that to youngsters these days and they wouldn't believe you. His own kids looked at him like he was a caveman when he tried to explain it. Hunter was dimly aware that he had a hundred channels to choose from today but there appeared to be fuck all on any of them. So he left the TV off and sat back, picked up the newspaper from the table in front of him and sipped his whisky. The drink warmed the back of his throat, but the newspaper failed to distract him. Instead he sat there, contemplating the situation he found himself in. Primarily he wondered if the siege mentality Blake seemed to be adopting had anything to do with the late, unlamented Tommy Gladwell.

It was Hunter to whom Blake had turned to dispose of the bodies of Tommy Gladwell, his wife and bodyguards. This he had done in the tried and trusted way, by taking them out to the farm and dumping them where the pigs could reach them. That was the great thing about pigs. They would get rid of everything for you, flesh, bones, cartilage, tendons, ligaments, the lot. If you wanted someone to disappear completely and forever, they wouldn't leave a trace. But the experience of getting rid of a Gladwell had rattled Hunter, for he was well aware of the family's reputation and he wondered at the time if this, far from being the end of things, might actually be the start of something. Now members of his firm were meeting with the Gladwells. Hunter didn't believe in suddenly trusting your enemies.

Hunter had worked for Bobby Mahoney for nigh on thirty years, starting as a teenager nicking cars, gradually working his way up the ranks until eventually he became the firm's quartermaster. He liked to think he was just like Morgan Freeman's character from *The Shawshank Redemption*; he could get you anything, could Hunter. To be fair though, the members of the firm didn't want just anything. They nearly always wanted a gun, and the particular variety of gun would depend on the job they were about to carry out. That was where Hunter stepped in. Shotguns were good for armed robberies and close-quarter kills in isolated places, or contained spaces like the backs of cars or lifts. Hunter frowned on automatic weapons; submachine guns were really only for the movies and if you tried to fire an Uzi without any training you were just as likely to kill your partner as the person you were meant to be aiming at. Mostly he provided semi-automatic pistols, like the Glock and the Sig Sauer, or the more traditional Smith & Wesson, Colt or Browning. He always advised against the .38, not enough stopping power, or anything you'd seen James Bond use like the Walther or Beretta, which were too fussy for his tastes. Magnums were usually unnecessary too, powerful, noisy and unsubtle, and he distrusted the new eastern European imports, like the Makarov, because he doubted their build quality and, if you were ever going to pull a gun on someone, the last thing you wanted was for it to jam on you at the crucial moment. Hunter would solemnly impart these opinions to members of the crew who were sent to him for weapons and they in turn would listen, because everybody knew that Hunter knew his stuff, whether the subject was guns, or the disposal of bodies.

Hunter couldn't get comfortable, so he rose to his feet and took another reflective sip of his whisky, then lowered the glass till he was standing with it at chest height as he looked out at the garden beyond. It was dark, but he could still see the overgrown hedge at the back of the garden being blown around by the breeze. Mary had been on at him to cut it back.

When the bullet came, it broke glass. First the thick glass of the conservatory window, which disintegrated on impact, leaving thousands of tiny fragments scattered all over the tiled floor. Next, the glass Hunter was holding in his hand exploded, taking two of his fingers with it as they were severed by the bullet's trajectory. Hunter didn't feel the pain though, for the bullet had travelled on through the tumbler and gone straight into his chest, piercing his heart. The cause of death would later be described as a severe traumatic injury to the aorta but, whatever the technical phrase, Hunter was dead before his body hit the ground.

27

I had the kitchen set up just right, the way I do when I cook something nice for Sarah. There were three chopping-boards on the work-tops; one for the meat, one for the vegetables and another just in case. I had the knife block within easy reach. I'd spent more than a few bob on my Sabatier knives, but they were worth it. They were tough, durable and razor sharp and when I was wielding these babies back in Hua Hin I felt like Michel Roux. That's why I had a second set at the Gosforth town house, a property I liked to stay in if I was in Newcastle for more than a few days.

I had the small cast-iron pan on the stove and the oil was heating up nicely. I usually have a drink while I cook but, because I was alone, I figured I'd at least wait until my food was done before I poured myself a beer or a glass of wine. It's too easy to drink on your own and you end up having more than you mean to. I made myself a coffee instead and put it on the work-top right by the stove.

I put the third chopping board by the oven and watched the oil heat up as I chopped a mound of coriander. Who says men can't multi task, I thought, and there was an answering creak from the parquet flooring in the lounge behind me. I turned up the heat in the pan and watched bubbles form in the oil, so I knew it was piping hot. I was still holding the big Sabatier, but I put that down, picked up my coffee cup instead, and took a small sip from it. As I lowered the mug I turned sharply on my heel and threw what was left of the contents right into the man's face and he gasped, then screamed in agony.

It was the merest creak of the wooden flooring that had given him away. If I'd had the radio on he'd have been up behind me before I could react and he would have had time to use the gun in his hand. He was tall and stocky, but I couldn't see his face as I turned. I just knew he was there, and that was good enough for me to throw the boiling hot coffee at him. No one in my crew would be stupid enough to walk up behind me unannounced, so there was little risk I'd hurt the wrong man. His free hand was up at his eyes and he was trying to clear them of the boiling water, his face red where the liquid had burned his skin. His gun hand was waving around while he tried to recover from the shock and the pain.

I grabbed the little iron frying pan, flicked the boiling hot oil at him too and immediately followed up with a blow that knocked the pistol from his grip. It careered into the far wall of the kitchen, but it didn't go off. His eyes were open now. He saw me, and went for me, but he was unarmed and I still had my weapon. As he stepped towards me, I hit him a crashing blow across the side of the face with the hot pan and he fell backwards, but managed to stay on his feet. I didn't know what level of damage I'd done but, from the gasping, blood-choked noises he was making, I was willing to bet I'd broken some bones in his face. I took a big risk and stepped towards him then. I raised the pan and swung at him again. This one was going to be the killer blow. I would finish him with it. But I didn't move quickly enough and he reached out and grabbed the pan, trying to wrench it from my grasp. He half succeeded, then howled in pain because he had forgotten it was hot. The pan fell from my grasp and it dropped to the floor. He bent to make a grab for the handle so he could use it on me and, as he lowered his head, I saw my opportunity. I grabbed clumps of his hair in both hands and pulled with all my strength, then twisted his body to one side. He tottered off balance and fell, head first, until his forehead smashed hard into the sharp corner of the granite counter-top. There was a sickening impact, and he dropped. There was blood all over his forehead and his head was lolling groggily. He was slurring incoherently like a drunk.

I reached back behind me then and grabbed the knife from the chopping board. I was on him in a second, pressing the razor-sharp point right up against his neck. I put one knee onto his right arm and straddled his chest, then managed to get my other knee onto his left arm. I pressed the tip of the knife further into his neck until it pierced the flesh. He'd know that any more pressure from me and he was a dead man.

'Don't move,' I managed to hiss, though the voice didn't sound like mine anymore, 'or I finish it.'

That got me his full attention and he froze. His head was at an angle and he was looking up, his left eye staring at me. He looked frightened and completely helpless.

'Who ordered this?' I demanded. He opened his mouth to answer, but seemingly thought better of it and said nothing. His breathing was coming out fast and shallow. 'Tell me,' I told him, 'you tell me who ordered this or I will finish you now.'

His one good eye was still fixed on me and I could almost see his mind racing. He was trying to work out what he could say that would save his life. I wasn't going to give him time.

'Five seconds,' I said, 'or the knife goes in.'

'Wait,' he said and I could feel the knife rise a little as his throat pulsed when he uttered the word.

'Four seconds,' I said, and I pressed the knife gently down into the flesh of his neck, 'who ordered this?'

'No one,' he said, and he could tell by my face I wasn't satisfied with that explanation. 'I mean, I don't know.' His good eye never left mine. I could tell he was terrified. 'I don't know who ordered it. I don't know who paid me. You have to believe me,' he urged.

I looked him deep in the eye and he stared back at me like he didn't dare to hope for anything now.

'I believe you,' I said, as I pushed the knife down hard.

28

I stepped over the dead man in my kitchen, ignoring the blood that had spurted from the wound in his neck and covered the entire kitchen floor.

I grabbed my mobile and dialled Palmer.

'I need a housekeeper,' I said.

Another one of his pregnant silences.

'Right away sir,' Palmer replied eventually, like it was the most natural request in the world.

I hung up and sat down on the sofa, then immediately stood up again. I didn't know what to do with myself. I thought for a moment then, instinctively, I called Kinane. I wanted him to be here when Palmer arrived.

Twenty minutes later, Palmer looked down at the body. It was lying in a dark pool of congealed blood now, the face red and blistered. I'd placed the gun on the counter-top and he clocked that too. 'What happened?' he asked.

I shrugged, 'I heard something, I turned around and he was standing there. I threw my coffee in his face,' and at this my voice cracked and faltered, which I put down to delayed shock. 'I had to use the knife,' I said and stopped. I'd intended to go into more detail but now he was here, and could see it with his own eyes, I couldn't see the point. I was glad to be alive, and I wouldn't have traded places with the guy on the floor, but I felt sick to my stomach. I kept thinking about the exact moment when the tip of the Sabatier pierced his skin, the desperate look he gave me while it was happening. I knew that was another image that would stay with me, to add to the ones that already kept me awake.

Palmer put his black leather gloves on and checked the dead man's pockets. He found nothing.

'What do you make of him?'

'Could be a local who is not on our radar, someone not long out of the forces perhaps, who needed the work? That's what I'm guessing because it looks hasty, a last minute job.'

'Why?'

'You heard him,' he said simply.

Palmer meant that if the guy had been any good I wouldn't have heard him, and I had to admit he was right. Maybe one day I could even pat myself on the back and say that the last man who tried to kill David Blake ended up dead. That might be a story we'd want to get round, because it wouldn't do my reputation any harm, but I wasn't fooling myself. I had the brains for this world, but not the brawn. If the guy with the gun had been anything more than mediocre, Palmer and Kinane would be moving my body now instead of his.

'Right,' I said.

'Someone probably called him in when they realised you were here.'

'I figured as much,' I said flatly.

'You going to be okay?' Kinane asked and I realised how bad I must have looked because this was the first time he'd ever enquired after my well-being.

'I'll get over it.'

When we were outside, Palmer asked, 'Can I have a word?' I nodded to Kinane and he headed for the car ahead of me.

'I know what you're thinking.' Palmer told me.

'Do you?'

'Yeah,' he said, 'you're wondering how a hit man got to you when you'd only been in the place for a couple of hours. You're thinking I was the only one you told.'

'Maybe I was,' I said. There wasn't much point in being anything less than honest with him. That was exactly what I was thinking.

'I reckon they've been watching the house. I think that somehow they have got hold of a list of places you stay in when you are up here and someone made a phone call when they saw your car pull in.'

'And how could they have got a list of places I use except...'

'...from one of our people.' He finished the sentence for me.

'There aren't too many, are there?'

'That know where you stay when you are over here?' he exhaled, 'there are a few. I mean it's not exactly top secret, is it?'

'No,' I admitted, 'maybe it should have been.' In hindsight, I'd been sloppy. It was a minor detail but it almost got me killed.

'I don't see how it could be anybody from outside the firm. I think we have a leak.'

'Then those tracking devices should come in handy.'

'If anyone has been anywhere they shouldn't have been lately I'll know about it. Someone's selling us out and I'll find him.'

'You could be right,' I admitted.

'But you're still not sure.' He meant I still suspected him.

I shrugged. As far as I was concerned everyone in my crew was guilty until proven innocent, not the other way around.

'There's something I need to show you,' and he jerked his head toward his car. It was parked a few metres away. I followed him over even though I'd reached the stage where I had no idea who to trust any more. Palmer looked round, popped the boot and held it half open, just enough so I could see inside. There was a man in there. He wasn't moving. I was no expert but, if I'd been forced to offer a diagnosis, I'd have said he had a broken neck.

'They came after me too,' Palmer told me.

'What happened?'

'I came home,' he explained, 'this guy was waiting for me, in the house.'

'How did you spot him?'

'I mark my door,' he was evasive, 'if someone's in there I know about it.' It seemed that was all the explanation I was going to get from him. I'd heard about people putting blocks or indistinguishable signs on their front doors and checking them when they came home each night but it was all a bit John Le Carré and I was wondering how a former solider had picked up the habit.

'Figured I'd get rid of them both at the same time.' It seemed there was still a lot I didn't know about Palmer but, wherever he'd picked up his skills, it was clear he'd been too good for the bloke in the boot of his car.

I wasn't really listening because a thought had struck me. Someone had been sent to kill me and another man to kill Palmer, at the same time, on the same night. Kinane hadn't been home so they'd not been able to get to him, but what about the others?

'Get on the phones to everyone,' I said, 'make sure no one

else has had a visitor tonight.' I picked up my own phone and dialled Danny. No answer. Where the hell was he?

It didn't take long before we got the news. I was in Kinane's car a few minutes later when my phone rang. It was Sharp, he sounded panicky. 'Are you okay? Has something happened?'

'You could say that,' I answered, 'but yes, I am okay. Why? What have you heard?' I was wondering how Sharp could have known about this latest attempt on my life.

'All hell's broken loose. It's like the Night of the fucking Long Knives. Someone got to Hunter. He's dead.'

'Hunter? Oh Christ, no.' I couldn't believe what I was hearing. Hunter had been part of Bobby's crew since anyone could remember and now he was gone. I felt like our world was caving in around us.

'There's more,' he told me, as if Hunter dying was the least of our worries, 'it's your brother, he's been shot.'

29

I should have known we wouldn't get anywhere near him. The Police were down at the hospital already, a couple of uniforms making their presence felt, ensuring they were visible in case anyone tried to finish my brother off, but they let me talk to the guy on the desk about Danny. He told me my brother was having emergency surgery and it was unlikely there would be any news for some time. I would have to prepare myself for a long wait. I told him I didn't mind. He also told me that my brother had been very seriously injured. He didn't add that I should prepare myself for the worst. He didn't have to.

I turned away from the desk to find DI Carlton facing me. 'I'm sorry to hear about your brother,' he said.

'Like fuck you are.'

'I am,' he said calmly, 'seriously. I've had a word with the docs because I thought you'd want to know. He's been shot three times, back and arm, it doesn't look good, even if he pulls through,' which I took to mean that Danny would be permanently fucked up. I had a sudden urge to throw up.

I managed to walk over to the row of bright red plastic chairs at the opposite end of the room. My brain was picking out little insignificant details, presumably as a coping mechanism, like the fact that all of the red chairs were screwed onto one large metal frame, which in turn was cemented to the floor. I surmised it was safer than having individual chairs that could be picked up and thrown about by Saturday night casualties who were still fighting drunk. It would be heaving in here on a weekend, full of people who'd been stabbed, slashed or glassed, but it was quiet tonight. I sat down heavily, put my elbows on my knees and brought my hands up to my face to rub my eyes. It looked like I'd be here all night.

I'd killed a man less than an hour ago. Now I was waiting for news of my brother's death or, if I was exceptionally lucky, they would come out and tell me he was paralysed or brain dead.

I realised DI Carlton had sat down next to me. 'You know that whoever did this to Danny is not going to stop, right?' he told me, in what he must have considered his most reasonable tone. 'They are going to keep on coming after you. It'll be you next,' he said.

I took my hands away from my eyes and sat up, but said nothing.

'Tell us who's behind this and we can stop it,' he assured me, which was a crock of shit. Even if I had a theory there'd be no proof, no evidence and nothing to go on. 'Let us protect you,' Carlton urged. 'It won't do you any good, this false code of silence, there's no such thing as *Omertà* in Geordieland, you know. Tell me what you know now and I can help you. That's the best offer you are going to get this century. You know that.'

'You finished?' I asked him.

'Yes.'

'Then can I please ask you, respectfully, to fuck off and leave me alone?'

He looked at me like I wasn't worth the effort of keeping up the nice-guy façade, then he climbed to his feet and went.

I waited there all night, and he was still in surgery when I left. I made them promise to call me the moment the surgeon emerged. Only then would I agree to leave.

I got in my car and went to meet Sharp at the Angel of the North. I'd sent him a cryptic text from my pay-as-you-go mobile and it was as good a venue as any to arrange to bump into him. There was a biting wind that morning so no one else was waiting beneath its rusting wings.

'What do you know?' I asked, as soon as he reached me.

'There's a witness,' Sharp said, 'young lass, a student at the Uni. She saw the guy who shot your brother on the way out of the bar. They're trying to get a photo-fit, but it's tricky. He wore sunglasses and a hat so I'm not sure how much use she'll be.'

'Can we get to her?'

'Course not, she's under twenty-four-hour protection. She's witnessed a shooting and clocked the hit man. They won't let her out of their sight.'

'Then you have to get me the CCTV footage for the place. I'm assuming it had cameras.'

Sharp snorted, 'Yeah, course it did, but I can't get it for you.'

'You're going to have to.'

'How do you expect me to do that? Detectives are poring over it right now. I can't just walk in and borrow it.'

'I'm not asking, Sharp,' I told him, 'it's an order. I give them from time to time, so you'd better start remembering whose payroll you're on.'

'Of course I remember – but I have to draw a line sometime

or they'll give me ten years. They'll put me in the cell next to your man Toddy.'

I leaned forward and grabbed Sharp by the lapel of his coat, pulling him towards me. I didn't hit him because I couldn't trust myself to stop, 'just get me the film!' I shouted the words into his face, then I pushed him back hard and he fell to the ground with a shocked look on his face.

I didn't hang around to watch him pick himself up. I strode back to my car, climbed in and drove away. I didn't know what to do with myself. I'd been up all night waiting for Danny to open his eyes and I was beside myself with worry for my older brother. Hunter, a man I had known since I was a kid, was lying on a mortuary slab and I was certain someone in our crew was selling us all down the river. How else could anyone know about the town house, Hunter's home address or Danny's protection money collection? I was so fucking tired I just wanted to curl up somewhere and forget the world, but somehow I had to keep my mind straight and work this one out because right now I couldn't trust anyone else to do it for me.

I suddenly realised I was driving at more than a hundred miles an hour, speeding past the other cars on the main road like they were standing still, and I hadn't even noticed. I forced myself to brake. I realised I was in a panic because I had no idea how to fix things, but I knew I had to stay alive, and there was one thing I was clinging to that would keep me going. I wanted revenge. I wanted to get hold of the man who had done this to my brother and I was going to make him pay.

30

The waiting room outside an intensive care unit is the most hopeless place. The patients on the other side of those big, grey double-doors with their porthole windows are nearly all in a permanent state of medicated sleep, which means they can give nothing back to the people visiting them. I'd see the visitors traipsing out looking lost, ruined and guilty all at once. Every time the doors opened I'd peer in, hoping for a glimpse of Danny, but he was out of sight. I wanted to march straight in there, but I knew the detective on the door would never let me do that.

I waited an age until the consultant finally appeared. He was a tall, authoritative man with an evidently unbending faith in his abilities. He was determined to leave me with the impression that whether Danny lived or died might be down to my brother's strength or the fates, but never the unquestioned skills of his surgeon.

'It was a very difficult operation. Daniel is lucky to be alive,' lucky wasn't the word I would have chosen, 'the position of the bullets made the procedure a particularly delicate one.' He went on to outline some of those complications in detail, but I didn't really take it all in until he ended a sentence with the words, 'and there is spinal damage.'

'We are far from certain that your brother is going to survive,' he told me, with an honesty I craved, but at the same time hated him for, 'however Daniel is a strong, fit man, which gives him a chance,' how much of a chance he wasn't prepared to reveal. 'You must be aware though that, if he does make it, the damage to his spinal column is so extensive that it is unlikely he will ever walk again.'

It's strange the tricks your brain pulls on you to keep you going. I heard the words, and instantly understood what they meant, but somehow I managed to rabbit on to the consultant as if it was all going to be alright. I wanted to thank him and his team for all of the work they had done to save my brother's life, I told him, and he reminded me there was no guarantee of that outcome. Nonetheless, I assured him, I was eternally gratefully to them all and would never forget their efforts. I took hold of his hand to shake it while I was talking to him and forgot to let go. I just carried on pumping it like a lunatic, until he looked down at his hand in mine.

'I'd like to see my brother now,' I said.

He told me I could go in, but he had to clear it with the man on the door. The man on the door was the plain-clothes detective, positioned there in case the assassin should attempt to pay a visit and finish my brother off as he lay in his bed, and I had to prove that I was who I claimed to be before he finally admitted me.

My older brother looked helpless. He was wired up to a machine that monitored his heart rate, and another that was helping him to breathe. His face was partly covered by the tube of the ventilator and there was a drip hanging out of one arm. He wore a loose-fitting, dark-green hospital gown that covered the incisions the surgeons had made during an eleven hour operation to remove the three bullets from his body. The only sound was a quiet beep coming from the monitor, and the low, repetitive whooshing sound of the ventilator as it did his breathing for him, keeping my brother alive, one shallow breath after another.

And now here I was, looking down at Danny, lying there with tubes and wires in him, and telling myself over and over that this was all my fault, when it hit me; the combination of muggy, warm air, the sickly-sweet smell of disinfectant and the sight of my brother's wrecked body before me. I felt the room sway and I had to reach out a hand to grab the metal frame of his bed to stop myself from falling. I sat down quickly on the hard plastic chair by his bedside and put my hand to my sweating forehead. I had to make an effort just to rise from my seat and walk out of there, feeling the nausea rising all the way along the corridor. Finally, I pushed open the last swing door, took the remaining yards across the waiting room at almost a run, and went out through the heavy glass door at the entrance. The cold air hit me and I gulped it into my lungs. I managed to walk a few more yards to a wooden bench and slumped down on it, putting my hands up to my eyes again so no one could see my face.

I went to a pub I'd never been to before. It was almost empty and I ordered a pint and a whisky. I had no plan except a vague notion I was going to sit there and drink until I fell off the bar stool and they called a cab for me, or the Police. Then I looked up and saw my ashen face in the mirror behind the optics on the bar. I realised that sitting here on my own, thinking about my brother and the fact that he was paralysed because of me, drinking myself sick in the process, was only going to make me feel worse. I needed company, but nobody from my crew would do.

It was raining hard when I pulled up outside the apartment block. I was drenched by the time I reached the communal front door. A woman of about thirty was just going in and she turned and held the door, then gave me a questioning look because she clearly didn't recognise me. I just muttered 'thanks' and followed her inside, without waiting for her to enquire who I was.

I didn't wait for the lift. I took the stairs two at a time until I reached the third floor, then headed for flat thirty two. I was only a little out of breath, but my heart was racing like I'd just run a marathon. All I could see right now was Danny wired up to his ventilator with tubes coming out of him. I was trying so hard to banish that sight from my mind because, if I didn't, I knew I'd start remembering all over again how it was my fault he was there. I just couldn't deal with that right now, which is why I was standing on the landing of a strange apartment block, pressing the doorbell for a second time.

'Just a minute,' came an impatient voice from the other side of the door, and there was the light sound of padding feet on the floor behind it then the door opened.

She was standing there with a white bathrobe tied loosely around her, pressing a towel up against the side of her head, dabbing at her sopping wet hair. She must have just stepped from the shower. It made her look pure and clean somehow. She barely seemed to take me in at first, but then Simone sighed and said, 'At least I don't have to ask how you knew my address,' and for a moment I thought I was in for one of her lectures. Then she looked at me more closely and frowned, asking, 'What is it? What's happened?'

Whatever she saw in my face was enough for her to admit

me. She stepped back and held open the door while I walked in.

She followed me through a tiny hallway and I walked on into the lounge of a neat little flat. I turned back to face her and saw the concern in her eyes. 'Sit down,' she said and I chose the only armchair. She leaned against the arm of her sofa and, as she did so, the bathrobe slipped a little, revealing the flesh of a long bare leg up to her thigh. She quickly pulled the robe tighter, which only drew more attention to the fact that she was naked beneath it.

'Do you want to tell me what happened?' she asked.

Somehow I dug deep inside me and found the words to explain that my only brother had been shot, three times, and it didn't look good for him. He wasn't expected to survive and, even if he did… But I couldn't finish that bit. Partly because I did not know what kind of life Danny would have if he didn't die in that hospital tonight – but mainly because I didn't want to even contemplate it.

Simone listened patiently, hearing me out, and unless she was the greatest actress on the planet she seemed genuinely shocked and concerned for me. When I finished she said, 'Oh my God, that's awful,' and, because she probably didn't know what else to say or do, she added, 'let me get you a drink.'

She walked out of the lounge and I followed her as she went back out into the hall, then into the kitchen. It was another small room with a fridge at the far end. She opened the door and took out a bottle of Absolut, then turned around so she was facing me. She hadn't heard me follow her in there and my presence seemed to make her start. Maybe she felt trapped with me framing the door like that, or vulnerable, wearing nothing but that soft, white robe. She turned away and opened a cupboard, then took out two glass tumblers for the vodka.

I felt a bit claustrophobic in this tiny kitchen. Somewhere

there would be one, or maybe two, bedrooms and a bathroom that was probably the size of our shower in Hua Hin. I'd noticed there were a couple of prints on the wall, modern art, nothing memorable, but no family photos or holiday snaps in frames. She reached for the vodka and I heard the metallic click as the lid of a brand new spirit bottle was forced open, followed by a thick, oily glugging sound as she poured a generous measure into the glass. Everything seemed heightened somehow; the noises in the kitchen, my senses. I was on edge.

I watched as she poured Absolut into the second glass. I wanted to pick her up, throw her down on the floor and take her right there until we'd both had enough of each other. Instead I walked slowly towards her, making sure she could hear my footsteps so I didn't scare her again. When I drew near she turned her head back towards me and there was uncertainty in her eyes. She avoided my gaze by turning back to the drinks. She screwed the lid of the vodka back on the bottle and said, 'I don't know what I've got to mix it with,' her voice wavering like she was nervous.

When she turned around again I was standing right in front of her. I put my hand out towards her, and she let out a little gasp, but I was only picking up one of the glasses from the work-top. She watched me drink, then turned her back on me again and picked up her own glass.

I reached my hand out again and this time I took hold of her wet hair and held it gently in my hand. Her body stiffened but she didn't say anything and I reached higher, placing my free hand under the hair I was holding so it rested on the back of her neck and I felt the cool, damp, olive coloured skin there and began to knead it gently. She pulled her head up at my touch and I began to slowly massage the skin at the side and base of her neck. I could hear her breath being drawn in deeper each time and she let her head flop to one side and rolled it with the movement of my hand.

I let go of her hair then and reached around her; I took the lapels of the robe in each hand and slowly began to open it until the soft material slid from her shoulders. She pressed her body against the work-top to keep the robe from coming off entirely and I began to massage her bare shoulders with both hands. She was breathing deeply now and I was alternating between her shoulders, back and neck, then bent forward to kiss the skin on the back of her neck.

She crossed her arms so the robe slipped no further and said, 'you shouldn't,' but her voice was low and she didn't move away from me. I continued to rub the skin on her back, then bent low to kiss her again. I took the collar of her robe in both hands and opened it wider, exposing her breasts. I put one arm over her shoulder and reached for her, rubbing her back with one hand and gently touching her breast with the other. As I did this, she pressed herself back against me and we stayed like this for a while.

If she still thought we shouldn't be doing this she was through saying it. I put my arm around her then, took hold of the belt and slowly pulled it until it came loose and the robe opened at the front. She bent her head back towards me. I kissed her on the mouth and she kissed me back, deeply, urgently.

She broke from the kiss and turned to face me then, letting the robe slide free and it fell to the floor behind her. Then she wrapped her arms around my neck and we kissed again. I had one hand pressed against the small of her back and I moved the other one slowly down her body until it was pressed against the smooth flesh high up on the back of her thigh. I let it trail up and down the top of her leg, softly stroking the skin with the palm of my hand. While we kissed, my hand got slowly higher each time before I let it fall again. Then I moved it round to her stomach and guided it gently down until finally, when I was sure she wanted me too, I slid it between her legs. She gasped and broke free from the kiss, closed her eyes and put her head back. I held her there, supporting her with my other hand. She wrapped her arms around me again and clung to me hard while I touched her. When she was finally through, she took my hand and led me to the bedroom.

31

'I'd forgotten it could be like that,' she told me.

'So had I,' and it was true. We were lying on the bed together; her robe and my clothes discarded on the floor somewhere. We were holding each other, still in the moment. I kissed her and she kissed me back, then she bit my top lip and laughed at the surprised look on my face. She looked very young then, shorn of the world-weary cynicism she always wore in public.

'Do you want another drink?' Simone asked, and I shook my head. She kissed me again and said, 'I'll be right back,' like she wanted to add, 'don't go anywhere,' then she got out of bed and went to the bathroom. When she was gone I realised I hadn't even thought about the rights, the wrongs or the wisdom of what I was doing. Climbing into bed with Simone like this was bound to complicate my life even further but it seemed insignificant compared to everything else that was going on around me.

Simone walked back into the room and lay down next to me. She was still naked and I was glad she hadn't tried to cover herself. There was just one thing. Now I'd finally had her, I wanted to leave. It wasn't her fault. It was the way I usually felt about women in fact, except for the early days with Laura, and with Sarah on the rare occasions when we did have sex these days. I was always like that when I was a younger man, back when I was single and every girl I saw was a possibility. I'd meet one, become intrigued by her and wonder what she looked like naked. I'd spend time wondering how she'd be in bed, trying to guess what her face was like when she came, or the noises she made in private, then when we'd finally end up in bed together, once the mystery was gone, I was never too bothered about a repeat performance.

Simone turned over and propped herself up on her elbow. She smiled at me, then asked, 'what are you thinking about?'

'I was thinking how amazing that was,' I told her and her smile broadened. I got the impression Simone had put sex, male approval and self-esteem together in the same basket a long time ago and now they were inextricably bound, 'and what a pity it is that I've got to go soon.' Her smile disappeared then, 'my brother,' I explained, and her face softened. She nodded like she understood he was my biggest priority right now and I realised I had sunk just that little bit lower, because I was using my brother's wrecked life as an excuse so I didn't have to spend all night in a girl's bed.

I didn't want to go back to the town house so I moved into the small apartment block we kept off Westgate Road. There were eight flats above an underground car park but no one lived there. We used them for clandestine meetings or to house visitors. Occasionally I stayed there when I was tired of hotels. The most important thing going for the site was security. There were toughened glass doors out front and a gated underground car park with an entry code that prevented anyone else getting in. I figured I was as safe here as anywhere.

I asked Palmer to show up early, but I made sure Kinane was there at the same time. I didn't want to be left on my own with either of them. Not until we had discovered the source of our leak. When Kinane went to the door to let Sharp in, I turned to Palmer, 'what did you find out from those tracking devices of yours?'

He looked sheepish, 'Nothing he said. I got Robbie to pore over everyone's movements and there's nothing that looks out of character.'

'Fat lot of use they turned out to be then.'

'Give them time,' he told me.

'That's the one thing we haven't got.'

Sharp walked in carrying a case and we watched silently as he set up a laptop and took a memory stick from his pocket. It seemed to take an eternity to fire up and we waited impatiently. Eventually he tapped the keyboard and an image popped up.

'Don't ask me how I got this,' Sharp said, but I didn't care how he got it. I just wanted to see the footage. 'I have to return it in an hour. There wasn't time to even copy it,' he looked stressed, 'an hour, tops.'

'Better get on with it then,' I said and he hit 'play'.

'What you can see is from the overhead camera in the bar,' he began, as the black and white, grainy image gave us a view of the whole pub. We could see the bar down the left-hand side of the screen, a girl and a guy in their twenties were serving behind it. The tables in front of it were largely unoccupied. It looked like there were four other people in the bar; a couple in their early twenties, holding hands over the table, and the teenaged girl, the only one who had actually seen the hit man's face, even though he apparently wore dark sunglasses and a baseball cap. She was dressed in an old, green Parka coat, and was reading one of her English set texts at the table, probably making her coffee last as long as it could so she didn't have to pay for another one.

Tucked away in a corner by the window, was Danny, looking a whole lot healthier than he had done the last time I saw him. Even from a distance he looked pretty chilled, and why wouldn't he be? He was expecting to see the bar owner to collect a little protection money just like he had done every month for more than a year. It was a routine job. I held my breath because, unlike Danny, I knew what was coming next.

It happened fast. One minute the hit man wasn't even in the room, next thing he walked briskly through the door, the baseball cap, dark glasses and long coat making it impossible to get a clear look at him. He marched straight towards Danny. Our young'un seemed to have an instinct that the guy was all wrong because he immediately climbed out of his chair and headed straight for the open French windows at the back of the bar. Unlike me, he didn't have enough time, because the guy sent to kill him quickly drew his gun and fired. The first shot missed Danny as he went into a stooping run. Instead it hit the large window behind him and shattered it. Somehow it stayed in place, but the impact of the bullet sent a spider's web of cracks spiralling across its surface. Danny kept moving, desperately trying to reach the French windows but he didn't make it. The second bullet hit him in the arm, spinning him round; the next two hit him in the back. He collided with a table and fell over it, then went head first into the nearest window, which gave way under his weight and broke completely, sending shards of glass tumbling down on him as he lay face down on the floor. The upended table knocked over a second table and a couple of chairs which may have made the difference between Danny being critically injured and dead. The hit man seemed to hesitate for a second, as he surveyed the scene in front of him. You could tell he was wondering whether he wanted to risk wasting valuable seconds clambering over the upturned tables and chairs to direct more shots into Danny's motionless body, or should he instead trust his instincts, the ones that said nobody could take three bullets and survive.

There was no volume on the CCTV but I didn't need it. The two young lovers leapt to their feet as the firing started, the girl's mouth was open in a scream, her boyfriend hopping about next to her like he didn't know where best to run to save their lives. The student girl was frozen, still clutching her book.

The hit man made up his mind. He turned and lowered his gun. He kept it held down by his side in his right hand, so he could quickly use it again if anybody tried to stop him from leaving. He moved towards the door at walking pace. The student had nowhere to go and he was bearing down on her. They both knew she was a witness, the only one close enough to get a good look at him. Maybe they each realised that the sensible thing for him to do was shoot her on his way out. It looked like he had the exact same idea for, as he drew close to her, he raised his gun, pointed it straight into her face, held it there for a moment that must have been a living agony for her, then he lowered it and walked away, disappearing off camera.

'Fuck! Is that all we've got? I couldn't have ID'd that guy if he worked for us.'

I couldn't believe we'd managed to view the footage, yet seen absolutely nothing.

'There's a second camera,' Sharp told us, producing another memory stick, 'this one's by the door. Because of the positioning it doesn't give such a good view of the shooting, but we see more of the guy when he leaves.'

'Show me,' I ordered.

Sharp changed the image and cut to the second camera; the one that must have been positioned high up on the wall that was just behind the girl with the green coat.

Sharp was right; the angle of the camera didn't give us such a good view of the attack. Some of it was obscured by the gun man himself, his tall frame blocking the sight of his hand pointing the gun at Danny, and my brother completely disappeared from view once he left his seat and ran towards the window. It was only when the shooting had stopped and the hit man made his decision not to finish Danny off that the recording got interesting. When he turned to head towards the door we got a far better look at the guy. Underneath the black raincoat there was a dark suit and a white shirt with no tie, black shoes and a black leather belt around his waist. He'd spent some money on those clothes. I could tell, even from this distance.

I watched once more as the gun man advanced on the young girl, then he raised the gun and held it there, pointing it at her face. It was then we noticed something we couldn't have seen on the other camera. The gun man's mouth opened, it formed a word and it closed again. We all saw it and didn't need any volume to know exactly what he said to her.

It was Palmer who spoke, and he sounded like he didn't quite believe it. 'Did he just say "bang"?'

No one bothered to answer. We saw it as clear as day, just as we saw the man's mouth transform into a deep, broad grin. He was smiling at the terrified girl, enjoying the moment. Then he laughed. He actually laughed.

'Pause it,' I said quickly, barely able to say the words. Sharp hit 'pause' and the image froze. The killer was still laughing, and the freeze frame caught him with his mouth open, teeth bared in a broad smile. Here was a man who was enjoying his day. I wanted to pick up my chair and hurl it at the screen.

'Sharp, I want you to get the best image you can of this guy and I want it circulated.' I wasn't looking at Sharp. I was too busy staring at the face of the guy who had shot my brother. Apart from his smile and the sunglasses, the only clue we had to his identity was the slight greying of his dark brown hair down both sides. The rest was obscured by his cap and glasses. 'I want every copper, bent or straight, and every grass in this city, and every other city in the country, to see this guy's face. I want you to trawl all the bars and nightclubs, whore houses and crack houses until you get me a name. I don't want you to do anything else, just this, you hear?'

Sharp was looking at me like I was deranged. Perhaps I was, but I wanted to find the man who had shot my brother in the back and walked out of a bar laughing about it. Even Tommy Gladwell's agonising end would have been a cake walk compared to what I was going to put this man through. All I had to do was find him. He was out there somewhere, hiding, in a country of sixty three million people, but that wasn't my problem, it was Sharp's.

'Just find him, Sharp, and quick.'

Palmer was staring intently at the grainy image on the screen, not saying a word.

'What?' I asked.

'I know him,' said Palmer, and he looked up at me, 'I know who he is.'

32

'Who is this man?' I asked Palmer, 'and how do you know him? Don't hold out on me.'

'His name is Thomas Mason,' said Palmer. 'When I was with the regiment we got sent on all kinds of missions. In this country and abroad, stuff we are not allowed to talk about,' he told me firmly, 'even now. When you work in hostile countries you are on your own. Deniable.'

'And you met this guy on one of those deniable missions?'

'Not met, exactly, but I did see him,' he admitted, 'and I heard what he did.'

'Go on.' I urged him.

'This was back in the nineties in Bosnia. He was supposed to assassinate a rogue Serb colonel who was planning another Srebenica. NATO didn't want the embarrassment of another massacre and the Americans gave us the green light to take him out. Our brass gave the job to Thomas Mason. The hit was meant to prevent the loss of innocent lives, but it didn't work out that way.'

'Because?'

'Mason flipped out.'

'What happened?'

'He killed everyone. I don't know what happened – maybe he was discovered during the job – but Mason killed everybody. He left eleven dead bodies in the Colonel's residence, including the chef, his driver, housekeeper, even his wife.'

'Why?'

'They never found out. Believe me, nobody really wanted to know. The whole thing was hushed up, buried and blamed on the Croats.'

'And Mason?'

Palmer shrugged, 'there's only three ways to deal with a man when he does something like that; promote him out of harm's way, quietly kill him or chuck him out.'

'And they chucked him out?'

Palmer nodded, 'I heard he went freelance.'

'So he's a fucking madman. Is that what you're telling me?'

'I don't know. A lot of guys in that business are wired tight and sometimes they snap. It happens, that's all I'm saying.'

I turned to Sharp. 'Find this guy,' I told him, and watched as my bent detective's face fell.

Despite everything, the club opening was a huge success. We made sure Golden Boots brought his team mates along with him for *Cachet's* first night party and they created just the kind of buzz we wanted, attracting the usual coterie of wannabe WAGs and hangers on. I did a deal with the biggest model agency in the area and hired two dozen stunning girls to pretend to be punters, making the place look like it was the first choice for the beautiful people. We paid half of them a bit extra to stand in a queue outside for an hour before we opened, so that anyone who walked by would think we were attracting the best-looking women in the north east to our doors on word of mouth alone. By the time we'd been open an hour the place was heaving.

Inside, our DJ had the place jumping. The dance floor was packed, the bars trading briskly and the pyrotechnics I'd invested in did the rest. The whole atmosphere was buzzing, helped by the four go-go dancers on the platforms raised high above the crowd. When the party was at its height, the huge glass-fronted lift rolled upwards, to the accompaniment of slow, atmospheric music and the animated chatter of the DJ. Once it reached the top, floodlights hit it and the doors slid open. An R&B star everybody in the room recognised stepped into it, accompanied by our best dancer dressed in a big red cape and a tiny gold bikini, over a sheer body stocking that was covered in what looked like diamonds. They sparkled brilliantly every time she moved. The R&B star offered her his arm. She took it and the lift slowly descended. The cheers from the crowd grew to a crescendo as the lift reached the ground, the doors slid open and they walked up a ramp until they were positioned right in the centre of the podium. She kissed him chastely and he, being an R&B star, took a fucking liberty and proceeded to rape-kiss her hard on the lips. The crowd went wild and our girl ignored the temptation to knee him right in the balls. I made a mental note to pay her extra for that. Motormouth grabbed the mic and shouted out a few inane phrases about burning up the dancefloor. As soon as he'd finished, he waved at the crowd and walked off. His few moments on the podium had set us back twenty grand.

The DJ started playing the opening bars to Snoop Dog's 'Sweat' and the dancers went into their act, in perfect step, arms and legs pumping, transmitting their energy to the dancefloor where the crowd joined in. They shouted, they screamed and cheered and I knew we'd done it. This place would be the best club in Newcastle for years. People would travel for miles just to get in, and we could launder all the money in the world through its doors, but all I could think of at that moment was Our young'un and how much he would have enjoyed this.

I turned my back on the scene below me and got one of the waiters to bring me a drink. I took it back to my new office and closed the door behind me to blot out the din.

I visited Danny in hospital the next morning but he didn't open his eyes. He'd been drifting in and out of consciousness but hadn't spoken yet. I was just glad he was still alive.

I was driving back through the city when my phone vibrated into life, 'Yes.'

'It's me,' said Sharp.

'What is it?'

'I found him.'

I felt a surge of adrenalin, the first positive emotion in days, 'you sure? That was quick.'

'It's what I do,' he reminded me, 'Palmer gave me a name, my contacts did the rest. The guy lives openly, under his real name, barely a hundred miles from here, which is surprising, but there you go.'

I asked him for an address and he gave it to me. Then I phoned Palmer and issued instructions. He, in turn, called Kinane, who collected his boys. I didn't want any delay; I couldn't risk the slim chance that our man might leave the country. It wasn't likely, but I knew I wouldn't be able to rest until I had reckoned with him and the men who had hired him. We left our city to hunt for the man who shot my brother.

The restaurant Palmer tailed him to from his apartment was upmarket, as was Thomas Mason's guest, a high-maintenance blonde in her late twenties with sunglasses resting on the top of her head. She was wearing one of those garish, yellow and blue, patterned Hermes scarves with a dark blue, blazer-style jacket with gold buttons and cream trousers, a Chanel bag at her feet. I couldn't see the manicured fingernails from here but I was betting they'd be immaculate. She'd be an expensive companion, one way or another, but it didn't matter because the man with her had money. I knew that because he would have been paid a great deal of it to gun down my brother.

Of course Danny was still alive, which meant that, technically, the assassin had failed but, if I was right, the man behind the shooting wouldn't care too much about that. Danny always said a wounded man was far harder to take care of than a dead one. He explained that, in battle, wounded guys have to be rescued, patched up and 'coptered out of there. The man's presence, his visible injuries and his screams would upset and unsettle the men and he would probably need months, sometimes years, of care from a large contingent of expensive personnel behind-the-scenes; including doctors, surgeons, and nurses and even the civil servants, who would eventually rubber-stamp his invalidity benefits before he was finally cashiered from the army. 'Wounded men are what the enemy really wants,' he explained to me once, 'they cause chaos and they fuck you up, mentally. It has a big effect on you when you see your mates carried off on stretchers with bullet holes in them and limbs missing. Why do you think anti-personnel mines are designed to blow legs off but not kill you? Wounded men are a burden. All you have to do for a dead man is dig a ditch and drop him in it.'

Now Danny was the wounded soldier and I figured the man behind it would be relishing the effect it was having on me. I wasn't sleeping, I couldn't eat and my mind was no longer on the business. I only cared about two things; Danny getting the best medical treatment it was possible to buy and me making the man who had done this to him pay in the worst way imaginable.

And now I was looking at that same man from the darkened window of my car, which was parked opposite the Michelin-starred restaurant where he had selected to take his female companion, watching him rise from the table and smile broadly as she rejoined him. His manners were good. You could tell he was ex-British army, officer class, even before Palmer confirmed this. He looked like the kind of man who wouldn't dream of staying in his seat when a lady entered the room, but he had no qualms about shooting my unarmed brother in the back

They were laughing at something now and I took a strange pleasure in that. I relished knowing what he didn't; that soon he wouldn't be laughing any more and she would be the final bit of female company he would enjoy. That this meal was going to be his last supper.

I turned to Palmer and said, 'Do it.'

When he left the restaurant, our target kissed his companion on the lips, walked back along the high street, paused to buy a newspaper, then took money from a cash point that he would never spend. He seemed relaxed enough, no visible demons, no haunted look caused by what he'd done, no noticeable fear that now he was the hunted one.

Palmer and I watched as Mason strolled back to his apartment on the edge of town. They were nice flats, just a few exclusive properties in a small block that had been built on the site of an old hotel. The apartments were occupied by commuters, young professionals who were never there during the daytime. There was no concierge, but there was an underground car park, which made it perfect for our needs. I sent a text message.

I was at the wheel of the car, so I could let Palmer out. He waited until our man walked through the front door of his apartment block then he left and went after him.

*

Palmer took the stairs slowly and quietly, making sure he would not be heard. He was in no hurry. He was just back-up, in case the guy caused any trouble that Kinane and his boys couldn't handle. He was armed though, and he took the gun out of a sports bag he was carrying and hid it behind a short raincoat that was folded over his arm.

He was about to round the corner that would bring him to his target's apartment when he heard the sound. It echoed down the corridor towards him, unbearably loud in the confined space of a corridor of a near-empty building. It was the unmistakeable sound of a pump action shotgun being made ready to fire. As Palmer came around the corner, he saw Mason standing by the door of his apartment with nothing more lethal in his hands than the keys to his front door. There were two Beretta shotguns trained directly on him by Kinane's sons and Joe himself was advancing on the man with a pistol in his hand. There were large holdalls on the floor to hide the shotguns. Blake's text had been the signal to release them. Mason held up his hands high in a gesture of surrender. Palmer tried to read him. Did he seem scared, rattled maybe? No, the look he wore was one of complete resignation.

Somehow the whole thing had gone according to plan and they had lifted the assassin without firing a shot. He was unarmed, outnumbered and, judging by David Blake's mood, his future was as bleak as could be imagined. There was just one thing that troubled Palmer. It was the look on his face – a calm, implacable look that seemed to say 'I knew this moment was going to come one day'.

Kinane walked right up to Mason and hit him hard with the hand that contained the pistol. It crashed into the side of his head with a sickening impact and he went down on one knee and put a hand up to the deep cut there. Kinane pulled the guy up by the lapels of his fancy suit. Blood was oozing down the side of his face. Kinane pushed him towards the door to the car park.

It was a risk doing it this way. There was always the possibility they'd be disturbed by someone pushing a leaflet through a door, or a resident coming home, but they'd reasoned this was their best chance. Sometimes you just had to do the daring thing that no one expects, particularly if you are going to take out a guy like this. He clearly hadn't expected to be lifted on his own doorstep. They clattered down the metal steps and out through the door that opened onto the car park. It was empty except for a silver Mercedes. Palmer guessed it belonged to the man they had just knocked senseless. The only other vehicle in the underground car park was a Transit van with blacked-out rear windows. The side door was dragged open and the semi-conscious man hauled inside. Both hands were cuffed to the metal racking on the far wall of the van and his feet were bound together with the kind of plastic cuffs the Police use. He was blindfolded and gagged. Even so, Kinane's sons sat on the bench seating opposite him with their shotguns ready. No one was going to take any chances with this one.

33

I followed the van all the way back to the old electrical plant. It parked up a few yards from the lock up and I stayed in my car for a moment and watched as the side door slid open. Kinane and his sons came out of the van and they dragged Mason out with them. They tore off the blindfold and he blinked at the light. Mason didn't look scared. His hands were still bound and there was dried blood on the side of his face but he walked unaided towards the lock up, past the newly-delivered breeze blocks and the cement mixer. Kinane started it up and it rolled round and round, making a convenient noise to mask any sounds that might come from inside the lock up. I climbed out of my car and followed them in.

I waited till Kinane took off the handcuffs and replaced them with an iron manacle that went round our man's left wrist. This was attached to a thick, linked chain ten feet long that stretched from a post cemented into the floor. He was tethered like a dog now. Kinane and Palmer walked back out while Kinane's sons stayed and covered the guy with their shotguns.

'Who paid you to kill my brother?' I demanded, 'or are you going to tell me you have no idea.'

He snorted, 'I don't know,' at least he didn't deny it, 'we never know. That's how it works. The job is sent, the money is wired. It's all done electronically.'

Jesus, he didn't even have a cut-out. He could have been lying, but I doubted it and I didn't want to waste my time trying to find out.

'You laughed,' I said and he looked up at me without comprehension, 'when you walked out of the bar after you shot my brother, you pointed your gun at that young girl, and then you said "Bang" and you laughed.'

'What of it?'

'You gunned down my brother and you leave the place laughing. How do you think that makes me feel?'

He looked down at his feet then like he was ignoring me. 'Why you don't just cut the chat and do what you have to do?'

'Kill you, you mean?'

'If you've got the balls.'

I couldn't fucking believe this guy. I knew he was crazy from what Palmer had said about him but it was clear to me now that he had a death wish.

'What if I choose to take my time? What if I get my guys here to beat the shit out of you in shifts for days, then I'll come back and stomp on the bones they've broken. How does that sound? I reckon we could keep you alive for a week, maybe two, before your heart finally gives out.'

'Like I said,' he mumbled, 'you do what you've got to do.'

'Reckon you're pretty hard core, don't you? You think you can cope with everything we throw at you, like this is some big heroic final test. Is that right?'

'Think what you want to think.'

'What if I get my men to pour a can of petrol over you, burn you alive in here and listen to your screams through the open window? What do you say? Does that sound like a good way to go to you?'

'You won't hear me scream.'

'Really? You sound pretty sure of that. You *must* be hard core. Burned alive and he goes without a whimper. But don't worry, it's alright. I'm not going to kill you,' I told him.

'Yeah,' he answered, 'course you're not,' before adding, 'I don't give a fuck.'

'You made that pretty clear. You've got your "it's all bullshit anyway" speech all worked out for me, haven't you, and that thousand-yard-stare is a dead giveaway. I knew it as soon as I saw you. You can't wait for it to finally be over, but you are too gutless to do it yourself. You had to wait till we came along to do it for you. Mission suicide. But like I said, I'm not going to kill you.'

Kinane walked in with a pack containing two dozen bottles of water covered in plastic wrapping. He dropped it on the floor within the guy's reach. Mason looked at it but, if he was wondering what it was for, he hid it well.

'I'm going to leave you here to think about what you did,' he frowned at me then, but I still don't think he understood. Palmer walked in and threw a large box of chocolate bars on the ground near the water.

'Okay,' he said. Did I imagine it, or was his voice cracking slightly? 'When you come back, we should talk. I could make a deal…'

'No talking, no deals. I'm not coming back.'

'I don't understand,' he told me, and he looked at the water and the chocolate bars trying to make sense of them.

'I'm leaving you here,' I informed him, 'chained up. I am going to leave the water and the food too, but not because I'm a nice guy. I want you to have them here with you, so you take a very long time to die. You're going to want to die when you've been down here for a while but you won't be able to stop yourself from drinking the water and eating the food, and that's what I want. That way you'll last a long while. I want you to think about how you ended up lying here with no hope, because that's how you left my brother. He's in a hospital bed right now, he can't move and he has no future. I'm going to show you how that feels.'

'You'll never break that chain. You probably think you can and I'm sure you'll try, but I'm telling you now there's no chance. You are never leaving this room and you won't see daylight again. When we leave here the door will be locked and padlocked on the outside. Then my lads will take the breeze blocks and the cement and they will seal up the door. No one will come because no one knows you're here and it's private land. You can scream all you like. I want you to scream, but no one will hear you. You are going to die in here but not before you've had a long time to think about what you did to my brother. I'm pretty sure you will be more than crazy by the time you eventually die – and that won't give my brother his life back, but knowing it will bring me some comfort.' All the time I'd been talking I was watching him, and now I could see the realisation slowly sinking in. He didn't look so calm now.

'I have two hundred thousand pounds in an account. Let me go and it's yours,' there was desperation in the words now because he knew it was a long shot.

'Keep it,' I told him, 'see how much good it does you down here.'

He started tugging at the chain then, pulling hard. It didn't budge. Palmer and Kinane walked out of the room, followed by Kinane's sons. I took one last look at the man who had destroyed my brother. I wanted to remember his fear and desperation. I wanted to see it written all over his face. He was still tugging at the chain.

'Please, don't leave me in here... please,' his voice was a croak and there were tears in his eyes, 'don't do this.'

I walked towards the door.

'Kill me,' he urged me, 'kill me now...'

'I just did,' I said and I took one last look at him. He knew the talking was over. I stepped outside the room and, as I closed the door, I heard him cry 'No!' Then I closed it firmly shut and clicked the heavy padlock in place. I threw the key away into the bushes. I nodded at the guys and they started to bring the heavy breeze blocks over to finish the job.

Kinane and Palmer joined me in the car and we drove away without a word.

34

It was the morning of our big meeting with Alan Gladwell. Today I had to decide whether I was going to share the proceeds of Edinburgh's drug trade with him – or decline his offer and risk going to war with the Gladwells. I had the TV on in the background while I showered and dressed in the apartment but I wasn't giving it much attention.

The news was all about Leon Cassidy that morning. It was the only story receiving any real coverage. The day before, he had been found guilty of all five murders and the Press were finally able to unleash all of their hyperbole on the Sandyhills Sniper, without fear of prejudicing the trial or risking a libel case. Cassidy was a misfit, a loner and a loser they told us. He was inadequate and lived in his own world. Former school friends and work mates queued up to denounce him with small, seemingly insignificant stories that, in hindsight, seemed like clues that they'd been sharing their lives with a killer all along. He'd blanked them, looked right through them, had a bit of a temper over silly little things, which clearly showed he was a nut job. Cassidy had been kicked out by the military, then by his wife, and couldn't hold down a normal job, and so it went on.

I was brushing my teeth with the door open, so I could hear the Strathclyde Police press conference. Their top brass could hardly contain their sense of satisfaction at the life sentence handed down to Cassidy.

I didn't really listen to the words of the Chief Constable. He was spouting the usual crap about 'the most important thing today is the sense of closure for relatives of the victims. Our hearts go out to the loved ones whose lives have been forever altered by the wicked and senseless acts of Leon Cassidy,' I walked back into the room while he was finishing his piece, 'I know it is some consolation to his loving wife Judy and their two wonderful children that Detective Chief Inspector Robert McGregor died bravely doing the job that he loved, protecting the citizens of his home against criminality of all kinds.' Every word must have been written by the press office in advance because it contained all of the pat phrases we'd heard a million times before.

I was buttoning my shirt when they finally allowed the arresting officer to have a word with the Press. When I heard his voice I stopped what I was doing and turned back towards the screen. I watched him intently. Detective Inspector Stephen Connor was a wiry man in his late forties, with a shock of white hair and a broad Glasgow accent. In other words, a working-class boy made good. He told the assembled journalists, 'the streets of our city are safe again, thanks to the conviction of the so-called Sandyhills Sniper. I would even go so far as to say that everybody in Glasgow can sleep sounder in their beds.' Connor went on to field questions from the Press but I couldn't focus on what he said. I sat down heavily on the sofa and tried to think, my thoughts churning. I was dimly aware of a noise somewhere that was not coming from the TV set and eventually realised that my mobile was ringing.

The meeting with Alan Gladwell was reconvened at the same venue. Virtually his whole crew was there, and so was ours, with the exception of Hunter and Danny. I'd had about an hour's sleep the night before, so my tolerance for bullshit was non-existent. When Amrein started to recount the main points of the previous meeting's discussion, I interrupted him.

'Mind if I say something Amrein, before you go through everything again?' I asked.

'Not at all.'

'I'd like to tell you a little story I heard once, Alan,' and I looked him in the eye, 'mind if I do that?' I didn't allow him to reply, 'it's all about a man who went a bit crazy last year and started shooting people at random. You'll remember it. After all, it happened in your backyard.'

'Of course I remember it. It was the biggest news story in Glasgow for years. You're right he was crazy, sick in the head in my opinion. Killed a couple of people who didn't deserve it.'

'More than a couple. He shot four civilians, but that's not what got him the biggest coverage, was it?'

'How do you mean?'

'It was the big cheese Police Officer he gunned down that got the tabloids really in a spin. What was it they used to call him? DCI Gangbuster?'

'I don't read the newspapers,' Alan said, coolly.

'Well then you'll just have to take my word for it. His real name was Detective Chief Inspector Robert McGregor. His speciality was taking down heavy-duty crews and locking up long-established crime families. His methods were a bit rough; a bit of blackmail, intimidation, paying large amounts of government money to grasses, then whisking them away into the witness protection programme. But the thing about him was, he got results. Every time he took a firm down he made sure it was his face on the Ten O'Clock News. Some even said he was a future Commissioner of the Metropolitan Police.'

'Yeah, I'd heard of the bloke.'

'I bet. The thing is, to the likes of you and me, DCI McGregor was a problem. He had a very good record of putting people like us out of business and his last port of call was Glasgow, where he told everybody who'd listen that he was going to take down the crime barons. Trouble was, he was so high profile he was untouchable. No one could get near him and, if anyone ever tried, the outrage would have been colossal. A firm like yours would have been rolled up in five minutes if you'd killed him. You and everybody else in your outfit would have been doing life before you knew it.'

'I agree,' he said calmly, 'so what's your point? The bloke who killed him was all over the Breakfast News this morning.'

'Except that we know it *wasn't* actually Leon Cassidy.'

'Come again?'

'Leon Cassidy. The man the police got for it, the fella the jury convicted, the one the judge gave a life sentence to. He wasn't the shooter.'

Alan Gladwell smiled as if I was a conspiracy theorist, 'of course it was him. They found the bloody rifle at his flat. Like I said he was a sick fuck. I mean if it had just been that copper he'd shot then I'd have given him a medal, but he took out innocent civilians in the process.'

'Collateral damage,' I told him. 'In the larger scheme of things, they didn't matter.'

'You reckon?' and he frowned at me, 'listen pal, this is all very fascinating but we haven't got all day. There's an entire fucking city waiting for you to make up your mind…'

I managed to ignore and interrupt him at the same time, 'Yeah, I reckon, they were chaff, cannon fodder, the PBI,' and when he looked blankly at me I explained, 'the Poor Bloody Infantry, you know, the ones who get sent into battle by the generals, sacrificed for the greater good.'

He was looking confused, so I carried on.

'Isn't that the way you viewed it, Alan? Leon Cassidy was the perfect patsy, your very own Lee Harvey Oswald. He couldn't hold down a job, had a history of mental problems, was booted out of the army as a young man, but not before he had weapons training. There were previous convictions for assault, a failed marriage and a lost custody battle, even a restraining order from the wife. You couldn't have invented a better suspect; a ticking time bomb just waiting to go off. Then one day he does – he becomes the "Sandyhills Sniper", gunning down a man on a petrol forecourt. No one sees him, all they hear is the shot. The next day he does it again. He's an impatient little psychopath is Leon. He waits all his life to commit a murder then he does two in twenty-four hours.'

'Is there a fucking point to this?'

'My point is you fucked up.'

'Did I?' and he shook his head, 'what the fuck are you talking about?'

'Yeah. I knew it was you the moment I saw the arresting officer on the TV news this morning, DI Stephen Connor.'

'What about him?'

'Connor has been on your father's payroll for years. Don't bother to deny it. Everyone in our world knows you own the guy. He didn't make a move in Glasgow without your dad's say-so and when he did move it was only to lock up the guys your father told him to.'

'So fucking what?'

'Getting rid of McGregor wasn't enough of a win for you was it? So Stephen Connor got to arrest Scotland's most wanted, when everyone knows he couldn't catch syphilis. Couldn't resist it, could you? You had to give your dog a bone.'

Gladwell looked like he couldn't even be bothered to argue with me, 'so what are you saying?'

'I'm saying that, all the while you've been bullshitting me about not wanting to kill anyone any more, you were setting up Leon Cassidy to take the fall for five murders you ordered, four of which were just random civilians used to cover your tracks for the real hit. You took out McGregor and no one batted an eye lid because they didn't realise it was you, but I did, this morning, the moment they gave the microphone to your bitch Connor. And it reminded me of another little case in Glasgow about two years ago. I'm sure you remember it. Two guys came up from London to try and take over a club and deal some drugs in your backyard. Unsurprisingly they ended up dead, shot in their car when they parked up on wasteland, for a meeting with a local crime lord, or so the story goes, but it wasn't close range, was it? No shotguns or semi-automatics like you'd expect. No, these guys were both shot with a rifle from distance, by a professional, someone good, who knew what he was doing, someone who had been hired to remove the competition. You've done it before Alan. I should have made the connection before now but I didn't. I made it this morning though. So how long before SOCA works it out and comes after you?'

'Is that your excuse for pulling out of this Edinburgh thing? Not got the balls to take on SOCA?'

'No,' I told him, 'I'm pulling out, but not because of that.'

'Why then?'

'Because I am not going to send my men up north so you can carve them up.'

'Fuck are you talking about?' I knew I was going out on a limb here.

'A man who can kill four innocent civilians to get at one copper isn't going to make peace with the guy who killed his brother. You know it's funny,' I said, 'I've heard a lot about you over the years. You're supposed to be a hard and ruthless man. A man to be feared, and yet when it comes down to it you can't even look me in the eye and admit it.'

'Admit what?'

'That it's you that's coming after me. You're the one behind it all, pulling the strings, ordering the hits. Your dad would have looked Bobby in the eye and declared war but you, you hide behind these talks like a bairn behind his mother's apron strings.' Alan Gladwell was looking at me like he couldn't quite comprehend what he was hearing, but I wasn't finished yet. 'I killed your brother, carved him up with a machete if you want to know, while he screamed for his life, and you're down here doing deals with me one day, then shooting my men in the back the next. What kind of spineless cunt does that? Your father would be disgusted. Shooting civilians in the street and gunning down men in bars, then pretending you know nothing about it? Take some responsibility for your actions, man, admit it and come at me in the open if you've got a pair.' I stopped for a moment and watched him absorb my words. I'd given him a lot to think about and some of it would have hurt, not least the bit about his brother and his father. If he wasn't looking to kill me already he would after today, that was for sure. If I'd read this situation wrong I'd just made myself another powerful enemy.

'Come on then,' I urged him, 'why don't you just say it like it is.' I'd barely finished my sentence when he lunged for me with a roar, hurling himself across the table towards me.

'Come here!' he screamed, 'come here, you bastard!' Amrein's bodyguards were already in between us and Gladwell's men were trying to pull him back. My lads were steaming in between us too and fists were flying. 'I'll fucking murder you! I'll put you in a fucking wheelchair just like your brother!' He was being dragged away by Fallon and his men, but he was still shouting. Amrein was trying to get a word in but Gladwell was having none of that. 'Fuck you Amrein, you fucking cunt!' then he started jabbing his finger at me as Fallon and two of his lads bundled him towards the exit door. 'There's contracts out on you,' his eyes were bulging, he was losing it now, 'on all of you! You're all fucking dead! Every hit man in the country knows your names and I don't care what it costs me! You're all fucking dead!'

With one last heave, Fallon and Gladwell's boys managed to manoeuvre Alan Gladwell out through the fire exit door and into the courtyard at the back of the hotel.

Amrein looked shattered.

'Thanks for setting this up, Amrein,' I told him sarcastically, 'it's been useful.'

Kinane walked up to me. He looked flushed, and I'd noticed he landed a couple of tasty blows on Gladwell's boys but he hadn't managed to get near Fallon, who had shown a cooler head than I expected by bundling his boss out of the way before he did something he could be arrested for.

'How did you know it was him?' asked Kinane.

'I didn't,' I admitted, 'but I do now.'

35

The days following our meeting with Alan Gladwell were chaotic in the extreme. Everything went wrong. The local Police started acting on tip-offs they would normally have ignored, meaning a couple of our dealers were arrested on the outskirts of the city and one of our pubs was closed down due to illegal gambling activities, because a few guys were playing cards in there for money. Meanwhile someone tried to set fire to one of our clubs and a bomb threat was sent to the hotel we were about to open, which resulted in our entire staff being evacuated during their training for opening night. There was barely a corner of our business that did not experience some form of assault, harassment or legal sanction and I could have traced just about all of them back to Alan Gladwell or Ron Haydon MP and his tame Chief Constable. Even Maggot was arrested and threatened with a charge of living off immoral earnings. He got quite upset about that and foolishly started threatening to name the names of Police officers who had visited the Sports Injury clinic in the past, until one of the detectives interviewing him gave him a slap. When Kinane found out he'd been so stupid he gave him another one, so Maggot went round for days sporting matching black eyes. He looked like a panda.

I took all of that on the chin because, right in the middle of it all, Our young'un finally opened his eyes. There was no way he was ever going to walk again, but at least he was alive and there was no brain damage. I can't tell you how relieved that made me feel. Danny was drifting in and out of consciousness while I was there and not really making much sense. I just told him everything was going to be okay and watched as he went back to sleep. I had no idea how I was going to be able to tell him he was paralysed.

That afternoon I was sitting with Palmer in my office in the Cauldron, getting updates on the latest outrages committed against our firm, when Kinane burst in.

'Our Kevin's been robbed,' he said, and he looked as angry as I'd ever seen him. I said nothing. I just let him speak, 'he was taking the stash down to Sunnydale. He'd barely got into the place when they jumped him; vans and cars pulling out to block him, shotguns and Uzis waved at him. They got him out of the car, smacked him about and drove off with it. We found it later, burned out, the stash missing.'

Kinane didn't waste any words.

'Braddock,' I said.

'Has to be! Who else knew our Kevin was coming down with the stash? We vary the timings and the vehicles but we have to let him know we're coming, so he's ready to unload. We give him the make and model of the car so his scouts can look out for it. A rival firm wouldn't have any of that information and how could they just sit there in their cars, tooled up like that, without Braddock's crew knowing about it and scaring them off? They know everything going on in that estate. It was him alright.'

'Is Kevin okay?' I was buying time with my question, trying to work out what to do.

'He's lost his front teeth,' Kinane said wearily, 'got a smack in the face with an Uzi.' In Kinane's world this was the equivalent of a grazed knee, 'he'll live, but he wants payback.'

'I'm sure he does,' I assured him, 'and I know you do too.'

'Well then,' he urged me, 'give me the go-ahead. Let me sort this cunt out once and for all.'

'No,' I said.

'What? Are you serious? He's just stolen the whole fucking consignment! You know how much that's worth. This is declaring war on you. And on us. After we went in there and you warned him, he goes and does this. He doesn't give a fuck about us. If we don't fix this then we are going to look like total mugs. Who else is going to steal from us if we let this go unpunished? They'll be lining up to take us on!'

Every word Kinane said was true but I couldn't go to war on two fronts right now, not with Danny in hospital and Gladwell's contract killers trying to take us all out.

'Here's what I want to happen,' I told him. 'Palmer is going to talk to Braddock. He is going to tell him I am furious that the drugs have been lifted from under Braddock's nose and he has to retrieve them and kill the bastards who've done it.'

'But *he's* fucking done it!' Kinane was bawling at me now.

'I know that, Joe. But don't you think Braddock has got his boys on full alert right now? He'll have them all pumped up from robbing your lad and now they're dug in waiting for us to race down there like General Custer and the Seventh Cavalry. If we do that it will be a bloodbath on both sides. It's not worth it.'

'Then what are we going to do?'

'We throw the ball back into his court, we wait to see what

he does, and we bide our time. We're already at war with the Gladwells, I don't want a war with Braddock's crew at the same time. So Palmer will tell Braddock there'll be no more drugs until the last consignment is recovered.'

'They've got enough to last them a month,' Kinane reminded me.

'And right now they are living large and spending money they haven't earned yet. When the drugs run out they'll feel it.'

Kinane was shaking his head, 'I don't believe this. I don't believe what I'm hearing. I've never even questioned you before…' he was talking to me, but he suddenly switched his attention to Palmer, '…you can't tell me you agree?'

This was a tricky moment. If Palmer agreed with Kinane I was pretty much finished. If I was lucky, the mutiny would be bloodless.

There was a long silence from my head of security. 'Well?' demanded Kinane.

'I think he's right,' he said, and for a moment I didn't know which one of us he meant, 'we can't go charging in there while they are expecting it. Let them drop their guard, then act.'

'Jesus Christ!' shouted Kinane. 'I would have expected better from you!' he told Palmer, then he stormed out of the room.

'Thanks,' I said.

'I told Joe you were right,' Palmer said, 'but I'm not sure you are. This waiting for the drugs to run out, it's a dangerous policy right now.'

I knew what he meant. Braddock would probably know we were at war with the Gladwells and had only acted now because he thought we were preoccupied with them. Once I'd let the drugs run out on his estate, Braddock's obvious next move would be to buy from Gladwell, giving our enemy a toe-hold in our city. It was the nightmare scenario for all of us. I just hoped he wasn't bright enough to spot it.

*

Sharp and I were back in the apartment because we didn't want to be seen together in public. 'What have you got for me?' I demanded.

He shook his head, 'Nothing.'

'That's not good enough Sharp. I told you...'

'Believe me, I am trying everything I can,' he snapped. 'I'm speaking to too many people on this one and sooner or later he is going to know there's a cop from your neck of the woods asking questions about him and then I'm a fucking dead man.'

'So you've spoken to a bunch of villains, all the bent coppers you know and even the honest ones and you've found nothing I can attack him with? I don't believe it. For a gangster, he's squeaky clean.'

'I'm telling you that's how it is. The guy just runs his crew, nowt else. He sells drugs but he doesn't do them, his men respect him, even the hardest ones like that Fallon do what he tells them to because he has things tight, the money keeps rolling in and they all get paid on time. He never goes anywhere without a few of his crew around him so a hit is out of the question. When he's at home he stays in with his missus, who he's known ever since they were at school together, and his kids.'

'What about a mistress, girlfriend, boyfriend even?'

'I thought of that too. I was hoping there'd be a bird somewhere, or at least some hooker he shags when he's bored, but there's no one. He's with his crew all day then it's back to the big house, set back from the road, CCTV everywhere and men watching over him. I guess he's learned from his brother's mistakes.'

I didn't say anything for a moment.

'What do you want me to do?' he asked.

'Get back out there, keep looking, there must be something.'

He looked like he was about to start crying, 'please, you don't know what you're asking me to do.'

'Yes I do,' I assured him, 'I need you to do this. It's important.'

He put his hands up to his head and pressed them hard against his skull like he was trying to stop his head from exploding, then he said, 'you don't get it, do you. You are going to get me killed.'

'In your game that's an occupational hazard, Sharp. Now get back out there.'

'Christ man…'

'Gladwell knows everything about us. He knows where I go, who I see and where I shack up when I'm over here. We've got nothing on his crew that I can use against him. I want something on Gladwell and I want it quick. Find me a weakness. Because if I don't get one his crew will keep picking us off one by one until there's nobody left, and you needn't think you're immune. If you don't deliver, I'll make sure he hears you are part of my outfit. You got that?'

'Yeah, course,' his head was bowed now. He looked terrified, but I couldn't tell who he was more frightened of; me or Alan Gladwell.

'Good, because you know something?'

'What?' he looked up at me then.

'You are on the right side, believe me. He might have three times as many men, but he's stupid. We are going to win and, when we do, I won't forget your part in it. You'll be well looked after.'

Sharp nodded, 'Yeah, cheers,' he mumbled, but he obviously didn't believe a word of it. I'm not sure I believed it myself.

36

It was getting dark when I walked out onto the roof of the Cauldron, which was turning into a second office for me. I could talk to people without fear of being overheard. I could smoke up here and clear my head. Palmer was out there already, gazing out at the city. 'What is it Palmer?' I asked him, even though I had a pretty good idea.

He turned to face me. 'How do you mean?'

'You've had a face like a smacked arse for days now,' I told him, 'so out with it. What's on your mind?'

'You really want to know?' he asked.

'I wouldn't ask if I didn't.'

He took a drag on his cigarette to fortify himself then said, 'I keep thinking about what we did to that guy,' he wasn't looking me in the eye. 'Him shooting Danny gave you every right to finish him but what we did?' He took another draw on his cigarette while he was choosing his words and said, 'it wasn't right, leaving him like that. We should have killed him. What we did wasn't right,' he repeated. Palmer turned away from me. He was leaning forward, head bent, elbows resting on the railing.

'It wasn't just spite,' I told the back of his head, 'what I did to that guy wasn't only revenge for my brother, though I'll admit that was a big part of it.' I stood next to him and we looked out over the rooftops together.

'I wanted him to suffer, really suffer, but that wasn't the only reason.' He looked at me doubtfully. 'Kinane will leak the story. Don't worry, he isn't going to be telling anyone who was involved, but he will let the word get out that the man who shot my brother died in the worst way imaginable, that we chained a man up and walled him in while he was still breathing. That way, the next time anyone even dreams of coming up against us, they'll think again.'

'Reckon it'll work?'

'How many times have you heard the story about Joe taking that gangster ten miles out into the North Sea on a fishing boat and chucking him overboard?' I asked.

'A few times,' he admitted.

'What did you think when you heard that?'

'That I was glad it wasn't me,' he admitted.

'Exactly. The same goes for the one about Alan Gladwell cutting that bloke's cock off. Well, now there's a new story doing the rounds that will make people realise we don't fuck about down here. Would you come up against us if you heard that death is the least of it?'

'I don't know,' he said, 'truthfully, I don't.' I had never even seen Palmer looking tired before now but tonight he looked all-in.

'Okay,' I said, 'tomorrow you go down there with a JCB or a bulldozer, whatever you can get your hands on at short notice. Take a couple of Kinane's lads with you to be on the safe side, make sure they have their shotguns. If the guy's as dangerous as you say he is, I want no fuck-ups.'

'I hear you.'

'Flatten the place. By nightfall tomorrow I don't want to be able to see a trace of that building, do you understand?'

'Yeah,' I could hear the relief in his voice. Personally I didn't give a shit about the grinning bastard. I reckoned he'd be at least half mad by now anyway, after all this time in that dark hole, but I needed Palmer back. I needed my main guy to be bright, alert and on my side again. I knew permitting him this small victory would change things for the better. Maybe he'd even sleep tonight.

'Palmer, make sure that nothing comes crawling out of that rubble, you hear me?'

He nodded slowly, 'I'll see to it,' he assured me, 'you won't have to worry about a thing.'

Me, not worrying about anything? That was almost funny.

I spent the evening at Simone's apartment or, more accurately, I spent it in her bed. Since that first evening together I'd not had much time to even speak to her on the phone. She seemed to understand that Danny's well-being was the most important thing to me, so she kept her distance but I got text messages from her and occasional voice mails; short messages that seemed innocent enough and never alluded to the fact that we had slept together. After a few days I went back there and I'd been twice more since then. I didn't see any harm in it. I don't have a normal life and my stress levels are probably a hundred times higher than a regular guy's, so why shouldn't I allow myself this little diversion? I didn't see us as a permanent item though. She was damaged goods, and not just because of her shifts down at the massage parlour. There were things going on in her head that I didn't think I'd ever be able to fix.

She dozed off next to me and I was just thinking about

leaving when Sharp phoned me, 'I've got something, it might not be much, but it's something.'

'Let's hear it.' I spoke quietly at first and left Simone's bedroom so I didn't wake her.

'It comes from a low-level grass, a street dealer who pays a man, who pays a man, who pays Gladwell.'

'Go on.'

'Alan Gladwell is going away for a few days. Out of the country. It's business, apparently, but he's not taking anyone with him,' that struck me as more than a bit odd, a man of Alan Gladwell's profile travelling abroad without protection. 'I know this because he's put his brother Malcolm in charge while he's away.'

'How do you know he's not taking anyone else with him?'

'I don't, for sure, but I did some digging and it turns out he has been doing this regular lately, just goes off and doesn't take his crew with him. Doesn't even tell them what he's up to but there's a rumour he's out east, negotiating with a new supplier about a shipment, and the word on the street is that it's a big one, a very big one.'

It seemed we weren't the only organisation seeking alternative suppliers after the arrest of the Haan brothers.

'He goes off without taking his own guys to watch his back?' This sounded all wrong to me.

'That's how the story goes, and I didn't buy it either, so I followed the guy.'

'You followed Alan Gladwell?' This was an even bigger surprise.

'I know. I was fucking terrified. I didn't want to do it but it's like you said, if I can't find anything on him, I'm a dead man anyway. I kept well back and I only hung on long enough to see where he went.'

'And where did he go?'

'That's the strange bit. He got his driver to park over the

road and made a big show of going into a Bookies, but he was only in there for a minute then he was out again. He glanced over at his car and, when he reckoned nobody was looking, he ducked into the place next door.'

Sharp paused to let that sink in.

'A knocking shop?'

'Nope.'

'Sharp, I know you are pleased with yourself but I haven't got all day. Where did he go?'

'A travel agents.'

'A what? Why would he do that?' If Alan Gladwell needed a flight booking there'd be a queue of people who'd want to sort it out for him.

'I figured he didn't want anyone to know where he was going, not even his right-hand men or his brothers, in case they worked out who he was talking to. You've had problems with leaks in the past, maybe he has too. Maybe he doesn't trust anyone with this deal, if it really is so big?'

'That's a big risk,' I said. 'Go on.'

'I waited till Gladwell came out, got back into his car and buggered off, then I took a gamble. I went right in there. I told the young lass behind the counter I was investigating a ring of stolen credit cards and could I look at the bookings she had taken in the past hour. There were only two and I assured her they were both legit. I didn't want his booking to be cancelled.'

'So where was he off to?'

'That's the bit you are going to be most interested in,' he told me. 'Thailand.'

I took Gladwell's flight details from Sharp, then I hung up and left Simone's. I called Sarah and told her not to leave the compound under any circumstances, and for once she didn't argue, then I spoke to Jagrit so he knew there was a threat. Jagrit assured me he would change the rotas and increase the guard on the compound. I got myself onto the first flight back to Bangkok. Then I phoned Pratin to arrange an emergency meeting there with my bent Thai detective. I didn't like the idea of leaving Danny but I had no choice. Palmer and Kinane said they'd visit him and I was gambling I wouldn't be away for long.

I quickly packed a bag, then left. I knew if I moved now, I had a couple of days head start over Alan Gladwell – I was going to need them.

37

I spent the flight from Heathrow to Bangkok thinking about Alan Gladwell and why he was flying out there. Either the story about the huge consignment from the new supplier from the East was true, or he had found out about my compound in Hua Hin. I couldn't gamble that Gladwell's trip to Thailand had nothing to do with me. I couldn't afford to take any chances where Sarah was concerned, so I planned everything like we were on a war footing.

I couldn't see Gladwell coming out to the compound on his own, but who else would be good enough to trouble my Gurkhas? Perhaps he didn't know about them, but if he'd found out about my place, surely he'd have had it watched – but wouldn't my Gurkhas have spotted his surveillance? The same thoughts were going round and round in my head and none of them made any sense to me. I was relieved when Pratin met me at the airport.

I supposed I could have had Alan Gladwell killed the moment his feet touched Thai soil, but that was a bad idea for a lot of reasons. British tourists being murdered in foreign countries always attracted the wrong kind of headlines, and the Thai authorities would come under pressure to investigate. Besides, if I killed another Gladwell, that would just leave two more brothers behind who'd want to become Top Boy and continue the war against me in Alan's martyred name. I explained this to Pratin, but I wasn't sure he took it all in. I gave him very clear instructions as to what I wanted from him but he just nodded a lot and left me to make some calls. Christ, I thought, I really hope he handles this one right. If he fucked this up we'd all be in the shit for sure.

I couldn't tail Gladwell all around Bangkok myself, so I left that job to Pratin, and hoped he was as good as he claimed to be. I told him to call me if he found anything we could use. Perhaps we could get a photograph of Gladwell having a cosy chat with one of the 'Golden Triangle's' most notorious suppliers. That alone might be enough to severely piss off the authorities. I doubted Gladwell would be stupid enough to be seen talking to the big players in the market out here though. Thai justice is notoriously harsh on dealers, and conditions are appalling. You wouldn't want to be banged up for life in a Thai prison, and when they say life here, they mean life.

With Pratin briefed and on the case, I could get back to Hua Hin to see Sarah. Jagrit met me at the gate and put my mind at rest. No one had been watching the compound. That would have been an impossibility, he told me, and I believed him. Sarah knew nothing of the threat against her. I walked into the house and she greeted me in a dishevelled state.

'Are you alright?' I asked, trying not to find her condition amusing.

'No,' she gulped the word, like it was an effort to get it out,

'I've been chucking up all day.'

'Nice image.'

'It was Joanne's idea.'

'Thought as much,' Joanne had stayed on long after the rest of Sarah's friends had returned home.

'It was our last night together so we did flaming Sambucas. Lots of them,' and she winced at the memory.

'That'll do it every time.'

'Sorry,' her face was pale, and her hair was hanging down in a straggle that obscured one eye, 'not much of a sight to come home to, is it?'

'You look gorgeous, pet,' and I wrapped my arms around her tightly.

'Thank you for lying.'

I laughed, 'have you been caning it all the time I've been away?'

'Pretty much.'

'Good,' I told her, 'that was the idea.' I drew her closer to me and kissed her on the forehead. 'Did you have a good time?'

'It was brilliant,' she looked up at me, 'thanks for sorting it.'

I instantly put any idea I might have had of telling Sarah about Danny being shot to the back of my mind. Why bring her down from the first genuine happiness she'd experienced in months? I'd have to tell her eventually, of course, just not yet.

'Well I only did it for selfish reasons,' I told her. 'I figured I needed the brownie points.'

'Oh you did,' she assured me, 'but you earned quite a few while you were away only…'

'Only what?'

'You are going to have to wait for your reward,' she gave me an apologetic look, 'it's just, I think I'm going to throw up again.'

'Nice.'

She broke from me without a word and walked quickly away.

A moment later I heard the unmistakeable sound of retching coming from the downstairs bathroom.

I turned on the TV so I could watch the football. There wasn't anything I could do now until Pratin called.

Pratin followed Gladwell all day, keeping his distance, and he was sure he had not been seen. He had tailed Gladwell while he checked into a four-star hotel and waited for him to shower, change his clothes, then emerge again on foot. He had followed the man as he sauntered past shops and markets and watched from across the road when he ate alone in a restaurant, waiting for his contact to show up. Blake had briefed him to watch out for someone joining Gladwell, particularly anyone known to be in the drug trade. Pratin assured Blake he knew every drug baron in the capital and all of their lieutenants. If they chose to join Gladwell at his dinner table, identifying them wouldn't be a problem.

But nobody showed. Gladwell finished his meal and paid the bill. Afterwards he walked on into the seedier side of the city, but he ignored the entreaties of the prostitutes, both male and female, when they approached him. Pratin followed him for an hour, waiting for Gladwell to do what western men always did in his city when they were killing time before a business meeting; buy someone and use them. But Gladwell ignored the dance bars and night clubs. He just kept walking. Eventually, when he was far from his hotel, he sat down at a table outside a quiet bar at the end of a dead-end street. It was small and squalid – not an obvious choice for a prosperous western male. This had to be the rendezvous point. Pratin selected his position carefully, watching from a seat set back from the window of a virtually empty restaurant, a discreet distance from Gladwell's bar. He ordered a bowl of Tom Yum Goong soup and waited for Gladwell's contact to show.

Gladwell drank his beer and ordered a second bottle,

looking like a man who was waiting for someone. Pratin was running the names of local crime barons through his head, wondering which one would have the balls to sell a huge shipment of heroin to a western gangster. He had to concede there were a few. A street kid wandered up to Gladwell's table then and started to chatter away at him, begging for dollars no doubt. Pratin was annoyed by the young boy's presence. He wanted the child to leave so he could get a clear view of Gladwell's contact when he arrived.

Then, something odd happened. Gladwell sat up in his chair, leaned closer to the boy as if to speak to him and smiled warmly. It wasn't the sort of smile you normally wasted on a beggar. It was the kind of smile a man would usually save for a woman. Pratin immediately understood what that smile meant.

I opened my eyes suddenly and realised I had dozed off while the match was still on. I sat up with a start to see Sarah standing there in the doorway. Her hair was still damp from the shower and she was wearing nothing but black lingerie.

'Hello.'

I was a bit groggy, 'that the underwear I bought you?'

'Yes,' she walked over to me and took my hand. 'I know I've been neglecting you and I'm sorry. Come upstairs with me,' she said, leading the way.

Later I cooked up some fish and we ate out on the terrace so we could watch the ocean. It felt like we were a proper couple again. I'd barely given Simone a thought since I'd flown out of the UK. She seemed part of a separate life that couldn't touch us out here.

'Did you ever go to Whitby when you were a kid?' she asked me.

'Whitby? Why do you ask?'

'You cooked fish. It made me think of Whitby. Did you ever go?'

'No,' I said, 'I never really went anywhere when I was a kid.'

'Dad used to take us there, for fish and chips. I mean it wasn't exactly just down the road but he'd say, "who wants fish and chips for tea?" and when I'd say "me!" he'd get the Jag out and we'd drive to Whitby. I'd say to him "Dad it's a very long way, don't they sell fish and chips round here?" and he'd say, "not like these, pet. Whitby cod and chips are the best in the world and do you know when they taste their very best? When you pinch them off someone else's plate, give us a chip!"' She was smiling now. I hadn't seen her do that much lately, but it gave me some mixed feelings, if I'm honest.

A lot of Sarah's conversations sounded the same and they usually started with the words 'Dad used to'. It was a nail through my heart every time she said it, since I was the one who killed him. It made me feel sick inside that she missed him so much. The fact that she didn't know it was me was the only saving grace out of a whole shitty situation.

'You don't talk much,' she told me, 'about the old days, when you were a kid, I mean.'

'Not much to talk about, really,' I told her. I didn't add that I tried not to think about my childhood because it wasn't that nice. 'We got by. My mam did her best, you know.'

'What was your dad like?' she asked me.

'Never knew him. He left, apparently, just before I was born, so if I had to make a guess, I'd say he was a wrong-un, wouldn't you? It was no big deal,' I told her, 'you don't miss what you never had, right?' There was a time when I did think about my dad, a lot, but I was little then and didn't know any better. I used to hope he'd run off and joined the army or he'd become a spy. One of my early memories was seeing that footage of the Iranian Embassy siege, those TV pictures of the SAS before they abseiled into the place and fucked up all of those terrorists, and I used to dream that one of them was my dad and, now that he'd rescued those hostages, they'd let him come home to me. Then he'd walk down the street in a shiny uniform with medals on it and he'd be carrying a new football for me. I get embarrassed thinking about it now. Soft lad.

'It must have been hard for your mum.'

'Yeah, it was, but she managed. Mums do, don't they? They just get on with it.'

She looked away then and I wondered if I'd been insensitive somehow. Had I reminded her about her own mother, who died years back and left her alone with the father she became so close to, before I ruined everything?

She forced a smile then. 'I've just thought, we are the same, you and me, we're both orphans.'

She was probably right there, but who knew? My dad walked out on me more than thirty years ago – he could conceivably still be alive, somewhere, but was probably dead. I didn't care either way.

'No,' I said, 'orphans are kids, and we are grown-ups. We can take care of each other.' I sat down next to her and put my arm around her. She snuggled up close to me and rested her head against my chest. She took a bit of taking care of, did Sarah, but it wasn't her fault. I knew that. I'm not entirely insensitive and I made myself a promise there and then that I would do whatever it took to keep Sarah safe from Alan Gladwell, or anyone else who tried to harm her. In fact there was nothing I wasn't prepared to do for her. No matter how bad.

Ten minutes later, Pratin called.

38

Pratin watched from his car as the boy led the man towards the small dilapidated hotel. Gladwell was trying to look inconspicuous, walking slowly behind the boy with his hands in his pockets, like any tourist taking in the sights.

As soon as he had seen that smile from Gladwell, Pratin had changed his plans. The foreigner wasn't stupid nor was he about to get up from his table in front of everyone and follow the child. He simply spoke to the boy and carefully palmed him a little money as a down-payment, but not so discreetly that Pratin didn't spot it, then he left and headed back to his hotel. Instead of tailing Gladwell, Pratin now followed the boy, caught up with him and paid generously for the information he needed. That was how Pratin knew the name of the hotel, the time they'd agreed, even the room number. He watched carefully as the boy opened the main door of the hotel and he gave them a few more minutes. He estimated how long it would take the boy to procure the key. Not long, since he'd done it many times before and the guy behind the counter was used to seeing him there. Gladwell would have to pay, of course. He'd be paying three times over; once for the room, once for the silence and complicity of the man behind the reception desk and once for the boy.

Pratin waited a little longer, checking his watch. He didn't really want to think about what was going on in that squalid room with the child, but he had to time this just right because he wanted to ensure Gladwell was entirely preoccupied.

When he felt enough time had elapsed, Pratin climbed out of his car, buttoning his jacket, making sure there were no tell-tale gaps through which the gun could be seen. Not that there was anyone else out here, as far as he could see. The place was almost deserted. He had only seen one other westerner enter the building since he'd pulled up outside its doors over an hour ago. In any case, Pratin was willing to bet that anyone using this hotel would be very unlikely to come forward as a witness.

Pratin walked around the building until he reached the rear. He stepped out from behind a cluster of trees with long golden leaves in full bloom that would hide his presence until the very last moment. It helped that it was dark with no moon and the street lamps were dim. He approached the designated window and drew his gun, inching slowly towards the window until he was standing right by it. The blind was tilted at an upward slant. He'd arranged that with the boy when he handed over the money. It meant that Pratin could not be seen from inside the room, but he had an uninterrupted view of it. Pratin recoiled in disgust at the scene on the bed and instinctively pointed the gun towards Alan Gladwell. It was so tempting just to squeeze the trigger now and end this, but Pratin forced himself not to. He had a job to do. He was being paid to do that job. He had to do it correctly or he would be in a whole world of trouble.

Slowly and carefully Pratin put his police-issue revolver back into his shoulder holster, then he reached into the little black bag he was carrying and drew out the tiny digital camera.

Alan Gladwell steered the car beyond an ancient bus, then accelerated past a VW Beetle that had seen better days. At this rate he was going to be really early for his flight, but that was no bad thing. He'd be home without anyone ever being any the wiser. It was always a risk flying out here, but no one in his crew, or his family, suspected a thing. This was just something that he needed – that they didn't have to concern themselves with. Nobody in Britain would understand it, which is why he had to come all this way. Thank God for Bangkok though, thought Gladwell. If it didn't exist you'd have to invent it. He was already wondering how long it would be before he could come out here again, when he noticed the car pull out in front of him. It was a Honda, with an instantly recognisable yellow and burgundy livery, and the words 'Highway Police' stencilled on it in blue lettering on a yellow background. Gladwell instinctively slowed, even though he had been keeping within the speed limit. The car slowed too, then pulled into the slow lane, allowing him to pass, which he did gingerly, not wishing to give them anything to be concerned about. As Alan Gladwell drove by he glanced to one side and noticed the uniformed officer in the passenger seat eyeing him intently.

No need to get paranoid, thought Gladwell, I've nothing to hide. He edged cautiously past and was on his way again when the police car pulled out once more and followed. Seconds later they were tailgating him and Alan Gladwell was frowning at the rear-view mirror, wondering at their sudden interest in him. He didn't have time to wonder for long. The red lights on the car's roof came on and started to spin wildly as the policeman in the passenger seat beckoned for him to pull over by the side of the road. Gladwell cursed and did as he was told.

Once Gladwell's car was stationary, the Highway Police car

overtook him and parked in front of his vehicle. The two officers climbed out and walked towards Gladwell's car. He wound down the window and asked, 'Is something the matter?'

They looked at him blankly, their eyes obscured by pairs of Ray-Bans. The younger of the two men was wearing a long, brown leather, presumably police-issue coat, even though Gladwell was overheating in just a T-shirt.

'Get out of the car please, sir,' the driver asked him in flawless English. He complied.

'Step this way, sir,' the passenger of the car gestured for him to accompany them.

Gladwell followed them uneasily. He figured he was about to become the victim of a shakedown, a suspicion that was confirmed when the passenger said, 'You drive too fast.'

'No,' answered Gladwell firmly.

'Yes,' contradicted the driver more forcefully, and they both took off their Ray-Bans.

'Look I have a plane to catch and….'

'You no catch plane today,' the passenger spoke again.

'Like I said, I have a plane to catch,' he sighed, 'is it possible to sort this out by paying a fine? I heard that was possible, when there has been a misunderstanding, to pay a fine I mean?'

The eyes of the police officers took on a sly look and the older man, the driver, turned to his partner and jerked his head to one side in a dismissive gesture. The younger man walked away. Gladwell followed the driver towards the Highway Police car. The rear door was opened and the driver gestured for Gladwell to sit inside. Gladwell climbed into the back seat of the patrol car and the driver went round to the other side, opened the door, and sat next to him.

No one spoke for a moment. In the end Gladwell felt compelled to break the silence. 'How much?' he asked, 'to clear up this problem?'

The driver looked at him sternly.

'I mean the fine,' Gladwell assured him, 'how much is the government going to fine me for going too fast?'

'Thirty thousand baht.'

'Fuck off,' replied Gladwell, without thinking, 'that's...' and he thought for a moment, converting their ludicrous currency in his head, '...over six hundred quid. That's fucking robbery.'

'Twenty-five thousand baht,' the driver amended his demand; all pretence that it was really a fine seemed to have disappeared now.

'Fifteen,' offered Gladwell, 'I'll give you fifteen thousand baht and that's all you're getting.'

Again there was a long silence. Christ, thought Gladwell, I don't need the grief. I just want to be on my way and off home. 'Jesus,' he hissed at the officer, 'this is fucking bandit country. Alright, okay, twenty-fucking-thousand, but that's it.' He reached for his money belt, pulled out a wad of currency and started to count it out in front of the officer, 'but I want a police escort all the way to the airport.'

The Thai policeman frowned at this at first and Gladwell wondered if he had overstepped the mark. God knows what he would do if the deal was off. Then, suddenly, the policeman roared with laughter, 'for twenty thousand baht we drive you to the airport!' He laughed deeper then, 'for twenty thousand baht we drive you anywhere!' and he carried on laughing.

Despite the delay on the highway, there was still no queue at the check-in desk. Gladwell dragged his suitcase along on its wheels until he halted in front of a young Thai girl who checked his ticket and passport, then asked him the usual routine questions about whether this was his bag, and if he had packed it himself.

She nodded in acknowledgement as he answered and he was about to hoist his case onto the conveyor belt when he became aware of a presence behind him. Gladwell turned to find four uniformed men blocking his path.

'What?' he asked them.

'Please come with us sir.'

'Eh? Why? I haven't done anything.' Gladwell felt a slight panic when he said this because he knew that what he had been doing was enough to get him a very long jail sentence – but they weren't to know about any of that, so he regained his composure long enough to ask, 'What's the matter?'

One of the customs men smiled at him politely and used a palm to indicate the direction he wished Gladwell to proceed. Gladwell glanced up at the departure time that was written on the board, then he looked at his watch. He still had ages before his flight. Long enough surely to clear up whatever 'misunderstanding' this lot might have concocted for him. He looked at the four expectant faces around him, 'Christ,' he thought, 'they'll all want paying,' and with a sharp intake of breath he followed their lead to a back office.

Once inside the office, Gladwell was asked to place his case on a table. He had no particular qualms about doing so. He wasn't daft enough to try to smuggle anything in or out of a country as hard core as Thailand. This was a nation that would imprison you for being mildly disrespectful to its royal family. Gladwell knew they didn't fuck about here.

He watched as one of the men began to slowly unzip the case, becoming aware that the room seemed to be gradually filling up with other people. As well as the four men who had approached him at the check-in desk, there was now a slow procession of officials and policemen filing into the room. Gladwell started to feel a little uneasy, not least because he didn't have any cash right now to pay this lot off in hard currency.

The man behind the table finished unzipping the case and turned it upside down. Out fell the contents, under the watchful gaze of what now amounted to more than a dozen people. Gladwell became more worried when he noticed the large bulky, brown envelope, an item that he had never seen before, in amongst his shirts and underwear. Suddenly he revisited the image of the police officer in the long brown leather coat with its deep pockets, standing by his unguarded car while Gladwell was bribing his colleague. Instantly he knew he'd been set up. Gladwell opened his mouth to protest but, just as he did so, the customs man tore open the envelope and allowed the contents to spill out onto the table in front of everyone. A dozen colour photographs confronted him. To Gladwell's horror, there for all in the room to see, was graphic and uncensored photographic evidence of his time with the young boy. He felt his face burn with shame and had to fight hard to quell the nausea as he suddenly realised the level of trouble he was in.

'That's not me,' he protested as he took in the looks of disgust from the officers who closed in on him, but it *was* him and everyone in the room knew it, thanks to the quality of the photographs, which were better than any human witness. Hands were on him now, pinning his arms behind his back. He didn't even struggle because he knew it was hopeless. How could this be possible? And just when the earliest realisation began to dawn on Alan Gladwell that David Blake might somehow have had a hand in it, a second package fell from the case onto the table. This one had been taped to the inside of the case. It was a black plastic parcel that looked like a folded-up bin liner and, when the customs officer tore that outer layer open, beneath it was a second covering made of brown wax paper. The officer reached into his pocket for a penknife, extended the blade and slid it into the wax paper. The parcel burst open and out poured thousands of granules of pure white powder in one steady stream. There had to be a kilo in there and Gladwell would have bet what was left of his worthless life that it was the purest heroin.

Gladwell knew for certain that he'd been set up. Only David Blake was capable of engineering something like this. It had to be him. The hands gripped tighter around Gladwell, pinning him down until his face was pressed against the table, his arms were dragged behind his back and there was a click as the handcuffs tightened around his wrists. There would be no escape now, and all because of Blake. Gladwell had been so certain that he had set in place the sequence of events that would ensure he'd outlive Blake; it wasn't supposed to end like this.

He tried to fight them, but the customs officers hauled him upwards and dragged him towards the door. There were too many of them and he couldn't fight back with his hands cuffed behind his back. Gladwell's legs must have given way then because strong hands grabbed him and held him upright. He was led from the room screaming that it was a set-up and the drugs weren't his, demanding to be let go. But Alan Gladwell already knew his situation was hopeless.

39

With Alan Gladwell safely under arrest in Bangkok I could return to Newcastle to conclude my business. The golf club was the best in the north east and the fees reflected its status. It took two minutes just to drive down the road to reach the club house and the greens on either side were all busy. I parked up close to the main door, in an area that wasn't supposed to be used for parking, but I wasn't planning on staying long.

Inside, the bar had oak panelling on its walls and pictures of hunting scenes hung in frames. There was a large plaque that had the names of all of the club's previous captains on it, next to the year in which they presided, and a display case full of ancient silver trophies. Men in blazers were standing in little groups, drinking scotch or gin and tonic before lunch, and the barman who served them wore a bow tie. It was the obvious place to find the north-east's most famous socialist and he was there, just like the old dear at his constituency office had assured me he would be, once I'd convinced her I had an urgent message for Ron Haydon.

My local MP was ordering drinks at the bar for his golfing mates while they were standing off to one side, laughing at what would be described in these parts as an off-colour-joke.

I walked right up to Haydon and showed him the manila file.

'What's this?' he asked gruffly.

'Some papers.'

'Got a file on me, have you?' he was squaring up to me again, puffing his chest out and drawing his fists to his side like he was preparing to knock me down.

'I'm just here to give you a preview of a story that will break later in the week. All of the red tops will run with it on their front pages. That's what you want isn't it, you politicians, to be on the front pages? Not this time though.'

'What are you banging on about?'

I handed him the file and he snorted, pretending not to care about its contents, but that didn't stop him from opening and reading it. After the first page, the colour drained from his face and he started to leaf quickly through the supporting documents I'd thoughtfully provided. He examined them one after the other. When he finally glanced back up at me, he was already a beaten man.

'Where did you…' then he stopped. I knew he would be wondering how I could have seen these damning documents. Me? Just a small-time gangster from Newcastle, accessing confidential papers from a giant US conglomerate; all courtesy of Amrein, of course, and some of his tame journalists. They might have been on Amrein's pay-role but they were bloody good at their jobs. What they'd unearthed was gold dust. Credit where credit was due, Amrein had finally come up trumps.

I'd just handed Ron Haydon the transcript of a story no newspaper could afford to turn down. It was a tale of corruption, and the headline was 'Former Government

Minister took massive bribe to change Iraq war vote.'

I nodded at the headline on the transcript he was holding, 'Of course the red tops will be more creative than that. I wonder what they'll come up with. Frankly, I'm disappointed. You're supposed to be one of the good guys, the principled man-of-the-people who stands up for the working classes. Who'd have thought that Red Ronnie would have taken vast sums of money from a US company so right-wing even the Yanks are uneasy about them? You know they are being investigated by the CIA, the FBI and the NSA all at the same time? They've been out in Iraq for years with their own private army, shooting any bugger who steps within a hundred yards of their convoys. They've killed more civilians than the US Air Force and you took their money.'

'It's lies,' but his voice was cracking so I knew the only lie here was his.

'You know, it's strange. When you changed your vote to support the war, after months of telling everyone who'd listen how illegal it was, we were all disgusted. I mean everyone up here was ashamed of you, but it was the oldest story in politics; politician sacrifices principles for political gain and self-interest. We figured you'd been got at by the Prime Minister. Now it turns out you were bought off with a bribe from a US construction company.'

'It's a mistake,' he told me, 'if anyone prints a word of this, I'll sue.'

'Then you'll end up bankrupt, because they are all going to print it, and you will lose.' I assured him. 'The trouble with taking kickbacks from American companies is that they are too damned bureaucratic. They even keep records of transactions they don't want anyone to know about. Your bribe was buried deep in the company accounts, but it was there. I mean they explained the payments to you as a consultancy or commission, they don't actually use the word "bribe", but that isn't going to fool anyone. You won't be able to provide an explanation for the work you supposedly did and you didn't put any of it in the Register of Members' Interests. It's not as if anybody could forget sums this large, and they are all going to want to know why the money went into off-shore accounts.'

'Alright,' he held up a hand to stop me, 'let's just say…' and he licked his lips nervously, 'let's say that I might struggle to prove that all of this is a lie, before the damage to my reputation is done. I mean people still believe what they read in the paper, even now, for Christ's sake,' and he rolled his eyes at the absurdity of it all, 'so let's say then that it would be in everyone's best interests if this story was buried.'

'Your interests, you mean?'

'Everyone's, bonny lad,' he forced himself to laugh, even though he was terrified. Ever the politician, he even slapped a friendly hand onto my shoulder. 'Yours too,' he assured me.

'Alright,' I said, 'what have you got in mind?'

He gave me his hundred-watt smile, 'well, a new hobby for me, for starters,' he laughed again, 'you know, fly fishing or golf.' I said nothing, letting him offer up more, 'I'll resign from the Police Authority; ill health, more time with the family, the usual shite.'

I frowned, 'Is that all?'

'I could be a good friend to you. I know stuff and I know people, important people. I'm well connected.'

'Important friends?'

'Important friends,' he agreed and he had a hopeful look on his face like he was connecting with me.

'But you wouldn't want to introduce them to me. I'm a gangster, remember? A gangster in *your* city.'

'Hey look, I got a bit carried away that night. I'd had a drink and I'd been doing my man-of-the-people act, so I gave you a speech to put the wind up you a bit, but I never meant any of it, not really. Look, I'm a realist, there's no bigger realist than me in this city, son. I know it's always gone on and always will do, long after you and me are both pushing up the daisies.'

'So we can be friends then?'

'That's what I'm saying, man,' he told me, throwing his arms wide and beaming at me like I was the prospective son-in-law he'd always secretly hoped for.

I stayed silent for a long while. He watched me expectantly, heart probably thumping somewhere near his tonsils.

'No,' I told him finally.

'Listen son,' he was pleading now, 'listen to me. I've got a wife and kids, Christ I've got grand kids, don't do this to me, don't do it to them. Please son, I'm begging you.'

It was my turn to put a hand on his shoulder. 'Fuck you Ron,' I told him, 'you're going to prison.' I left him standing there in the bar. As I walked out there was another burst of laughter from his friends at the golf club. Someone must have told another off-colour joke, but Ron wasn't laughing.

40

If Ray Fallon had worn a cap it would have been in his hands. For a gangland enforcer he looked pretty humble.

'What the fuck do you want?' demanded Kinane. He got to his feet and took a step towards the man who had appeared at the hotel without warning. I was next to Kinane and I raised my hand to prevent him from kicking off in the cocktail bar. Kinane stopped, and gave me a sour look, but I wasn't about to let him start tearing the room up in front of me. Besides, the demeanour of the man put me at ease. He looked calm, humble even. What he didn't look like was a man who had travelled all the way down here to start something.

'I'm wanting a word,' explained Fallon quietly, 'if that's alright with you?' He directed the question at me, and I nodded. Fallon was alone, which was dangerous for him, but not as dangerous as coming to see me when witnesses could report our conversation back to Malcolm and Andrew Gladwell.

They'd have cut him to pieces if they'd known he was talking to me.

'Leave him be, Joe,' I commanded, 'we're just talking here,' I motioned Fallon over to a quiet corner of the bar which had no windows, safer for him and for us. We sat down and I offered him a drink.

'You've got some fucking nerve coming here,' Kinane told him, 'after the stuff you said.'

'Maybe so,' admitted Fallon, 'but that was just bluster. He knows that,' he nodded at me, 'and so should you. It comes with the turf.'

Kinane grunted as if he couldn't really argue the point. Fallon was right. He and Kinane were like boxers during the pre-fight weigh-in, always sizing each other up and putting each other down, looking for an advantage.

'So Fallon, why are you here?' I asked.

'Well,' he looked a little uncomfortable, like he didn't really know how to explain it. 'It turns out I've had my money on the wrong horse.'

'You can say that again,' Kinane told him, but I knew they were talking about two different things. Kinane meant we would have won no matter what, and I admired his confidence. Fallon was talking about the character of the man he used to work for.

'I assume it's fair to say you had no idea?' I asked him gently and he flared.

'Christ, no,' he glared angrily at me. Then, abruptly, the anger evaporated, to be replaced by something like incomprehension, 'do you think we realised we were working for…for a nonce. I mean the man was married with three bairns for fuck's sake,' he shook his head, '… it just shows you can never really know anyone deep down. It turns out he'd been flying over there for years, raping little boys, then coming home again to the missus and his daughters. They never had an inkling. Arthur must be spinning in his grave. I mean,' and he shook his head again, 'old Arthur couldn't even tolerate a bender, let alone a kiddie fiddler.'

'I can understand your disgust,' I told him, 'but I'm not sure how it involves me.'

Fallon's eyes narrowed and he looked directly at me. This was his big moment. He wouldn't have put it like that, but Ray Fallon was about to cross the Rubicon. I knew it as soon as I watched him walk through the foyer of the hotel.

I figured I'd better encourage him, 'what have you got in mind?'

'I'm a loyal man,' he began and I knew we were in for a speech, a little bit of self-justification before the knife went in. 'I worked for Arthur Gladwell for years and I always knew where I stood with him. If he asked for someone to be sorted, I sorted 'em, square-go. If you stepped out of line with Arthur you'd get filleted and you usually had it coming.' I nodded like I understood and I supposed I did. 'People said he was a grass,' and he frowned like the very notion was an affront, 'but I never heard anything'. I nodded again. Arthur Gladwell had been a grass for thirty years. It was how he made his way up the food chain, by shopping his competitors to bent coppers in return for them turning a blind eye while he raped Glasgow for three decades but I kept silent. Fallon had been disillusioned enough for one lifetime.

'Tommy was meant to take over when Arthur died, but we all know what happened there,' he said nothing further on the matter. I nodded again and let him continue, 'Alan looked like a different matter. He was a chip off the old bloke, or so we thought,' his eyes told me how conflicted he was about Alan. 'What you said about the Sandyhills Sniper made me think. I didn't want to believe it at first. When you are working for a man you don't want to see the bad in him but now, I reckon you had him just about tagged. I reckon he paid someone to kill all those people, just so he could get at that copper.'

'I know he did,' I assured him. Fallon was like a man who has finally woken up one morning and realised his missus has been shagging all of his mates. Previously he had refused to acknowledge anything but good in Alan Gladwell, now though, he was looking back on every incident and noticing only the bad.

'Aye,' he said, 'and now he won't be coming back. Me and my lads, well, we're all feeling like proper numpties.'

'I'll bet.'

'I mean just because Arthur was capable of running a city doesn't necessarily mean his boys are up to it. Tommy wasn't, Alan we know about, and the other two...' he folded his arms, 'well, I just can't see it somehow,' and he gave me a meaningful look. What interested me most was the way he had said 'me and my lads'. He was speaking for the others, with authority.

'Someone more experienced, perhaps?' I offered, 'someone who has been Arthur Gladwell's right-hand man for fifteen years and knows how the city works?'

He snorted, 'you don't mess about do you? Trouble is, you need money,' he continued, 'for a takeover, and Arthur was tighter than a Gnat's arsehole, God rest him. It's all tied up so that only his boys can reach it. I mean we'll get most of it... Eventually...' Just then I wouldn't have wanted to be the Gladwell brothers. They'd be given two choices, tell us how to get Arthur's money and die quick – or die slow and tell us anyway, when you can't take any more.

'I'm sure you will need funds to tide you over,' I said, anticipating his question. 'There must be a large number of people on the payroll, suppliers who have to be paid?'

'Yeah,' he told me, 'people who don't like to wait for their money.'

'Let's call it a bridging loan,' I told him, 'or we could avoid calling it a loan at all.'

He smiled slightly. We both knew that was why he was here, 'a partnership?'

'A sleeping partner,' I assured him, 'I've enough on my plate down here.'

'It isn't just the money,' he explained, 'I can handle the boys, they can look after the streets, it's that Amrein,' he was frowning again like he didn't really understand our mutual fixer, 'I need someone to explain it all to him. I don't want the Euro mafia trying to take control of my city.'

'Leave it to me,' I assured him, 'you won't have any problems from Amrein.'

Palmer and Kinane stayed silent while we went on to talk terms. There was a loose discussion about the level of funding I was prepared to provide, and the return I would expect on my investment. Fallon knew he was out on a limb, so I could get good terms, but not so brutal that he didn't stand to gain a lot from this. It's only ever a deal if both sides are happy. I didn't want Fallon resenting me more and more over time and then finally coming after me years later when he eventually decided I'd shafted him.

In the end he just said, 'Right enough', nodded, and got to his feet. Then he shook my hand.

'I've got to get back. Stuff to attend to.'

'You'll need to see the Gladwell brothers.'

'I'll have a word,' he assured me.

I knew then that the Gladwells were finished.

'That was some deal you got us there,' said Kinane when Fallon had gone, 'when this goes through we'll be untouchable.' From the look on his face, I could see he couldn't believe that our problems had instantly come to an end, all because of a quick chat in a hotel bar on the Quayside. I was happy about that. I knew there had been times lately when Kinane had privately and publicly questioned my judgement. I needed a coup like this to get Palmer, Kinane and everyone else I employed remembering I could do deals none of them were capable of. They were all as hard as nails, but not one of them could handle Amrein or negotiate an agreement like this one with a Glasgow firm.

Palmer drove me back to my apartment. 'I'll have a word,' he said, when we were in the car.

'What?'

'That's what Fallon said when you told him he'd need to see the Gladwell brothers.'

'So?'

'It's what you say,' he reminded me, 'just before something bad happens to someone. I'll have a word,' he repeated.

'Coincidence,' I said.

'And it was all tied up real quick, wasn't it – your deal with Fallon? Smooth as you like.'

'Meaning what?'

'You knew he was coming down tonight, didn't you?'

'Perhaps.'

'That's why we got such a good deal. You'd worked it all out beforehand?'

'Most of it,' I admitted, 'but I needed him to come here, to make sure he was serious about it. What else is a man like Ray Fallon going to do with himself? With a whole city of enemies just waiting for retribution, he won't last long if he's not protected by a large firm.'

'Is that why you invited him down here?'

'What makes you think I instigated it?'

'He wouldn't have the nerve to chance his arm like that, not after all the things he has said,' Palmer told me, 'not without clearing it with you first.'

'Let's just say I sent up a flare so he could see it. I put myself in his shoes and I didn't think he had many options. The

Gladwells are history, with or without our intervention, but with them gone we'd have the same old problem. Someone new running Glasgow and Edinburgh, right on our doorstep.'

'Better the devil you know,' he said, 'but can you trust Fallon?'

'No,' I admitted, 'we can't trust anyone, ever, which is why I employ you.'

'So why the cloak and dagger?' he asked me, 'why not just tell us he was coming?'

'Kinane.'

'You think he would have blocked it?'

'Blocked it?' I asked him, 'since when does he get to block a decision I make? No, I just didn't want to listen to him moaning about it all year.'

Three days later, Ray Fallon drove his car into the underground car park of the same hotel and left it there. He made sure the boot was unlocked. He knew that when he returned later there would be two large holdalls in there containing his start-up cash. All he had to do was assure me the situation in Glasgow was back under control. It didn't take long.

'The brothers are gone,' he explained simply. He didn't need to elaborate further. I wondered if the Gladwell brothers had retained the sense to tell him what he needed to know about the money they'd spirited away. I doubted it though. They wouldn't have believed their eyes when their father's old crew turned against them. Whatever their answer, it would take him months to free up all the cash. Much of it would have been lost to him forever without the relevant passwords, documents, signatures and passports needed to drain the accounts. That suited me fine. It meant he needed me.

'Good,' I told him, 'then we can make a new start. Glasgow is well rid of the Gladwell boys. Here's to a new era.' We clinked our glasses together and sipped our whisky. We were drinking in the cocktail bar again but this time the place was half full. We had to be discreet so we spoke softly. I had not bothered to bring Kinane with me this time but I did have Palmer at my side. I wasn't going to sit down with a man like Ray Fallon on my own.

'Cheers,' he told me and he looked relaxed.

'The money will be in your car by the time you've finished your drink. There'll be more when you need it. I'll take care of your first three payments to Amrein so you'll have enough working capital to get by,' I meant he could pay his suppliers, dealers and muscle without any of them kicking up a fuss.

'Thanks,' he said simply.

'There is one last thing, before you go.'

'Aye, I thought as much.'

'I want his name,' I told Fallon.

Fallon was obviously expecting this and he came right out with it. Palmer and I heard the name of the man who had been betraying us to Alan Gladwell in silence.

Fallon drained his drink and said, 'I'll be away then,' leaving us to digest the information he had given us. We looked at each other but didn't bother to say anything. I knew Palmer would be feeling as sick as I was. Even after everything we had been through, I was still shocked rigid by it; of all the people.

Eventually a waiter walked by and Palmer nodded at him to gain his attention and summon the bill. 'What's the damage?' he asked.

I've read a lot about the Cold War over the years. Spies and traitors always fascinated me. When I was young I thought agents were like James Bond, tough guys who could always beat the villains. Then, when I got older, I realised they were usually squalid little men who took big risks to give secrets away to the other side, sometimes for money, sometimes for women and sometimes for the so-called glory of their cause.

Often these guys would end up dead or serving long prison sentences, but sometimes they would get away with it and live to a ripe old age. It seemed to be almost entirely down to luck. Often they only got caught because a defector came over from the other side and brought their names with them. It wouldn't matter how clever or resourceful you thought you were, if the man who was handling you defected to the other side you were finished.

Ray Fallon had done just that. He was with us now and the price of our friendship was the name of the man who had been handing the Gladwells all their information on us, including Hunter's address, the location of my town house and the bar where Danny did his regular pick-up the night he was shot. I couldn't allow that to go unpunished. He'd have to be dealt with and people would have to know why. We couldn't let this happen again. I gave the order that night.

41

Toddy could at least be philosophical about one thing. There were some perks that came from being a member of Bobby Mahoney's firm. No one messed with you for starters. The freaks, the queens and the nut jobs all left you alone. Men who would normally have been keen to extort money or cigarettes, to bully and assault you, steered clear of you and picked on other, weaker men.

There were also small privileges that Toddy enjoyed. They might be scant consolation right now but, as the memory of his freedom began to recede over time, he knew they would take on an increased significance. Perhaps the best perk was some time alone in the shower. Everyone else had to queue up in line to use it. Then they shuffled forwards in groups, were given a few minutes to wash themselves, which was a nervous time for all concerned; the last thing you wanted to be in a prison was naked. Then they shuffled out and had to wait days to use the facilities again. But it had been fixed for Toddy to go in before all of the other men. The prison guard, Hinds, had been paid to fetch him from the recreation area early, then escort him to the shower and leave him there while he took his time. Toddy would often stay under the water for twenty minutes or more, until Hinds got nervy, and told him he had to come out because the others were on their way.

Toddy took full advantage of his perks. He was serving a long stretch because he had kept his mouth shut. The least David Blake could do was provide the basics; money to his girlfriend, groceries to his mum and her bills paid, some money for Toddy to get the stuff you needed when you were on the inside; books, cigarettes and of course the drugs, which were necessary to numb the boredom. It wasn't much though, not compared to everything Toddy had lost and the resentment burned in him. He tried not to think of the life he should be leading on the outside. He especially tried not to worry about Kathy and who she was with right now. How long would it take her to give him up as a bad lot?

This was all David Blake's fault. Toddy blamed the man for all of the time he had spent on remand and every day he would have to do between now and the completion of his sentence. Toddy was just a foot soldier and the time he was doing should have been Blake's, which is why Toddy felt no guilt over what he had done. One day he would finally be free of this place and, if he was ever going to be able to pick up his life again, which included persuading Kathy to take up with him once more, he was going to need money; a lot of money. Of course the deal he had struck with Alan Gladwell had not been without risk, but he didn't think Blake would ever suspect. He had played fair right through the court case, not that he had any choice but to keep schtum and take the full rap. Blake would have given him a lot of credit for that but, once Toddy was tucked away inside Durham jail, he would be out of sight, out of mind.

One of Gladwell's guys had approached him while he was on remand and done the deal right there and then. Toddy wasn't an idiot. He had been caught with kilos of H and knew he would be made an example of. The money the Gladwells offered him would be the right level of compensation for losing so many years of his life. They promised him protection too, and a bonus once they effectively seized control of Newcastle. All he had to do was talk to them about Blake's business; his safe houses, routines and the main men in his organisation, guys like Palmer, Kinane, Hunter and Danny and what they did for Blake. If any of this led to the death of David Blake, well that was the price that would just have to be paid if Toddy was going to win back his life. He no longer cared what happened to his former associates, or the city he'd lived in. Toddy was pretty sure they had all forgotten him by now and Blake was probably already trying to get Kathy into his bed.

So Toddy spilled it all. He laid out everything on Blake's organisation, up to, and including, minor players who held grudges against the Top Boy, like Billy Warren and Peter Dean. He told Gladwell's firm what they wanted to hear, which was everything.

Toddy heard a noise behind him but it was nothing to be alarmed about. It was just the sound of the gate swinging shut at the other end of the corridor. The rest of the guys must have been on their way to the showers already. Toddy reasoned he'd better finish off and dry himself. Everyone knew he got special privileges because he was one of Blake's men but he didn't want to rub their noses in it. Better to be out of the shower by the time they were lining up.

Toddy grabbed the rough towel and gave himself a quick dry then hastily wrapped it round his waist and left the shower. He had been right, the guys were lining up. There were a couple of familiar faces; Don Watts, who was doing a life stretch for accidentally killing someone he beat up during an armed robbery, Harry Harris who was employed as muscle by a London-based firm, with a side line in torturing people, and finally, Henderson, a complete headcase, doing life with little prospect of parole, for a series of gangland killings all over the north of England. These guys would have intimidated most men, but Toddy always held his head up high when he walked by them because he was protected.

Strange that there were only three of them though? Come to think of it, where was Hinds? He was usually at the rear of the queue, ensuring the blokes kept moving, but today he was nowhere to be seen. Seeing him, Watts turned and walked back the way he had come. At the exact moment that Toddy started to realise something was wrong, Harris stepped out in front of him, blocking his path with his huge presence. Toddy opened his mouth to say something and that was when Henderson stepped out and grabbed him from behind, slamming both of Toddy's arms together and pinning them behind his back. Toddy tried to struggle free, but he couldn't budge. He was terrified, his first thought that they were trying to rape him. Had they forgotten he was a protected guy? The fact that vicious retribution would fall on them all afterwards would be little consolation to Toddy if he ended up gang-raped by them. He struggled to break free again but Henderson merely tightened his grip.

'What the fuck are you doing?' he demanded.

It was then that Harris looked him calmly in the eye. 'He knows you betrayed him,' he said simply. Harris was careful not to mention Blake's name but Toddy didn't need to hear it to understand. Before Toddy could utter a word in his defence, Harris brought his hand out from behind his back. In it was a shank, a toothbrush sharpened into a vicious point until it could cut through flesh easily. Toddy pushed back with all of his might, fighting against Henderson's grip. It worked, and

Henderson was propelled back a few feet, but he grunted and pushed hard against Toddy, holding him now in a grip he couldn't escape from, no matter how he struggled. Harris advanced towards him, the sharpened shank at his side.

Toddy struggled desperately but the more he fought, the tighter Henderson's grip became.

'No,' he managed, but Harris was on him now and his hand shot forward in a blur. Toddy felt the thump of the man's fist as it collided with his guts, then the pain of the shank as it went deep inside him. He managed a terrified scream, quickly silenced by the second blow, which went into his side, piercing his kidney. Henderson held him up while four more blows were struck, the razor-sharp point of the hard plastic shank piercing Toddy's skin again and again, travelling deep into his stomach, chest and finally his heart. Toddy's head shot back then and his body went limp. Henderson released him and he slumped to the floor.

When it was over, Watts walked back from his look-out position. The three men surveyed Toddy's corpse, then calmly walked into the showers to wash the blood from their own bodies. There was no need to advertise their crimes. Why make it easy for the prison authorities to investigate? Still, none of the men were unduly concerned. You can only do life once.

Each one of them had been well rewarded, with money sent to family members and prison privileges promised in return for a minute's work. After their shower, they passed Toddy's body on the way out, careful to step over the little rivers of fresh blood that rolled from it and slid down into the gutter.

42

'What do you want doing about Toddy's other half?' asked Kinane. He was sitting opposite my desk in the Cauldron.

'Nothing,' I told him, 'let the prison authorities explain to her that Toddy was killed in a fight with another inmate.'

At first Toddy's girlfriend would be devastated. Kathy would demand an enquiry into his death, she'd want answers, but she wouldn't get them. Nobody would ever be able to prove anything and we'd chosen the men carefully for their silence. In time she'd get over Toddy, meet someone else and start a new life. 'Give her a settlement,' I instructed Kinane, 'a lump sum, see the accountant. I don't want her on the pay roll.' He nodded like he understood. Nobody wanted her hanging around like Marley's ghost, reminding us about Toddy.

'And his mum' he asked, 'take her off the pay roll?' Kinane expected me to cut Toddy's mother loose as a punishment for her lad's treachery. After all, if it had been down to Toddy, I'd be a dead man now. 'Tell everyone that's what we've done,' I said, 'don't want anyone thinking we're a soft touch. They have to know the consequences.'

'Right,' he looked a bit uneasy.

'The woman has just lost her only son,' I explained, 'she's getting on and she'll be in bits. Do we really want her evicted too? I don't think she'll live forever, do you?'

'You're all heart,' he said dryly, which was his way of telling me he thought I was out of my mind.

It was almost over. I still had the problem of Braddock to contend with, and the Turk's shipment still hadn't arrived, but at least neither man was behind the hits against my crew. That was down to the Gladwells and they were finished. Everything else was just detail and I could handle that.

I was tired though; the kind of tiredness that comes from living off your wits all of the time. I just wanted to eat something and crash. I parked my car in the underground car park and got out. The electronic gate completed its slow, lazy arc, then it closed with a metallic clang. I felt safe here.

I started to walk towards the main door at the other end of the car park. It was quiet. We stored a few cars down here for convenience but I was the only one actually staying in the apartment block just now.

I didn't hear a thing until he was right up behind me. He moved so quietly. Then there was a click, as he drew back the hammer of the gun and cocked it. It's incredible how fast your mind can work when you're in danger and I realised straight away that I was a dead man. I wasn't even surprised when I heard his voice, just very, very scared.

'Don't move,' he ordered me, 'not until I tell you to.' The voice was so familiar. I'd heard it a lot over the years – but this time he was the one giving the orders. 'Bring your arms up slowly and place the palms of your hands on the top of your head. Go too quickly and I'll kill you. Do you understand?'

'Yes.'

'Do it then.'

I did as I was told, bringing my hands up with agonising slowness while my mind raced. I was looking for possibilities, but there didn't seem to be any right now. I couldn't see any way out for me other than a bullet in the back of the head.

'It doesn't have to be this way,' I told him, 'you know that'. No reply. 'You know I'll pay you,' he didn't say a word. Instead he used his free hand to pat me down, first one side, then the next. 'I'm not armed,' I told him, but he ignored me. He didn't find a gun, but he did find my phone. He took it out of my inside jacket pocket, dropped it on the floor and kicked it so it slid under my car.

'We'll take mine,' he told me.

'Are you listening to me?' I asked him, but my voice didn't sound like mine any more. I was trying so hard not to sound scared but I was terrified, and we both knew it. I carried on talking, reasoning with him, but I already knew it was no good. 'Did you hear what I said?' I asked him, 'you know I'll pay you.'

Jack Conroy spun me round and pressed the gun right into my face. His eyes were fixed on me intently, but they seemed dead, and I realised why he had always given me the creeps. Up close, I could see right into him and I knew he was a psychopath. He didn't care what happened to me. I was just another job.

'That can't happen. It's a question of credibility. If word got out I could be bought no one would ever hire me again.'

'But you came to see me,' I said, 'you told me someone wanted me dead but you didn't want to do it.'

'Would you kill a man on Billy Warren's say-so? Nobody would. But they contacted me again and this time they didn't use a numpty like Billy. They sent someone who knew what he was doing and they are paying me a hundred grand.'

'I know who offered you that hundred grand, Conroy, even if you don't, and he isn't in a position to pay you anymore.'

'Oh please,' not only did he not believe that, but he obviously thought the lie was a poor one.

'You're being paid by the Gladwells and they are finished. There *is* no hundred grand Conroy.'

'I am being paid by a fixer, a man I have done business with for more than ten years.'

'But you don't know who the client is, and I do.'

'No,' he corrected me, 'I don't know who my client is and you only think that you do. There's a lot of men want to see you dead, Blake.'

'Walk over to the car,' he nodded at the vehicle he was using. It was parked up in the far corner. I didn't recognise it and realised he had hired it from somewhere.

'Pop the boot and get in.' I didn't move. He pressed the gun right up into my eye.

'Why would I do that?'

'Because if you don't I'll kill you here, which will make things more difficult for me, so I'll make you pay by putting the first bullet in your balls and the second in your stomach, then I'll smoke a cigarette while you think about the mistake you made in not listening to me. If you get in the car it'll be easier for me, so I'll make it easier for you.' I looked at him questioningly, 'a head shot, nice and quick. No pain.' He was selling the idea to me. 'It's the best deal you are going to get. Besides, I know you. You'll be thinking the longer you delay this, the more chance you have of somehow getting yourself out of it, so why not get in the car, eh?'

I lowered my hands and slowly, reluctantly, walked towards the car. When I got there I clicked the catch on the boot and turned back to him. He gestured with his head for me to get in and, even though it terrified me to climb in there, I did as I was told. When I was lying down he peered in at me and, for a moment, I thought he was going to shoot me there and then, but he just looked at me, then slammed the boot shut.

A moment later I heard his door open and close, then the car moved off and I lurched to one side. I felt every bend as we shot round the side streets. I tried to lie flat so I wasn't bounced around too much, but most of all I tried to think. I flailed my arms around looking for anything that I could use as a weapon, knowing full well that Conroy wasn't that stupid. The boot was empty.

Then the car stopped turning and we must have been on open road. I lay like that for twenty minutes, scared to death, just thinking about what I could do to dissuade Conroy or overpower him, but nothing came to me. The fear was choking me now.

The car lurched suddenly, and I slid round as it turned violently to the right, banging my head against the floor in the process. The car started bumping up and down like we were on a dirt track. I was bounced around as it took deep ruts. Where the fuck was he taking me? It had to be farmland or woods, somewhere isolated, somewhere he'd prepared in advance, where no one was ever going to find me. I was trying to stifle the panic that was rising in me now. I had to stay calm, in control, figure out a way to get myself out of this somehow; but I couldn't see how. Conroy wasn't like other people. You couldn't reason with him. All he wanted to do was finish the job and go home. Jesus, how had I got myself into this? I couldn't believe that after everything I'd been through it was going to end this way. I'd tried talking my way out of it already and it hadn't worked. And nobody knew I was out here. No one. Christ.

Abruptly the car drew to a halt and I heard the creak as the handbrake went on. I froze as I heard the door handle click and the car moved slightly as Conroy opened his door. He popped the lock and the boot swung upwards. He looked in at me dispassionately.

'Get out.'

I didn't move. I couldn't move.

'Get out,' he told me, more firmly this time.

I couldn't even speak. Instead I just shook my head like a child who doesn't want to do what his daddy tells him. I felt so small, so scared.

He pointed the gun at me and spoke again, quietly, patiently, reasoning with me, 'get out or I'll shoot you in the guts and haul you out.'

I forced myself to climb out, but when I stepped down from the car my knees buckled and I almost fell to the ground. My legs were no longer working properly and I found I was gasping for breath like each lungful would be my last.

'Walk,' he dragged me up, then gestured with the gun for me to lead the way along a tiny path that went into some trees. The half-moon lit the way for us. The path was almost covered over by long grass on either side of it and I realised it had been a long while since anyone had walked here. God knows how he had found this place, but he had chosen well. You could kill a man down here and nobody would ever find him. I wanted to weep. Christ, I was never going to see Sarah again. I wanted to reason with Conroy, make him understand that he had to let me go for her sake, but I knew he wouldn't give a damn. He had taken me out into the middle of nowhere and he was leading me along a path that had only one destination. At the end of it he was going to shoot me and bury me out here. I fell onto my knees and started to retch.

'Get up, you cunt,' he ordered me. He aimed a kick at me and it connected with the back of my leg. The pain was searing, but it wasn't enough to make me stand up, 'on your feet in two seconds, or I do you here and now.'

Somehow I managed to climb to my feet, desperate to steal myself some time, praying for a miracle that I knew could never come. The wind was up around us, shaking the branches of the trees. They were rising and falling like waves and the noise was so loud that I barely heard him when he told me, 'keep walking.'

I walked as slowly down that rutted little path as I thought he would allow. Without moving my head, I let my eyes dart around, desperately searching for anything I could use as a weapon, a rock or a fallen tree branch, anything, in case he took his eye off me for a second, but I already knew there'd be nothing. He'd have made sure of that – there would be no way Jack Conroy would take his eye off a target, particularly one like me.

There was nowhere to run to either. He was right behind me and I wouldn't get two yards before the bullet hit me in the back. There was no point even trying. I kept thinking about Sarah. There wouldn't even be a headstone to mark the spot where I lay.

'Just a little further,' he told me, 'it'll soon be over and you won't feel a thing, just so long as you do this my way.' He meant I'd die in agony if I did it any other way.

I didn't say anything in reply, just trudged forwards. Then I saw it. At first it looked like little more than a dark shape by the side of the dirt track but, as I drew nearer, I realised what it was; a deep hole, dug a few yards from the path in a clearing by the trees, a large mound of dark brown earth piled next to it. I stopped in my tracks. I was looking at my grave.

'Don't stop,' he told me, 'keep going. Go right to the edge and kneel down. Do that and I'll make this quick.'

'Fuck you,' I said and I realised I was sobbing. I didn't sound as brave as I wanted to.

I didn't hear him make a move behind me but I did feel the gun as he brought it across the side of my skull and smashed me to the ground. I fell forwards and to the side, a searing pain lancing through me.

'I won't ask you again,' he told me, pointing the gun down at me. I wondered how many men Jack Conroy had led sobbing to their freshly-dug, unmarked graves. 'Get up, get over there and get down on your knees by the hole, or so help me...' I began to think that maybe I should just do what he said. The end result would only be the same and at least I'd be spared the pain. I climbed to my feet as slowly as I dared, turned back towards the hole and walked slowly forwards. I only had two choices; kneel down and take his bullet, or try to lunge at him, a course of action I knew he'd be prepared for. A man like Conroy could easily repel me. If he couldn't, he wouldn't last a minute in his profession. Once he'd done that he would make me pay for it, putting bullets into parts of me that would cause maximum pain.

Then, all too quickly, I was at the graveside and right then I made my decision. I dropped to my knees.

'That's it,' he said and he sounded relieved, like he'd been spared a burdensome task, although I could barely hear him above the din the wind was making. I looked up at the branches of the trees in front of me and tried to think only of them. I watched as they swayed and swirled helplessly, buffeted by the wind. I felt the first spot of rain on my face, then I thought of Sarah and, for the first time since I was a little boy, I prayed.

I heard the dull snick as he cocked his gun. 'Soon be over,' he told me and I held my breath. I noticed there was a large, heavy shovel to one side of the grave but it was too far away for me to make a grab at it. The rain started in earnest and I felt large heavy drops hit my hands and face.

The trees were being tossed violently now, the wind rising, but even I heard Conroy move. I turned and realised he had spun round to the side, suddenly alert. Then I heard what he had been listening to; footsteps. Conroy had his arm raised, gun pointing to one side and out into the darkness, back the way we had come. He was aiming at something, hesitating like he was trying to pick out a clear target in the darkness. There was a shot and it took me a moment to realise it hadn't come from Conroy's gun. I only really understood what had happened when Conroy took the bullet in his chest and was thrown backwards, landing flat on his back, his gun bouncing away from him in the long grass. He gasped, and tried to get to his feet, but he couldn't manage it. Instead he fell back and his head rolled from side to side, his eyes widening as he struggled to stay alive. I stared into the blackness so I could see where the shot had come from, but there was nothing. I couldn't see anything and I couldn't hear anything now either, because the wind was still violently swirling the branches and the rain was falling hard, but then I saw the darkness change, and a shape began to form in front of me. The man was holding a gun out in front of him. Palmer.

He didn't even look at me, just advanced slowly on Conroy, never taking his eyes off the man he had shot, holding his gun out straight, keeping it pointed at the assassin. Palmer waited till he drew close enough for Conroy to see him clearly. He was still desperately trying to pull himself upright, but it was no use. Palmer noticed the gun in the grass and the tension seemed to ease in him, though he kept his own weapon trained on Conroy. He stole a quick glance over at me and saw the hole in the ground, then he looked back at Conroy, who was wincing and gasping.

'Stupid bastard,' he told Conroy, 'you're going in that hole now.'

I could tell from Conroy's eyes that he understood Palmer's words. Palmer took a step forward and put two more rounds in him, just to make sure.

43

Palmer didn't say a word to me. He just put his gun away, took everything out of Conroy's pockets, then dragged his body to the edge of the hole and rolled it in. He picked up the shovel in his gloved hands and started to throw soil on top of the body, moving incredibly quickly.

I collapsed on the wet grass and lay there with my eyes open, staring up at the sky as the rain continued to fall. I didn't have any energy left. I lost all sense of time and all I could hear was Palmer grunting slightly in exertion as he shovelled all of that earth on top of Jack Conroy. I turned my head and watched him as he walked into the trees, pulled away some branches and bits of bushes and used them to cover the freshly-filled grave. Hopefully no one would ever walk down here but, if they did, this rudimentary camouflage might be enough to keep their eyes away.

I forced myself to sit up as he walked back over to me. He

picked up Conroy's gun, unscrewed the suppressor and stowed both items in the outside jacket pocket of his leather coat. Then he hauled me to my feet and shoved me back down the path. I didn't understand how he knew to come here. 'How…?' I asked him.

'Not now,' he said, and instead of an explanation all I got was a shove in the back which propelled me down the rutted lane. My head hurt and my ears were ringing but I was alive.

Palmer put Conroy's keys in the glove compartment of the hire car and called one of our people so they could collect and return it to the rental company. Palmer drove me back into the city. It was a while before I could speak.

Eventually I managed. 'How did you find me?'

'I chipped your car.'

At this point I would normally have pulled him up for not obeying my wishes, but I knew that if Palmer had listened to me I would have been the one lying in a grave in the woods instead of Conroy. So all I said was, 'I don't understand. He didn't take my car.'

'I chipped his car too,' and he glanced over at me. 'I didn't trust him, after Conroy came to see you and volunteered the information that he'd been asked to kill you,' he shrugged, 'well, I just didn't trust him.'

So it was Palmer's instincts, his innate distrust of his fellow human beings that had kept me alive. If I'd had a less cynical right-hand man I'd be a goner. 'I still don't get it,' I said, 'it wasn't his usual car. It was a rental.'

Palmer exhaled like he really could do without this right now, but I needed an explanation, even if that involved pissing off the man who had just saved me; a man who was probably preoccupied by the fact that he had just killed another man, left his body in the woods and wanted to get the hell away from the place before anyone else showed up. 'I chipped your car,' he explained, 'because it's my job to keep you alive, and your refusal to cooperate with that compromised me professionally.'

'Fair enough,' I conceded.

'I chipped Conroy's car because I didn't trust him, and I asked Robbie to keep an eye on his movements. When his car didn't move for two days and it wasn't at his house, I checked out the location and it turned out it was parked outside a rental company. Now, since he drove his own car down there, there was clearly nothing wrong with it mechanically, so I figured he was using the rental car for a job, so I went down to his house one night, watched him arrive in the rental car, waited till he had gone to bed and I chipped that too.'

Most people I know are too scared of Conroy to walk within a mile of his front door but Palmer messed with the guy's car, as cool as you like. Unbelievable.

'I told Robbie and his guys to check on it every half hour. Another few days went by, presumably while chummy waited for his opportunity to get near you, then I got a call from Robbie. The chip on the rental car showed it was ten feet from your motor and the location was your supposedly secure apartment. We need to get that looked into, by the way. Conroy got in there way too easily, which means someone else can.' That was a cheering thought. 'As soon as I got the call from Robbie I pegged it round there, but you were on the move again before I could reach you. Robbie kept tracking you and I caught up as fast as I could, but there wasn't much in it.'

'Christ, you're not joking.'

'I would have been quieter,' he explained, as if a point of professional pride was at stake, 'but I had to be quick.'

'I didn't hear you.'

'No, but he did. Lucky I got my shot off first.'

That word again – lucky.

'Palmer?'

'What?'

'Thank you.'

Palmer shrugged, 'It's what you pay me for.'

'I know,' I said, 'but even so.'

I closed my eyes then and slumped back in my seat. I kept them shut until we were back in the city once more.

The next morning I called Kinane. 'I've made a decision,' I told him.

Everyone was there, and I made sure they all saw Kinane. I kept him with me as I went from table to table, shaking hands and shouting in ears above the din of the crowd's chatter. There was a palpable sense of excitement among the gilded folk of Tyneside's business community; the men in their penguin suits, sweating in their bow ties and cummerbunds, beneath the arc lights that shone down on us all, lighting up the boxing ring which dominated the centre of the room. They were out in force to celebrate the opening of our new five-star, six-storey Quayside hotel and witness the bloodshed from our exhibition match. It was mostly men, but here and there the monotony of black and white was broken by a flash of beige, green, even scarlet from evening dresses worn by chubby wives or expensive mistresses.

As I shook hands, I introduced Kinane. 'This is Joe!' I shouted above the din and he played the part, grasping hands, almost crushing them in greeting, and I bawled over the din, variously describing him as: 'the brains behind our fighter', 'the coach', 'the man in the corner', 'the guy who makes it all happen in the ring'. 'It's all down to Joe!' and they noticed him alright. Who's going to forget a guy who looks the way Kinane does? All those flabby, dinner-jacketed captains of industry felt inadequate when they stood in front of him. Even some of the women were impressed by his bulk, eyeing him up and down. We took our time getting to our seats and by then Kinane had been patted on the back by half of Tyneside's movers and shakers.

Despite my claims that Kinane was 'the man in the corner', he left that job to 'Big Auty', the silver-haired trainer who walked out in front of our fighter, and Joe and I headed to our table. There was a master of ceremonies in the middle of the ring and he was using a microphone to loudly announce the arrival of our man. Kinane gave me a questioning look and I told him, 'Not yet'.

My phone bleeped then, another text from Simone. 'Am I likely to see you later?' I wasn't deliberately ignoring her but I had been understandably preoccupied lately and, now that I was back on more normal terms with Sarah, I felt like I didn't need an arrangement with someone as complicated as Simone any more. It would have been easier if she didn't still insist on working down at the parlour. It seemed she wasn't prepared to accept my help. I slipped my phone back in my pocket without answering her, but made a note to call her in the morning.

I waited until the challenger, a tattooed meat-head from Lewisham, was booed into the ring, and the two fighters went toe to toe, but still I didn't give Kinane his signal. Then the fighters returned to their corners and the braying from the audience reached its peak, the lights were dimmed and a blonde glamour model climbed into the ring. The male section, which made up the majority of the crowd, went wild for her. The volume of the whistling, shouting, braying and cheering rose. I waited till she reached the centre of the ring and, as she stood straight to raise her sign with the words 'Round One' written on it, I gave Kinane the nod. He slid from his chair, as discreetly as a man his size could, and left. I had ensured our table was in a corner and there was very little light above us. Kinane only had to walk a few feet before disappearing behind a curtain and he was gone. I was prepared to bet that no one in the room noticed. Not while they were busy speculating on the cup size of our bikini-clad lovely as she strode confidently around the ring, holding her sign high, reminding everybody that bloodshed was imminent.

There was a conference room that backed onto the main event room, and Kinane used it to get out of the building unobserved. The lights were out, but he used the light from the streetlamps that shone through the curtains to guide him as he crossed the open, carpeted floor purposefully. He reached the fire door and pushed down on the heavy metal bar, triggering its release. No alarm sounded. It had been disabled in advance and would be reactivated later that evening, on his return. Investigating officers would be able to report that nobody had triggered the alarm that evening and, if they enquired, they would be helpfully presented with last night's CCTV footage, edited by Palmer's watchers to include today's date. The hotel reception was busy that night. Blake had ensured there were four members of staff manning reception and an equal number of glamorous PR girls in the foyer, to meet and greet guests for the fight. That was at least eight people who could testify they did not see a man of Kinane's memorable bulk leave the event, via the front door. Blake ensured there were witnesses at every other exit; the kitchen was full of chefs, the restaurant packed with diners and, in the underground car park, valets had been employed to assist VIP guests – as well as help Kinane with his alibi.

The only matter left to chance was the fight itself. It was crucial for Kinane that it went the distance. He required enough time to leave the fight, do what needed to be done and return to witness its end. His alibi would be destroyed if the bout ended in a first round knock-out. Phil 'The Warrior' Watson's opponent that night had been carefully chosen, handpicked from a small selection of fighters able to put up a good enough show, but with the kind of punching power that was never likely to trouble a future British and Commonwealth Champion. Watson was fiercely loyal to Kinane and his backer David Blake and, since they weren't ordering him to lose the fight, only delay its inevitable outcome until the final round, Kinane knew Watson would do what was asked of him. He would dance around his opponent, land a selection of underpowered punches, scoring points in the process, without knocking him through the ropes, and make it look as if he was struggling to finish the man.

Local newspapers might report that the championship contender had underachieved that night, but nobody would get bent out of shape over it, particularly in an exhibition match. Kinane had led Watson to believe it was merely a question of money, and he had nodded like he understood. Watson presumed thousands had been wagered on a tenth round knock-out and assured Kinane that this would be delivered.

Kinane pushed the fire door a little harder, eased it open, stepped through and pulled it almost closed behind him, careful not to shut it entirely. Instead, he dragged a wheelie bin so that it now blocked the door and prevented it from swinging wide open. From a distance it would appear locked, but all he had to do was remove the bin and it would swing open again, enabling him to silently re-enter the building.

Behind Kinane an engine started, and a van drew slowly towards him down the side street and parked by the kerb. His son Chris was at the wheel and Kevin was sitting next to him. Kinane drew back the side door and climbed in, then closed it behind him. He took the bag his third son Peter passed him and unzipped it. He sat on the floor of the van and began to remove his dinner jacket and tie, which went into another bag, keeping it clean for later. Kinane pulled on a set of oversized overalls, then he gave the word to move. The van pulled away from the kerb.

*

Braddock eased the big Mercedes out of the garage and set off on his usual route. It was raining hard now and the roads were slick with it, the street lights reflecting back off shining pavements. He was driving too fast for the conditions, but it wouldn't have crossed his mind to slow down. Instead, he pressed on towards the city.

Braddock was pissed off. The day had not been a success. He had started to realise that some of his crew were probably too stupid even to make money dealing drugs on the Sunnydale estate and he was perturbed by David Blake's reaction to their little robbery. He had expected Blake to come straight down there and have it out with him, but it seemed the guy didn't even have the balls for that, sending messages instead and skirting round the issue. It would soon be time to explain to Blake that he no longer held any influence over Sunnydale. It was Braddock's territory now and if he could just sort out a regular supply of H from those guys in Liverpool he'd been talking to, then he would be up and running on his own in weeks. Still, he hadn't expected it was going to be this easy.

Soon Braddock would have exactly what he wanted; complete control. Despite this, his future seemed uncertain now, and he was beginning to wonder who he could really trust in his crew. It left Braddock feeling uneasy. He knew he had been on edge – he had given Suzy a backhander when perhaps he shouldn't have. True, she had unwisely ignored his command to get him and a couple of the guys some beers but, it had to be admitted, she was a bit out of it on some of that Dutch skunk he'd given her. Demanding for a third time 'get…us…a…fucking…beer…Suzy!' he'd lost his rag and clipped her one right across the chops. She recoiled like she'd been shot, then scampered straight over to the fridge, dug out three beers, pulled the tops off the bottles, handed them over to the lads and silently crept out of the flat with tears in her eyes.

She hadn't been seen for a couple of hours. It was the first time he'd cuffed her one and, from her reaction, it was probably the first time she'd been hit by any bloke, but she would have to learn. Suzy got free board and lodging from Braddock and as much dope as she could handle. All he expected her to do in return was screw him and fetch him a beer. Surely that wasn't too much to ask? A man like Braddock couldn't be seen walking over to the fridge to fetch beers for guys who worked for him. It sent out the wrong signal. It sent out a worse signal if the girl he was with didn't do what she was told *when* she was told.

It looked like she'd actually walked through the Sunnydale estate and away down the road, silly bitch. People would know that Suzy was the latest in a fairly long line of Braddock's girls so they wouldn't touch her, but it wasn't the best neighbourhood for a lass to be walking through on her own. These posh girls could be bloody stupid and he made a note to take up with something a little rougher next time; something that wouldn't question him, or ignore him, or take exception to a slap when she was clearly bang out of order. Suzy would be back, he was sure of that. She liked a bad boy too much and, realistically, where was she going to go with no job, no money and a one-fifty-a-day coke habit?

Robbie was on a pay-as-you-go phone and he used to it to dial Kinane's equally untraceable mobile. 'Elvis has left the building,' he said solemnly.

'Talk properly,' Kinane told him, 'this isn't a fucking movie.'

'Sorry,' said Robbie, 'vehicle sighted, heading east, into the city, as expected.'

Not just as expected, thought Robbie, but almost to the minute. Braddock had a weakness Blake had spotted. Here was a gangster who was tough and ruthless, but he went to visit his grey-haired old mum, who lived in a ground-floor flat at the other side of the city, once a week, regular as clockwork.

'Never have a routine,' Palmer always said, 'that's how they'll know when to come after you,' and he was right. Now Robbie was tracking the robbing little bastard who had beaten Kevin Kinane and stolen the stash, and Joe Kinane and his sons were waiting to spring the trap.

For the next five minutes, Robbie never let his eyes leave the CCTV, switching from camera to camera as Braddock's car progressed, keeping up a running commentary involving street names, pub names and the number of the B and A roads that Braddock took, so Joe Kinane could ready himself. Occasionally Braddock's car would disappear for a few moments when there was a gap in the network, but Robbie soon learned to anticipate the reappearance of the car and he would notify Kinane whenever he picked up the Mercedes as it crossed the city.

Braddock was halfway there when he saw her. She was all alone at the bus stop standing in the pouring rain. She didn't even have a coat on. He pulled the car over by the side of the road and slowed to a halt beside her, but she didn't react, still obviously furious at him. Braddock slid down the window 'Get in,' he told her and when she made no move towards him he frowned, 'don't be fucking stupid girl, it's pissing down. I said get in.'

'We've lost him,' said Robbie.

'What?'

'That's odd,' Robbie sounded like he was talking to himself, not Kinane, 'his c...c...car has disappeared. It should have been back on line by now and...oh...wait a minute...yeah... that's it. G...g...got him.'

'Keep me posted,' ordered Kinane gruffly.

*

Phil 'The Warrior' Watson was dancing around his opponent, landing punches at will. The Lewisham pub brawler looked out of his depth, but he was a game lad and he stood up to the blows, before being smothered by Watson's grip until the referee made them break. It was a strange fight. Watson seemed to be lacking his renowned punching power and he was affording his ill-matched opponent too much respect. When the bell sounded at the end of Round Three, both men were still standing.

'What is it now?' asked Kinane, clearly irritated by Robbie's flustered stammer.

'He's d…d…diverting,' answered the young man nervously, 'v…v…veering off.'

'Shit,' answered Kinane. He hadn't anticipated that. Palmer had chipped Braddock's car and he had never once deviated from the usual route to his mum's flat before, 'where's he going? Tell me. Hurry up.'

'He's heading south now. I don't know where he's going but if he is still off to see his mum he must be taking the s…s…scenic route.'

Kinane ordered his son to start the van and get moving. He knew Newcastle like the back of his hand and the direction Braddock was travelling in wouldn't bring him out anywhere near the ambush they were planning.

'Listen carefully Robbie. Tell me every street the bastard takes and don't lose him, you hear.'

By Round Seven the crowd were getting frustrated. They expected that the north east's best boxer since the great Glenn McCrory was going to put on a show tonight but, just when it looked like he had rocked his opponent and could move in for the kill, he seemed to lose confidence in himself and falter. The two men traded weak punches, then immediately clung onto each other, like a drunken couple at a dance. The first catcalls could be heard.

Braddock's Mercedes came around the corner and he cursed as the lights turned to red up ahead of him at the crossroads. This wasn't his usual route, he had diverted because of the girl, but he knew the road well enough, everyone did, and the lights here were a pain in the arse. You were always likely to be stopped by them and they took an age to change to green. He was tempted to run the red light, but he didn't want to raise his profile any higher with the police so he slowed to a halt.

It was then that the van drew alongside him. He couldn't see the driver and he gave it scant attention. Then he heard a metallic scraping sound and he turned to see what was going on.

As soon as the van pulled up alongside the Mercedes at the red light, the side door slid wide and the passenger door was flung open. Joe and Kevin Kinane jumped out, and ran up to Braddock's car. Before he had time to react they raised their Beretta shotguns and pointed them at the darkened glass of the windows. Kinane couldn't see Braddock through the tinted window but he took a grim satisfaction in knowing that the drug dealer would be able to see him alright. In fact, Joe Kinane would be the last thing Braddock ever saw.

Both men fired their shotguns at point-blank range, straight into the front and side windscreens of the Mercedes. There were two huge bangs and the accompanying sounds of shotgun rounds destroying metal and glass. The Mercedes alarm went off, adding to the din.

Kinane advanced on the car and peered in through the shattered windscreen – but any satisfaction he might have felt at Braddock's death was instantly tempered by the sight of two bodies in the wreckage of the car.

Kinane froze, unable to believe the scene that greeted him. Kevin had already turned and run back to the van. Chris was calling his father, urging him to leave now before it was too late. Kinane took one last look at the damage the shotgun blasts had inflicted on the young woman sitting next to Braddock, then he too turned and ran back to the van.

44

They were two-thirds through the final round when Big Auty glanced over at me and I nodded my agreement. He caught Phil Watson's eye and nodded too. Our fighter suddenly became a different man, easily side-stepping a wild punch from the Lewisham lad, then landing three consecutive blows to the head in quick succession that knocked his opponent senseless and dropped him to the floor. The guy tried to get up but he was still on one knee when the referee counted him out.

As the crowd rose to its collective feet to acknowledge the devastating finale to the fight, banging their hands on the tables in the process, Kinane slipped silently through the drapes and back to our table, then sat down between Palmer and myself without a word. Eventually Palmer asked, 'Well?' and when he received no immediate answer he prompted Kinane, 'Braddock?'

'GNV,' answered Kinane, but he looked a little rattled.

'Eh?' asked Palmer.

'Good Night Vienna,' Kinane told us, but he didn't look as happy as I'd have thought he might. He lived for nights like this, which is why I needed him in my crew. 'How'd he get on?' Kinane asked of Watson, like he was deliberately changing the subject.

'Textbook,' I told him.

Kinane just nodded like he expected nothing else, then he reached for his beer and drank deeply.

'What is it Joe?' I demanded.

He ignored me at first, took another big glug of his beer, then set it down on the table.

'There was a hitch,' Kinane finally admitted. 'He had company.'

'What?'

Joe shook his head, 'the car was supposed to be empty apart from him, but there was a passenger. It wasn't easy to tell after what we did,' he continued, 'but I'm pretty sure it was a woman'.

'Jesus.' I immediately got a mental image of Suzy, the pasty little junkie who had been hanging around Braddock when we visited him in the high-rise. She might have looked like she was on a one-way trip to oblivion, but I didn't think we'd be the ones to finish her off. 'The poor little bitch. How the fuck did that happen?'

'I don't know,' he said it in a dead voice like he couldn't believe it either, 'the watchers said he was on his own. I don't know what happened.'

'We met that poor young lass,' I was exasperated, 'she was a bloody civilian.'

'A civilian shagging a drug dealer that was robbing from his supplier,' said Kinane. 'I'm not saying she had it coming but she got caught in the crossfire. It was his fault, not ours.'

I knew Kinane was trying to rationalise what he had just

done. I couldn't imagine how it must have felt to peer into that car and realise you'd just killed a young girl. I knew Kinane felt bad about the lass so I let it drop, even though it would increase the heat on us tenfold.

I forced myself to be the life and soul of the party that night. I laughed loudly at the celebrity comedian who came on after the fight. He was one of those nasty little fucks who mocks the old, the fat and the handicapped but does it in an oh-so-knowing and ironic way, so it's alright really. I got to my feet to command waiters to fetch more wine and champagne, then I spent lavishly in the charity auction that was the climax of the evening, shelling out for drive days in Formula One cars, balloon rides and the shirts of former Newcastle players – and I did it all so that no one doubted I was a country mile from Braddock when he was killed.

'There's going to be a riot on that estate,' Palmer said afterwards when we were all back at the Cauldron, as if I hadn't known it already. Braddock's lads would go berserk once they heard he was dead. They'd want to vent their anger at anyone who might be behind his murder and, when they couldn't find the guys responsible for it, they would smash up everything, even the homes they lived in. Like it or not, the Police would have to go in to restore order and they'd take a pasting for a few hours, hiding behind riot shields as bottles rained down on them from the high-rises. Their commanding officers, mindful that the media was watching, would not want to be too heavy-handed to begin with, particularly if the riot had been triggered by the death of a 'community leader' like Braddock. Some would try and portray him as a cross between Ronnie Kray and Joan of Arc, defender of the oppressed masses of the Sunnydale estate. It would probably take serious injury to a Policeman before the top brass ordered their men to remove their kid gloves and go in with the batons. There is nothing that makes a copper angrier than standing impotently by while Molotov cocktails are hurled at him, and his mates are stretchered off to hospital. By the time they were finally allowed to use 'reasonable force' their anger would sweep across that estate like an avenging tide. Everyone would be caught up in it, innocent and guilty alike.

'What do we do?' asked Kinane.

'Nothing,' I told him, 'we stay well clear of the place. Let them vent their anger. The Police will have to crack some heads to get them back in their cages. It'll be a week before the place calms down.'

'Then we go in?' asked Kinane.

'No,' I told them, '*then* we turn off the tap. No drugs for the Sunnydale estate, which means no supply for the junkies, no cash to pay the dealers, the look-outs and the bully-boys who handle security. There'll be no money for the loan sharks either. Braddock's boys need to learn who pays for all the cars, the women and the nights out on the town. Give it a week and the junkies on that estate will be clucking, desperate to get their hands on anything that'll get them high. Another week and you'll get rival dealers coming in from the other estates. The guns will come out and they'll be shooting each other every night. We won't do anything to stop that. It'll be Armageddon. We'll just spread the word that Braddock tried to rip us off; that turning the tap off is punishment for the whole estate, and we won't be coming back. Let's see how long Braddock's 'Robin Hood' image lasts when they are blaming him for the shit they are in.'

They listened intently while I continued to outline my plan for regaining control of the Sunnydale estate. 'After a month, go down there with your sons and the boys from the gym and restore order. Speak to Braddock's men, tell them you'll turn the tap back on if they toe the line and stop dipping into our profits. Get the rival dealers out. It will be messy for a week or two but I suspect your boys will enjoy the work.'

'I expect they will,' agreed Kinane.

'My guess is that everyone on that estate will be thrilled to see you by then. You'll be the liberating army come to save them from themselves.'

'I like the sound of that,' he agreed.

'I'll get Sharp to talk to that journalist on the local paper. He can be a 'highly-placed-police-source' who reveals the authorities are acting on the theory that Braddock was killed for supplying them with information about rival dealers. The journalist will make that sound like a good thing, which would get Braddock a bit of sympathy from normal folk.'

Kinane interrupted, 'but on the Sunnydale Estate…'

'They'll think he's a Judas cunt,' added Palmer.

'Braddock a grass?' laughed Kinane. 'He'll be spinning in his grave at that. He'll probably come back and haunt you.'

'He's dead,' I assured him, 'you can't harm the dead and they can't harm you.'

'You've got it all worked out, haven't you?' said Kinane wryly. 'As usual.'

'If you're going to get rid of someone in our world, you've got to do it twice,' I explained, 'first you kill the man, then you kill his reputation. That way it ends.'

They knew I'd done it, when they hauled me in. Of course they did. They're not stupid. The Police usually do know what's going on. Proving it? That's the difficult bit.

I was brought in for questioning and made to wait. I suspected they knew they would never be able to pin this one on me, not if they threw questions at me from now till the end of time, but they brought me in to make a point. They knew I had an alibi, several hundred in fact, and they would have been pissed off I chose the night of a high-profile charity do to put an end to Braddock. I suspect they would have been particularly annoyed to learn their own Chief Constable was in attendance as the guest of a children's charity, while I entertained some of the great and the not-so-good a few feet from him on a different table.

'Shall we dispense with the usual bullshit?' Carlton asked, 'and maybe just cut to the chase for once.'

'Okay,' I said, 'it's that parking fine isn't it? I could have sworn I'd paid it but, if I didn't, you've got me bang-to-rights.'

'No,' he said reasonably, doing his best keeping-calm-in-the-face-of-extreme-provocation act, 'it's the murder of Frank Braddock, but I think you know that.'

'Frank Braddock?' I asked, 'no, the name doesn't ring a bell.'

'I thought we'd agreed to dispense with the bullshit, but no,' he was trying to sound pained, 'in a moment I'll be forced to tell you that Frank Braddock was shot in his car last night by at least two unknown assailants and killed instantly. You will continue to deny you've ever heard of him, when in reality he was your top man on the Sunnydale Estate; has been for a year or more. I'm assuming you'll then deny knowing where the Sunnydale estate is, even though we have film of you down there.'

So they'd been filming me. That proved nothing in itself and I was surprised he'd admitted it to me. 'I was thinking of investing in some of the private properties on the outskirts of the place,' I explained patiently, 'I went down there to see if the stories about the estate had been exaggerated. I didn't want to invest in an area with a reputation for petty crime and drug use. In the end I decided it probably wasn't worth the risk.'

'Really? Well that's just fascinating,' he was nodding to himself, 'and I suppose, when I tell you Braddock was killed at around ten o'clock yesterday evening, you will helpfully point out that you were at your grand hotel opening, watching the boxing with a few hundred local dignitaries.'

'And your Chief Constable,' I reminded him.

He ignored that, 'and I suppose you never left the building? And you can provide dozens of witnesses who'll say as much? That's all just fine and dandy,' he told me, 'except it isn't – because we both know you killed Braddock or, more accurately, you had him killed. He'd been robbing from you and bad-mouthing you for months. The only thing that surprised us was how long it took you to get rid of him,' he leaned in right close to my ear then, 'we were beginning to think you'd gone soft, Davey boy, but we shouldn't have worried about that. I mean, Bobby Mahoney's protégé all these years? How could we ever have doubted you? You're proper gangster, you are.'

'Yeah, that's right,' I sighed, 'I'm a wise guy, a made-man, I work for Don Corleone.'

'What if I told you there was a woman in that car,' said DI Carlton quietly. 'Would you believe me?'

I'd been waiting for this and I was prepared. I still felt bad about that young girl, but to be brutal about it, little Suzy couldn't have chosen worse company. I reckoned she'd sealed her fate as soon as she started sleeping with Braddock. Carlton probably thought I didn't know she'd been killed too. He was hoping I'd be shocked into saying 'no there wasn't' or 'there can't have been' and he could then leap in with a flourish and shout something like 'Ha! How do you know?' like something out of a third-rate detective series.

'Why would I believe anything you say to me?'

'Oh yes,' agreed Carlton. 'She was beautiful, though you'd not know that now of course, with her face blown off and half her head missing. We had to identify her from the credit cards in her purse and the picture from an old ID card. One of our officers went round to her flat, came back with a picture in a frame from her university days. Looked to be a bit of class, she did. God knows what she saw in Frank Braddock, though I'm told he had a way with the ladies. I guess you're going to tell me she was in the wrong place at the wrong time. Did she just get in the way, or was it your intention to kill Simone Huntington for some reason we are not aware of? What did the poor bitch do to deserve that, eh?'

He paused while he waited for me to answer and frowned when I said nothing. 'What's the matter Blake? Feeling ashamed are we? I doubt that. You've got to have a heart to feel shame. I mean, come on, your lot don't give a fuck who you kill.' He turned back to look at me and frowned again. I was still trying to digest what he'd just told me. Then DI Carlton did a funny thing. He actually smiled.

'He didn't know,' he sounded triumphant, 'look at his fucking face. He didn't know!' and he shook his head in wonderment. 'Well, how about that. You look like someone just punched you in the guts, Mr Blake. You look a bit sick.'

'Should we bring you a bucket, Mr Blake?' asked his Detective Sergeant, with a sneer. 'Don't want you to make a mess all over those expensive shoes of yours.'

Carlton wasn't through yet. 'What's the matter? Was Frank Braddock's old girlfriend not meant to be caught in the crossfire? You telling us your lads fucked up and shot a civilian when they were only supposed to take care of Braddock?'

'You do look a bit rattled Mr Blake,' added the DS. They were enjoying this. 'Feeling a bit remorseful about causing the death of an entirely innocent girl?'

'Is there something you want to tell us?' prompted Carlton. 'Well, is there?'

I steadied myself before I said, 'I've nothing to say to any of you, nothing at all.'

45

For a few days after they told me Simone had been killed, I actually thought I was going a bit mad. I didn't leave my hotel room. The more I thought about it all, the more I was convinced my head was going to explode. I even started blaming the God I don't believe in for my bad luck. What the fuck had I ever done, I asked him and myself? All I ever tried to do was my best, for my family, for my friends, for the people who depended on me. Everything I did, I did for them. And this was what I got in return. I kept playing the last few seconds of Simone's life over and over in my mind. Did she die instantly, or did she suffer? Had the rounds from the shotgun made a bloody mess of that pretty face of hers, like DI Carlton said? Was she frightened? Did she scream before she died?

There were a few dark days I can tell you but, in the end, I realised it really wasn't my fault. I didn't order Kinane to kill her. She just chose the wrong moment to step into Braddock's car, that's all. Call-me-Tanya's story is as sad and simple as that. She never once told me he was the guy who got her so messed up, so how was I to know she'd be there that night? For fuck's sake, I was the one who was trying to save her. Why would a woman like Simone fall in love with a man like Braddock? What the hell did she see in him, apart from the danger – the danger that cost her everything in the end?

There was a stage when I was thinking so much about Simone and poor Danny that it felt like my brain couldn't cope with it all anymore, but I got through that low point and carried on. What choice did I have? There are still too many people who rely on me, who need me to make the right choice, for me to just switch off from the world. If I do, everything would come crashing down around me.

Simone's picture appeared in all of the papers, unsurprisingly, because she was a young, beautiful and tragic victim. The newspapers all printed stories on her, but they couldn't make up their minds how to describe her. Some ran pieces saying that she was a bright, educated young woman who had inexplicably befriended a man with a secret life she was wholly unaware of. To back this up, they printed accounts from a friend of hers who said she thought he was a property developer. But others ran much darker stories about the perils of drug addiction, safe in the knowledge that you cannot libel a dead person. They quoted anonymous sources who said Simone snorted cocaine in nightclub bathrooms and even at tables in bars, which was clearly a crock of shit. I mean, Simone did a bit of coke now and then but she was hardly likely to snort it in a crowded wine bar.

Her father was widely quoted on his desire to start up a charitable trust in her name. The Simone Huntington foundation would devote considerable resources, pledged by her dad and his city backers, to getting young men and women off drugs. There would be school visits to persuade children to refrain from using them altogether. 'Perhaps then,' her father was quoted as saying, 'my daughter Simone will not have died in vain.'

Not long after I read that piece I got a call from Palmer, 'it's here,' he said, and I could hear the relief in his voice, 'the shipment's finally arrived.'

'Right,' I said and hung up. It looked like I wouldn't have to kill the Turk after all. The heroin drought was over.

The trial of Ron Haydon came and went with astonishing speed. He was an embarrassment to the region and his party, in particular those who'd backed him or worked for him for the past twenty-nine years, all of whom either abandoned him or turned on him. Everyone just wanted this case to be over and for Ron to go away.

Someone persuaded Ron Haydon that it might be better to plead guilty under the circumstances and, seeing no way out, this he duly did. The media consulted the legal world and the consensus was that he would get a couple of years in prison.

The judge accepted his plea and made a long speech about the seriousness of the crimes, pointing out that they were not just illegal in themselves but a breach of the public trust and that, as an MP, he was expected to be 'whiter than white' in the eyes of both the law and the electorate. This made me smile, as most people I know think politicians are all in it for themselves; spend their entire working lives lying, to ensure they don't contradict official party policy, and have their noses stuffed so deeply into the trough it's amazing they don't choke to death on their own greed.

Ron was told a custodial sentence was almost inevitable, then bailed until sentencing. Finally he was allowed to leave the building with his wife and son, to face a posse of cameramen eager to capture the exact moment of his downfall for posterity. I was there too, standing on the steps of the court room, right where he could see me.

It was early evening by the time he emerged to a broadside of flash bulbs, and he tried to walk down the steps with as much dignity as he could muster. His wife clung to his arm to support him, which would have taken some courage on her part as he was being bombarded with questions like, 'what happened to the money Ron?', 'what did you spend the cash on Ronnie?' and jibes of 'what did you do Ron-Ron?' all of which he studiously ignored, but you could easily see the hurt and humiliation in his face. Photographers walked backwards in front of him, snapping away with their cameras like he might suddenly disappear and rob them of tomorrow's front page. He was halfway down when he saw me standing there. Ron stopped, looked at me, opened his mouth as if he was about to say something, thought better of it, and gave the tiniest of nods before walking on. It was the nearest I would get to an admission of defeat.

Detective Sergeant Wharton made the front pages too. The copper who was paid to arrange the disconnecting of the CCTV in the Quayside, so I could be gunned down with no witnesses, received a bit of a shock one morning when the BBC called to tell him he was the subject of that evening's *Panorama* programme. It seemed he was part of a small group of detectives in the north east of England who had been taking money from crime barons, one of whom was formerly based in Glasgow and now resided in a Thai prison.

The BBC are a thorough lot. Once they were tipped off about Wharton they set to work. They had footage of him having cosy conversations with the Gladwell brothers, shaking hands and drinking together, and film of Wharton extorting money from drug dealers, together with recorded phone conversations of him agreeing to intimidate a witness in a murder trial. To seal it all, there was hidden camera footage of DS Wharton snorting coke and kissing one of his many mistresses in a seedy club. Wharton refused to cooperate with the BBC and instead jumped into his car and fled, leaving his wife and two kids in their semi-detached, wondering what the hell had just hit them. Fortunately the programme's contents had been leaked in advance to the Northumbria constabulary who, though acutely embarrassed by its allegations, weren't about to be humiliated further by their inability to arrest their own man. He was picked up at the end of his street and charged with a wide variety of offences. They reckon he will get at least ten years.

My visits to Danny became harder and harder. It was the consultant who broke the news to him that he would never walk again so at least I was spared that. The doctors talked to him about eventually moving from the hospital to a rehabilitation centre about sixty miles from Newcastle. The idea was to work as hard as possible to restore as much movement as they could, using physiotherapy and all manner of high-tech electric pulse machinery. In Danny's case this seemed to be a complete waste of time. He had already given up.

As soon as I knew he was paralysed I threw money at the problem. I didn't skimp on anything. I got medical reps in who must have thought it was their lucky day. Everything they tried to sell me I said 'Yes' to and never once tried to beat them down to get a deal. Then I got the builders round and they set to work. I had them double-up their work gangs and I paid bonuses for early completion, but I made sure the work was sound. I didn't want anything to come off in someone's hand when the job was done.

When the work was finished, I'd transformed Our young'un's house. It had everything; ramps at the front and back and there was a lift that he could wheel a chair into that took him upstairs. He had special showers on both floors and beds that moved up and down then sank to floor level at the touch of a button. I put plasma TVs in each room, along with anything else I could think of that might keep him amused or occupied.

When it was done I showed Our young'un the photographs of the conversion. 'Thanks' he said like I'd just brought him that morning's paper. I was a little annoyed at first. Not everyone comes home from an accident to that kind of set-up. I reminded myself what happened to Danny, for a man like him, who'd been a soldier, who liked getting around town, who enjoyed pubs and girls and his mates around him, well, it was about as bad as it could be for him.

Eventually he said the words I knew were coming and had dreaded hearing. 'You should have left me where I was, bro. I'd have been happier than this.'

He meant I should have left him to carry on slowly drinking himself to death, shambling round the seedier pubs of the city for the rest of his life. No job, no friends to speak of and no prospects. Now he told me he would have been better off like that, 'at least I could walk,' he reasoned. I couldn't think of anything to say in reply to that.

'I can see you don't want me around at the moment, Danny,' I told him, 'and I understand why. You blame me for this.' He didn't contradict me. 'Maybe you're right too. I'll leave you in peace, but there are some people I want you to meet first.' I went out through the door without another word but I didn't close it. I wasn't going to introduce them to Danny. I figured it would be better if they did that without me around.

Sergeant Johnson and Corporal Connelly had been back from Afghanistan a while now, but not so long that they'd have fully come to terms with what happened to them. Both were victims of an IED, 'which sounds like a venereal disease, I always reckon' Corporal Connelly said, which was when I knew he was the right man for me. Most importantly, they were both former members of the Parachute Regiment.

I nodded at them then and they took that as the signal to go in; Sergeant Johnson hobbling on crutches because he had one leg blown off in Afghanistan and Corporal Connelly in his wheelchair because he had lost them both. They'd taken the trouble to wear their uniforms to come and visit Danny and for some reason that made me feel tearful.

'Hello brother,' called Corporal Connelly to Danny, as he wheeled himself into the room. 'No, it's okay, don't you get up on our account!' and he started laughing at his own joke. I knew that if there was anyone Danny might listen to in his despair it would be these guys. They were my last hope.

I was sitting in the first-class lounge at Heathrow, waiting for my flight to be called. I had a newspaper open, lying flat on the table in front of me. There was a picture of Alan Gladwell next to the headline 'British Paedophile gets record sentence in Bangkok Hilton'.

'Bangkok Hilton' is the catchy little nickname for Bang Kwang Prison, six miles outside the Thai capital. Seven thousand inmates, all lifers, spend fifteen hours a day locked down in cells there, each containing two dozen people. Being a new arrival, Gladwell will have to spend his first three months in leg irons.

The newspaper article explained how 'evil sex tourist' Alan Gladwell 'preyed on underage boys by offering them money and gifts in exchange for sex,' which was of course true. The piece continued that he shot videos, then offered the boys to other middle-aged, white westerners as part of a sophisticated but twisted paedophile ring that had just been busted wide open by the Royal Thai Police. Of course that last part was not true and neither was the assertion that 'Gladwell was carrying large quantities of heroin when he went through Bangkok

International Airport' because the heroin wasn't his. That had been planted on him by Pratin's highway patrol man when his car was pulled over.

There was no need to bribe the customs men. They were actually only doing their job and the tip-off they received came from Pratin. When the customs guys found the H and the photos of Gladwell with the young boy, they made him a top priority case. He eventually managed to get hold of a lawyer and the British Embassy, who rather stiffly commented that he would receive 'the usual consular assistance' due to him, but he could hardly deny everything could he? I mean it was *him* in those photos after all and, if he was guilty of that, then he could just as easily have been guilty of peddling drugs and heading up a paedo ring. We had some very nice, convincing material planted onto a memory stick which Pratin 'found' in Gladwell's hotel room. There wasn't much outrage expressed against the Thai authorities when Gladwell was arrested and charged, even from the men in his own firm, who were still trying to come to terms with the fact that they had been 'working for a poof' all this time, as Fallon put it. The man clearly didn't make any distinction between sex with consenting adult males and sex with conspicuously underage boys, but I did, and so did the judge in Thailand. The two things they hate most in that country are drug dealers and Western paedophiles, hence the sentence Alan Gladwell received. Forty-two years in jail. Everybody agreed the sick bastard deserved it.

Neither of the remaining Gladwell brothers was the sort to go quietly. Fallon had convinced them Amrein wanted a meeting to discuss their joint stewardship of the city. On the way to that meeting they were diverted to a warehouse at the edge of Glasgow where Fallon's boys tortured them until they gave up the details of their money. Then they were both beaten to death with pickaxe handles and their bodies dropped into the Clyde, so that everybody knew there was a new man in charge of the city.

We now have half of the Edinburgh drug trade and a significant share in Fallon's entire Glasgow operation, though I prefer to see myself as a sleeping partner in the latter. I'll leave Fallon to get on with it, just so long as he pays me my dues every month – and he will too, because he knows what will happen if he doesn't.

I glanced down at the blurred picture of Alan Gladwell and wondered if I could even contemplate what it must be like to be in his shoes right now. Forty-two years. There's no way he can last that long in a place like the Bangkok Hilton and I very much doubt he would want to. It's ironic. He wanted me dead, and now he must be praying for death every minute of each new day.

EPILOGUE

Hua Hin

As soon as I saw the compound up ahead I knew something was very badly wrong. Usually the gates were closed, and one of my Gurkhas would be walking the perimeter, with another just inside the metal gates. Today the gates weren't just unlocked, they were gaping wide open and our bodyguards were nowhere to be seen. My first thought was Sarah.

I didn't have time to worry if it was a trap. I'd seen a fair number of my enemies killed or jailed lately but there were still plenty of people in this world who might want me gone. The easiest way to hurt me was to come at me through Sarah. I drove straight into the compound.

As my car passed through the gates and rolled swiftly along the driveway, I looked frantically to left and right and saw no one. Where the hell was Jagrit? If he and his men had been taken out by someone, I didn't give much for my chances. I parked as close to the front door as I could, leapt out of the car and went into the house. I stopped in the hallway and listened. Absolute silence.

'Sarah?' I didn't shout, just said her name loud enough for her to hear if she had been in the living room or upstairs in a bedroom. No reply. I started to get a feeling of complete dread. I was already responsible for Simone's death and my brother being paralysed. If anything had happened to Sarah I didn't know what I would do. Maybe I deserved to lose her, but she didn't deserve this.

'Sarah?' I called her name this time, loud enough for anyone in the house to hear it. I ran up the stairs, two at a time. Her bedroom door was open and I burst in to find… Nothing. The place looked normal, no signs of a struggle, but no trace of Sarah either. My mind was churning over every possibility. Jagrit had realised there was a threat and they had gone. He just hadn't bothered to tell me about it. No. That was impossible.

But who could have taken out Jagrit and his men without a pitched battle in the compound? I ran back down the stairs and checked every room in the place. The living room looked like Sarah could have been in it moments ago, and the kitchen was spotless, except for a single, unwashed mug in the sink.

I went out through the front door and checked the outdoor pool but I wasn't hopeful. Sarah would have heard my car if she'd been sunbathing and she'd have come round to greet me. There was no sign of her.

I walked towards the only room I hadn't checked; the indoor pool. If I didn't find Sarah in there, then someone had managed to do the impossible. They'd killed all of my bodyguards and taken her.

I grabbed the handle and slid the door open. The shades were drawn over the windows and there wasn't much light in the room but it looked empty.

Then an indistinct shape at the end of the room stirred. When it moved I realised to my intense relief that it was Sarah – but something was wrong.

'Sarah?' I called and I walked quickly towards her. She moved then and slowly turned to face me and, as I drew closer, I could tell she had been crying. 'What is it?' I asked as I reached her and put my hands on her shoulders. 'Who has done this? Tell me what happened,' but she could only shake her head and fresh tears fell.

'What happened' I asked again, 'where's Jagrit?'

'Gone,' she managed, 'they've all gone,' and she must have seen the panic in my eyes because she added, 'I'm alright. Nobody hurt me.'

'I don't understand,' I said, 'where are the bodyguards?'

'Jagrit and his men had some sort of meeting last night. There was an argument and it got heated. I mean, I don't know what they were saying but it sounded like they were having a row. This morning Jagrit came to see me and said, "so sorry missy. We have to leave." I said, "Leave? Leave when?" and he just said "Now, so sorry missy."'

'I don't believe this.'

'He offered to take me with him into Bangkok but I didn't think I should leave here without you. I didn't know what to do. He kept banging on at me about it.' There was a flash of anger in her eyes, and I got a glimpse of the old Sarah. 'In the end I said "Jagrit, go fuck yourself, I'm not leaving."'

'Have you got any idea why they left?'

'Well he kept saying they couldn't work for you anymore,' she explained. 'It was something to do with their honour.'

Great, so Jagrit and his men had finally worked out who they were working for and there had been some kind of mini-mutiny. They had left Sarah out here in the middle of nowhere, all on her own.

'It's okay,' I told her, 'it's fine,' but she knew I was lying, 'pack a couple of bags, do it quickly,' I said, then corrected myself, 'I mean, there's no panic, but let's not hang about, eh?' Word of what had been going on back home must have somehow reached Jagrit and they just weren't prepared to carry on working for a man like me.

'I'm taking us away from here,' I told Sarah, and she brightened at that. I knew then that we wouldn't be coming back. 'Dry those tears,' I told her, 'I know it was frightening, being here all on your own, but you're safe now.'

'That's not why I was crying,' she told me, 'I've done something really stupid.'

My mind started to race again. 'It's alright,' I lied, 'just tell me what you've done and I will deal with it.'

'You can't,' she said, really sobbing now.

'Just tell me,' I urged her gently.

'I think it's because I was sick through drinking,' she explained, as if that would make me understand. I just looked at her and frowned, 'it didn't work because I was so sick. I was chucking up for two days but I never gave it a thought, I'm so sorry.'

'What?' I was trying hard to understand, but I was no nearer getting it from this explanation. 'What didn't work?' I asked her, 'tell me.'

'The pill,' she said, 'I'm pregnant.'

It took me an age to convince Sarah I wasn't angry. She really thought I was going to be furious with her for being so stupid, as she put it, but instead I found myself walking around with a permanent smile on my face.

I had always wanted kids eventually, but there was no hurry because she was so young.

'You're sure you're not angry,' she kept asking me, 'you're sure you want this?'

'Yes,' I told her a thousand times, 'yes, I want this.'

We finished packing and loaded up the car. I locked up the house, then the front gate of the compound and we drove off together; Sarah, me and the 'bump', as we had already started to call it, even though she wasn't showing at all yet.

I felt hopeful for the first time in months. If there was one good thing that could come out of this whole terrible time it was this. Sarah was going to have our baby and that changed everything.

For a moment, when I drove into that empty compound, I thought I'd lost Sarah, but I've got her back now and I'm never going to let her down again. It all came back into focus when she told me she was pregnant. It seemed fitting somehow, like a new life could mean a new start for all of us and I just know Sarah will be the best mother in the world. She'll dote on that child, though she reckons it'll be me that does the spoiling. She could be right about that. I'm already thinking about one of those big teddies from Hamleys in London, the really soft, expensive ones that are about the size of a five-year-old and Sarah tells me not to be so daft, that the baby will be frightened by it, but she's smiling when she says it and it's great to see her looking so happy now. Sarah looks great in fact. Her skin is so clear and there is a real sparkle in her eyes.

I'm going to make everything alright for her and the baby. I really am. I just need a bit more time.

But it will all be okay because Sarah is having our baby, which is a thought that makes me smile and, at the same time, takes my breath away, filling me with a panic I feel so acutely it's like a physical sensation somewhere deep in my chest. I have to tell myself over and over that it will be alright. I can be strong enough for all of us; for Sarah, for me and our baby. I will stay strong and I won't make any mistakes.

I hope it's a girl though. I know it sounds bad but I really do. I mean, who would want to bring a boy into a world like this?

THE END

Howard Linskey on **'What's your perfect writing environment'** and **'What is your actual one like?'**

Howard's debut novel *The Drop* was one of the top reads of 2011 according to the *Times*. Originally from Newcastle, he has gained many fans for his excellent portrayal of the North East's seedy underbelly of crime.

'I write straight onto a laptop. Life's too short to write long-hand then transcribe it all onto a computer screen like I used to,' he says. 'I have a desk by a window in a ground floor room of my house. I've done a lot of writing there but I have probably written just as many words sitting on the sofa, laptop perched on my knee, while family members watch TV in the background. I get used to writing wherever and whenever I can – coffee bars and even pubs – if I can find a quiet corner away from everyone. I play five-a-side football and if I arrive with 20 minutes to spare before kick-off, I'll sit in my car and write. The words might be rough, need editing and may even be discarded at the eleventh hour during the final edit, but as I nail down another chapter involving my gangsters, bent coppers and assorted Geordie low-lifes, I know that if I just keep going, one day there will be a finished novel with my name on it. I completed the latest one (*The Damage*) last night in fact, and I can tell you it's a damned nice feeling.'

crimefictionlover.com